IN the cool of the evening they dined on roast peacock and quails' eggs dipped in gold dust. As the curfew tolled they toasted the future in tawny spiced wine. Then Lotus Flower played the mandolin and sang for him. All the while Diego marveled at her beauty. But he kept wishing that she would give him some sign of desire.

Later that night, Diego lay awake listening to the howl of wolves prowling on the edge of the city. Suddenly Lotus Flower appeared, walking barefoot in the moonlight, dressed only in a diaphanous robe. Not wishing to startle her, Diego breathed deeply as if he were asleep, his body tensing as she knelt at his side. First Lotus Flower kissed his hands, then his chest, then his throat and the curly gold beard. Then, hungrily, she sought his mouth and Diego knew that it was not the kiss of a child but that of a woman impatient to be loved....

To hold her forever—the girl with the emerald eyes.

Cathay

by

Helene Thornton

FAWCETT GOLD MEDAL • NEW YORK

CATHAY

Published by Fawcett Gold Medal Books, CBS Educational and Professional Publishing, a division of CBS Inc.

ISBN: 0-449-14471-2

Printed in the United States of America

First Fawcett Gold Medal printing: June 1982

10 9 8 7 6 5 4 3 2 1

AUTHOR'S NOTE

The names of Chinese cities have changed many times over the centuries. For the purpose of this book I have used modern city names for Peking, called Cambulac by Marco Polo and variously Khan-Baligh and Taidu by the Mongols. I have also used the modern name for Hangchow rather than King-sze or Quinsai or Lin-an, which were also used at that time. For the Emperor I have used the name Kublai Khan rather than Kubilai Khaghan for ease of reading. The facts about the Khan's wealth, the size of his army and military strategy are taken from contemporary accounts. The journey of Diego Mazzarini in detail and route is taken from the Marco Polo account of his travels.

Lady from Cathay

One morning before dawn as Kublai Khan rode out alone, far away from his encampment, he saw a young boy crouched by a wildfowl lake. There was intense eagerness in the set of the boy's body as he stood with bow at the ready. Soon the young hunter had shot three ducks and a bird on the wing. The Khan smiled indulgently, pleased to be able to witness the hunter's skill. He strode forward, intending to startle the lad with a glimpse of the Divine Ruler of China. But as the boy waded back to the bank and undressed, in order to dry his jacket and trousers, the Khan stepped hastily behind a tree, his heart pounding, his eyes wide with pleasure. The "lad" was a girl with a tempting body that excited the Emperor to ecstasy. As he examined her, the Khan saw that the girl had the body of a courtesan but the slender thighs of a Tartar youth. He closed his eyes and tried hard to regain his breath.

The huntress threw down her cap and shook her hair, which was black and fine like silk. Her eyes appeared to be an impossible green. As the sun rose she held up her clothes so they would dry more quickly. Then she hung them on a bush. As she dried her body with an old cotton cloth, the Khan's mouth watered at her innocence, at the creamy skin of her body, at the nipples like rosebuds closed against the early-morning chill. Suddenly he forgot himself and, stepping out from his hiding place, walked toward the spot where the girl was dressing.

At his approach the girl realized that she had been spied upon and ran to her horse, pausing only to snatch the birds and fishes on her hook. The Khan pursued her, forgetting his age and the harsh beating in his chest. But the huntress eluded him. For a brief moment, he saw her naked body outlined against the cherry blossom, her hair flying in the breeze like a triumphal banner. Then she was gone. The Khan cursed his stupidity. His pulse was pounding, and he could think only of the tantalizing beauty of her body, the spring in her step and the lusciousness of her breasts.

As he rode back to his encampment, the Khan knew the encounter with the girl had disturbed him greatly, and he swore he would send his minions to learn the identity of the beautiful huntress.

Part One:

The Journey

Gadflies swarm on the weary horse.
Streaming blood, it can go no further.
The color of night rises on the road behind:
Ahead, uphill, hear the tiger roar.
These times, the traveler's heart
Is a flag a hundred feet high in the wind.

Meng Chiao (751–814)

Chapter One:

Venice

The young man was tall and broad-shouldered, with a strong face above a beard of fair curly hair. His eyes were blue, a fathomless azure like the sky when a storm is brewing. His expression was full of anticipation and excitement, yet wistful because he was about to leave home. This, he told himself, is the most important day of my life. The young man was going in search of a fortune to replace the empty family coffers. He intended to find this fortune in a country few Europeans had ever seen or would ever visit. Sending his servant ahead to the ship that lay anchored below in the lagoon, the young man walked in the garden of his home, looking up at the gray stone mansion that had been the domain of the Mazzarini family for generations. As he looked at the house, Diego thought of the idyllic days of childhood, the lessons he had disliked, the sports he had adored, the

11

tutors he and his brothers had teased, the parties his mother had given in the pink marble salon. Remembering the past lit his face with happiness. There had been good times in the days before death and ruin came to those who lived in the elegant palazzo.

Life had changed dramatically for Diego Mazzarini in the past three years. First his parents had died of a mysterious fever that had taken many lives in the Venetian islands. His sister had succumbed to the same malady shortly after her parents. Then Diego's elder brother, the heir to the Mazzarini title, had gone down in his ship that sank off the coast of Genoa. Suddenly Diego, a lover of beauty, writer of poetry and chaser of women, was responsible for everything and everyone in the Mazzarini household. Only too soon he had learned of the seriousness of the family finances. In order to boost the ailing exchequer he had sent his younger brother, Pierluigi, to trade in the Far East with the party of Niccolo and Maffeo Polo.

At the time Diego had thought that an excellent idea. In retrospect he knew he had made a mistake. Pierluigi was only nineteen and not of a serious turn of mind. He had the habit of falling in love with every pretty women he met and would probably be tempted to marry and forget his responsibilities.

Diego sniffed the heady fragrance of lemon blossom and thought of the land of which the Polos had spoken. Did that country really exist? Or was it a figment of the Venetian imagination? A land no man would ever see?

Early springtime and colors and fragrances were everywhere; the mimosa by the garden wall was already in bud. It hurt Diego to think that he would not see its golden fronds this year nor for many years to come. He might, in fact, never see Venice again, because he had, after weeks of deliberation, decided to follow Pierluigi to the East. It was Diego's intention to travel across the roof of the world to be reunited with the members of the Polo party. He would then help his brother to return to Venice with a new fortune. As Diego mulled over his decision, an elderly servant walked through the courtyard. The man spoke reassuringly, though it was obvious he was apprehensive about his master's departure.

"Have no fear, my lord. Maria-Innocenta and I shall guard the house as if it were our own."

"I have confidence in you, Duccio."

"Take this with you, sir. I found it when I was walking near the Arsenale."

Diego looked down at a prayer book heavily studded with amethysts. He wondered which careless lady had lost it and if she was as beautiful as her missal.

"It's very valuable, Duccio."

"It will help you, when times are hard. I only wish I could persuade you to stay here in Venice where you are safe."

"If I stay we shall soon be hungry. What then, Duccio?"

The old man shook his head despairingly as Diego voiced his thoughts.

"The Mazzarinis have never been reduced to begging or soliciting favors, and I would not have them do so now."

"I have been in this house all my life, and my father and his father before him. The Mazzarinis have always survived."

"If I am successful in my quest, the Mazzarinis will prosper as never before."

"I shall pray for you, sir."

A tear fell down the old man's cheek, and he stepped back against the wall, watching as Diego's eyes roamed longingly, lovingly, over the facade of the house. Duccio's daughter appeared on the balcony of the uppermost floor and called merrily down to her master.

"Bring me back a yellow songbird, sir, and some silk for a dress so I can look like a lady."

"I shall try, Maria-Innocenta."

"I will wave with my red scarf as your ship passes the house. And my father and I will pray for you every morning and every night before we sleep."

"Look after your father, Maria-Innocenta."

Diego swung his cloak around him and hoisted an antelope-skin bag to his shoulder.

"Till we meet again, Duccio."

He shook hands with the old man, hugging him to his chest.

"God bless you, sir."

As he strode toward the gate, Diego paused to run his

fingers through the water of the fountain. Then he walked down a flight of uneven stone steps leading toward the waiting ship. He felt at once afraid and elated, eager to prove himself in this test of a lifetime. The greatest of the Mazzarinis long ago had founded a dynasty that had been respected and honored for generations. Then a common swindler had deprived Diego's grandfather of the family fortune. Diego nodded graciously to passersby as they raised their caps or bowed low. Respect, he believed, had to be earned. It was not a man's due regardless of his behavior. Diego was anxious to warrant the respect of those who had loved his parents and of the men with whom he would have to do business in order to increase the fortune he hoped to bring home. The youthful head of the Mazzarini family walked toward the harbor, his heart full of hope, his face grave with determination.

In a square near the dock, local men were using public target boards for compulsory archery practice. Enthusiastic cries heralded each fine shot. Diego paused for a moment to enjoy the sound of the twanging crossbows and the camaraderie. Far below him, in a shrimp-pink sea, he could see the bleached larchwood poles of cavane that supported the wattle-and-reed houses of Venetian fishermen. His servant, Giorgio, had been born in one such precarious dwelling. Diego thought fondly of Giorgio, who had volunteered to share his perilous journey. With Giorgio along, Diego knew he would never lack loyal encouragement whatever the unknown wastelands might present.

In the distance the bells of the campanile chimed the end of the working day. Diego tried not to wonder if he would ever see Venice again. Others who had traveled to the East had carried letters and seals of authority from the Pope or the barbarian Khan. Diego had nothing of the kind. He thought wryly that if all he needed to keep him safe was letters he must surely write some to himself. Then he was serious, because most of the people who had essayed the unknown countries to the east of Constantinople had never returned to tell their story. Was the journey a foolish scheme as Duccio had warned? Or would he return with riches as he hoped? Like the other young nobleman of his day, Diego had

14

learned to fight with the sword. In lessons, he had excelled in history but not in science, and had ignored logic, metaphysics and philosophy to concentrate on diplomacy, climbing and archery. Would what he knew and the desperation of his need be enough to keep him alive? Diego shrugged resignedly. What would be would be.

The galley was a fine ship owned by friends of the Mazzarini family and captained by their youngest son. Well-provisioned and crewed by men from the parish, it was rowed out of the harbor by galley oarsmen. Then, as the wind was favorable, a lateen-rigged sail was hoisted and the ship proceeded through the islands of the Venetian lagoon. The channel was marked with *bricole,* massive wooden piles erected to keep the mariner and his ship away from weeds and sandbanks. But the tides were capricious and the sands constantly shifted, so only the most experienced captains knew how to negotiate the seaway that had helped make Venice omnipotent. The water was pale green in patches, sapphire in others and surging with frothy white foam as the ship cleared the canal. Depending on the light, the sea around Venice could turn gray or pink, wine or gold. Local people said that the lagoon had as many moods as those who lived on the islands. Fascinated by the expertise of the navigator, Diego stood at the rail watching the ship's progress. As they proceeded toward the outer islands, he was unaware of his servant Giorgio's increasing queasiness.

Diego's companion on the journey had the reputation for being the rudest servant in Venice. In a city where a nobleman could frequently be seen being berated by his serf, that was a considerable distinction. Giorgio had escaped the fishermen's cavane where he was born because he hated the idea of living on stilts above water, which he feared. He had enrolled in the police force, where he had expected to remain for life. Young Mazzarini had first come to his notice ten years before when Diego, then a handsome fourteen-year-old, had been accosted in the Piazza by a demented woman. As the woman clung to him, determined to be heard, Diego had melted her anger with an irreverent poem about luck that changes too soon. Giorgio had watched the incident with interest, charmed by the diplomacy of the victim. He had asked the young man's name and remembered it. Then, when he lost his job for refusing to bathe, Giorgio had presented himself at the Mazzarini mansion and asked for work. Shortly afterward, Diego's parents died and Giorgio realized he was needed; so he had stayed, unpaid, often unheeded, a pillar of strength whenever things went wrong. He had agreed to accompany his master on this perilous trip across many seas because he could not bear to let Diego go to his death alone. Giorgio pulled his surcoat about him, thankful for the four layers of wool he wore winter and summer, and ran through the items he had packed for the journey, checking to be sure he had forgotten nothing . . . salt and goods for trading, extra clothing, dried fruit, leather vessels for wine, mule saddles, horse saddles, boots for snow, pitchers for water, arrows, swords, daggers and his master's finest clothing and cutlery. Giorgio was forty, unmarried and without a home or coin with which to bless himself. His ambition was to find a woman who loved him passionately. He believed sincerely that he had seen everything there was to see, that he had experienced everything a man could experience and that nothing in the world could shock him. Giorgio had much to learn.

There were 119 islands in the Venetian lagoon, each one different, each in its way a citadel against any enemy foolish enough to brave the sandbanks. Diego listened to the crewmen chanting . . . *"Sempre diretto . . . sempre diretto,"* "Straight on . . . straight on," the fishermen called whenever they saw strangers. The misleading cry lured intruders and their craft to destruction; the wrecks were prizes to be pillaged at leisure by the islanders. Diego watched as the ship passed Murano and the island of San Michele, a small, silent place mysteriously veiled in gray. The sun was setting as Burano appeared in the distance, and Diego remembered the summer he and Pierluigi had visited the lacemakers' island, where the houses were full of songbirds, the gardens merry with flowers and the streets busy with women who knew how to dazzle the senses. He had had difficulty persuading his brother to return home from Burano, and even his own control had vanished in the face of the women's taunting, beckoning ways.

Suddenly there was nothing ahead but a rolling sea and
16

an ephemeral mist that shrouded the coast. Giorgio leaned over the side, gazing helplessly into the water. Diego went below to eat dinner with his friend, the captain, Arnaldo della Frascati. The two men ate heartily of almond soup and a stew of venison, chicken and quail. A pastry sprinkled with ginger, sugar and nuts pleased them, and a dozen toasts in fine red wine made them merry. Then Arnaldo confided that he was soon to marry, and Diego congratulated his friend.

"All Venice is talking about your decision to leave the sea, Arnaldo."

"I am going to manage my father's shipbuilding yards."

"Why are you leaving the water, which you have always loved?"

"I love Lucilia more than I love the sea. I cannot bring myself to think of leaving her once we are married. She is beautiful, and men follow her with their eyes. I should die a thousand deaths thinking of what might be happening."

"But she will be a virtuous wife, not one of those women whose husbands grow horns."

"I know Lucilia is virtuous, but I am jealous, Diego. Every time a man stares at her I want to throttle him, and if I were to go away for many months I should be insane before very long."

Diego thought about that for a while. Then he poured himself more wine and said confidently, "I could never be jealous."

"So says a man who has not been in love!"

"I hope I cannot be jealous, for all my emotions run to excess, and in jealousy I should surely take to my bed!"

"Then I hope you remain free from infatuation. But if you are ever unlucky enough to fall in love, I can promise that you will enjoy the experience."

At first light the two men walked arm in arm to the deck, where they were greeted by Giorgio, who was suffering from seasickness.

The servant called out wearily, "Are we nearly there, Captain? Tell me we're almost there!"

"Not for a week or two, my good friend."

"God's punishment is on my innards."

17

"You'll mend, Giorgio. All my sailors mend sooner or later."

Diego walked to the prow of the ship and looked out at the nearby mainland. He saw only a few shepherds' huts and a rough stone jetty where fisherfolk were gathering. A small girl playing on a sandy beach cried out. Diego turned to Arnaldo.

"Did you hear what the child said?"

"She was wishing you good luck and good fortune."

Diego waved back and called a greeting.

"I shall need her luck, Arnaldo."

"You will indeed, my friend. Are you sure what you are doing is wise?"

Diego watched the sun rising in a pale-lemon sky.

"I am a Mazzarini. Once my ancestors were great men. Some were diplomats and dukes, others were crusaders. Then, as you know, our fortune was stolen by the swindler Cachetti. That was in my grandfather's day. He was old and very ill, so we make excuses for his lack of courage. But for me there can be no excuse. I must survive and bring sons into the world to inherit the title. I cannot do that if there is nothing in our coffers. That is why I am going in search of my fortune, Arnaldo. It's a gamble, and I am not a gambler, but I have no choice."

"What exactly are your plans, Diego?"

"I shall travel to the East and bring back merchandise of value and a thousand tales to tell my grandchildren."

"I pray you live to have grandchildren, my friend. You deserve the best. But what will you do if there are no jewels and merchandise to bring back?"

"I shall return to poverty and the Mazzarinis will be ruined for ever."

"Can it really be so serious?"

"It is indeed. All the money I have left is here in my bag. There is nothing more in the house or in the treasure chests my grandfather once owned."

It was a fine day with a bracing breeze, and Diego's spirits rose with the sun. He stood at the bow of the ship impatient to be at his destination, remembering the little girl's cry ... "Good luck and good fortune go with you."

Chapter Two:

Constantinople to Tabriz

The ship docked in Constantinople—a noisy, colorful city full of amazing sights. Golden domes and minarets formed the skyline, above cypress groves and lovenests of carved and gilded wood set by the side of the sea. At the docks' edge Jews and Armenians, Turks and Ethiopians, Phrygians, Nubians and Anatolians watched as the passengers alighted. Merchants offered goods, pickpockets robbed and ran away, asses brayed and small boys wrestled with baggage too heavy by far for their tender years. A lad named Ismail led those he considered wealthy enough to an inn where hot food was waiting. The inn was well run and clean, and from its windows guests could see the simmering blue of the Bosphorus.

Diego looked out on the citadel of Constantinople, then at the water with its heavy traffic of barges, caiques, merchantmen and quinqueremes. For a moment he thought of the

Venetian lagoon and longed for his home. Then he asked Giorgio to bring their belongings along to his room. Diego was soon alone in a comfortable room dominated by a cedarwood bed. Gilded screens covered the windows, and the floors were bright with woven rugs. Diego threw himself down on the bed and closed his eyes. After weeks at sea he imagined he could still feel the ship undulating beneath him. He remembered how Giorgio had cursed the captain, the waves, his stomach and every evil spirit that had persuaded him to make such a journey. Giorgio had been relieved to see the end of their association with Arnaldo della Frascati. But to Diego it meant the end of security, the final severance with Venice.

While Diego dozed, a servant girl appeared with water in an earthenware jug. She placed sugared rose petals at Diego's bedside. Then she began to tug at his doeskin boots and the woolen surcoat he was wearing. Diego was surprised when she spoke not in the dialect of Venice but the pure tones of Rome.

"Take off your clothes, sir, so I can wash you."

"I can wash myself."

The girl giggled happily.

"Here in the Inn of the Blue Dragon I must wash and anoint you. You are traveling east, are you not? In the East you will encounter many strange customs and you must learn to enjoy them."

The girl looked no more than sixteen. Her hair was dark and curly, her skin the cinnamon shade of the Levant. She was plump but winsome, her arms well muscled and firm. Diego sighed resignedly as he allowed her to remove his clothes. From time to time he eyed the door, fearful that the irreverent Giorgio might appear to scoff at his predicament. The towels were scented with lemon oil, the water warm and inviting. Soon Diego decided that it was a pleasurable experience, one to be repeated often. As the girl washed him he questioned her.

"Are you from Italy?"

"I am from Constantinople."

"What is your name?"

"They call me Halima. I learned to speak a tongue like your own when I married a sailor from Gaeta."

"How old are you?"

"I am twenty-two, too old to marry again now my Gianni has left me."

Diego looked surprised. She certainly didn't seem too old to him.

"At what age did you marry?"

"When I was fourteen, sir. For six years Gianni and I were happy. Then he fell in love with a rich and cultured woman and began to follow her wherever she went. He had such a conscience about his behavior that he began to mistreat me. Then one day he vanished, and I have not seen him since. Now I work here at the inn. I cook and clean for the guests, and I am happy and content because my heart is at peace. Sometimes I think of my husband when the nights are warm and the scent of jasmine is in the air...."

Halima covered the Venetian with a cambric robe, lingering as she admired the slim, hard body that was so sensitive to her touch. Diego felt his pulse quicken with desire. Their eyes met. Then Halima curtsied and explained that the noonday meal was ready in the hall below.

"Food awaits you, sir. Some say it is the best food in Constantinople."

"I shall come at once."

That afternoon Diego wandered alone in the bazaar, admiring silver trays and jars, jeweled clasps, silk carpets, priceless furs and uncut emeralds. All the goods were displayed in shops and stalls so crowded and untidy that the merchandise appeared worthless to its owners. Diego made only two purchases, both in a shop near the Great Mosque. First he bought an icon of solid silver, then a brooch of turquoises in the form of a jasmine flower. As he walked back to the inn he smelled the scent of Constantinople, a potpourri of spice and fruit, sweat and aloe wood and perfumes of Araby. For the first time since his departure, Diego forgot Venice and enjoyed the new, the unknown, the unexpected.

In the servants' quarters of the inn, Giorgio was once more counting his store—the bags of dried apricots and raisins, the wine, clothing, swords, containers of salt and items for trade. He had developed a fear of thieves and refused adamantly to leave his master's belongings for a moment. If his eyes closed, he opened them at once, staring as though bewitched, because he believed that in this alien land every stranger was a villain, every servant a liar, every rich man a rogue. He conveniently forgot that in Venice lying was looked upon as a fine art. One never told the truth to a foreigner, a stranger or a woman. Indeed, one rarely even thought the truth for fear of upsetting oneself.

When Diego informed him that they would be departing for Mersin the following day, Giorgio was unhappy.

"Must we leave so soon, sir? I have only just settled my stomach from the last voyage."

"There is no time to be wasted, my good Giorgio, if we are to avoid the heaviest snowfalls of the year."

"The servant girl asked after you, sir."

"She insisted on bathing me."

Giorgio's eyes widened in horror.

"Bathing you! I never heard of such a thing. Are we paying to be so ill treated, sir?"

Once in his life Giorgio had been forcibly bathed by fellow officers of the hotel inspection unit. Water had entered his every orifice, and for days he had imagined himself deaf, blind and without taste because of contamination. He shook his head apprehensively.

"I hope she does not come to my room, sir, for I shall never bathe again."

"You have said so many times."

"I had a grippe that continued for days after my last submersion. My balance was affected and my eyesight ruined. Bathed indeed! And I thought her such a gentle girl. I shall return to my quarters now, sir. I have arranged to eat there so I need not leave our supplies."

That night Diego lay in the sandalwood bed looking at the moon and listening to the cry of a distant muezzin. How strange the city was, he thought, how alien and different in every way from Venice. The door opened and he saw Halima enter. Without a word she slipped off her robe and for a moment stood outlined against the dark-blue evening sky. Then she knelt at the foot of the bed and kissed Diego's

22

toes, and continued upward until her face was resting on his chest, her stomach pressing against his thighs. Soon they were lovers. The night was warm, their kisses intoxicating, and the tension within Diego made the experience memorable. As the sky lightened, Halima rose and looked longingly at him. Then, reluctantly, she put on her shift and turned to leave the room. Diego called her back.

"I bought something for you, Halima."

Diego handed her a velvet pochette that contained the turquoise brooch. Halima examined the gift, and looked questioningly at the Venetian. It was unheard of for a nobleman to buy a servant a gift. Halima struggled to find words. Then she ran from the room, returning with a leather-bound book handwritten in an educated script.

"And this is my gift to you, sir."

Diego kissed her hand. "Each time I read it I shall remember you."

Halima placed her hands together as if in prayer. Then with a bow she was gone. Diego walked to the window and read the inscription in the light of the early morning. It was a book of words, partly in Italian, partly in the language and signs of a tongue he could not decipher. Puzzled, Diego dressed and prepared to go downstairs to find his servant. First he tucked the book into the bag he carried everywhere. Then he paused to look at the carved bed, to enjoy the scented air and the sounds of the city that drifted constantly over the water.

Giorgio was sitting at a table loaded with cheese, grapes, bread and rose-leaf jam. He was eating noisily and belching contentedly. When Diego appeared, the servant inquired innocently, "Did you sleep well, sir?"

"Perfectly, as always."

Diego avoided the inquisitive eyes, unwilling to submit at this early hour to one of Giorgio's inquisitions. They ate in silence. Then, when they had had their fill, they walked toward the harbor, marveling at the sights of the city, enjoying the strangeness of its atmosphere and making plans for their arrival in Mersin. At quayside Diego was appalled to discover that the freighter they were to travel in was filthy. The sailors

23

were foul-smelling Lascars whose vicious manners made him caution his servant.

"Take care not to antagonize these fellows, my good Giorgio."

"I shall ignore them, sir. By the Virgin I will."

"Come with me while I inspect the sleeping quarters."

Giorgio stepped back in alarm at the thought of sleeping in the bowels of such a disreputable vessel.

"I intend to sleep on deck. The cabins will be alive with rodents."

Diego went alone to the room allocated to him for the journey. First he lifted the bedcover. He watched with distaste as fleas jumped around the linen sheet. The floor was muddy, and there were rodent droppings on every surface. Diego returned to the deck and asked to see the captain. Few understood him, and those who did affected not to. When he made his way toward the bridge a swarthy seaman barred his way. Diego pushed him aside. The seaman pulled out a knife. Diego grasped the sailor's wrist and bent the fingers back till the weapon fell to the floor. Giorgio kicked it aside, watching with admiration as his master proceeded upward to the captain's cabin.

Glad to be away from the prying eyes of the crew, Diego looked down at the sleeping man and knew his efforts had been in vain. The captain was drunk and asleep at his desk, a stream of saliva dripping from his open mouth on the log of the ship he commanded. Diego inspected the captain's quarters, which were as dirty as the cabin he had been assigned. Then he walked below and looked over the galley. Minutes later he returned to tell Giorgio what he had decided.

"The ship is foul and full of rodents, as you said. The food would be inedible, and I shall not travel on this vessel."

"But sir, there is no other ship to Mersin for weeks."

"Then we must sail elsewhere, my good Giorgio."

"But where?"

"To Cyprus perhaps. I recall my brother's mentioning that the ships of Cyprus were fine ships, well run by men who had learned their seamanship from Venetian captains."

They collected their belongings, and Giorgio counted them yet again as they reached the quayside. An hour later they had secured passages on a well-ordered ship due to leave Constantinople for Cyprus that evening. To celebrate, the Venetians bought violet and honey sherbet from a street vendor, and ate squares of rice jelly—a treat Giorgio adored because it was flavored with rose water. Then Diego deposited his servant at the inn and went on a tour of the Grand Bazaar. After wandering for some time through the maze of stalls, he found a wise man writing letters and giving advice to those of lesser education. Diego showed the man the book Halima had given him and asked what its purpose was. The old man peered inside and then exclaimed.

"This is a wondrous object. It is a finder of words. It was written by one of your own countrymen for use on his travels, and no doubt he curses its loss."

"Which words can I find in the book?"

"They are the words of Persia and Turkestan, sir."

"And how do I find them?"

"If you wish to ask for water you look for the Venetian word for water and then to the opposite side of the parchment, where there is written the word in Persian and in the dialect of Turkestan. It is written in the script of those countries with a way of pronouncing the word in your own language."

Diego examined the book with renewed interest. The scribe smiled politely.

"Will you travel far, sir?"

"I am going to Cyprus and then through Persia to the East."

"Many moons ago men came to this city and spoke of a country far to the east, but I did not believe them. You must take care on this journey. The Turkomans are rude fellows, slow-witted and uncongenial. The Persians are the opposite, too clever by far. They will have that fine robe from your back and you none the wiser."

"Did the travelers say anything of the people who live in the country far to the east?"

"They told stories of those people being ruled by an emperor who is hated throughout the land. They said that the houses of that country are all palaces and that there is gold and rubies and pearls as big as pigeons' eggs to be had without effort. That is why I did not believe them."

25

"I thank you for your advice, sir."

Diego put a coin in the scribe's bowl. The old man weighed it in his hand. Then he warned Diego again of the dangers he would encounter.

"When you reach Cyprus you must hide the gold you carry so openly, sir. Put the coins in your shoes or, better, sew them in your clothing. And you must buy daggers and poison to conceal about your person. That sword will surely be stolen and you will be left defenseless. Once you leave the island of Cyprus you will be at the beginning of the most uncivilized part of the world. If the lands of the East exist, the people there may not welcome you. I have heard some fearful tales about a race of horsemen whose joy is killing, who boil their enemies in oil and split them asunder with specially forged swords. Watch your shadow, my son, for you will never know when you can trust it."

Diego returned to the inn, where he and Giorgio were served with fruit soup, aubergine stew and a dish of Azerbaijan pears. Halima listened eagerly as the Venetian spoke of the condition of the ship they had abandoned, clucking sympathetically when Diego told her what the scribe had told him. When the meal was over, Halima brought sherbet flavored with musk and amber. As she served Diego she whispered encouragements in his ear.

"You must not worry, my lord. I am sure you will succeed. Think of nothing but achieving your ambition. That is the way. One thought of failure and it will fly over the mountains to plague you."

Giorgio watched and waited for his moment. Then, when Halima had returned to the kitchen, he leaned across the table and whispered irreverently, "I hope your brother, my lord Pierluigi, did not rest in this inn, sir."

"Why?"

"He might have married that eager one."

Diego laughed. They had often joked about the possibility that his young brother would marry a woman in every town and return to Venice with a harem. Giorgio wiped his face and went to the door to look out on the busy thoroughfare.

"When shall we depart, sir?"

"Soon—we must board our ship before sunset."

Giorgio counted the packages swiftly in case something had been spirited away while he ate. The commercial quarter near the dock was said to be full of rogues and vandals. Giorgio tried to take his mind from the worry of his responsibilities by thinking of a woman he had seen that afternoon. One brief glimpse of her limbs through the diaphanous wrappings had made his head whirl, and he had remembered with dismay that he had not made love to a woman for months. No one wanted such an uncouth and dirty individual, and without money Giorgio knew he would never change a Venetian woman's mind. He looked guiltily at his employer, afraid lest the wind had ears for his thoughts. Then he spat. Women were nothing but trouble. He must learn to be content without them.

From Cyprus the two men sailed to Acre. From Acre they proceeded on steppe ponies to Tabriz. By late summer, they came to the chief city of Azerbaijan province. The landscape as far as they could see was covered with yellow dust. Fellow travelers rode by in voluminous clothing, their faces resembling carnival masks of brown and ocher. Women in the villages near Tabriz were winnowing grain by tossing it in the air. And everywhere there were piles of chaffless corn outside pink-walled farmhouses.

Giorgio rode at the Venetian's side, wondering if Diego would allow them a brief rest in Tabriz. He looked at the dark-eyed women as they passed and wished he had Diego's powers to attract them.

After the grueling 750 miles of journeying, in which the hatred of Christians was apparent in local eyes and religious fanaticism bubbled close to the surface of daily life, Diego was relieved to find Tabriz a large and stately city. The thieves who had dogged his trail, trying to steal the horses and traveling packs, took flight as the Venetian rode into the courtyard of a busy inn in the city center. Ostlers took care of the animals. Servants carried the packs inside for Giorgio to count. Others hurried to remove the saddles, which, at Diego's insistence, were placed in his bedroom. Women in chadors could be seen passing like black phantoms through the courtyards, their eyes downcast, their faces hidden from the infidel's gaze. Diego decided that the only woman lucky enough to lead a normal life was the owner's wife, whose laughter could be heard from the depths of the building. Someone told him the woman came from a far country and that she was not imprisoned in the zenana with the other women. Diego never saw her but in the sullen silence all around he was often thankful for the sound of her merriment.

A few days after their arrival in Tabriz, Diego was walking down the hill, past the vendor of rose petals and sturgeon eggs, when he heard a voice calling to him in Italian.

"Sir! Sir! Please, may I speak with you?"

Turning, Diego saw a young boy dressed as perfectly as any Venetian son. In Tabriz it was a strange sight and a welcome one.

The boy bowed. "Tassilo Viglioni, may it please you, sir. My mother asked me to invite you to our home. We heard that you follow Niccolo and Maffeo Polo to the East and we would like to assist you in any way we can."

"I shall be delighted to visit your home, Tassilo."

"And will you tell me stories of Venice, sir? I am always thinking of La Serenissima, wondering what it would be like to visit the home of my parents."

The boy was not more than eight or nine but seemed wise beyond his years. Diego was touched by his desire for knowledge of a city he had never seen and delighted to be in contact with a family familiar with Venice. He followed as Tassilo led him to a Venetian-style mansion behind ornate black iron railings.

"This is our house, sir. Please come inside."

Diego looked around in admiration at masses of pink Persian roses growing over the facade of the house. Their perfume filled the air, and the sound of a tinkling fountain added to the romance of the place in the Venetian's eyes. As he approached the house, Diego saw an old lady watching him from the balcony. She was sitting with a haughty young woman dressed in white and green. Tassilo tugged Diego's hand and led him forward.

"This is my grandmother, sir, and this is Mama, the lady Marella. Mama, meet Count Mazzarini from Venice."

Diego bowed. The old woman touched his hand with her

gnarled fist. Marella nodded coolly at the newcomer. Despite her hauteur, however, Diego was pleased to see a flush spreading from the lady's neck to her alabaster cheeks. He examined the silver-blond plait that framed her face, the voluminous robe that hid her body. And as he looked in admiration at her beauty, Diego wondered why the lady was so unhappy and unwilling to smile. Marella greeted him in a soft voice.

"We are happy to welcome you, Count Mazzarini. My husband is away in Tiflis and will not return for many days. When Tassilo heard about your expedition and learned that you were Venetian, he begged me to invite you to our home. Tassilo has never seen Venice, and as it is ten years since I visited my parents, I feel I cannot tell him of its present appearance. That is why I invited you here."

Diego looked to the matriarch's blank face and then back to Tassilo's mother.

Marella motioned for a servant to take the old lady to her room. "My husband's mother cannot speak and she hears nothing, because she is very old. She will rest now after the excitement of meeting a fellow Venetian. May I invite you to dine with us this evening, sir?"

"I should be honored, my lady."

"Tomorrow Tassilo will take you to meet a man who will help you arrange the next part of your journey. My son is already well versed in the customs of this area, so he can guard your interests. If you go alone I fear you may have some difficulty with the language. These people are less than scrupulous in their dealings with foreigners."

"I have come this far alone, my lady."

Marella smiled mysteriously.

"My dear friend, Tabriz is only the beginning. Tabriz is the rose. The desert of Dasht-i-Lut and the mountains of the Pamirs will be your thorn."

Stung by her reproachful tone, Diego turned away. When he had collected himself he found Marella watching him closely.

"Will you return to Venice someday, my lady?"

"I do not know. My husband enjoys life here and loves to travel. My son also wishes to travel, as is the custom in the

Viglioni family. The business is prospering and my husband and his brothers are well established. They will surely never leave Tabriz."

"Are there many Venetians in the city?"

"Yes, there are many, all linked together in this small community. There are also Genoans and Armenians, Georgians, Persians and Saracens as well as the natives of India, Kashmir and the Uighur. Tabriz is not only for the Tabrizis, though they would like to believe that it is."

Diego was fascinated by the autocratic tone and the contrasting twinkle in the lady's eyes.

"At what time do you dine, my lady?"

"In the cool of the evening."

"How shall I know the hour at which you wish me to arrive?"

"Come when you wish, sir. Tassilo and I will be looking forward to entertaining you."

On his way back to the inn, Diego was accosted by a ruffian who snatched his hat and tried to drag the pearl-and-gold fastener from his mantle. Diego hurled his attacker aside. Then others appeared and surrounded him, their eyes full of loathing for his fair skin and fine style. As the beggars taunted him, Diego fought gamely, but he was no match for their number and they knocked him down. Soon the scarlet mantle was gone and with it the boots from his feet and the doeskin jerkin. As Diego lay unconscious and bleeding in the roadway, the people of Tabriz passed by, amused by the heathen's downfall. Children threw dust on the unconscious man and a traveling water carrier tried to remove the ruby ring from Diego's finger. When the ring would not move the man berated the unconscious figure with every curse he knew.

Diego awoke and blinked uncertainly. When he realized what had happened he was thankful that he had left his most valuable belongings with Giorgio. Amazed that even his boots had been stolen, he stumbled back to the inn, trying to wipe the blood from the cut on his forehead.

Giorgio, who was watching for his master's return from the window of the inn, saw Diego's condition and rushed outside to help him. Scolding and grumbling like an irate mother with a recalcitrant child, Giorgio took Diego inside.

"What did I tell you would happen if you insisted on going out alone? Mother of goodness, what blood! Boy, run for water and linen to dress my master's wounds."

The servant returned with strips of cambric, a bowl of water and healing herbs for the gashes on Diego's head and body. Gently, Giorgio dressed the wounds and staunched the bleeding. All the while he complained bitterly about embarking on such a futile journey.

"I knew it would end badly, and now this. We're but a quarter of the way to wherever we're going, and here you are injured from head to toe. I wouldn't care if I knew the place even existed, but who knows if it does? We could be walking forever and then never reach our destination. How many of these ruffians were there?"

"Seven or eight."

"What cowards they are that they attack only in packs like jackals."

"I intend to go out again this evening to dine with the Viglioni family. You had better stay close to our belongings and see you guard them well, my good Giorgio. There has been talk of our arrival in Tabriz. That is why I was attacked. I believe these fools think me a rich man!"

"I advise you to change your plans, sir."

"Indeed I shall not. I promised the lady Marella I would dine with her."

Giorgio glowered at his master's stubbornness.

"Your brother calls you mulish. I think you are unable to change your mind. What's to be done? I am servant to a man determined to accomplish his own destruction."

Diego arrived at the Viglioni house in the cool of the evening. He was surprised to find the enclosure lit with torches. There were pretty women on the lawn, and Venetian men on the terrace, and Tassilo was waiting impatiently for him by the gate. When the boy saw Diego's injuries he flinched.

"Did the beggars attack you, sir?"

"They did indeed."

"Mama will have them whipped. She is very angry about

31

the beggars, because once they tried to take her parasol. She will make Papa have them all arrested."

"I hope she does. And now, Tassilo, tell me, who are all these fine ladies and gentlemen?"

"They are Venetians, sir. Mama thought the surprise would please you."

The boy hesitated. Then he whispered to Diego, "Mama is wearing a new dress, sir. Be sure to tell her how much it becomes her so she will not cry as she does when Papa forgets to notice such things."

Diego remained silent as Tassilo led him toward the terrace.

"When Grandpapa was alive he paid Mama the prettiest compliments, but Papa does not know how. I suppose that is why my mother cries so much."

Diego greeted his hostess with a bow and a kiss to the bejeweled fingers. Marella curtsied and smiled enchantingly.

"You look like a warrior, Count Mazzarini, with your injured head and bandaged hands."

"And you, my lady, look like a goddess. The color of your dress suits you more than you can know. Or perhaps you *do* know the effect it has upon those privileged to be in your company."

Diego held out his arm. Marella took it and led the way into the dining hall, where a table festooned with fruit and flowers groaned under the weight of the banquet she had ordered for her guest's honor. Wild boar sat on gold servers amid rows of honey-basted lamb. Grapes and peaches were piled into a cornucopia of carved ivory, and there was wine from Italy. Diego toasted Tassilo, then his hostess. A young Venetian merchant seconded the toast and proposed another of his own.

"To Venice! To La Serenissima!"

Everyone rose and cried, "La Serenissima!" and Diego noticed that some of the ladies grew tearful at the mention of their beloved city.

After the meal a troupe of dancers performed to the accompaniment of wind bells and gembris. Some of the men retired to the gaming room, others reclined in the garden on

32

couches littered with rose petals. Diego walked with Marella amid the trees.

"May I ask why you are so unhappy, my lady?"

She took a deep breath and walked on without answering. Diego persisted.

"Forgive my curiosity, but I hate to see any unhappy woman, and an unhappy, beautiful woman should not exist."

"My husband is often away seeing to matters of business in Tiflis, Baghdad and Maragheh."

"Are you unhappy because you are lonely or for other reasons connected with his absences?"

"You presume, sir. We have only just met!"

For the first time Marella's composure vanished, and Diego felt her arm trembling in his.

"You invited me here when we had only just met, my lady. You wore a new dress for me when we had only just met. Will you not confide in me? Is there nothing I can do to make you happy?"

Marella picked a rose from the hedge and inhaled its perfume. Then she threw it away as though she were not conscious of her actions. Suddenly the secret she had kept for so long became too much to bear and she began to speak.

"My husband is in love with a Persian woman. For two years he has visited us here in Tabriz only rarely, and when he does he avoids all contact with me. I long for another child, sir, that is why I am unhappy. For months I have been hoping that my husband will tire of this woman, but I fear he is besotted with her. I do not wish Tassilo to be my only child. I have always prayed for a daughter ... but ... I have said too much! I must return at once to the house."

Marella turned to run away, but Diego held her arm.

"Stay with me. Don't hide from the truth."

"I cannot stay. I have spoken indiscreetly."

"I am a Venetian gentleman, my lady. Your desire is my command. If you tell me to go away I shall go at once. If you tell me to love you I shall love you with the homage your beauty deserves. If you ask me to be your cicisbeo for a few days until my departure, I shall be deeply honored."

Marella laughed delightedly.

"When I was a young girl in Venice I went to see a play

33

in which the lady's cicisbeo was also her lover. He danced attendance on her as a cicisbeo should, opened doors for her as a cicisbeo should, picked up her fan when she dropped it and helped her into her gondola as a cicisbeo should. Then, in the darkness of the night, when the husband went to see his mistress, the cicisbeo came to Madame's boudoir and cuckolded the old goat!"

Suddenly Marella remembered her manners and covered her face with her fan. "I talk too freely. I am alone so frequently it has become easy to forget that I am a lady."

She was trembling so violently Diego took her in his arms. "Say no more, my lady."

He led her back to the house, and they listened as a troubador sang melancholy songs of unrequited love. Marella tried not to watch the Venetian for fear of causing a scandal. But often she found herself examining the clear skin, the golden hair, the curly beard and twinkling blue eyes that had made life suddenly more interesting for her.

As dawn came, the ladies were sent home in their carriages. The men of the Venetian party insisted on accompanying Diego back to his inn. When they reached the corner of the street they found their way barred by a line of swarthy beggars. Cackling and rubbing their hands, the beggars were delighted by the prospect of the fat pickings to come. Six elegantly clad Venetians looked at each other and then back to the ruffians. Then, to the beggars' surprise, they shouted for the attack to commence and fell on the thieves with their swords. The air was loud with screams, shouts and the clanging of metal. One beggar was hurled over a wall to the marketplace below. Another ran down the hill to get away from his aristocratic pursuer and fell into the fountain, almost drowning. The most dangerous met his match when he tried to use a dagger on Arturo di Fellipe, once the finest swordsman in Venice. The ruffian disappeared, screeching like a fishwife, his gut split from side to side. The foppish di Fellipe wiped his blade and was heard to complain that it would forever be contaminated. In minutes the encounter was over. The beggars were unconscious on the ground or running to far parts of the city. The Venetians were soiled but otherwise unharmed. They gave three delighted cheers of victory and carried Diego back to his inn on their shoulders. Then they returned to Marella's house to tell her of their adventure.

Alone in her bedroom, Marella lay dreaming of Diego Mazzarini. As the sun rose over the tamarisk trees she thought of what her Venetian friends had said: *Mazzarini is a fine fellow and brave of heart.* The more she tried to put Diego from her mind, the more he appeared like a phantom to taunt her. Then, as the clock struck eight, Marella looked up and there he was, smiling down on her. She gave a small startled cry.

"Is it really you? You frightened me almost to death. I did not hear the bell."

"A cicisbeo comes secretly to his lady by climbing the branches that touch her window. He would not ring the bell for fear of compromising her virtue."

Marella smiled happily and ran to Diego, throwing her arms around his neck and kissing him warmly.

"Be my lover and love me till the sun sets in the sky."

"I am yours to command, my lady."

"Then I command you to pleasure me."

The room smelled of lilies. The lady's skin was smooth as the blush of peach down. Diego loved her as she had always longed to be loved, eagerly, gently, with the confidence of one whose pleasure is to please. As the sounds of morning began to filter into the room, the couple burrowed further into the bed, unwilling to be interrupted by reality. They titillated each other with promises they knew they could never fulfill but which both enjoyed as children enjoy forbidden games. Lunch was served by a discreet maid in the boudoir, tisanes at four in the conservatory. At nightfall, as they were dining by candlelight, a strolling minstrel came to play under the window. Pleased by the love song he sang, Marella threw him a coin and the white rose from her bedside. Then she turned to Diego and spoke about the morning.

"We should have arranged your journey, sir."

"Tomorrow will do as well."

"I may not wish to let you go."

"I hope to return someday so we can dine together and tell each other secrets."

Marella was silent, and Diego knew she was struggling to retain the taste of happiness, to reject the sadness of parting. He held her in his arms, stroking her hair and kissing her shoulders.

"Would it not be wise for you to return to Venice?"

"I long to return home. Indeed, I am forever dreaming of it."

"Why do you stay if you dislike Tabriz?"

"Tassilo loves his home, sir. He dreams of Venice, but not as much as he dreams of traveling to the East, to the lands where no other man has been. In Venice he would know no one. The customs would be alien to him and he would feel confused and lonely without his friends. Soon he would be unhappy—of that I am certain."

"And so you stay?"

"When my son is old enough to begin his travels I shall return to La Serenissima; that I have promised myself."

Tears fell from her eyes on Diego's chest, and he spoke reassuringly.

"When you are back in Venice, I shall call on you and be your cicisbeo again."

"By the time I return to Venice I shall be too old to be loved."

"You will never be old, my lady. Never."

"Don't talk of the future. Tonight is our night. Tomorrow Tassilo will take you to the agent who can arrange your journey. Then you will be gone. Blow out the candle. The moon is full and I want to remember you as my own silver god of the night."

Diego blew out the candles and opened the shutters to the moonlight. Then he went to Marella's outstretched arms, and she whispered her innermost thoughts to him.

"They say girl children are conceived on the night of the full moon. Do you think it can be true? I shall pray that my cicisbeo fulfills all my wishes."

The following morning Diego went with Tassilo to the rooms of an agent who arranged passages to Herat and Balkh. The agent suggested that Diego and his servant join one of the silk caravans traveling west through Kerman and Tabas.

As the man explained the dangers of the journey, Tassilo looked up uncertainly at the impassive face of the Venetian, then back to the grinning agent on the rug. The native's smile widened as the perils about which he warned increased. Tassilo wondered if there was going to be another fight, but Diego listened to the outpourings with a calm expression.

Annoyed by his visitor's sang-froid, the agent spat and continued his pessimistic harangue.

"You will pass through the lands of the Bakhtiari. They are very fierce. They may kill you or they may let you pass, it depends on how they are feeling. If they kill you they will play *buzkashi* with your corpse and will find it very amusing. Usually they use the body of a goat, but an infidel's body is much more interesting."

"Is there water in the area through which we'll be traveling?"

"The waterholes are far apart and salty. You must take with you as much water as you can carry."

"And what of the cities?"

"In Herat you will find very few people. Years ago there were as many in that city as on the face of the earth. Then the Mongols came and killed almost all. Now there are only the descendants of the forty who remained after the Khan's horsemen departed. The Mongols are murderers, sir, each and every one. Never forget that. If you do not have tablets of authority from the Khan you will almost certainly be killed as you pass through his lands."

"I do not intend to be put off by your warnings, sir."

The merchant looked in wonder at Diego's defiant face.

"By the stars, sir, you are a foolish fellow to contemplate such a journey. Ah, I remember one thing more. The flies. See you do not get bitten by the flies, for if you do you will suffer a fever for the rest of your life."

On the way back to the house Diego sensed that his companion was troubled. "Is something wrong, Tassilo?"

"My father is returning home today, sir."

"You seem upset. Surely you should be happy?"

"I am happy to think of Papa's return, but my mother always cries when he comes back. Why do women cry so much, Count Mazzarini?"

"Women are like cobwebs, Tassilo. They are fragile in some things and strong in others. Perhaps your mama is tired? Women are given to small but frequent maladies which pass like a ripple on the water."

"When you visit our house she sings, sir."

"And if you look after her well your mama will be happy and sing all the while. She needs your attention, Tassilo. I fear my lady misses her home in Venice much more than she likes to admit."

"I shall do my best, sir. Will you be coming tonight to meet my father?"

Diego ruffled the dark hair.

"I start my journey tomorrow at dawn, and I must retire early to be fresh for the morning. So, time will not permit it."

"I shall remember your tales of Venice, Count Mazzarini."

"And I shall remember you, Tassilo, and your beautiful mother. Bid her my fondest farewell."

On his way home Tassilo tried to walk like Diego. And when his mother summoned him to her boudoir he recited the Venetian's conversation word for word. The boy's heart leaped with pleasure at his mother's happy smile, and he kissed her and told her he thought her especially beautiful. As Marella hugged her son, he was busy thinking of ways to keep her content.

Marella looked dreamily out on the parched plain, her thoughts with the handsome young man who had warmed her heart and stolen her wifely virtue, but whom she would never see again. Still, the sadness of the past was replaced by a sense of well-being and confidence. Marella closed her eyes and prayed that her dream of having a daughter would come true.

Chapter Three:

Persia to Balkh in Bactria

The first twelve days on the trail were interesting by their very strangeness. The party passed mud villages on the way to Isfahan and fire worshipers in the hills. They ate the staple food of the area, boiled chicken and sour-milk dish called mast, supplementing it with green and yellow melons which they bought at every busy junction. The stars in that part of the world were the brightest the travelers had ever seen, and they took that as a good omen. For weeks their luck held and they met only merchants, water carriers, camel drivers and beggars on the route. Their sleep was peaceful and the weather neither too hot nor too wet for comfort.

Then, without warning, they came to the black burned terrain the agent of Tabriz had mentioned. Salty waterholes exaggerated the thirst of those foolish enough to drink the contents, and the sun burned down relentlessly. There the party encountered a group of mounted brigands. First the raiders circled the party. Then they charged, screaming like dervishes, into the travelers' midst. Two of the merchants were killed. Three women were abducted, never to be seen again. Then the brigand leader dismounted and surveyed the confusion he had caused with immense satisfaction. He called orders in a language Diego could not understand, and cracked his whip when he was not instantly obeyed.

The caravan master informed what remained of his party that they must form a line and hand over their most valuable possessions. Some protested and were beaten by the brigands. Some walked meekly into line with everything they owned. One young woman cowered under blankets in a wagon, praying she had not been noticed. And a child began to cry for its mother, who had been abducted. Diego was distracted to see one of the brigands carrying the baby away.

As his fellow travelers handed over their valuables, Diego weighed what to do. The gold he had left had been sewn into Giorgio's clothing on the assumption that no one would wish to touch such foul-smelling wrappings. His supplies for the journey were in no way remarkable. Only the case of silver cutlery embossed with the Mazzarini crest would have value enough to interest the raiders.

When the brigand leader reached Diego, he held out his hand for the Venetian's valuables, astutely weighing the young man before him. Diego shook his head to indicate that he had nothing of value. The brigand screamed to the caravan master to translate. Diego explained that he was a poor man with nothing of value to give. Five brigands held him down while the leader searched his clothing. When he discovered a stone that Diego had found on the day he left Tabriz, the leader roared in triumph. The stone glinted like gold in the sun, and Diego was relieved when the brigand pocketed it and passed on to his servant, Giorgio.

Giorgio beamed at the brigand and pawed his coat. All the while he jabbered like a simpleton and allowed saliva to drip down his chin. The brigand recoiled as Giorgio touched him and, fearful of catching whatever had addled the servant's brains, passed on to demand the valuables of the next in line. Giorgio sighed with relief that his acting had been successful.

Soon the raiders rode off, leaving behind them broken families and the sound of women wailing. The mother of the girls who had been abducted was prostrated, the wives of the murdered merchants inconsolable. Diego reassured the girl who had hidden in the wagon. Then the party moved on. Diego's eyes scanned the horizon, but there was nothing to see, only a village and a traveling ass dealer who offered them splendid animals at thirty marks of silver apiece. Impoverished now, most of the travelers could not buy and the caravan continued toward Kerman.

Before long, they were happy to see that they had left behind the salty waterholes and desert terrain for a more verdant area with date groves and numerous partridge and quail. The men went hunting. The women cooked feasts and commiserated with each other in their distress. Diego felt only an increasing impatience to be away from the party. Alone with his servant he would run the risk of being an easy prey for robbers and brigands in the hills. But two men on horseback were a minute target in the vast panorama of mountain and sand. The Venetian calculated that he had traveled three hundred miles from Kashan to Yask and another two hundred to the city of Kerman. Diego was adamant in his belief that he had traveled far enough with such an unlucky party.

"I think we should leave the party when we reach Herat," he told Giorgio.

"I agree, sir. If the bandits don't kill them they will like as not kill each other. Since they found turquoise stones in the province of Kerman there has been nothing but squabbling. I am tired of listening to them, indeed I am."

"There's a desert ahead; are the water pots filled?"

"Aye, sir, I made the others fill theirs too so they wouldn't try to steal from ours."

"How long is the desert? Did the leader tell you?"

"He said it would take eight days to pass."

The desert of Dasht-i-Lut had no trees, no fruit and no water. Surprisingly the quarrels ceased as exhaustion and the possibility of death united the travelers. One of the widows began to cook for the Venetians, and the young woman

41

who had hidden from the brigands explained that she was on her way to be married in Balkh.

"I have not met my future husband, sir, but I dream of him every night."

Diego looked at her docile face and nervous, trembling hands.

"What will happen if you do not like your future husband when you meet him?"

The girl seemed startled by the suggestion.

"My parents say I shall love him, and I know that I shall. I am happy with my future, sir."

After this conversation the girl's parents prevented their daughter from speaking with the Venetians again. Diego accepted their decision without argument. But often the girl could be seen peeping tearfully out of the covering of her caravan at the handsome traveler who had aroused her curiosity.

One day Diego and his servant rode away from the main party, which had camped on a plateau. It was their intention to hunt game to replenish their supplies. The clear mountain air was invigorating, and Diego felt happier than he had felt for many weeks. It was elating to be so far from civilization. For the first time since he had left Venice Diego felt like a great explorer.

The two men shot fawns and some gray-winged birds like partridge. Then they gathered mushrooms, which grew all over the area. In the heat of midday they descended into a green, heavily forested valley to search for more food. Relieved to be free of the party, Giorgio grew reckless. He rode ahead of his master at high speed, through the forest, singing Venetian songs and irreverent ditties learned from fishermen in the days of his childhood. Thinking of the conversations he had had with his master about life and the love of women, money and the evils it caused, religion and the burdens of goodness, Giorgio was grinning happily as he rode along the path that led to a village in a clearing. Suddenly his horse reared and he fell to the ground half stunned. Then, to his horror, he heard the roar of a tiger.

Diego galloped forward in time to see the tiger leap from a tree branch onto his servant's shoulders. Appalled by Giorgio's agonized screams, Diego quickly took his crossbow and selected the strongest arrows. When he had fired six arrows Diego felt it safe to approach his servant. It took all his strength to roll the dead tiger from Giorgio's legs so he could examine the unconscious man. The ashen face was covered with blood, Giorgio's breath was shallow, and one of his legs was broken. His chest was covered with claw marks and he was bleeding profusely. Diego carried the injured man to his horse, placed him over the saddle and rode to the nearby village, where he begged help with the assistance of his book of words.

Soon the silence was replaced by excited shouts. Old women appeared from the huts, young men from the forest where they had been cutting wood. Cries of jubilation rose as some of the natives dragged the tiger's body into the clearing, and gradually Diego came to understand that the animal had been killing children from the area for many months. Some of the villagers fell to their knees and kissed the Venetian's feet. Women who had lost children to the tiger garlanded him with flowers, and the village elder sought words in the book with which to welcome the new arrival. Diego looked to where the old man pointed and read in Italian... "Sir, greetings, thanks."

Giorgio was placed on a makeshift bed in one of the huts. His wounds were dressed, his leg splinted with bamboo, and green liquid poured into his mouth to calm the fever that would come with the night. Then young girls garlanded the sick man with necklets of yellow frangipani. When Giorgio recovered consciousness he turned weakly to his master and asked what had happened.

"Your leg is broken. You were mauled by a tiger, but you'll live, my good Giorgio."

"You saved my life, sir."

"And my own."

"Don't try to diminish what you did. You are a most noble gentleman and it is my privilege to serve you."

Leaving his servant to sleep, Diego walked to the clearing, where he studied the book of words. He asked the village elder to ascertain from the woman who had dressed Giorgio's wounds how long it would be before he could move on. The

43

woman replied that in two days the sick man would either be recovering or he would be dead. Diego decided to return to the caravan with news of the accident. Then he would ride back to the village with his belongings and wait until his servant was well enough to continue the journey. Despite all that had happened, Diego was cheerful. Now, at least, they would be able to travel on alone, free from the dangers connected with a caravan traveling through hostile territory.

Diego saw no one as he rode back through the forest, and no one passed him on the high ground that led to the plateau. As he drew near the spot where he had left his fellow travelers, he saw an ominous pall of black smoke. Diego stopped suddenly, his face paling with horror. Below in the clearing two of the caravans were still burning, the rest were charred remains. The mules and horses had been stolen. The men lay staring at the sky, their throats cut. A thousand flies buzzed over the corpses, and vultures were already circling overhead, impatient predators incensed to be delayed.

Checking to be sure he was alone, Diego led his horse through the remains of the camp. At first he could not find the cart of supplies Giorgio had driven from Tabriz. Then he saw the young woman who had hidden in fear from the first brigands. She was dangling like a rag doll from the branch of a carob tree, her body mutilated and defiled. His cart lay beyond her, hurled into a thorn bush, and Diego knew the assassins had stood her on its boards before pushing the wheels from under her and slowly strangling her. He cut down the girl's body and covered it with a blanket. Then he walked to the cart and took what remained of his supplies. The water jugs were all smashed. The dried fruits had been tossed on the sand and were alive with ants. The silver cutlery with the Mazzarini crest had vanished, as had the salt and most of the items for trade. Only his clothing had been left untouched. Diego looked helplessly down at the surcoats and cloaks of fine velvet and silk. To men intent on murder, the finery of a Venetian nobleman had seemed useless, so they had left it untouched. Diego packed his clothes into a bag. Then he went around the clearing collecting what he could salvage, a barrel of salt, a cask of wine, a case of dried figs, a Bible chased in gold. After he had said a prayer for the

44

dead he rode away, his heart thundering with shock and anger. On the edge of the plateau an ass ran out of the bushes. Diego fastened a rope around the animal's neck and led it back to the village.

Darkness streaked the sky with carmine as Diego neared the clearing where he had left his servant. Often he heard the sound of wolves howling at the sunset, and that increased his melancholy frame of mind. The people with whom he had traveled were all dead. He had lost everything but his life, his servant and his frivolous Venetian clothes. Would he still be able to reach the East? Diego thought of the ducats still sewn into Giorgio's jacket and the book of words in his saddlebag. There could be no turning back. But what lay ahead for men with no supplies and nothing with which to trade? Diego rode into the village trying not to think of the girl who had died so ignominiously, but her image haunted him like a phantom.

The villagers brought food, rice and a hammock so Diego could sleep out of the way of snakes and scorpions. They gave advice on how to proceed to Herat, reassuring him as much as they were able. In the firelight glow the women hummed a lullaby that sent their tired guest to sleep long before the moon was high. They watered Diego's horse and ass and gave Giorgio more of the draught to cure his fever. The villagers had tried to warn Diego about the dangers of Mongols and assassins who took pleasure in killing Christians foolhardy enough to venture on the silk route. But Diego's book of words had only the translations for food and water, the means to ask help, direction or simple advice. Only the elder could read, and he could understand only the simplest signs. Feeling responsible for the stranger, the village men mounted guard throughout the night in case someone returned to harm the man who had killed the tiger.

In the morning Diego woke to see yellow sunlight dappling through the branches of a red-leafed tree. The village was a hive of activity. Women washed clothes on stones in the river; children played contentedly in the mud, and the old women of the community sat grating coconut and making ghee. A young girl appeared with food for the Venetian. First she laughed at his attempts to eat the strange mixture. Then she showed him how to take nourishment in the manner of her people, with the fingers, using only the right hand. Diego saw that she grabbed a handful of rice which she molded into a ball; the rice was then dipped into sauces and other dishes and eaten. The simplicity of the action belied the intricacy of its execution and it was with difficulty that Diego ate anything.

When he had finished, Diego went to the hut where Giorgio was being fed by a huge, fat woman. The sick man was feeling better and was no longer troubled by the fever.

"I think I am almost well again, sir."

"God be praised."

"This is Arya. She is fond of me, sir. She says I am a fine man and a great warrior to have so strong a scent."

"How can you tell what she says?"

"She talks with gestures and I understand almost everything. Is she not magnificent, sir? They do not have women like Arya in Venice."

Diego shuddered at the rolls of fat around the native woman's waist.

"When will you be ready to leave, my good Giorgio?"

"Yesterday you thought I was dying. Today you become impatient to leave. I'm sick of hurrying."

"The caravans have been destroyed by marauders. I returned to the plateau yesterday to collect our belongings."

"And what of the people?"

"They are all dead."

Giorgio fell silent, and seeing his unease the woman left the two men alone. At last Giorgio summoned the courage to ask about the possessions he had guarded so zealously.

"The antelope bag is here with us, and my clothing was untouched. No doubt the murderers thought it unsuitable for the climate of this land. Everything else was gone," Diego replied.

"What shall we do, sir?"

"I shall go on. I cannot turn back."

"I will come with you when I am well, sir."

"Then we'll remain here until your body has healed. Each morning I'll ride out in order to forage for supplies."

46

"I think the people hereabout are poor. They have only enough food for themselves."

"We need vessels for water more than anything, and clothing for the snowy wastes. I do not know how far ahead the snow is, but the elder told me there is snow in some parts throughout the year."

"You will not find what we need here, sir. We must search for those things in Herat or Shimbarghan."

Each day Diego left his servant in the village and went to search the countryside for anything he could find in the way of supplies. He found only simple villages full of elderly folk without possessions, and in the south some caves that once had been inhabited. The massacre of the caravan party still weighed heavily on the Venetian's mind, and often he went over conversations he had had with the girl who had been murdered. Diego was thinking of her one morning as he rode near a lake surrounded by high gray hills. Suddenly, he saw a horseman looking down on him from the heights. Unused to meeting anyone on his daily journeys, Diego paused and looked questioningly up at the stranger.

The horse on which the man was sitting was short-legged with a thick, muscular body and a circular saddle. The rider's head shone hairless in the sun, though his beard and side-whiskers were exceedingly long. He wore a loose coat belted at the waist and gathered pantaloons tucked into boots of black skin. A curved sword swung at his side, and across his breast there was a gracefully shaped bow as flexible as a reed. When Diego moved toward the trees, the rider moved on a parallel course. When Diego paused, the rider paused. When he retreated, the rider mimicked his every move. Diego decided that the rider must be one of the assassins of the caravan party. Could others be near? And how many would there be? For a moment Diego sat facing the rider high above him. Then he made what he considered a wise decision.

The Mongol tribute collector smiled a savage smile, his black eyes glinting in the sun. Every autumn he and his band came along the silk route and through the Pamirs into Turkestan. It was their duty to collect precious stones, grain and money from townspeople in the provinces. They also removed cows and horses, corn and barley from farms along the way, which they sold for their own profit without the Khan's knowledge. The Mongol wondered what an infidel was doing riding so proudly by the lake. And how dare he look as if he owned the land? Suddenly he saw Diego galloping through the trees. The Mongol galloped down in pursuit, crowing at the prospect of capturing the stranger. The Mongol was surprised when Diego turned to face him.

As he turned and reined his horse, Diego saw the Mongol raising his bow. Something the wise man of Constantinople had told him came to his mind and he thought of the race of horsemen whose pleasure was killing. These barbarians were the horsemasters of the world. They could fight with the sword or the bow while riding at high speed, and some could ride for a day and a night without rest. Diego drew his sword and charged his adversary at full gallop.

The Mongol fired two arrows. He was pleased when they struck Diego in the chest but mortified to see the infidel riding on as if he had not felt them. For the first time in his life the Mongol knew fear. His superstitious nature told him that a man who could not be killed by an arrow was a God to be worshiped, not harmed. Diego ran the Mongol through before he could communicate his feelings, and the tribute collector died without uttering a word.

The Venetian stepped down from his horse and walked to where the dead man lay. In a fold of the voluminous jacket there was a jade tablet on which was inscribed a flying horse. As Diego took it and put it inside his own coat, he discovered the holes where the Mongol's arrows had torn his clothing. Diego laughed and pulled out the solid-silver icon bought in the bazaar of Constantinople. He had carried the icon with him to be used as currency if the need arose. Now the holy picture was dented in two places, and Diego thought wryly that it was better the silver be damaged than his heart. He returned the icon to his inner pocket. Then, leading the Mongol horse behind his own, he returned to the village.

As Diego entered the clearing his servant called to him.

"We must leave at once, sir!"

Diego ran to where Giorgio was lying near the fire.

"You said you would need five days' rest."

"Sir, a party of Mongol horsemen came here today. They

took what the villagers had in the way of food, and they would have captured me too if Arya had not hidden me. Arya carried me to the river and pushed me under the water and remained there with me until the horsemen had gone. I fear she is an idiot. I shall never recover from the immersion. I shall dream of it to my dying day."

"You would have reached your dying day sooner than you expect, my dear Giorgio, without that woman's strength and presence of mind. I hope you showed your gratitude in a suitable fashion."

Giorgio grinned sheepishly.

"We must leave at once. But Arya wishes to marry me."

"Can she wait until your return?"

"No, sir. She wishes to marry me at once."

"Then marry her. We have no time to lose. This morning on my journey in search of supplies, I killed one of the Mongol band. I have his horse and I would not be surprised to see his companions come in search of him."

"They left the ass. I think it was not large enough for their intentions."

"We can use the ass to carry supplies."

"What shall I do about Arya?"

"What does your heart tell you to do, Giorgio? Do you love her?"

"I believe I do, sir."

"Do you wish to remain here? Say what you feel."

Giorgio lay thinking. Here there was greater poverty than ever there had been in the cavane where he had been born. Giorgio was tired of poverty, tired of the fear that comes when there is no food in the house. And yet he wanted the velvet-voiced giantess who adored him above all other men. He looked uncertainly at the Venetian, then fell again to reverie. As he was wrestling with desire and duty, Giorgio saw Arya peeping through the window, her face flushed with excitement. He turned to Diego and gave his answer.

"I do wish to marry the woman, sir. But I also wish to continue on the journey with you. When I return I hope to be a rich man, able to live out my life in comfort. It would give me pleasure to share my riches with Arya."

Diego gave Giorgio his blessing. Within minutes Arya had

told everyone she was to be married. A hunting party, a fishing expedition and a root-digging group left the village at once. Women began to decorate the clearing with flowers, and Arya hurried away to dress for her new husband. Despite his protests, Giorgio was washed and dressed in a flowing robe. Then, as the time for the ceremony drew near, he began to have doubts. Sensing his unease, Arya sent her brother to guard the prospective bridegroom until it was time for him to come to the clearing to marry her. Arya had accepted that Giorgio wished to leave her to seek his fortune. She had agreed to wait for his return, but she was anxious to have the special local rights of a wife, not the secondary status of one who has been used and abandoned.

By the light of the campfire Arya and Giorgio were married. Windbells tinkled as a holy man intoned the formalities. Giorgio did not understand anything of the proceedings, and Arya cried like a child throughout the ceremony. For his part, Diego provided a ring from his own finger for the bride. It was not the custom of the area but it reassured Giorgio that the ceremony was legal and made the villagers cheer excitedly. As the feasting began, local dancers performed provocative wedding rituals. Women from the village served fruit and roast game on leaf plates, and men set off firecrackers to liven the proceedings.

The men drank rice spirit and laughed uproariously. Then Arya led Giorgio away, half-carrying him as he stumbled on the makeshift crutches. Diego sat at the elder's side, applauding the dancing of local women until it was almost morning. Exhausted, he dropped into a hammock and slept peacefully.

At sunrise Diego awoke with a fearful headache. Giorgio was emerging from the hut on the far side of the clearing. He was already dressed for the journey, and Diego saw that his servant was as sick as he from the effects of the rice spirit. Arya walked at her husband's side, teasing him affectionately. Giorgio kept kissing her shyly, and Diego realized that his servant really was in love with the woman. He was moved to pity Arya as she sat watching them prepare to leave.

The custom of the area demanded that the host ride seven miles with his guests before returning home. But it was not possible, as the only ass was loaded down with what remained of the Venetian's belongings. Despite that, one of the village men insisted on accompanying them on foot. Now and then he beamed delightedly in Giorgio's direction until the servant wondered uneasily what the fellow was up to. As he watered Diego's horse, the native whispered to the Venetian and made signs so he could understand. It was all Diego could do not to laugh out loud at the shock in store for his servant.

At a busy market, the native negotiated the purchase of new water containers, snowshoes and clothing the Venetians needed. Then he bade them goodbye and returned to his village, waving and bowing as he disappeared from sight.

Diego and Giorgio wandered among the stalls of the bazaar, admiring mother-of-pearl pieces from Damascus, camel bridles, Turkoman rugs, silver ornaments of the Kuchi and sheepskin coats favored by those living above the snow line. With the villager's help they had bought two of those heavy garments with hats and leggings of the same skin. Now they bargained for chapons to wear underneath the sheepskin. These were padded cotton garments with long sleeves extending far beyond the tips of the fingers. Diego was about to cut the sleeves to size, but he was stopped by the frantic gestures of the trader.

Diego and Giorgio returned to the trail that would lead them to Balkh in Bactria.

Diego and his servant made their way out of Shimbarghan in the direction of Balkh. As they approached the mountains the weather turned cold. They put on the chapons and soon saw the reason for the disproportionately long sleeves. Inside them, their hands remained warm, not chapped and frozen, as they held the reins. As they rode, Giorgio talked of the wife he was missing.

"I love Arya dearly, sir. She is such a virtuous woman."

Diego smothered a laugh.

"You have always said a virtuous woman is one who has a husband and only one lover."

Giorgio scowled. "That was my opinion before my marriage."

Giorgio began to think again of the man who had traveled the first seven miles of their journey with them. Why had the

51

native been so amused? Had there been some jest he had not understood?

Giorgio turned to question his master. "What did that man say to you, sir? The one who accompanied us on the first part of the journey?"

Diego decided to tell the truth. "He told me that he had been chosen out of all the men in the village to be Arya's reserve husband in your absence."

Giorgio struggled to retain his equanimity.

"I am not amused by your joke, sir. If I thought you were telling the truth, I would be obliged to ride back and kill the rogue."

"You are too far away to think of riding back, my good Giorgio, and I have saved you a shock on your return. You must live by the theories you have expounded for so long. You have a wife who is a virtuous woman, one who has one husband and only one lover. Be satisfied and don't be a hypocrite."

"I shall succumb to a broken heart."

"Nonsense, you will reap the advantage."

"I don't understand, sir."

"Arya is allowed by her village custom to have a reserve husband if her first is absent for long."

"Say no more—it hurts me."

"You must be allowed also to be a virtuous husband."

Giorgio looked out of the corner of his eye at Diego. Did he detect a smile? For a while he mulled over the situation. Then he, too, began to smile. If Arya had a temporary husband he could, given the opportunity, take a temporary wife. Soon Giorgio was singing merrily.

There were long-horned sheep on the mountain passes, and a camel train with two thousand animals passed them en route to Balkh. Often the two men encountered a foraging ass which they soon learned meant they were near fresh water. The local asses were small and nervous, with a high, braying laugh and a black stripe from head to tail. Giorgio amused himself trying to catch one, but he could never get within touching distance. Not all the animals of the area were harmless. The hills were full of wild boar, hyena, wolf and the lynxlike caracal. To guard against attack, the two men took turns sleeping, one always mounting guard during the hours of darkness. During his periods on watch Giorgio dreamed of Arya and of returning to the village with riches beyond description.

Diego occupied his watch composing poems and bringing his journal up to date, because he wanted to describe everything while it was fresh in his mind. As they climbed higher into the mountains, Diego thought the trail majestic and beautiful. The road ran between blue mountains so high they disappeared into the clouds. Men appeared small and insignificant in the shifting light of the sepia chiaroscuro. Pink Turkestan lilies scented the air of the mountain passes, and barberries provided color in the sand beige landscape.

The journey continued to be enjoyable until the Venetians were ten days' ride from Balkh. Then, without warning, the air filled with flying insects, moths and stinging predators. Diego remembered the agent's warning that if they were bitten they would suffer from the fever for the rest of their lives. At first he swatted furiously and slept wrapped in gauze. But gradually the onslaught overwhelmed the two men and they were both bitten on the ears and around the eyes. From that moment on it seemed as if they would never stop itching.

Three days from Balkh the snows came, and the red poppy meadow through which the two men were traveling was soon covered in white. Diego paused to admire the beauty of the scene, the scarlet valley, the falling snow against the pink of a winter sky. He bent to pick one of the poppies from the couch grass, but withdrew his hand hastily as a cobra slithered by. Diego saw the encounter as a warning, an omen. In the midst of peace and beauty a cobra had appeared dangerously close. Was there trouble ahead or to the rear?

The Mongols had taken the road leading to Kabul and Peshawar but, hearing nothing of strangers in that area, had turned back and were now not more than a week's ride behind the Venetians. Unaware that Diego and his servant were ahead of them, the tribute collectors were returning with all haste to the Court of Peking. They rode like the warriors they were, closing the gap between themselves and the Venetians. Sometimes they paused to elicit supplies from unwilling villagers along the route. Night and day they rode, often sleeping in the saddle. The Mongols stopped only to rest their horses.

By the time the Venetians reached Balkh in Bactria it was obvious that Diego was ill. He had a raging fever that soaked him with perspiration despite the freezing atmosphere. The illness made his mind wander back to Venice, the city he loved, and he talked disjointedly of seeing his parents again.

Fearing that his master was dying, Giorgio made the decision to obtain lodgings in the home of a merchant of Balkh. Diego was put to bed by one of the widower's daughters, and a physician was called. Giorgio hid the animals in the merchant's stable and put Diego's belongings in the attic of the house. He thanked God a thousand times that the Venetian had taught him to read and write. Painstakingly, as he waited for the physician to arrive, Giorgio fumbled with the book of words, selecting one here and another there until he could tell the man about their journey, their adventures and his master's valiant quest for a new fortune. There were not enough words for what Giorgio had to say, but that night, after dinner, he regaled his lonely host with stories. The merchant was delighted to have such an interesting person in his house, and when he took Giorgio to the room next to Diego's he bade him goodnight with a sweeping bow.

Alone, Giorgio prayed that they were out of danger. He still feared the Mongols who had pursued them so relentlessly, and his instincts told him to take care. No one in the city had seen his master, because Diego had been lying on a pallet covered in blankets when Giorgio rode with him to the merchant's house in the outskirts. Giorgio had taken care to arrive at night and had made a point of finding lodgings outside the city center. As he lay in bed, Giorgio decided he had better stay inside the house lest his alien appearance betray the man to whom he was devoted. Finally he slept, dreaming of Arya.

The Mongols arrived in Balkh a week later and elected to rest their horses. People closed their shops and retreated to their homes in fear of the tribute collectors. Soon the city was as silent as the tomb. Icy winds cut the air and the snow fell thick on the mountainside. The leader of the Mongol party studied the weather and decided they would have to leave as soon as their animals were fed if they were to clear the roof of the world before it became impassable. Ten hours after their arrival, the Mongols sped east, leaving behind a trail of sadness.

Diego cried out in his sleep. He could see tigers on the bed, giant ants on the wall and a thousand demons dancing before his eyes. He was cared for with dedication by the eldest daughter of the house. The physician came daily, but left full of despair because none of his remedies was having any effect on the patient.

Giorgio spent his time pacing the room, convinced that his master was about to succumb. Sometimes tears fell down his cheeks and he no longer cared who saw them. Often, in the stillness of night, when the girls had fallen asleep, Giorgio would go to his master's bedside and whisper encouragement to the sick man.

"Fight, sir! You must fight or you will be dead before you know it. We are almost there. You cannot die now. Soon we shall pass the roof of the world, and then we shall be with your brother, my lord Pierluigi, filling our pockets with pearls and rubies. Will you not speak to me, sir? Insult me if you like, but say *something*, I beg you."

Diego remained too ill to move, too weak to communicate. Slowly, surely, his resistance deteriorated and his weight dropped alarmingly. The fever continued unabated, immune to the medicine he was being given. Giorgio grew desperate, and he prayed a dozen times a day. Please Lord, give Diego a chance, for he is worth saving. Must you be so foolish as to allow only hypocrites to live until they are old?

But the sick man remained in peril of his life. Outside the house, winter took its grip on the mountains. Reluctantly Giorgio admitted that they had lost their chance of traveling through the high passes before the snow closed them. Unwilling to face defeat, he sat at Diego's bedside talking of the old days in Venice, telling jokes, making plans and doing everything in his power to revive the ailing spirit. Often Giorgio asked himself if they would ever reach Cathay as they had once dreamed. Unhappiness and uncertainty made Giorgio angry, and with renewed vigor he urged Diego to get well. Somehow the servant swore to provoke a response from his master.

Chapter Four:

The Emperor of Cathay

Winter was over, and for two months Kublai Khan had been camped with his hunting party on the plains. He was enjoying life in a tent—the only life his Mongol ancestors had ever known—though this encampment of ten thousand tents pitched around the imperial lodge bore little resemblance to the felt-flapped yurts of the Tartar plains. The tents of the Emperor's party were neatly arranged in geometric design, in much the same plan as the streets of Peking, because Kublai Khan was a man who loved order in all things. The court tent housed a thousand nobles and attendants. It was raised on gilded poles, its exterior covered with tiger skins. Inside, the walls were lined with cloth of gold, the divans and pillows covered with sable. In the Khan's private audience tent a tame cheetah prowled from silken rug to silver table, springing onto an emerald-studded treasure chest and calmly surveying the scene.

Accompanying the Khan on this hunting expedition were his sons, nobles, concubines, physicians, astrologers and the craftsmen who maintained the massive community. To assist him in the pleasures of the hunt, the Khan had brought with him ten thousand mounted falconers, five hundred gyrfalcons and a hundred goshawks to catch birds on water. Tame leopards and lynxes prowled the periphery of the camp, and fourteen thousand experienced huntsmen were preparing for another day of slaughter.

The province in which the party was camped was low-lying and marshy, abounding with game, roe deer, wild hart and boar. The game caught during these months would feed the court not only during the hunting season, but during the journey back to Peking and the stay in the capital. In Peking the Khan would hold feasts to celebrate his safe arrival. Then after a few days he would depart for the summer palace of Shang-tu.

On this fine spring morning the Khan was up early and looking forward to his final week of hunting. Only one cloud darkened his horizon, making him moody and given to outbursts of untypical bad temper. The Khan was fifty-nine and suffering from gout. He was no longer able to ride from dawn to dusk in the time-honored way of his forefathers, and this year, for the first time, elephants had been brought with the hunting party to transport the Khan when the rigors of the saddle grew too painful for him. As he thought of the future, Kublai Khan frowned. Old age was not amusing, and for a ruler less so than for an ordinary mortal. A ruler who was no longer able to outride and outthink every man in the kingdom was a man diminished, a man revolutionaries plotted to cut down. The Khan looked at the howdah his carpenters had constructed, a boxlike contraption covered in beaten gold. Inside the howdah, atop the imperial elephant, he presented a splendid sight, but was that enough? The Khan hoped that his nobles believed that he rode on the elephant because he liked doing so, not because his body was no longer strong.

The Emperor sighed. The nobles knew the true reason for

his occasional departure from tradition, and talk would already have reached the capital of his diminished strength. He drank a pitcher of koumiss and lay down to rest before the evening feast.

At dawn the Emperor rose and threw on an ermine-lined robe that had cost him two thousand bezants of silver. Stepping over a sleeping concubine, he roared to his hunting captain: "What say the astrologers?"

"They say it will be another fine day for the hunt, if it pleases you, sire."

The Khan breakfasted on spit-roasted turkey and fried prawns, washing the food down with a flagon of plum-flower wine. Obsequious servants removed the dishes, their faces covered with white gauze lest their breath offend the Omnipotence. While the imperial physician bandaged his gouty toes, the Khan sat thinking of the summer palace of Shang-tu and the feast of a hundred virgins which would be held for his pleasure during the summer. A hundred exquisites from the province of Onggirat, where all the women were lovely, would come to bow down before him. What more could any man desire? The Khan shook his head, aware that he was lonely and dissatisfied with life. His four wives lived in splendor at a discreet distance from each other and from him, each waiting to be visited at a given season of the year so the succession would be assured. In the Imperial Palace of Peking the Khan had a thousand concubines to adore him and who were kept busy satisfying his lust when no wife was near to spoil him. Still, he longed for something he could not define. As always when he thought of the emptiness in his heart, the Emperor grew impatient, and when the hunting master told him the men were assembled he hurried out of the tent.

At first the Khan enjoyed the chill air of morning. But as the horse galloped on he began to feel tired and dispirited. Sweat ran down his sallow face, dripping from the points of his mustache. The black silken tunic bunched around his waist felt suddenly too hot, too tight and constricting for his exhausted body. The Khan called a halt and rode ahead to a quiet spot by the river where he sat looking at the gray landscape, catching his breath. He was relieved that his nobles were not there to see how worn he was, how saddened by the decline in his own condition.

When the Khan had recovered, he rode his mare back and forth, inclining his head approvingly at red-clad court hunters who raced past him to the plain, white bows at the ready. They shot a hail of arrows, cheering each time they killed, and then returned to their line. The Emperor gazed at his noblemen, their banners flying in the breeze, then at the grooms in their gourd-shaped hats. The grooms were leading spare horses to the fore, saddling them to replace the huntsmen's tired mounts. The Khan's eyes softened when he saw his horses. Even now, when the joy of the hunt had begun to pall, he looked on the horses with something close to love.

Suddenly the sun faded and a yellow mist crept over the plain, obscuring the Emperor's view. He could see no more than five strides in any direction, and, turning his horse, he tried to return to the spot where the huntsmen were waiting his imperial approval. As he turned, he came face to face with a wounded cheetah; a brace of winged arrows protruded from the animal's breast. The Khan's eyes narrowed and he sat very still, aware that the wounded beast was more dangerous by far than anything he had encountered in the hunt thus far. The cheetah's ears folded back, her legs tensing for a spring. The Khan remained motionless, his snakelike eyes hynotizing the angry animal. For a moment he thought he had controlled the danger. Then the cheetah sprang, embedding her teeth in his horse's neck. The Khan leaped down, appalled by the injury to his favorite mare. He swung his sword, cutting the air with such fury the cheetah's head was severed from its body.

In the eerie yellow light of the marshes, Kublai Khan surveyed his prize and his sorrow. The horse had been the foal of a Mongol warrior mount, an animal of courage and discipline. No command had ever been disobeyed. No journey had ever proved too long or too hard for this loyal creature. In the final moments of its life the horse had remained obedient, even in the face of death. The Khan knelt at its side and wept as he had not wept for many years. Then he took off the saddle, the gilded bridle and panoply, and walked back through the mist to where his nobles were waiting.

As he raised the cheetah's bloody head, the Emperor acknowledged ringing cheers. He smiled and bowed low. Then, mounting one of the spare horses, he led the huntsmen back to camp. As he rode he gave instructions to the captain that his horse's body be returned to Peking to be buried under the persimmon trees in his private orchard. Word of his valor and strength would filter back to the capital quickly, he hoped. For a while the revolutionaries, assassins and political plotters would stay their hand, fearful of his all-powerful rage. He had been fortunate to be able to prove his strength once more, and he was grateful. He rode into camp like a noble warrior, calling for concubines to amuse him and wine to slake his thirst. That night he feasted until the small hours.

A week later the royal hunting party returned to Peking. Their stay would be a short one, because in three days the Khan was due to travel to the summer palace of Shang-tu. When the Emperor saw the rooftops of the imperial city he smiled; the bright colors cheered him, and the despondency that had of late dogged his every move abated. The rooftops were scarlet, sun-yellow and peacock-blue, glazed to a high sheen and elegant. Cypresses lined the Imperial Way, their pointed shapes reaching up to a deep-blue sky. The Khan took in the scene, enjoying it, because it was *his* city. He inclined his head graciously to rich merchants bowing before the imperial cavalcade, and he waved to young children standing by the wayside.

The streets of Peking were scrupulously clean and lined with lime trees which were in blossom. Closing his eyes, the Khan sniffed the perfume of the blossom. Then he frowned as he looked out at the impassive Chinese faces. The Chinese were a conquered race, subservient of necessity to his whim but never loyal. Since the conquest of China he had ruled with compassion, he felt, protecting learned men and aiding farmers with gifts of free grain after bad harvests and plagues of locusts. Despite his enlightened way, there was something in the manner of his subjects that warned the Emperor he could never cease his vigilance. He was annoyed by this affront to what he considered liberal ways. The Ruler of Half the World found it impossible to understand the desire for freedom inherent in every captive heart.

By twilight, the Khan was settled in the inner sanctum of the Imperial Palace with his favorite wife, Jamui. For three days Jamui would entertain the Khan, but when he departed for Shang-tu, she would return to her own house to the north of Peking and would not see her husband again until winter. The couple walked together in the garden, watching as the sun set on the lily pond and listening to the sounds of wild beasts roaming the no-man's-land between the outer and inner gates of the enclosure. Jamui had heard of the Khan's act of valor and, kneeling at his side when he sat under the pomegranate tree, she flattered him. "You are the sun and the moon and the great white star, my lord."

The Khan sighed. Every day his subjects flattered, his wives and concubines cajoled and his nobles fawned. Where were the warlike friends of times past? What had happened to the fights and arguments he had so enjoyed when young? The Chinese were silently watchful, forever aloof and relentlessly cold. Now even his favorite wife had become a bore. The Khan spat into a porcelain vase, looked at Jamui and asked, "Why must you forever agree with me?"

Startled, she replied with cool dignity, "You are my master, sire."

"But why do you never disagree with me?"

The Khan's wife frowned, uncertain whether she dared speak the truth. "You would chastise me, sire, if I disagreed. You do not like people who disagree with you, and especially you do not like *ladies* who say you nay."

"You are wrong!"

"I am right, sire."

"Fiend! Do you dare disagree with the Emperor?"

Jamui smiled a secret smile, infuriating the ruler. "You see, sire, you do *not* like me to disagree. Your color changes, your juices ferment, and before long we shall have to call the physician. If you do not like those who agree with you and yet cannot bear to have them disagree, you are a man who cannot be pleased. May I beg to withdraw from the Imperial Presence?"

The Khan knew that his wife was right. He watched her tiny figure retreating, bowing low in obeisance, and felt guilty. What was wrong that he was behaving in such a strange fashion? Was old age making a fool of him? Was it that he missed the warlike days of the past or was it that he was sick of life in an alien land where treachery was rife and no man spoke the truth except under torture? The Khan called for the feast to commence and strode into the banqueting hall, determined to forget his annoyance and the fact that Jamui had been right. Tomorrow he would give her a pearl necklace and allow her to disagree with him once at least.

Cymbals crashed. Drumbeats announced the arrival of the ruler. The Khan clapped his hands impatiently for the feasting to begin. Magicians appeared, eating fire and creating illusions. The Khan turned his back on them, and silenced his nobles when they tried to compliment him further on his bravery during the hunt. As the Emperor ate a murmur of consternation spread through the hall, because it was obvious he was in an ill humor. Harpists appeared to serenade the ruler, but they too earned nothing but an angry gaze. The harpists disappeared, to be replaced by jugglers, who performed outrageous feats which the Khan applauded briefly. Then the astrologers were called. The Khan leaned forward eagerly, anxious to know his luck during the journey to Shang-tu.

The first astrologer foretold joy, peace and the coming of a period of bliss.

The Khan roared his disapproval. "Take the fool away. He says those very words each time I see him."

The second astrologer trembled so violently he could not speak at all. The third committed the sin of repeating the first's prediction. The Khan shouted for Tai Cheng, the unpopular Chinese astrologer who foretold evil as well as good. Tai Cheng had been banished for some years from the court because it displeased the Khan to be told so often of disasters. Now he was back in Peking.

The Khan watched as the old man folded his arms across his chest, his dark eyes watching the ruler impassively. "Well, Tai Cheng, what have you to say?"

63

The astrologer remained silent, his face pale, his arms still crossed in a position of what appeared to the Khan to be defiance.

"Speak or you will die before the dawn."

"I beg permission, noble lord, to tell the truth. I can tell no other."

The Khan leaped to his feet, choking with annoyance. "Speak, damn you!"

Tai Cheng spoke softly, forcing the Emperor to draw near in order to hear the details of his strange prophecy.

"Your journey to the summer palace of Shang-tu will be a pleasant one, my lord. Your spirits will be high and the sun will shine on all your hopes. I see that before the twenty-eighth day of the eighth moon something will happen which will relieve the tedium of your life, something that will make you both happy and sad."

The Khan was delighted by the news. The twenty-eighth day of the eighth moon was his birthday and the day of the Feast of the Virgins. He waved impatiently for Tai Cheng to continue.

"I see that before that day you will meet a woman whose eyes will captivate you and you will remain forever her servant."

The Khan sat very still, his heart pounding with annoyance. "The Emperor of Half the World cannot be enslaved."

"I tell only what I see, my lord." The astrologer bowed.

"Continue. This woman, is she one of the hundred virgins who come from Onggirat?"

"She is not, my lord. I see the woman living somewhere in the country in exile with her father. She is not one of the women brought for the imperial pleasure."

"But she will love the Imperial Majesty?"

"No, my lord. The Imperial Majesty will love *her*. The lotus flower will rule the sword."

The Khan's eyes narrowed. It was not possible for a woman to be favored by the Emperor and then to ignore him. It was not possible for a warrior to be challenged by a flower. He was Kublai Khan, God and Almighty Ruler of China and Half the World. His word would be obeyed. He turned to the astrologer and asked icily, "Say *why* this woman cares nothing for the Imperial Majesty."

"She is impressed by your power and your courage in battle, sire. But she does not love you."

"Whom *does* she love?"

The astrologer paused while the hushed assembly waited for his reply. "It is written that the girl will love a man who comes from across the world to meet her. He will not come alone but with another, perhaps with many men."

"At the head of an army?"

"No, my lord, he is not a warrior. I cannot tell who he is, but surely he will be your friend and stand in awe of your almighty power."

Kublai Khan sat back, trying to envisage what manner of man would travel across the world to meet a woman. "How shall I know this woman when I meet her?"

"You will know her by the color of her eyes, which are green like the emeralds in the imperial treasure chambers."

"I dislike green eyes. They are unlucky."

"You will adore her eyes, sire."

"Never! And this stranger who travels across the world, what shall I think of him?"

"You will know him because he is a man like no other you have seen, my lord. Your heart will go out to him in admiration of his courage and his wisdom."

The Khan stared at the imperturbable face of the astrologer, willing Tai Cheng to enlarge on this intriguing prediction. But the old man bowed and withdrew at once from the presence. The Khan, infuriated to hear irreverent titters following the astrologer's departure, glowered at the nobles, silencing the assembly with an impatient wave of the hand.

Two days later the Khan left Peking. He rode north accompanied by an entourage of thirty thousand nobles and twelve thousand men of his personal guard, the Keshikten. Musicians, palace retainers, cooks, physicians, saddlers and soldiers accompanied this massive expedition with some of the ladies of the court and the children of the noblemen. As they rode they sang and chanted warlike songs. Often they paused so the Emperor could slake his thirst with a gourd of koumiss or a flagon of rose-petal wine. When the day was fine the Khan called a halt so he could enjoy an hour's shooting. Then the party rode on in the merciless heat of the plains.

The palace of Shang-tu lay 170 miles north of Peking in a cool place far removed from the stifling humidity of the capital. It was not an easy journey, but as the sun grew hotter and the distance shorter, members of the party were relieved to find the air becoming cooler and clearer than the damp air of the south. When they reached the Kin Yung Kwan pass with its golden Mongol archway they knew the greater part of the journey was over. Ahead lay the red poppy steppes and the summer palace. At Chagan Nor the Emperor called a halt so he could spend a few days wildfowling. Renewed by the invigorating freshness in the air, the Khan imagined himself young again and strong as he had been in times past.

One morning before dawn the Khan rode out alone, far away from his encampment. He saw a young boy crouched by a wildfowl lake. There was intense eagerness in the set of the boy's body as he stood with bow at the ready. Soon the young hunter had shot three ducks and a bird on the wing. The Khan smiled indulgently, pleased to be able to witness the hunter's skill. He strode forward, intending to startle the lad with a glimpse of the Divine Ruler of China. But as the boy waded back to the bank and undressed, in order to dry his jacket and trousers, the Khan stepped hastily behind a tree, his heart pounding, his eyes wide with pleasure. The "lad" was a girl with a tempting body that excited the Emperor to ecstasy. As he examined her, the Khan saw that she had the body of a courtesan but the slender thighs of a Tartar youth. He closed his eyes and tried hard to regain his breath.

The huntress threw down her cap and shook her hair which was black and fine like silk. Her eyes appeared to be an impossible green. As the sun rose she held up her clothes so they would dry more quickly. Then she hung them on a bush. As she dried her body with an old cotton cloth, the Khan's mouth watered at her innocence, at the creamy skin of her body, at the nipples like rosebuds closed against the early morning chill. Suddenly he forgot himself and, stepping out from his hiding place, walked curiously toward the spot where the girl was dressing.

At his approach, the girl realized that she had been spied upon and ran to her horse, pausing only to snatch the birds and fishes on her hook. The Khan pursued her, forgetting his age and the harsh beating he felt in his chest. But the huntress eluded him. For a brief moment, he saw her naked body outlined against the cherry blossom, her hair flying in the breeze like a triumphal banner. Then she was gone. The Khan cursed his stupidity. His pulse was pounding and he could think only of the tantalizing beauty of her body, the spring in her step and the lusciousness of her breasts.

As he rode back to the encampment the Khan knew the encounter with the girl had disturbed him greatly.

The summer palace was built of pink marble. Every corridor, banqueting suite and audience chamber was gilded and painted with pictures of birds and orchids so the Emperor could think himself at one with nature. Around the palace there was a park, and in the center of the park a less substantial pavilion constructed of bamboo, its walls and roof guyed on two hundred silken ropes. At the end of each summer the pavilion was dismantled and stored in the palace.

The Khan lay indolently dreaming, his vast frame reclining on a pile of cushions beneath the white silk draperies of the bamboo pavilion. In the garden parrots squawked, larks and myrtle birds sang and concubines played their flutes. But he kept thinking of the girl he had seen by the wildfowl lake, and began making plans for her capture. Soon, he was confident, she would be the most beautiful pearl in his harem.

The palace servants were busy unloading ivory from India, rhinoceros horns from Bombay, pearls, agate, incense, cloves and cedarwood brought from the kingdoms of the south by traders from Burma and the islands of the unknown sea. Ladies of the royal household sat admiring silks from Suchow, jasmine from Fukein and fans from Nanchang. A visit from the traders was a treat to be enjoyed, and the sharp voices of the concubines could be heard all over the imperial enclosure.

In the courtyard of the lion fountain, two men hidden in a doorway were plotting to assassinate the Khan. Nearby, in the palace kitchens, cooks were wrestling with the preparations for the Feast of the Keshikten when thirty thousand guests would gather to eat in the lapis-lazuli assembly hall. The cooks shouted and fought, jabbering and cursing because the kitchens were too small, the heat oppressive. To displease the ruler could mean an ignominious death. The head cook shrilled his orders and everyone ran to obey him.

While his subjects busied themselves, the Khan remained on the cushioned dais thinking of the huntress. He was wondering if she had really had green eyes and why she had fled. Was it possible that a man could be enslaved by one glimpse of such a creature? The Khan savored the memory of the girl's body and was happy.

In the courtyard of the lion fountain the two assassins decided that the Khan could be killed in his private apartment after the Feast of the Keshikten, when he would be full of rice spirit and less able to defend himself. The two men nodded in agreement, unaware that their conversation had been overheard. They returned to their duties, satisfied that they would be successful.

The Khan's horsemaster hastened to the bamboo pavilion to tell what he had heard, prostrating himself at the Khan's feet. When bidden, Badriak rose and took his place at the ruler's side, proud to receive such a warm greeting from his master. The Khan was fond of the horsemaster, and admired his legendary appetite for women as well as his gentleness with the valuable Mongol horses.

"Tell me your news, Badriak. I'll wager it is bad from the look of your complexion."

"My lord, there is another plot to kill you."

The Khan remained quite still. Then his fingers began to pluck grapes from an ivory bowl.

"I was walking in the courtyard of the lion fountain when I heard men plotting," the horsemaster said. "They were Yen Fa, the keeper of the munitions store, and Wan P'eng, from the royal library."

"I have noted their names."

"I hid myself near the stables of the white camels and listened as they made their plan. They will try to kill you tonight, sire, when you are alone after the Feast of the Keshikten."

68

"So soon."

"I fear so, sire."

"How many will come?"

"I know no more, sire. I heard only the end of their conversation."

The Khan wondered how best to deal with the news. Would the plots never cease? Was there never to be a moment of peace for the Ruler of Half the World?

"You have done well, Badriak."

"My life is yours, sire."

"Take as your reward one of the mares from Changchow."

The horsemaster's face lit with pleasure.

"One of the white mares, sire?"

The Khan nodded. The white mares had been given as a tribute during the New Year White Feast. For some reason Badriak loved one of the animals more than all the others and was forever fussing over it. Now it was his. The Khan dismissed the horsemaster and sat alone looking into space. Outside, in the garden, bees were buzzing in ziziphus and azalea. The Khan thought how sad it was to think of murder and rebellion in such an idyllic place. Minutes later he sent for the captain of the royal guard and ordered the arrest and torture of the two plotters. If they revealed that there was going to be a coup or an invasion, the Feast of the Keshikten would be postponed. If, however, they were acting on their own initiative they would be used to provide some unusual entertainment for the soldiers during the evening celebrations.

Handmaidens were summoned to prepare the Khan for the feast. As they dressed him, he listened to their gossip, amused by the lies they told. Was there anything in the world as delicious as a woman who knew her place? The Khan's mind wandered yet again to the huntress of the wildfowl lake.

The Feast of the Keshikten was held thirteen times a year and was a tribute from the Emperor to the members of his bodyguard. Heavy drinking took place at this bawdy gathering, and a dozen vats holding more than six barrels of wine apiece stood in the center of the arena to be emptied during the evening. In addition, spiced mare's milk, camel milk livened with coriander, rice wine and plum-flower spirits made the soldiers merry and the Khan relaxed in his vigilance.

During the meal, swordfighters from the royal guard displayed their skill, archers their accuracy and dervishes from the mountains their frantic dances. Then a troupe of girls appeared, provoking the assembly to raucous hilarity with a toe-tapping bell dance of the temple goddesses. The Khan roared his approval, and those present sighed with relief that he was in such a good humor. By tradition, the warrior barons kneeled whenever the Khan drank. Tonight many grumbled out loud that they were forever on their knees because the ruler's thirst seemed unquenchable.

When the feast was over servants removed plates of honey pastry and piles of chewed meat bones, and replaced any empty flagons of wine. A sudden hush fell on the merrymakers as the master of proclamations announced a contest between two of the Khan's best swordfighters. The Khan rose and walked to a terrace overlooking the rose garden. Then, motioning for the two men to take their places below in the courtyard by the fountain, the ruler ordered lanterns to be grouped around the pair so the soldiers could see what was happening.

Members of the Keshikten put down their goblets and fell silent, their faces apprehensive at this departure from tradition. As they muttered among themselves, the guards watched the two assassins being escorted through the banqueting hall and down the steps to the paved court where the two swordsmen were waiting.

Silencing the babble of voices with a motion of the hand, the Khan announced, "Below are two men who were discovered plotting to kill me. The first swordsman to present me with the trophy of my enemy's head will win my royal approval and with it a gold tablet of authority incorporating the royal seal."

The plotters knelt, their bodies trembling with fear. The Emperor raised his hand, dropping a white silk kerchief to the ground as a signal. In the silence of the night a swishing sound and dull thud heralded the demise of first one then the other assassin. The Khan smiled as the plotters died, their blood mingling with fallen petals in the courtyard.

Chao Yung, the Chinese court artist, sighed wearily as he watched the beheadings. He was aware that his fellow countrymen had not acted alone. In villages around the palace of Shang-tu and amid the red poppy fields of Manchuria men were plotting to rid China of the Mongol Khan. They were too numerous to all be killed. Most of the assassination attempts were masterminded by a Buddhist priest, the powerful Ch'eng Ch'i, who taught that man's destiny is decided by his own actions. Thus the freedom of China was in the hands of its people and they alone could free themselves. Chao Yung was a patriot with a secret admiration for those who sought to be rid of the Khan. He had no such admiration for the Japanese Shogun of Kyushu, who had roasted Kublai Khan's emissaries alive and who continued to send agitators to disrupt the kingdom. The court artist had an overriding fear of the Japanese, who were known to use a divine wind, the Kamikaze, to scatter invading ships. And so, superficially, Chao Yung supported the Khan's rule because he was sure that life under the ambitious Shogun Junichiko Minamoto would be infinitely less secure than life under the Mongol Emperor.

While he was preparing to retire, the Khan heard one of the concubines force the others to withdraw. When she was alone with the Khan, the girl moved to his side and begged him to listen to her.

"I have news of great importance to your royal self, sire. I did not wish to speak of it before the others."

"Tell me what you know."

"I have heard of a young lady with eyes the color of the Khan's emeralds."

The Khan scowled at the girl's unctuous manner. Then he looked into her face and at the thin-lipped, avaricious mouth, which interested him greatly. It was the mouth of one who would dare anything for money. He handed the concubine an ostrich fan and told her to cool him. Then, acting as disinterested as he was able, he ordered her to tell him what she had learned.

The concubine explained, "I have questioned my friends, the jewel traders, sire."

"And what did they tell you?"

"They told nothing because they know nothing of a woman with green eyes."

The Khan sighed. Was it possible the girl was a fool pretending to have information?

"The food purveyors knew nothing and neither did the sweetmeat vendors."

"Say what you have to say!"

"When I had almost given up hope I met someone who knew the girl. He goes fishing with her and sometimes they shoot wildfowl together."

The Khan swallowed his criticism of the concubine's intelligence and asked her to continue with her story.

Satisfied that she had the imperial attention, the girl continued, "My friend says the young woman goes wildfowling above Chagan Nor. She is a wonderful huntress."

"I could never admire a woman who went hunting!"

The Khan clapped his hands and ordered a servant to bring his rose water. The concubine knelt at his side, watching the Emperor's every move.

"The girl is only fourteen years old, sire. Her family were exiled from Peking when your Omnipotence came to Cathay. Now she is alone in the world but for a father, who is blind. That is why she hunts. If she did not they would surely starve."

"And where does this vision live?"

"I do not know, sire."

"Why did you not ask?"

The concubine flinched at the Khan's sudden change of humor. "I have spoken only briefly with the boy who met this young girl. He has gone trading to Manchuria with his father, so I am not able to question him further. He is the son of Zak the silk merchant and but a child himself. He met the girl in one place only and could not make her tell where she lived."

The Khan closed his eyes, unwilling to let the concubine see the extent of his longing. Surely the girl was the same one he had encountered by the wildfowl pool. The astrologer's forecast had come true, though he had not recognized her as the woman he would love in vain. The Khan had seen the

72

girl's body, her hair and the swiftness of her stride. But he had not been sure that she had green eyes. Suddenly the ruler felt tired.

In order to lift his spirits, the concubine began to play a love song on her guitar. As she played she encouraged the Khan. "My lord, the girl has the habit of shooting wildfowl on a certain lake. Would it not be clever to send guards to watch for her? Then, when you have captured her, you can have her brought to the palace to please you. It cannot be impossible for the Ruler of Half the World to overcome the lady Lotus Flower."

"Is that the girl's name?"

"That is what she calls herself, but I think she has another name, one which she wishes to conceal for some reason."

Dismissed with the promise of a ruby bracelet to reward her vigilance, the concubine returned to her quarters and ordered green mint jelly and her favorite honey cakes. As she ate the girl plotted to extort more than a ruby bracelet from the Emperor before she finished with him. She was sure the Khan would beg her to tell him the precise location of the lake where the lady Lotus Flower hunted. On either side of the road from Chagan Nor there were dozens of lakes, perhaps hundreds, and she knew which was the right one. She began to giggle, thinking of the riches that would soon be hers.

The Khan lay blissfully back on the silken cushions, resolved to capture the delectable huntress within the week and have her for his own. All other thoughts vanished from his mind at the prospect of the encounter. He envisioned the jewels he would give her, the exhibitions of horsemanship he would arrange to impress her. Then, falling asleep, he dreamed of enslaving the huntress and making her love him.

The following day a dozen men from the elite imperial bodyguard were dispatched to the area where the Khan had camped, their orders to watch and wait for the huntress to return. As time passed, the soldiers reported back that there was no sign of the elusive girl. The Khan began to sink into a deep depression. Sometimes he was so angry with his servants that they feared for their lives, and life became purgatory in the palace of Shang-tu. Courtiers, concubines and guards foraged for information about the enigmatic Lotus

Flower, but the girl had vanished, never to return to the lake that had once been her haunt. The Khan thought of nothing but capturing her. Each night became a vigil until the dawn when he could hope again to have news of her. But as the summer heat reached its climax and the dry plains shimmered like the sea, the soldiers admitted that they had failed in their mission. The lady Lotus Flower had vanished.

In a field of buttercups, Lotus Flower lay giggling at the continued presence of the soldiers. In the heat of midday the men were sitting on burning rocks cursing the futility of their mission. Lotus Flower was greatly amused by the comedy, and each day as the sun set she returned to lie in wait for the soldiers' departure. When they had gone she fished for an hour before creeping back to tell her father all the exciting things she had heard that day.

After a vigil of many weeks, the soldiers were ordered to return to the summer palace. On their last night by the wild-fowl pool, after a drinking bout which lasted until the small hours, they slept like dead men. The next morning they stumbled to their feet and broke camp, watched from the distance by a joyful Lotus Flower. When the men were only specks on the horizon she rushed to the pool, shouting delightedly as she leaped into the water. This was *her* secret place, *her* hunting domain, her personal lake of a thousand birds. As she swam, Lotus Flower sang a song of love and longing. Then she rushed home with a string of rainbow fish for her father's noonday meal.

The Khan strode into the barracks of the Keshikten to question the men who had returned from Chagan Nor. The leader of the party saluted, bowing to the ground, before addressing his ruler.

"The lady did not come, sire. We moved not an inch from the lake, except to report at night to your Omnipotence."

"Did others come to the lake?"

"No, sire. We saw not a soul in the weeks of our absence."

Just then a startled cry came from the inner hall of the barracks and the Khan saw some of his officers emptying their saddlebags of flower petals.

"I found *flowers* in my saddlebag!"

74

"What can it mean, sire?"

"My clothes are gone, replaced by these pink flowers."

The soldiers stood staring askance at the Emperor as he picked up a handful of the petals and sniffed them. The Khan fondled the flowers to his cheek and smiled a secret smile. She had wit, that little girl of the lake, and courage to mock the Ruler of Half the World. The scent of the lotus petals beguiled the Khan, and he walked quickly back to his private apartment to change into traveling clothes. If the lady Lotus Flower wished to tease his men she could do so, because Kublai Khan wished her to be happy. But she would not tease *him!* The astrologer must be proved wrong and he, Khan of the Mongol Horde, Ruler of China, would have his will with the lady. He could not be outwitted by a mere girl. The sword could not be conquered by the flower, of that he was certain.

Chapter Five:

The Roof of the World

Spring arrived, and Diego realized a whole year had passed since he had sailed from Venice. The Venetians were sitting together on a crag in the Pamir region called the roof of the world. Around them wild tulips nodded alongside buttercups in valleys between the mountain ranges. Overhead, eagles wheeled, and far below they could see sheep following farmers hauling sharpened-stick plows through the rocky terrain. Ahead, there were mountain peaks twenty thousand feet high through which the two men would soon have to travel. Behind were the white clay houses of Badakhsh province. During their journey to this spot, the Venetians had passed through areas of empty countryside littered with the bones of animals, and valleys where the sounds of wolf and mountain lion were heard.

Diego had spent the winter months recuperating from his

illness. He had occupied himself by helping the merchant in whose house he and his servant lodged, and by learning the language of the province from the man's daughters. But now he was relieved to be on the road again. Surely, he thought, the end of the journey cannot be far away. Legend said that after the roof of the world there was nothing, and that men who ventured on fell into the fiery pits of hell. The Venetian looked at the road ahead, shielding his eyes from the sun and the bright reflection of snow still deep in the highest passes. If the legend was correct there would be nothing beyond the mountains, but Diego was sure that the country the Polos had described was there. Spurred on by that hope, he and Giorgio were able to keep going.

They passed through a village where they were given tea by friendly locals who lived in huts damp from the steam of perpetually boiling kettles. Then they came to an area of rope bridges perched over ravines and raging mountain streams. Only the Mongol horse and the ass would cross the first bridge, which was sixty feet long and two hundred feet above a dry riverbed. Diego had no option but to leave behind the second horse. From that moment Giorgio rode the ass, grumbling endlessly about the uncomfortable riding position, with his legs pushed out at the animal's sides by the packs containing their dwindling supplies. Often, as they ate by the campfire, Giorgio swore that he would be permanently affected by the rigors of the trail. He wished he had not come on the journey, and the only time he appeared cheerful was on days when his master was depressed. Then Giorgio made jokes and rallied Diego's flagging spirits.

Soon the two men saw ahead the yurts of a Kirghiz village. The tribesmen were of legendary duplicity, and Diego viewed the encampment with caution. All around the valley there were large fur-covered animals as tall as horses and heavier by far than bullocks. Their feet had cloven hooves and some ran lightfootedly up sheer rock faces to find especially tender roots and hidden berries in the heights.

Diego and Giorgio rode into the encampment and met the Kirghiz chief, but Diego learned from an old woman that if they did not leave immediately they would be held for ransom.

The friendly old tribeswoman also told them about the land ahead. They were about to come to the desert of Takla Makan, which was a place without a single waterhole. Few survived it, and she advised that they avoid the worst part of the desert by following the base of the mountain. They lingered only long enough to gain one further piece of information from the old woman—the name of the strange animals with the cloven hooves. Yaks, she announced, and said that they were not strange at all.

The Venetians hurried away from the village with their animals. Then, as Diego planned, they rode on in the cool of evening, finding their way in the darkness by skirting the foot of the mountain. In this way they followed an arid route which was relieved by brief patches of greenery, avoiding the impassable desert.

For days they continued to ride only at night and in the dusk hours to avoid being seen by any Kirghiz horsemen. Once, four days after leaving the encampment, they saw a rider peering intently over the cliff at the valley floor below. For hours the Venetians hid from the tribesman in a scorpion-ridden cave. Then they galloped on, relieved to have eluded pursuit.

Twenty days later the two men reached Lot, a once-prosperous place in a plain which had been ruined by Mongol visitations. Though the people were suspicious of strangers, there was grass for the horses and fresh water to drink, so Diego decided to remain for a few days before journeying on through the only desert he could not avoid. He begged lodgings in many houses, but the inhabitants were fearful of strangers. Only an old woman welcomed them, and for two days the two men ate and slept and thought of nothing but regaining lost energy.

So the two men were well rested as they entered the barren wastes. Diego smelled the warm dry air and thought of a Turkoman proverb—"The desert is as warm as a prayer and as dry as a curse." How long, he wondered, would it be before they reached the land of fabled riches? Or would they forever travel from snow to sand in countries that looked like lands God had forsaken? Weary of the journey, Diego rode on without complaint, praying that he would soon have some sign that they were nearing the end of their quest.

The Venetians were able to trade the Mongol horse for a camel of appalling ill temper. Its whim became their command, and often Giorgio relieved his feelings by kicking the animal furiously. One day the camel turned on Giorgio and bit off the tip of his right ear. As Giorgio wailed, the camel wandered away and settled to eating the prickly alhagi shrubs which were its only sustenance in the wilderness. Giorgio dressed his wound, comforting himself with the thought that he would tell everyone he knew that his ear had been bitten by the tiger his master had killed.

After twenty days of traveling through the desert the Venetians were close to collapse. After twenty-six days their water ran out and the ass fell dead at their feet, a victim of the heat whose bleached bones would decorate the landscape. Diego and Giorgio took turns riding the camel. Diego's eyes were forever scanning the oscillating, shimmering horizon for signs of civilization, but there was nothing to see but leafless saxaul trees, their white branches outlined against the dark-blue sky. In the beginning Diego thought the desert empty of life. Then, gradually, he noticed burrowing beetles and rodents, lizards, desert tortoises and green vipers that hid in the noonday sun like all the animals of the waterless plain. He had tried to learn survival from these creatures, resting in the heat of the day under a canopy of cloaks spread over dry tree branches, traveling distances only in the cool of the evening and at night.

On the twenty-seventh day, Giorgio began to hear voices. His tongue was swollen, his legs bloated, and he could barely walk. Again and again he cried out as demons wailed in the emptiness all around.

Diego too heard the phantom sounds of the desert, but he pressed on, dragging the camel along grimly, determinedly heading for the town he felt sure would be near. Sometimes, as thirst tormented him, Diego's mind turned to thoughts of Venice, and he berated himself for the wasteful life he had once led. In the face of death, a change came over Diego and he felt pangs of conscience that he had not acted long ago to help regain his family's fortune. He was twenty-five and until recently had never suffered physical harm. He had not thought of illness or hardship and had never considered the possibility of failure. Now the true strength of the man was revealed, and Diego strode on, his face burned brown by the sun, his lips cracked and suppurating, his body crying out for water. He would *not* be beaten by the desert. He would march until he fell dead on the ground. Such was Diego's truculent mood as he and his servant struggled to survive another night.

On the twenty-eighth evening in the desert, Giorgio became delirious. In a brief moment of lucidity, realizing that he could go no further, he begged his master to leave him behind.

"You can return later for me, sir. But in truth I am too old for such harsh exertion. My heart is willing but my flesh weak."

"I shall not leave you."

As he sat at his master's side, Giorgio heard again the wailing phenomena that had plagued him for days. He clutched his fingers to his ears and screamed in agony. Then, with one last desperate burst of energy, he ran until he could run no further. In a sandy hollow he collapsed and lay like a corpse, half conscious and longing for death. Suddenly, out of the moonlit stillness, he heard a different sound, the sound of someone playing the flute. Giorgio blinked to clear the sand from his eyes and crawled to the top of the hollow. On the other side there were the lights of a town.

Slowly, painfully, Giorgio dragged himself forward so he could be sure that it was not a mirage or phantom of the distracted mind. It was not. There were men walking in the town. Their faces were sallow and pale, not leathery and brown like Mongol faces. To the sick man they appeared civilized and kind. Overcome by relief, Giorgio buried his head in his hands and sobbed like a child.

When Diego caught up with his servant, he too saw the town. He wiped Giorgio's face and loosened the thonged sandals cutting the servant's swollen feet.

"We are saved, my good Giorgio."

"Oh, sir, I am reborn. If you can help me walk I will beg water and recover my health at once."

"You are too weak to go further. I will bring men to carry you to the town."

The Venetian led his camel into the main street, looking around with relief, because the town was peaceful, the people dignified and courteous. He tied the animal to a wooden bar over the horse trough. Then, as the camel drank, Diego immersed his head in the water, closing his eyes and thanking God for his delivery from the desert. When he felt stronger, he filled a gourd with water and took it back to Giorgio.

An old man who looked like a scholar was passing through the square, his arms folded, his face politely inquiring. Diego took him to the place where Giorgio lay unconscious on the sand. One look at the burned face, one touch of the swollen legs, and the scholar hurried away. He returned with some young men who lifted Giorgio on a cart and pushed him to the house of the local physician. People appeared in the doorways and at windows of nearby houses. Someone handed Diego a bowl of jasmine tea, and a little girl held his hand as though to reassure the weary traveler that he was safe. Suddenly the Venetian felt very tired. His eyes began to close, and he was barely able to understand what was going on around him. The babble of high-pitched, singsong voices pleased him, and he smiled hopefully at the warmth of his reception.

Diego was given shelter in the home of a widow. The woman was in the middle years of life, delicately boned and full of smiles. It was her pleasure to rescue this stranger in distress, and she called endless orders to her three sons. First they filled a washing tub with water and immersed Diego in its depths. Then they bathed him from head to toe. When they had oiled his tortured body, they placed the Venetian on a floor pillow and covered him to keep out the chill drafts of night. Diego was asleep before the young men had left the room.

That night the Venetian dreamed of a girl with black hair who berated him for loving too many women. He had dreamed of her before, but in previous dreams the girl's face had been hidden. Now he was thrilled to see the diminutive virago's green eyes and bow-shaped, rosy mouth. Diego woke with a start, confused and bewitched by the girl of his vision. Then,

82

realizing that he was exhausted and prone to strange imaginings, he lay back, enjoying the sweet smell of the persimmons at his bedside. Was this the land of which the Polos had spoken? Surely not? Here there were no pearls and rubies to be gathered in the streets. Here there were only honest people in a small, pleasant community. Diego fell asleep, unable to resolve his uncertainty.

In the town of Kangchow there was a spy named Ho Shan, and a few days after the Venetians' arrival he sent a message to the Khan informing him of the arrival of strangers in the town. Ho Shan kept continual watch on Diego from his house next to the Venetian's lodgings. He noted Diego's every move and daily checked the condition of the sick servant. Often, as he stood watching from his window, Ho Shan would see Diego bowing to him from the garden of the next house. When this happened Ho Shan would also bow, pleased to have been acknowledged by such a noble lord. Soon he ceased making notes on the stranger's actions because he was fascinated by Diego's bearing. Finally some weeks after the Venetians' arrival, Ho Shan engineered a meeting with the newcomer and was immediately overwhelmed with admiration.

Diego's hostess was amused when the two men became friends.

She confided what she knew to Diego. "Ho Shan is a spy of the Mongol Emperor, Kublai Khan."

"Does he spy on me?"

"I think so, sire."

"Why does he spy?"

"The Khan likes to know of all strangers who come to his lands."

"What will Ho Shan tell him?"

"I do not know, sire. But I believe he wishes that he had said nothing. You must speak with Ho Shan when I have taught you more of our language. He will tell you much about life in the Mongol court."

For hours each day Diego studied the language of the East. When he was tired, Kai-Kai, his hostess, treated him with special food and intoxicating plum-flower wine. She arranged outings to beauty spots and bought potions from the apothecary to renew Diego's strength. Summer's heat turned to the warmth of autumn. Then bronze leaves fell and blew along the pathways. Diego knew that he should continue his journey, but he believed Kai-Kai to be right. The language of Cathay was hard to understand and impossible to assimilate quickly. He would do well to learn it before he reached the Khan's land in order not to be at a disadvantage. And so he continued to take lessons from the occupants of the house.

Diego often visited Giorgio in the home of the apothecary. The servant was still very sick. His kidneys had been damaged by the deprivations of the desert. Neither man knew, as yet, if Giorgio would be able to continue the journey with his master.

Sometimes Ho Shan accompanied Diego on these visits to the sick man, and he was forever offering advice and bringing experts from neighboring towns to see the sick man. When Giorgio began to improve, no one was happier than the spy, and soon Ho Shan's conscience forced him to admit to Diego that he was working in the pay of the Emperor Kublai Khan.

"I would like to be your friend, Count Mazzarini, but I have done you the disservice of reporting your arrival to the Omnipotence."

Diego gave Ho Shan a ring seal of gold from his own finger. "This is a gift for you, Ho Shan. I give it because I like you and because I admire your honesty."

Ho Shan bowed his head in shame.

"You are not like the people of Cathay, Count, and you are as unlike a Mongol as the rose is unlike the sword. I hope to learn from you and perhaps someday I shall be able to be of service to you when you need a friend."

Outside Diego's window a blossom tree showered petals on the spring earth. Kai-Kai was crying, and Diego knew she had heard he was making preparations to resume his journey. He went to the garden to comfort her.

"Why are you crying?"

"I do not cry, my lord."

"We are friends and we shall always be friends. There is nothing to cry about."

"Yesterday Ho Shan came to see you, but you were out visiting your servant. Ho Shan knows much of the Emperor, and he wanted to tell you something very special before you departed. He said that the Khan has been waiting since the last spring for a man who will travel to his kingdom from across the world."

"Why is the Emperor waiting for such a man?"

"I do not know, and Ho Shan does not know either, but he told me the Khan watches from his window for the traveler and sometimes rides out of the capital with soldiers and courtiers to greet the stranger's arrival."

"Perhaps he expected the Polo family, who have been in his kingdom before?"

"It is possible, sire, I do not know. Ho Shan also told me that when you have traveled twenty days from this town you will reach Chagan Nor. From that place a road leads to the Khan's summer palace of Shang-tu. Ho Shan advises you to put on your finest robes and display your tiger skin once you reach that road."

"Did Ho Shan say why I should do this?"

"He says that you may meet the Khan's party en route to Chagan Nor. The Khan expects much of the stranger he seeks, and it would be bad for you to disappoint him. He admires strength and determination, so you must appear as mighty a warrior as he has ever seen, sire."

Ho Shan appeared as the couple were talking.

"I hear you are leaving us, Count Mazzarini."

"I am, Ho Shan, but I shall return before winter comes to collect my good Giorgio, who is not yet strong enough to travel."

"Have no fear, we shall care for your servant as if he were our own kin."

Ho Shan fumbled in his jacket and brought out a silk-wrapped gift. "I wish to give you this, Count Mazzarini, as a token of my esteem. It is the most precious thing I have ever owned and may be of use to you someday."

Diego unfolded the kerchief and took out a chain of tallow-pale jade on which was hung an oddly shaped sign. Ho Shan put the chain around Diego's neck and explained its significance.

"This is an imperial messenger's chain. I found it many moons ago when I was riding near the desert. With that chain you can pass through any of the lands governed by the Emperor Kublai Khan. Hide it when you reach Peking, for you are not supposed to possess such an object. The fellow who lost it surely paid with his life for the error of losing it."

Diego thanked Ho Shan for the gift. Then he went inside the house, and returned with a gray velvet cloak lavishly edged with fox—a garment the spy had coveted since the day of their first meeting. Diego handed the cloak to Ho Shan, who bowed low and stammered his thanks.

When the spy had gone, Kai-Kai said, "Ho Shan will try on the cloak you have given him and fall in love with his reflection. Then he will close his house and mourn your departure. He is a lonely man, sire, with no family and few to care for him. Since poverty forced him to accept the role of spy to the Emperor, Ho Shan has lost the respect of his neighbors. You are the first person who has treated him as a gentleman, and he has tried to win your admiration."

In the early evening, Diego went to visit his servant in the house of the apothecary.

Giorgio sprang up when he saw his master. "My lord, I am so happy to see you. I have been trying to speak with the apothecary's son, but he is a stupid fellow who cannot learn the Venetian tongue, though I have persisted in teaching him for many weeks."

"I leave at dawn, my good Giorgio."

"Would I could come with you, sir."

"You will, I give you my word. Expect me when the leaves turn red."

"I pray you ride safely, my lord."

The two men shook hands. Then Diego returned to complete his preparations for the journey and bid farewell to Kai-Kai.

Briefly, Diego slept, waking with the dawn on a sunny spring morning. Within the hour he was gone, riding boldly along the road that led to Cathay.

Chapter Six:

Chagan Nor

The city of Chagan Nor was built around a lake in an area beloved by the Khan because it offered the finest wildfowling. The Emperor had a hunting lodge and an estate there where partridge, duck and pheasant were raised and fattened for the royal table. The countryside was beautiful, with willow trees, waterfalls and blue mountains framing a fertile plain. Poppies bobbed in the fields and yellow orchids climbed around hedgerows of scented scarlet flowers. Chagan Nor was also the place where Kublai Khan had first met the girl who had dominated his thoughts since the previous year's visit.

Once again, the imperial entourage was on its way to the cool of the summer palace. As he rode, the Khan's breath came fast at the thought that he might see the elusive Lotus Flower again. He thought of the gifts he would give her, the estates he would present and the pearls he had hoarded for a decade which he would offer only to her. There was nothing the girl could not demand if only she would love him as he longed to be loved; as he *demanded* to be loved! The procession passed on and the Emperor's eyes continued to search the distant landscape. Courtiers observing him wondered why the Omnipotence was so excited.

Diego had camped on a hill above Chagan Nor, after he had hidden his horse in a nearby cave. Below the camp was a pool inhabited by cranes and swans, and not far away there were woods noisy with wildlife. The Venetian was satisfied that he could eat well and rest in peace until the Khan's party arrived in the area. An old charcoal vendor in the market of Chagan Nor had told him that the Mongol court would be arriving in the town within a few days. Diego's impatience knew no bounds, and often he ran to the edge of the clearing and looked searchingly to the plains below.

One day while Diego was hunting by the wildfowl lake he heard a rustling in the undergrowth behind him. Looking around, he saw nothing, so he rose and parted the acacia bushes at the edge of the water. There he found a primitive bow and some arrows of a type used to shoot small birds. He was puzzled, but he continued hunting until he had some pigeons and a hare. Then he trudged through a meadow on his way back to the camp. As he walked, the Venetian began to feel that he was being watched. Every few minutes he turned, without warning, to see if he could catch the culprit, but each time the field seemed empty. Shaking his head, Diego made his way back to the camp. Still he could not rid himself of the feeling that someone was spying on him, and he wondered if loneliness had made his imagination run riot.

In the cool of evening, Diego sat by the campfire cooking the birds and the hare he had caught earlier in the day. He drank the last of his wine, upending the flagon, disappointed that there was no more. He ate hungrily, then wrapped what remained in muslin and put it in one of the saddlebags for the morning. By the light of the fire he wrote in his journal, and then sat looking dreamily into the embers. Chagan Nor had surprised Diego by its modernity, forcing him to reassess the Mongol ruler. A man who could build such a city, with

88

postal institutions for sending letters and a system of aid for the poor, was no barbarian. Sleepily, Diego tried to envisage what the Emperor would be like, how he would speak, what his interests would be and, most important of all, if he would be friendly. Impatient for the morning, the Venetian finally slept until the sound of birdsong woke him.

At dawn Diego walked to the stream, undressed and plunged into the water. The sun was already warm, and there was the promise of burning heat to come. Diego enjoyed the freshness of the air and the bubbling of a waterfall at his feet. When he had washed, he walked back to the camp, where he selected his best clothes, a tunic of scarlet crepe, a tabard of bejeweled brocade and a black Genoese velvet hat. Over these he planned to throw a cloak of white silk lined with silver tissue. Diego thought affectionately of Kai-Kai as he put the clothes aside. He was not ready to dress yet. Shaking his hair dry, he rubbed his body with a coarse linen towel which he wound round his waist as he prepared to make breakfast. He looked in his saddlebag for the meat left over from supper. The meat was not where he had left it. He went to the cave and searched in a box where he kept his reserve food, but the meat was not there either. Diego tried to imagine what kind of fool would steal two cooked hare's legs and other leftovers. Then he sat by the fire, warming his hands and wishing he had something appetizing to eat.

It was not long before a luscious smell drifted his way. Diego walked in the direction of the smell and entered another cave, which was empty but for a bubbling stewpot over a wood fire. He looked round suspiciously, half cautious for his safety, half longing to rush to the pot to eat his fill. On the floor he saw his wine flagon, and was delighted to find the flagon full again. Was it possible Giorgio had ridden behind him all the way?

Smiling at the thought, Diego called softly to the emptiness of the cave, "Are you there, my good Giorgio? Show yourself and we shall celebrate your arrival."

A chirruping sound answered his cry. Diego inclined his head, wondering if this was the sound of a bird or a squirrel. The sound came again, this time in merry, regulated rhythm. Intrigued, Diego sat on the floor of the cave and waited, for what he was not sure. As he waited he pulled a chicken leg from the pot and ate hungrily. Then he drank some of the wine, impressed by its amber clarity. He was about to leave the cave when a shadow crossed his path and, looking up, he was surprised to see a young woman in the ragged clothes of a peasant boy.

The cave was dark, and Diego could barely make out the girl's face, though he saw the white of her teeth as she smiled at his confusion. He greeted her with an elegant bow. Then, realizing he was wearing only a towel, he blushed.

"I am Diego Mazzarini, Count of the Venetian Empire. May I ask your name?"

"I have no name. I am an animal of the forest in the cave where you hide."

"I am not hiding. I am waiting."

"Why are you waiting?"

"I am here because I wish to meet Kublai Khan, the Emperor of Cathay. I have heard he is due to pass through Chagan Nor today."

The smile vanished, and Diego felt the girl was distressed. He held out his hand to her.

"Will you not come down? I can barely see in this darkness."

The girl stepped hastily back, and Diego realized that he must treat her gently, for she was shy.

"Thank you for the wine and food. It was the finest stew I have ever eaten."

"Where are you from? I saw you riding out of the sunset when I was fishing the other day. Do you live in the country beyond the mountains?"

"I am from a great empire situated in the middle of the sea many thousands of hours' ride from Cathay."

There was a pause while the girl assimilated this startling information. Then she spoke with great vehemence. "The Emperor Kublai Khan is a villain. Why do you wish to meet such a person? Are you a fool that you travel from across the world to pay homage to him?"

The edge in her voice startled the Venetian, and he looked more closely at the tiny, doll-like figure in the shabby jacket and shapeless pantaloons.

"I have not come to pay homage. I am here to find a new fortune. I am a poor man whose family was once rich. Then a swindler deprived my grandfather of his wealth. My parents are dead and with them my sister and elder brother. In order to rebuild my family fortune I have come to Cathay to find merchandise which I can take back to the city of Venice to trade. I cannot hope to do that without the permission of the Emperor."

For a moment the girl was silent, and Diego wondered if she was crying. When she spoke her voice trembled with emotion.

"My father was also deprived of his fortune. Kublai Khan appropriated it and sent us into exile. My mother and my sisters died of a fever they caught living here in the marshes. Now my father and I live alone as if we were peasants. But I do not care. I love to hunt and fish. I want nothing of Kublai Khan. *Nothing!*"

Saddened by the calamity that had ruined the girl's life, Diego called gently, "May I ask you a special favor?"

"You may ask, but I do not know if I will grant your wish."

"I would like to see you for a moment."

The girl smiled like a child. "Close your eyes and you will see me when you open them."

Obediently Diego closed his eyes. When he opened them the girl was gone. Disappointed, he turned toward the entrance of the cave, and there, framed in the gray rocky arch, was the sprite with emerald eyes and a rose-red mouth. Diego gasped at this embodiment of his dreams. While he stared in disbelief, the girl mounted a white horse and galloped away, her dark hair flying in the breeze like a satin banner.

As Diego sat by the fire, his face glowing with pleasure, he thought what an extraordinary creature the girl was, what a demon of mischief and intrigue. He tried to remember everything she had said, but his mind was confused, his memory inaccurate. He could only recall that she had been exiled by the Khan and that she had emerald eyes, creamy skin and a mouth the color of a rose. An hour passed like a minute. Then Diego roused himself from his daydream and returned to the place where he had put his clothes.

As he reached the clearing, the Venetian noticed dust

clouds below on the plain. He felt sure that they were caused by the approach of the imperial party at last. He dressed with care. Then he drank more wine and served himself more stew. As he ate he remembered his early-morning bath. Was it possible the girl had seen his naked body? Diego's chagrin was intense. He had loved many women and had never been shy, but the thought of revealing himself to such a beguiling innocent filled him with unease. He looked uncertainly round the clearing, wondering if the girl was still watching him. For the first time in his life Diego felt himself at the disadvantage of a lady.

When she had had her fill of watching the stranger, Lotus Flower crawled through the undergrowth and returned to her horse. She was elated to have encountered such an intriguing and noble person. As she rode, she thought how the traveler had enjoyed the food she had prepared, how great had been his appetite and how sweet the smile when he tasted the wine. She resolved to go at once to steal more wine from the drunken merchant in the marketplace. Then she would catch some fish for her father's meal.

Lotus Flower carried out her plan adroitly and without conscience. After she had served her father his midday meal, she returned to the woods to steal a pair of ducks from the Khan's hunting estate. The ducks, she knew, were kept in special wooden houses of their own, not far from the lodge in which the Khan often stayed. Lotus Flower crept into one of the huts and picked up a pair of fat, sleepy birds. She was thinking happily of the dinner she would make the stranger when she found her way barred by the Khan himself.

The Emperor's laughter filled the air, and he held the girl close to his chest, determined not to let her go. No matter how much she struggled, the ruler continued to hold her. Lotus Flower bit him, and he roared with annoyance.

"So! Not only do you offend the Imperial Personage but I see it is your habit to steal my birds."

"As you stole my father's property. You are a bigger thief than I."

The Khan deposited Lotus Flower in the buttercup meadow, his face softening at the sight of her tears.

"You need not steal. Tell me what you want and I shall be happy to give it to you."

"And what must I do in return?"

"You must love me as I have never been loved before."

"I could never love you, not if you gave me the sun and the moon and the stars."

Perplexed, the Khan looked down on the face of the girl he adored. "Why could you not love me? Tell me, *why?*"

Lotus Flower hesitated. Then she decided to tell the truth. "I am fifteen summers old, sire, you are at least a hundred and your face is painted like the face of a singing girl to make you appear younger than you are. I could never love a man whose face is painted, a man whose body is large and rolling. I could only love a man whose skin was fresh and whose breath smelled of grass and flowers."

Roaring with annoyance, the Khan grasped Lotus Flower to his chest, again, intending to take her where she stood. Then he grew pale and his eyes stared until they seemed to bulge from his head. Lotus Flower followed the imperial gaze.

Above them, appearing like a vision from the rocks of the hillside, was a rider with golden hair. The man was magnificently dressed, and as the Emperor stared in amazement, a playful gust of wind blew the stranger's cloak so it billowed out like a silver, shimmering cloud, catching the sun and almost blinding the onlooker. The Khan stepped back, shielding his eyes from the spectacle. While his attention was diverted, Lotus Flower ran away, still holding the two ducks firmly under her arms. When she looked back from the safety of the bushes, the Khan was still rooted to the spot, staring in disbelief at the approaching figure of the Venetian.

Unaware of the stir he had caused, Diego rode through the meadow, reining his horse before the figure of the Emperor. He looked commandingly down at the massive figure dressed in yellow.

"Sir, I seek Kublai Khan, the mighty Emperor of Cathay. Do you know if he has arrived in Chagan Nor?"

"Who are you? What is your name?"

"My name will be told to the Khan and to no other."

The Khan looked at the stern face of the young man, at the signs of suffering around his eyes and the lines of laughter around his mouth. Suddenly he felt very old and unequal to dealing with this proud creature of another world. Dejectedly, the Khan turned his back and mounted his horse so he could at least speak from the same height as the stranger instead of peering up at him like a servant.

The ruler called haughtily, "You will meet the Khan by the imperial arch of Chagan Nor at sunset. He invites you to visit him as he invites all strangers to his land."

Diego watched as the rider disappeared. Then again he heard the chirruping sound he had heard that morning in the cave. Looking around, he was delighted to see the girl standing before him, her face shining with pleasure, her eyes alight and under each arm a contented, jade-winged duck.

Diego knew that he had never seen anyone so beautiful, so entrancing. As their eyes met, he felt an earthquake of the soul that left him full of longing. It was with great effort that he spoke calmly. "What is your name?"

"I have no name."

"How can I find you again if I cannot ask for you by name?"

"No man can find me. I prefer to find whom I wish to find. I do not like to be pursued."

Diego wondered how to deal with such an independent creature, whose ideas on life were so unlike his own. The girl came closer and whispered gleefully to him.

"The Khan was upset by your appearance, sire. He has now gone back to his encampment to dress himself in splendor in readiness for your arrival. The next time you see him he will be bejeweled like a rich old woman."

"That was the Emperor?"

"Yes. Only the ruler can wear yellow. But no matter, the Khan felt himself inferior to you. It made him angry and that is why he would not tell you his name. I was so happy I almost crowed like a cockerel."

"I must meet the Khan at sunset. That is what he said."

The girl stepped eagerly forward and held the reins of Diego's horse. "Will you be sleeping again near the cave?"

"If the Khan does not invite me to lodge with his party."

The girl was disappointed, and Diego realized that she wanted to see him again.

94

"If you were to tell me I must sleep in the cave I should do so," he said.

"Then I command it."

"I am yours to command, my lady."

The green eyes flashed defiantly at this flowery statement. "When you are gallant you speak like one who loves too many women and who says the same words to each of them. I do not care for such locusts."

Diego remembered the girl in his dreams who had berated him for loving too many women. He wondered if he could control such a headstrong one by arousing her jealousy.

"I have loved many women, and no doubt I shall love many more, for I have never found one who could keep my attention without diversion."

Lotus Flower scowled at the Venetian, uncertain if he was teasing her. Then, to Diego's surprise, she raised her chin and said defiantly, "I have decided I do not wish to see you in the cave tonight. It is obvious that you would do better to remain with the Khan. In his encampment you will be given the choice of the imperial concubines."

Realizing that his strategy had failed, Diego tried to retrieve the situation. "I spoke falsely of my love of women. And I do not wish to enjoy the Khan's concubines when I can have your company."

"I do not believe you, sire."

Lotus Flower retreated toward the bushes, her face pale with annoyance.

Diego called to her, "You are too lovely to spoil your looks with so many frowns."

"Now, surely, you talk like one who chases women. Goodbye, sire. No doubt I shall see you again someday, but I do not know if I shall remember your name."

With that insult, Lotus Flower ran away into the heart of the forest. Diego tried to follow, but soon he had lost her. Depressed and angry with himself, the Venetian waited patiently for her to return, but Lotus Flower did not reappear, and reluctantly he rode away toward the archway of Chagan Nor. As he rode, Diego felt a heaviness in his chest that he had never felt before, he could think of nothing but the eager face of the girl who had offered friendship. In return he had offended her with his foolish bragging. Diego comforted himself with the thought that he would wait for the girl in the cave that night and every night until she deigned to return. He remembered Giorgio's praising his abilities in love and telling him there was not a woman in the world he could not love for the asking. Now he had met a woman no man could demand, a goddess who was unwilling to confide even her name. Diego told himself he was better off without such a monster, but his heart continued to sing her praises and his mind to dwell on the petal softness of her skin.

At sunset the Khan was sitting on a dais covered in cloth of gold. Twelve thousand members of the Keshikten were lined around him, forming an avenue of approach to the Royal Personage. Members of the court had been ordered to appear in their best and musicians commanded to play martial music in order to raise the ruler's spirits. The Khan's face had been painted, his fingers covered with the imperial emeralds. His robe, bejeweled with rubies, was so heavy that he could not rise. Instead, he kept nodding regally, and ordering the concubines fanning his face to take care not to permit perspiration to dwell on the Omnipotent countenance. Handmaidens waved scarlet ostrich fans attached to gilded poles to keep the Royal Personage happy. And all the while the Khan kept remembering the girl who had thought him a hundred years old.

As Diego approached, the imperial sorcerer released a flight of doves to flutter in the air, their wings forming patterns against the orange-gold of the sky. Some of the doves flew away, one flew to the Khan's dais and settled at his feet, two landed on Diego's shoulders and remained there as he rode down the avenue of heavily armed guards. When he reached the foot of the steps leading to the Khan's podium, Diego stepped down from his horse, bowed and knelt to kiss the ground.

"I salute you, Emperor of Cathay, Khan of the Golden Horde, Ruler of Half the World, and I salute the land that is yours."

Pleased by this show of humility, Kublai Khan nodded the imperial assent. "What is your name?"

"I am Diego Mazzarini, Count of the Venetian Empire."

"And why have you come to visit us in Cathay?"

"I seek my brother, sire, who is come before me."

The Khan leaned forward, keenly interested in this surprising statement. "Who is your brother?"

"His name is Pierluigi Mazzarini, sir. He traveled to your land before me with the party of Niccolo and Maffeo Polo."

The Khan beamed and clapped his hands, turning to silence the clamor of excitement that rose from the assembled court. "This noble lord is brother to our guest Sir Piers."

The Khan turned again to Diego. "Are you come with many men, Count?"

"No, my lord. I left Venice with only one, my servant, Giorgio. He has remained in Kangchow, still suffering from a sickness contracted in the desert. I hope to return for him in the fall, with your permission."

The Khan brooded on this information. The man had come from across the world with only one servant to assist him. Was it possible? Surely it was not. Had the stranger crossed the deserts and the precipices of the roof of the world without the aid of an army? Had he eluded the brigands and bandits without safe-conduct tablets from the Emperor? Was he bewitched? Was he a God and not a mere mortal? Could this be the man about whom the astrologer had spoken? The Khan felt sure that it was. He took note of the tiger skin on which Diego rode and asked his chamberlain to order information to be collected from all corners of the kingdom about the stranger. A man who could kill such a tiger and ride unharmed across the last great desert of the world was a man the spirits favored above all others. The Khan's superstitious mind balked at the idea of harming such a person, though he disliked the thought of admitting his rival to the kingdom.

After long deliberation the Khan spoke. "I shall be pleased to invite you to join my party, Count Mazzarini. Your brother has already ridden to the summer palace of Shang-tu. Tonight you will feast with us and tell me of your travels. I shall be interested to know how you traveled from across the world without the aid of an army."

The Khan's chamberlain dismissed the nobles. Then, as the sun slipped over the horizon, the two men looked at each other, the young handsome stranger and the old campaigner who had come from early days in a Tartar tent to old age in the exotic palaces of Cathay. The Khan thought sadly that at this moment he would trade all his palaces and concubines for Diego Mazzarini's youth.

The Venetian looked into the Khan's eyes and was troubled because there was an aura of concealed anger in the man facing him. The Emperor's body was no longer young, but it was said he could still wield the heaviest broadsword and there were those who swore that he could outride the fastest horsemen in the kingdom. Diego's instincts told him he must tread warily with the master of Cathay.

That night the Khan presided over a feast by the campfire. Though he had lived many years in the luxury of royal palaces, the Emperor still loved to sleep under the stars. He watched as servants carried in bowls of steaming noodles, with chicken and kid, fresh fish, guinea fowl and fallow deer, thirty courses to be approved by the Omnipotence. But he was not interested in food, and many of the nobles feared that he was about to have an attack of ill humor.

In truth the Khan was impatient to dismiss the party. He had decided to visit the wildfowl lake where he had first seen Lotus Flower. All day he had been willing the girl to appear. The Khan's astrologer had foretold that a meeting would take place, that the lady would come to the court of Peking and that the Emperor would be given the opportunity to know her. The Khan had taken this to mean that he would have his heart's desire, and he could barely keep himself from hurrying away into the moonlit darkness, the sooner to be with the object of his passion. Then he remembered Lotus Flower's acid comment of the morning, and his eyes misted with sadness. The spirits were paying him back for desiring a woman who always spoke the truth.

The Emperor's gaze wandered to Diego, who was enjoying a leg of wild turkey and a goblet of wine. The Khan looked enviously at the Venetian's sunburned face with its golden frame, the laughing eyes that missed nothing and had already enraptured the ladies of the court. The Khan admired the muscular body and thought furiously that Diego Mazzarini's breath probably smelled of flowers and fresh-cut grass, just as Lotus Flower had described. He hoped fervently that the

Venetian would never meet the sprite of the wildfowl lake. As soon as he thought of that alarming possibility, he ordered members of the court to be ready to move on at dawn to the palace of Shang-tu. Murmurs of consternation greeted the ruler's sudden whim, and many were relieved when the Khan strode away into the forest.

When the feast was over, Diego returned to his camp on the hill. He was touched to see that the fire had been lit and a bed made for him of clover flowers. He longed to see the elusive girl again. As he walked to the pool and watched the swans gliding by in the moonlight, Diego recalled the pure lines of her face and the shabby clothes she wore. His ears strained for the familiar chirrup, but the night was silent and he heard only the distant sound of the Khan's party below on the plain.

Disappointed that the girl had not appeared, Diego undressed and wrapped himself in a woolen robe. Then he threw some pine cones on the fire and poured himself wine from the flagon by his couch. As he drank he looked thoughtfully into the flames, wondering if she would return with the dawn or if he would never see her again. He could not bear to think of losing her, and he thought that if she did not appear he would search until he found her.

Finally, Diego lay down on the bed of scented flowers, comforting himself with the thought that the girl had forgiven him for his unmannerliness of the morning. For that he was thankful. As the moon moved behind a cloud darkening the clearing, Diego fell asleep to dream of the dark-haired beauty.

The Khan rose before dawn and set off yet again for the wildfowl pool. Members of the court preparing for the last part of the journey looked askance as the Emperor rode away. At once there were rumors of a secret meeting with envoys of a foreign power, of a clandestine love affair or a malady of the mind which made the Omnipotence so uneasy he paced the nights away.

Kublai Khan knew nothing of this speculation about his abrupt behavior as he leaped off his horse and walked stealthily toward the lake. His heart missed a beat when he saw

Lotus Flower bathing in a pool, her arms upstretched in delight as she splashed the icy water on her face. The Khan looked hungrily at the girl's newly developed breasts, so full and round and tempting. When the girl stepped out of the water, he crouched behind a bush and continued to peer at her through the dense branches.

The Khan vowed to control himself so he could watch what Lotus Flower did, where she went and with whom she met. Once he knew who her friends were he would persuade them, by bribes and threats, to influence the girl in his favor. The Khan was puzzled to see the girl putting a lotus blossom in her hair and securing it with a pin shaped like a silver butterfly. Was the vixen going to meet a secret lover? When Lotus Flower had put on the trousers and jacket which were her only clothes, she took from her pocket a green silk scarf that matched the color of her eyes. She tied the scarf around her waist, retying the knot three times before she was satisfied. The Khan sighed, recognizing her preparations. The girl *was* in love!

He would put the object of her admiration in chains for a year and then cut off his head, he raged. When he looked again, he saw Lotus Flower pulling a large earthenware pot from the water. Struggling to lift it, she staggered off up the stony hillside. The Khan followed.

Diego woke with sunlight streaming into his eyes. He leaped up, concerned that he had overslept. Had the Khan's party already left the plain? He rushed to the edge of the clearing and peered across, relieved to see that the group had not moved since the previous evening. Hastily he dressed and as he raked the embers of the fire, wondered if there was time to catch a fish in the pool before rejoining the imperial party. Hunger made Diego decide there was time and he got his fishing rod. Making his way to the water, he smelled again the intoxicating odors he had enjoyed the previous morning. He rushed toward the cave, halting by the campfire to stare at the bewitching creature he had feared he might never see again.

Lotus Flower looked up, her eyes shining with happiness.

Diego bowed and asked hopefully, "Is there enough food for a stranger to share?"

She smiled at his formal tone, pleased that Diego had not persisted in asking her name.

"What is your name, sire? I have forgotten."

"I am Diego Mazzarini, Count of the Venetian Empire."

Lotus Flower rose and curtsied gracefully. "I am Lotus Flower, Princess of the House of Sung, now a shabby peasant with no home."

Diego held his breath, uncertain if the girl was teasing him. "Is that our real name, my lady?"

"It is not my born name. I dislike my given name, so I call myself Lotus Flower. It is a pretty name, is it not?"

"I should prefer to know your real name, but no matter."

Lotus Flower served him a bowl of duck steamed with feather-light dumplings. As they ate, she explained, "I stole these ducks from the estate of the Khan."

"You should not steal. You could be executed if the Khan's guards apprehend you."

Lotus Flower laughed merrily. "The Khan would not execute a woman he desires."

Diego flushed with annoyance—a reaction that made the girl happy. Yesterday the Venetian had made her jealous by boasting that he had loved many women. Now he too was feeling the agonizing barbs of the soul. She gave Diego more of the meat and ate her own, looking up at the sky to appraise the weather.

"It will be a fine day for your journey to Shang-tu. The Emperor has a wondrous palace there where he will entertain you as you have never been entertained before. He is the richest ruler of the world, and generous with those he favors. Soon you will be rich again if you obey the Emperor's commands."

"If the Khan desires you, why are you poor?"

Lotus Flower frowned as she put down her bowl.

"If the Khan offered to return my father's estates in Peking and all our wealth, I would not love him. I shall never love any man."

Diego finished the food and poured himself some wine. He was sorely tempted to kiss the girl, because he was sure she had no knowledge of how passion aroused the soul. The thought of teaching Lotus Flower about love and developing

101

her appetite for pleasure excited him. Diego rose and walked uneasily to and fro in the clearing, uncertain what next to say to this enigmatic child of the forest.

Finally, he spoke. "I shall soon be leaving for Shang-tu as a guest of the Emperor, and I hope to be reunited with my brother, Pierluigi, there. Thank you for allowing me to share your meal and also for the delicious wine. I would like very much to be your friend, but as I shall be in Shang-tu until after the twenty-eighth day of the eighth month I think it is impossible."

"I am always here near the wildfowl pool if you should wish to see me."

"And when you are old, my lady, will you still be here alone by the wildfowl pool?"

Lotus Flower turned away, and Diego saw that her hands were trembling. "You are no gentleman, sire!"

"I ask only to show you that a woman who is foolish enough to say she can never love ends her life alone and lonely."

"I have no money, nothing in which to dress myself, and to add to my distress my father is dreadfully ill. If he should die, I shall be alone in the world. Then, sire, I shall send a message to you in the palace of Shang-tu and you may come to rescue me."

Diego bowed his assent. "I shall be honored to come to your rescue, my lady."

He kissed the girl's hand and returned to the clearing where his horse was waiting. Every second that put distance between them hurt Diego and he longed to run back and throw himself at the girl's feet, but he knew this would only frighten her. Instead he raised his hand in salute and rode down the mountain to join the Khan's party.

Lotus Flower watched until the Venetian disappeared. Then she returned to the cave and, kneeling on the ground, cried until her eyes were red and swollen. She did not know why she was so distressed. She was aware only that her heart felt heavy and her soul full of phantoms. As she cried, Lotus Flower wiped her tears on the ragged sleeves of her jacket, and soon the sleeves were soaking wet. She continued to sob as she tidied the camp and washed the cooking pot. She wished she had never met Diego Mazzarini. Until she had met the Venetian, Lotus Flower had felt content with life and resigned to the futility of her exile. Now she raged at the hopelessness of her desire, and at the thought of Diego cavorting with the grasping concubines and devious noblewomen of the imperial court.

When she had wiped her eyes for the last time, Lotus Flower made her way back up the hill to the place where Diego had camped. There, on the floor of his cave, she found a miniature fallen from his baggage. She examined this treasure with avid curiosity. On one side there was a portrait of a haughty woman with white hair. She assumed that to be the Venetian's dead mother. On the other side there was a painting of a palazzo overlooking the Venetian lagoon. The house was enclosed within high walls covered with yellow hanging blossoms.

Lotus Flower took the miniature and hid it in her jacket. Each day she would look at it and remember Diego Mazzarini, and someday, when they met again, she would beg him to tell her all about his mansion by the sea. As Lotus Flower was hurrying back down the hill, she came upon the Khan. She was about to run away from him when something in his ashen face prevented her from moving.

The Khan staggered three paces and collapsed on his knees. He had been hiding in the forest, listening to Lotus Flower talking with the Venetian, when a pain like molten lead struck him in the chest. He had tried to call for help, but no voice had come from his throat. Now, as he sat suffused with pain, the Khan knew that his life depended on the caprice of the girl whose family he had wronged.

The Khan closed his eyes resignedly. But he looked up, surprised to see Lotus Flower kneeling at his side, offering him a flagon of wine.

"Are you ill, sire?"

"My chest burns with agony."

Lotus Flower gave the Khan a sip of wine. Then she put both hands together and punched him a resounding blow to the breastbone. The Khan gulped, relieved to feel something shift within him, releasing the obstruction that had prevented his breathing.

"Dearest child, you have saved my life."

"No, my lord. I only released the stone from your heart."

"Where did you learn this trick?"

"I saw a wise man do that to my father when he was ill a few days ago. Do not rise yet, sire, you must rest awhile. Shall I cover you with your cloak?"

The Khan sat upright, leaning against a tree. His eyes followed Lotus Flower's every move, and he wondered how to tell her that he wanted to make amends. The girl's thoughts seemed far away as she sat stroking his hands to soothe his pain. The Khan imagined she was thinking of the man who had come from across the world to love her. Lotus Flower wiped the Khan's brow and apologized for her haste.

"Soon I must leave you, sire. My father is very ill and cannot be left for long."

"I shall not forget what you have done."

The green eyes gleamed angrily. "You will forget before you reach Shang-tu!"

The Khan stumbled to his feet. "The Lord of the Mongol Horde does not forget. He can wait a thousand moons to kill an enemy or to reward a friend. It is one of the advantages of being one hundred years old."

Lotus Flower covered her face to hide her smile, and the Khan mounted his horse to ride away.

"Say nothing of my illness this day or you will be responsible for my death," he commanded.

"I speak only to the birds and animals of the forest, sire."

"You will see me again before the full moon."

Lotus Flower watched as the Emperor rode away, down the stony hillside to his camp. Soon she heard the conch shell summon the court procession to move on, and at its rear she could see Diego Mazzarini.

She waited until the party disappeared along the road to Shang-tu. Then she ran through the woods, past the wildfowl pool and the meadow of poppies, to a wooden shack in a damp, leafy clearing. When she reached the door she called, "I am home, Father."

Hearing no reply, she went inside and found her father gasping for breath. She covered his body with sacking and held him in her arms.

"Shall I go for a physician?"

"No, I command you to stay. I am dying, Mo-ch'ou. By nightfall I shall be gone, and there is much I must still tell you. Bring me wine so I can be strong."

Lotus Flower poured some of the wine she had stolen into a cup, and held it to the dying man's mouth.

Her father spoke calmly, in a low voice. "When I am gone you must go to Hangchow."

"But why? I know only this area and the street of our home in Peking."

"My sister lives in Hangchow. She is now your only relative and she will care for you."

Lotus Flower rebelled against that idea, but she remained silent as the old man continued.

"You were the child of my middle years, born after a great interval when I thought happiness had gone out of my life. I love you dearly, Mo-ch'ou, but I see that my misfortune has changed you. Ladies of gentle breeding should not fish and shoot. They should never lose their innocence by riding wild horses around the countryside like Mongol women. I fear it will be impossible for you to marry a nobleman. My sister may disagree. She is younger than I by twenty years and you will like her. Her address is written in my book of the stars. It is the Street of the Green Dragon, in the House of the Singing Kite. Say you will go there."

"I will, Father."

"When I am gone, burn this house down around me. It is full of the sickness which has weakened me. And remember I want only for you to be happy and content."

The old man struggled to find something in the folds of his robe. Lotus Flower gasped when her father handed her a gold key.

"This fits a box buried in the garden of our home in Peking. The box lies buried under the yellow rose at the side of the well. I have ascertained that no one is living in our house. If you can find some way to go there, you will unearth an object of great value which will keep you for the rest of your life."

"Why did we not take this precious object with us into exile?"

"The Khan's men took me by surprise and I had no time to remove it from its hiding place."

"And why have we not returned to collect it, Father?"

The old man's eyes closed and he was barely able to reply. "The Khan said that if I or any of my family returned to Peking we should all be executed. I was not willing to risk your life for a mere bauble."

Within an hour the old man was dead. Lotus Flower dressed him in his only remaining silk robe, and after she had removed her belongings from the hut, she locked the door and set fire to the building. She waited in the forest nearby until the hut was a mass of powdery rubble. Then she led her horse to the road Diego had taken. She had told the Venetian that if he wished to see her she would be in the vicinity of the wildfowl pool. But now Lotus Flower had to tell him that her father was dead and that she had other plans for her future.

With her belongings tied in a kerchief on her shoulder, Lotus Flower rode after the imperial party. As she rode she was sad, because of her father's death, and happy, because she had just made a decision which would change her life. She no longer needed to be rescued. But she wanted to make sure the Venetian could find her if he wished to.

Diego was watering his horse at a wayside trough when he heard the chirrup he had noticed whenever Lotus Flower was near. He walked away from the rest of the party and stood behind some rocks, hidden from the Khan's gaze. Soon the girl appeared, leading her horse, and Diego saw that her face was tear-stained and pale.

Alarmed, he rushed to her side. "What has happened? Has someone harmed you?"

"I am well, sire, but I have ridden hard to catch up with you and I am tired. I wanted you to know that my father died this day, and I will be returning to my home in Peking."

Diego paused to assess the risks involved in this bold action. "How do you know your house is not occupied?"

"My father said it was still empty."

"And what of the Khan? What will he do when he discovers your defiance of his orders?"

"I shall not know what the Khan will say or do until he knows that I am back in Peking."

"Why must you go there?"

A look of sadness haunted the beautiful face. "When I lived in Peking I was learning to be a great lady. I had a hundred dresses of the finest silk and jewels for each day of the year, though I was but a child. My time was spent learning to play the lute and the mandolin. I also learned calligraphy and the art of flower arrangement. I was happy then as I have been happy fishing and shooting in Chagan Nor. But now I am growing too old to be the boy. I am *sick* of exile. I am sick of these old clothes I must wear every day. I want to be a lady again."

"But how will you live? You cannot hunt and fish in the city, and you have no money."

Diego suddenly had visions of the men who would want this enchanting creature, the villains who might try to take advantage of her. His mind whirled at the idea of leaving her, and he said so. "You must not go to Peking alone."

"You are not my husband to forbid me, sire."

"I mean well. I am concerned only for your safety."

"And I for my future. I have plans to make and many changes to bring about in my situation before we meet again. I must be brave and clever or I shall perish."

Diego looked at the determined face and knew that nothing would dissuade Lotus Flower from her plan. He took what gold he had left from his coat and offered it to the girl. "Take this to help you on your way. If we should meet again you may repay me."

"I hope we shall meet again, sire."

Lotus Flower examined the gold. She was pleased when Diego told her of his intentions.

"Say that I may visit you in Peking before the month is out. I must be sure that you are safe. If you say no, my lady, I shall be compelled to disobey you."

"I am not your wife to forbid you anything, sire! And I thank you for your generous loan of these gold coins. I hope to be able to repay them with interest."

Lotus Flower mounted her horse and with a mischievous chirrup was gone. Diego returned to the Khan's party subdued by the encounter. Should he ride after the girl? Or was he, too, falling into the trap that had impeded his brother's progress, by longing for love at the least opportune time? Diego rode on with the entourage, and soon he saw ahead the shimmering marble towers of Shang-tu. Around the palace there was a park full of tame leopards, wild hart, deer and gyrfalcons used by the Khan while hunting. Diego looked but did not see. He was thinking that as soon as he had been reunited with his brother he would follow Lotus Flower to Peking and stay there until her safety and security were assured.

Diego watched as servants ran out of the palace and kowtowed to the Emperor. Then a group of noblemen appeared, among them Diego's brother, Pierluigi. With a hoarse cry, the Venetian leaped down from his horse and ran to embrace the astonished young man.

Pierluigi responded by throwing his arms around his brother's neck. "My dearest, dearest Diego, can it really be you?"

"Are you well, Pierluigi? Oh, how glad I am to see you."

"I am well and I have many surprises for you. But surely you have not come alone? Where is our good Giorgio?"

"He remained in Kangchow to recover from an illness he contracted in the desert. I will return for him at the end of the summer."

"Come to my quarters, Diego, and tell me about your journey. I am so happy to see you that I could cry like a milkmaid."

The Khan watched the reunion closely. Then he instructed his spies to follow Diego's every move. Ever cautious of the stranger who appeared out of nowhere, he felt the need to know all Diego's intentions.

During the evening, Pierluigi regaled his brother with stories of the court. They were joined by Marco Polo, with whom Pierluigi had traveled to Peking.

Marco eyed Diego and began to question him. "How long did your journey take, Count?"

"Too long by far. I thought I should never reach Cathay. Indeed I had begun to wonder if stories of a land beyond the rising sun were invention."

"My father's party traveled easily because they had visited the Khan on a previous occasion. They are certainly the world's greatest explorers."

"I hear you are going to act as the Khan's traveling envoy, Marco," Pierluigi said.

"I have been appointed to such a role. I am trusted above all others by the Omnipotence. Someday I hope as a result of my work for the Khan to return to Venice as rich as the Doge."

"The Doge may not like such competition."

"You mock me, Pierluigi, but I *am* clever and hard-working, and I feel sure that I *shall* return to Venice the richest of all men."

Diego interrupted, "Where is your uncle tonight?"

Diego's question embarrassed Marco, and he blushed. "My uncle is with one of the ladies of the court."

Pierluigi spoke to his brother. "Maffeo Polo has been hailed as the greatest womanizer in Cathay. He has won the admiration of all the Mongols because they have never before met a man so generous with his favors."

Marco looked at his feet, displeased by Pierluigi's remark. "My uncle is a great man. However, he has not yet learned to withstand the presumptuous advances of the women of the Mongol court. They may appear demure, but they are *not* ladies."

Diego and his brother laughed uproariously. Then Marco departed after bidding Diego welcome to Cathay and inviting the two men to drink with his family the following day.

Pierluigi poured his brother more orange-blossom wine. "Maffeo Polo is a rake and young Marco a prude. All the women adore him, but he tarries with none of them. On one thing he is right, however, and that is that he *is* the very cleverest fellow. He speaks the tongues of a dozen tribes and understands the history of the world as well as the Khan. No doubt he will tell you a dozen times a day that he is a wonder."

"And you, Pierluigi, have you found our new Mazzarini fortune yet?"

"I have begun to assemble a treasure chest. I have

these...." Pierluigi displayed five magnificent pearls in a velvet casket. "And these...."

He showered Diego with uncut diamonds and then handed him a chamois purse full of rubies. Diego touched them wonderingly. "Where did you find these?"

"The pearls were a gift from my lady friend. The other things are the Khan's payment for my advice on certain matters concerning Venice."

Diego was pleased that the foundations of a new Mazzarini fortune were already laid.

After the initial pleasure he had felt at being reunited with his brother, Diego fell into uneasy despondency. He decided he would ask the Khan's permission to visit Peking. Then he would ride as he had never ridden before to catch up with Lotus Flower.

As dawn crept over the horizon, touching the hills with gold, Diego admitted to himself that he was in love. The thought alarmed him and he tried not to think what his friend Arnaldo della Frascati had said about the agonizing pangs of jealousy that accompanied the condition. Despite all his efforts to persuade himself that love was not his malady, Diego knew that it was. He looked out on the perfumed gardens of the palace of Shang-tu, thinking not of their beauty but of that of his love. Suddenly everything was linked with her, every action dictated by his longing to be with her. As Diego dressed, he prayed fervently that he would catch up with Lotus Flower before she reached the perilous streets of Peking.

Part Two:

Cathay

A Tartar horn tugs at the north wind,
Thistle Gate shines whiter than the stream.
The sky swallows the road to Kokonor.
On the Great Wall, a thousand miles of moonlight.

—Li Ho (791–817)

Chapter Seven:

Peking

Lotus Flower waited until after the curfew to enter the outlying districts of Peking, in order to avoid being seen by too many inquisitive eyes. She had decided to use the gate to the Suburb of the Prostitutes, because it was open later than the others. And there would be none of her family's aristocratic old friends there—the men who had shunned her father when they heard of the Emperor's decision to exile him. Lotus Flower was anxious that no one should know of her return, until she was settled in her home and in possession of the valuables her father had mentioned. As she led her horse through the gaudily decorated streets she trembled with fear. In order to stay calm, Lotus Flower kept telling herself that by passing through this forbidden quarter she would reach her home more easily and without risk. Still, she kept asking herself what she would do if someone accosted her.

Merchants and foreigners who patronized the women of the area looked curiously at the girl with the white horse. Some debated whether to approach her. Others looked condescendingly at Lotus Flower's shabby boy's clothes. But none came near her, because something in the autocratic tilt of her chin and the defiance in her eyes made an impression. So they bowed as the girl passed by instead of molesting her.

Lotus Flower was trying to decide how she could get through the gate that led from the Suburb of the Prostitutes to the Inner City of Peking. It would be easier there than to attempt getting in from the Suburb of the Merchants or that of the workers in jade, but still a risky affair. Deep in thought, Lotus Flower did not notice a woman in a sedan chair watching her intently. As the girl passed the scarlet-lacquered chair, the woman tapped with her fan on the sill to draw her attention. Startled, Lotus Flower looked into the alluring black eyes of the most expensive courtesan in Peking. Her first thought was to run away. Then she looked right and left to see if she was being observed. To be seen talking to such a person was to commit social suicide by placing oneself in the same category.

The courtesan, Hsu Lan, smiled at the innocent one's dilemma. Then she began to question Lotus Flower. "Why are you out after curfew and in this area? I'll wager you have no business here."

Lotus Flower replied in a breathless voice, "I have ridden many days from Shang-tu. I ... I wish to return home, but I do not know if I can pass the guards at the gates of the Inner City."

Skeptically, Hsu Lan examined the shabby clothes and the dirty, dusty hands. "Ladies of Peking do not ride horses."

Lotus Flower examined the woman's rice-powdered face with its blood-red mouth and glittering eyes. Was it possible this notorious woman could help her? She decided there was nothing to be lost by confiding her problem to the courtesan.

"I am Lotus Flower, daughter of Wen-Fai of the House of Sung in the Street of the Almond Blossom. I am returning to Peking because my father and all my family are dead."

114

Hsu Lan caught her breath, turning away so she could collect her thoughts without the girl's realizing her distress. "The Khan appropriated your father's land, as I recall?"

"He did, and now he has offered to restore it to me if I will love him."

"Then your future is assured, is it not?"

Lotus Flower's voice revealed her disdain for the Khan's demands. "I shall *never* love that obscene old man."

Hsu Lan laughed delightedly, and looked with renewed interest at Lotus Flower. "If I were to take you through the gate, would you promise to listen to my advice?"

"I shall listen, but I do not know if I can heed it."

"If you are as wise as I think, you will heed what I say, because I speak from many hard years of learning about the world."

Hsu Lan ordered one of the sedan-chair carriers to return for her carriage. Within minutes the servant was back with an ornate gig pulled by two miniature horses. The courtesan made Lotus Flower sit at her side, covering the girl's clothes with a velvet rug and calling for the servant to bring the white horse behind.

As the two women rode toward the gate, Hsu Lan told her companion to remain silent. "Say nothing, no matter what the guards ask."

Each entrance to the Inner City was guarded by a thousand soldiers. Through the archway, Lotus Flower could see the familiar streets full of tall, narrow houses built around courtyards of polished cobblestone. The streets were deserted but for the occasional physician making a night call or a midwife attending a birth. The lanterns of these privileged people seemed to move by themselves in the darkness, wobbling along the streets, throwing light on the curves and pillars of the houses. Lotus Flower looked with longing through the gate, praying she could soon be home.

Suddenly a sentry called out from the wall, "Who passes the gate?"

"Friends ask to pass the gate," Hsu Lan replied in a firm voice.

"In what name?"

"In the name of Kublai Khan, Emperor of China, Ruler of Half the World."

"Have you a pass?"

"I have."

Four soldiers appeared, grinning sheepishly when they saw the courtesan. Under her disapproving gaze they swaggered to the side of the carriage and challenged Hsu Lan.

"And what have we here?"

"This child fell from one of the bridges and was unconscious for many hours. She lives in the house of my friends and wishes to return home."

The soldiers turned to where Lotus Flower was sitting half buried in the rug.

"Can the girl not speak for herself?"

"She is too shocked by her fall."

"And you? Are you now assuming the role of nurse? Or are you trying to recruit this innocent for your secret salon?"

By way of an answer, Hsu Lan brought her whip down on the soldier's head. Then she took a jade tablet and showed it to the captain of the guard. "Here is my authority. Now do you dare deny me entrance?"

The soldiers took one look at the tablet and without further discussion opened the gate. Hsu Lan urged the horses forward, and within minutes she and Lotus Flower arrived in the Street of the Almond Blossom. The courtesan watched as Lotus Flower stepped down and took her horse's reins from the servant. Hsu Lan was impressed by the girl's poise as Lotus Flower turned to thank her.

"My thanks to you, my lady Hsu Lan. Without you I would not have succeeded in entering the city."

"My pleasure is to help you. And remember this advice: You should never say yes to the Khan, but you should also never say no."

Lotus Flower listened without understanding as her companion continued.

"In Cathay the Khan can demand whatever he wishes, so everything he obtains without effort bores him. However, because he is the Omnipotent he does not like to think there is something he can never have. If he is led to believe that

116

in time you may come to love him, he will wait many moons for you to change your mind."

"Then what should I do?"

Hsu Lan shrugged contemptuously at the thought of the Mongol ruler. "If you are lucky, the Khan will die of the gout or the dropsical swellings or his heart will grow so weak he cannot accomplish that for which he yearns. I must return home now—it would be unlucky for you to be seen with me. If you should ever need advice, I live in the House of Violets, on the Street of Laughing Voices. And now goodbye, sweet Lotus Flower."

When Hsu Lan had gone, Lotus Flower found herself trembling violently. She had spoken to the most forbidden lady in Peking! As Lotus Flower hurried along the empty street lined with chestnut trees and almonds in full bloom, she kept thinking of the rumors about Hsu Lan. It was said that the courtesan charged five hundred pounds of silver for her services and bewitched men by her touch. Some of the lady's lovers had willingly ruined themselves to gain admission to her perfumed court, and many had never recovered from her caresses. Lotus Flower thought with amusement of how Hsu Lan had whipped the offending guard. She tried to still the trembling of her limbs, but she was unnerved by all the excitement she had experienced.

A high wall surrounded the House of Sung in the Street of the Almond Blossom. Its gate was made of a special hardwood called iroko, imported from the southernmost provinces. Lotus Flower touched the gate lovingly. Then she inserted the key and stepped inside, turning the rusty key on the world. The first thing she noticed was the familiar smell of rose and orchid. Then she walked slowly, wonderingly, up the path, looking at the outline of the home she had missed so cruelly during the five years of her exile. The blue tiles on the roof shone like ebony in the moonlight. The upcurved gables were intact, the watchful dragons of carved jade unchanged. The steps leading to the entrance were littered with petals and a mold of dead leaves left over from the previous autumn.

Lotus Flower walked to the door and entered the house, shivering because it felt as cold and damp as a burial cavern.

117

She decided to sleep outside on the terrace in the balmy spring air. As she stood inhaling the scents of home, she heard a woman singing in the distance to the tune of a mandolin. Content, Lotus Flower curled up on the wooden floor and closed her eyes. She was home in the house she loved; the house she would never leave again. She made one of her squirrel noises to the horse tethered inside the gate. Then she fell asleep and dreamed of capturing the heart of Diego Mazzarini.

A butterfly with dark-red wings settled on a yellow orchid. Outside the wall, watchmen cried: "Arise! Arise! It is a fine day and sunny!"

Lotus Flower leaped up and looked about her. Then a smile of inner peace lit her face. The garden was untidy and overgrown but ablaze with blossom. There were wild strawberries among the weeds and radish plants around the edges of the flower beds. She picked some of the radishes and, after wiping them carefully on her jacket, ate them. As she was preparing and eating the strawberries an old man appeared.

Lotus Flower watched while the ancient climbed down a ladder inside the garden wall. Then, forgetting herself, she ran to him, calling excitedly, "Li-Huei, Li-Huei, I am home."

The old man's eyes twinkled and he bowed respectfully. "My lady, you are come back to lighten our days. Forgive the state of the garden. I have tended it carefully in your absence, but I myself have been away from the city until a few days ago. Only the radishes my grandson planted are flourishing; the rest is overgrown."

"I am happy to see it whatever its condition."

"And your father? Is his excellence well?"

"They are all dead, Li-Huei. That is why I left the northern province of our exile and returned home."

"The Khan will have your head when he is informed."

"Then he may have it and welcome."

"So be it, my lady."

Lotus Flower laughed, grateful that the gardener remembered to tease her willfulness. She took one of the Venetian ducats from her pocket and handed it to the servant. "Take this. It is gold and must be sold to one of the dealers in the

Street of the Coin Merchants. Our survival depends on your obtaining the very highest price."

"I shall do my best, my lady."

"And Li-Huei, say nothing of my return to your friends, for they will gossip. No one will recognize me now I am a woman, and that is how I wish it to be."

"They will recognize you, my lady."

"I think not!"

"Do not plan on it, my lady. There is only one woman in Peking with emerald eyes."

Lotus Flower frowned at the servant's presumption. Then she said, earnestly, "When you have sold the coin, go and find my nurse, Hanan. Also order food to be delivered, enough to withstand a siege. I have made a list for you. Buy it from different places, not all from the same dealer."

"Are there more of these, my lady?" Li-Huei looked questioningly at the gold piece.

"I have not many. We must make them go far."

The gardener disappeared through the gate. Lotus Flower made her way to the yellow rose bush near the wall. For a moment she looked at it curiously. Then she took a spade and dug until she was covered with sweat. Finally, the spade struck something hard and she lifted out an etched gold casket the size of a roof tile. She did not examine the contents, but began to return the rose bush to its former position.

Lotus Flower then went into the house and opened the shutters so she could determine its condition. Inches of powdery dust covered everything. Moths had eaten the silk upholstery of the couches and termites the footstools. Even the floors looked unsafe. She trod cautiously as she wandered from room to room, opening the shutters to the light, touching faded brocade and tattered velvet. The silver and jade vases had remained intact, along with the calligraphy scrolls hidden in ivory cases in her father's cabinet. The lacquer furniture was also safe, and Lotus Flower polished it with a cloth, happy to see it restored to its former sheen. The rest of the contents of the house were ruined. She fought back tears, comforting herself with the thought that her father's precious objects had not been stolen. Remembering the box unearthed from the garden, she collected it from the table and went to her room to examine it.

As the sun shone, warming the house, Lotus Flower looked in puzzlement at the contents of the box. In her hand were six large pebbles. She turned them this way and that, sniffing them, biting them and then shouting with unladylike exasperation. She made an effort to be calm, thinking of her father's last words. He had told her the stones were valuable and that their price would keep her for the rest of her life when he had given her the gold key to the box. But their worth was one Lotus Flower did not recognize. She wondered who to consult about the puzzle and could think of no one but Diego Mazzarini. The Venetian was a gentleman who would not stoop to thieving or malicious advice. She was sure Diego would know everything there was to know about precious pebbles and items of alien appearance.

For a moment Lotus Flower thought wistfully of the man who had so impressed her, grinning as she recalled Diego's jealousy when she told him how the Khan wanted her. Then she remembered what Hsu Lan had said—she must never say yes to the Khan and she must never say no. She wondered what the Venetian would think of such tactics, sure that games of cunning and calculation were not for him. Only the Khan would enjoy being tricked, and Lotus Flower had already decided to play him as she played salmon in the river, expertly, tirelessly, with all her wiles.

Li-Huei visited three dealers in the Street of the Coin Merchants without coming to a satisfactory price. Perplexed, he walked through the crowded quarter, wondering how to raise the price. Then he saw two foreigners arguing over the ownership of a newly purchased coin. Sensing an opportunity for business, Li-Huei made his way to their side. When he had listened for a while to their discussion he begged leave to speak. "Sires, I am your humble servant and seek to resolve your differences. I beg leave to show you something of value which I am willing to offer to the man who does not get that fine coin you are quarreling over."

Taken by surprise, the two men looked at the gold ducat Li-Huei was holding. Then the gentleman from Burma gave back the original coin to his companion, the Circassian. At once the two fell to arguing as to who should have the opportunity to own the new ducat.

Li-Huei silenced them with a devious suggestion. "I will sell this gold specimen to whoever bids me the highest price. In that way there will be no further dispute."

The bidding began, and soon Li-Huei had twice the ducat's worth in his money bag. He chuckled as he thought of the quarrelsome pair who had offered him far more than the coin's worth, not to win a valuable article but to triumph in an argument. Li-Huei thought solemnly that all foreigners were demented and was relieved that he need have nothing to do with them. As his mistress had instructed, he bought food supplies, plants for the garden, dried fruits and crystallized ginger. These he purchased from different shops and markets in the trading quarter. Li-Huei kept a meticulous account of everything he spent, asking that the goods be delivered to a friend's home. That evening he would ask his grandson to help him transport the supplies to the Sung house, in that way avoiding unnecessary gossip, which would endanger the lady Lotus Flower. When he had finished ordering food, the gardener made his way to Hanan's home.

He found Hanan sitting in a crowded courtyard which was her only home. She was dreaming of better days and wishing she did not have to exist in full view of a hundred neighbors. She greeted Li-Huei with surprise and pleasure. First she offered him tripe soup from a communal pot, then a pipe of tobacco, which made him cough.

When Li-Huei explained his reason for calling, Hanan pushed everyone aside and announced that she was leaving at once. Li-Huei hurried along behind the nurse, trying not to laugh at Hanan's gray hair, which was so unruly from sleeping under the stars that it resembled a hayrick.

As though she had read the gardener's thoughts, Hanan turned to face him. "Give me money so I can buy a new robe. I cannot serve my lady in this condition."

"I have no money."

"You are a liar. If you do not give me some at once I shall upturn you like a newborn and shake you till your money drops out on the floor."

Li-Huei handed over two coins, and Hanan disappeared

121

into a bazaar. By the time the old man had invented an excuse to tell his mistress about the missing money, Hanan emerged resplendent in a blue cotton robe, her hair neatly coiled and held with a shark's-tooth comb. Ignoring Li-Huei, she hurried on toward the Sung house.

As she walked, Hanan was recalling happy times in the past with the child she had loved and nurtured. She thought how hard the years of exile must have been and knew that Lotus Flower must be irrevocably changed. She resolved to make no unfavorable comments and to help her mistress in every way during the period of rehabilitation.

When the two were almost at the gate of the house, Hanan had a sudden thought, and turning to face Li-Huei she asked, "Did the Khan give permission for my lady to return to Peking?"

He answered that the ruler had not given her permission.

"Ha! So you bring me here to my peril?"

"I said you would not wish to come under the circumstances."

Hanan spat in disgust at the statement and entered the house through the garden gate. She recalled the ceremonial swords on the wall of the master's study and planned to make Li-Huei practice using them. Then she looked at the old man and frowned. Li-Huei had lived almost sixty summers. It would be wiser to bring her son, who was twenty, to guard the precious one.

Hanan marched through the garden, halting abruptly to stare at the terrace where a vision in violet silk stood chirruping at a squirrel on the maple branch. Lotus Flower was dressed in one of her mother's robes, which now fitted her well, and Hanan thought proudly that her charge was no longer a child. She was a woman of beauty and presence; a woman who could change the destiny of a nation if she so desired.

Lotus Flower turned to welcome her nurse with a loving embrace. Touched, Hanan noticed the radiant skin, the sparkling eyes, the exquisitely dressed hair pinned with flowers and the hands covered with calluses like those of a washerwoman. Tears sprang to her eyes, and it was some time before she found her voice.

"I am deeply honored to return to you, my lady."

"I am grateful that you are here."

Li-Huei presented his accounts and disappeared, glowing with pride. It was like old times to see his mistress so elegantly robed. If their association ended in the executioner's square, so be it; he had no desire to live until his brain became addled. Li-Huei went to the home of his grandson, and the two men spent the rest of the day ferrying food supplies back to the Sung house.

By nightfall, Li-Huei was snoring peacefully in the garden shed. Outside, his dog growled at the sound of footsteps in the street. Inside the house, Hanan and her son were busy cleaning and polishing, getting rid of damaged furniture and making note of what had to be done before the property could return to its former glory.

Alone in her room, Lotus Flower listened as her nurse sang a song she remembered from childhood. She could still barely believe she was home, and often she ran to the window and looked out in wonder at the garden. She was home, home, home. Lotus Flower whirled delightedly like a tiny dancer. Then she went to the cupboard and began taking out the toys and playthings she had used as a child. These she intended to keep in one of the unused rooms of the house so they would not litter her boudoir. When she had done that she went to what had been her mother's room. There she sat on the couch, sniffing the elusive perfume of carnations that had followed the mistress of the house everywhere. Lotus Flower looked at her mother's robes, touching them lovingly and hugging them to her cheeks. Then she opened the jewel box, hidden in an ivory stool, and ran her fingers through strings of pearls, brooches in the shape of lions and dragons, butterfly slides, jade combs, émerald chokers and breathtaking opals embedded in gold. Lotus Flower thought again how miraculous it was that the contents of the house had not been pillaged, that decay and the effects of disuse were the only hazards to be righted. She returned to her room, hugging the jewel box to her chest, and sat on the floor, playing as she had done as a child with the precious baubles.

The curfew tolled, and Hanan appeared to say goodnight. "What do you wish me to do in the morning, my lady?"

123

"I would like you to move my mother's clothes into my room and the clothes I wore as a child into one of the other bedrooms."

"Would it not be easier if you occupied your mother's suite?"

Lotus Flower hesitated. Then she answered shyly, "Mama loved her room. I would not like to change it in any way."

"Very well, I shall bring the dresses here and the combs and hair ornaments too."

Lotus Flower was happy. Then looking around her room she asked the servant, "Have you any idea how long it will take to make the house whole again, Hanan?"

"It depends on what money is available, my lady."

"I have little money and none for the future."

"You have your mother's jewels. You can sell them for a fortune."

"I shall never sell Mama's jewels. I intend to give them to my own daughter someday. They have been in the possession of this family for generations."

"Then you will have to sell your own jewels, my lady."

"You are a dear friend, Hanan, and my heart is light now you are here."

Lotus Flower slept until dawn, when she lay listening to the sound of birdsong and the cries of watchmen calling the day. Suddenly she felt restless, and she realized that she missed the open spaces of Chagan Nor. She sat up and looked around at the beautiful rose silk boudoir with its ivory ornaments and gilded screens. She kept telling herself that her unease was due to the shock of the change in her circumstances. Then, impulsively, Lotus Flower rose and put on her patched trousers and faded jacket. Before anyone in the house was awake she had led the white horse out of the city and was riding on the road that led north from Peking. Exhilarated by the freedom and the fresh air of the plain, she crowed like a cockerel, throwing her arms up in delight. Then she reined her horse and looked down, astonished to see Diego Mazzarini riding below on the dusty road leading from Chagan Nor. At some distance behind the Venetian were two of the Khan's men.

Without hesitation, Lotus Flower galloped down the hill

and called to Diego, "You are being followed by two of the Khan's spies. Ride behind me so we can lose them."

Diego galloped behind the white horse through an orchard of mulberry trees where women were tending silk worms, and on to a village crowded with people. Leading him to an old barn, Lotus Flower galloped inside, slamming the doors as Diego followed. Within minutes the Khan's spies rode past, their faces grim with determination.

Diego turned to Lotus Flower and held out his hands, thrilled when she touched his fingers with the tips of her own. Then she turned away and looked cautiously through the planks of the barn wall, relieved to see no sign of the spies returning.

"What are you doing in Peking, Count Mazzarini?"

"I told you I would come to see that you were well. I was delayed because the Emperor seemed reluctant to give me permission to leave his court."

"And when you left he sent spies to watch where you rode and with whom you spoke. The Khan trusts no one, because many plot to see him dead."

"Is he so evil that people wish him dead?"

"The nobles hate the Khan because he confiscated their lands and sent them to die in exile. The scholars tolerate him because he reveres them. The peasants, who have most to gain from his bounty, dislike any ruler who is not Chinese. But you did not ride all the way to Peking to talk of Kublai Khan?"

"I rode to Peking to tell you that I love you, my lady."

Lotus Flower blushed with pleasure. Then she walked to the center of the barn and sat down on a pile of dry fodder. After a moment of deep thought she looked up at Diego. "When you want a woman do you tell her that you love her?"

"I have not loved women with my heart, only with my body."

"But in Venice you said you had loved many women."

Diego shifted uncomfortably. "I love you. Must you question me like a magistrate?"

"I wish to know if you say that you love every woman who catches your eye. I am Chinese and do not know the ways of your people."

"I do not say it to every woman."

"Then I thank you for the compliment, sire. I am honored by your remark."

Aware of the tense attitude of Lotus Flower's body, Diego sat at her side, wishing he could touch or kiss her. Romancing this mercurial creature was going to be a dangerous game with compliments forbidden and contact unthinkable. He wondered if he should pay a visit to the famous courtesan Hsu Lan, about whom Pierluigi had spoken. She would soothe and reassure him of his masculine powers. She would be predictable, like other women, and the relief of her familiarity would be profound. But Diego looked again at Lotus Flower and, smelling the petal fragrance of her skin, knew he had lost his taste for the more exotic perfumes of sin. He smiled as he remembered his brother's comments about Hsu Lan— "You will need five hundreds pounds of silver if you are to enter her salon, unless she is charmed by the color of your hair, in which case she may permit you to pleasure her once, for no cost." Stirring from his reverie, Diego asked if Lotus Flower would show him her home.

"Do you know a road into Peking that will let us avoid the Khan's spies?"

"I do, and I shall be pleased to show you my home. The house is decayed through neglect, but someday it will be a fine home again. I hope you will make allowances, sire, for the fact that it has long been unoccupied."

From the barn, they took a route through the fields where water buffalo were working. Diego looked about him, charmed by the quaintness of this alien landscape. Many of the small-holdings were market gardens growing melons, gourds and ginger root alongside garlic, onions and vegetables. Soon Lotus Flower pointed out a red bridge, which they crossed, and led him through the Suburb of the Workers in Bronze.

"This is a shortcut to the street of my home. Next we shall pass through one of the inner gates of the city. If you stay too long in my house, the curfew will prevent you from leaving."

"Then I shall stay late and beg your hospitality, my lady."

A twinkle lit Lotus Flower's eyes and for a moment the two stood facing each other. Then Lotus Flower led on and

Diego looked with interest at people buying and selling, at storytellers, astrologers, craftsmen and street urchins. Suddenly, the massive inner wall of Peking appeared before them. Excitement pounded in Diego's chest as he passed inside the imperial city. A poet walked by, reading his compositions aloud to a group of admiring ladies. An executioner in black strode past, preoccupied with the volume of work that would be heaped upon him with the return of the Omnipotence from Shang-tu. And in a square of ornate houses a gig driven by a beautiful woman passed them. The lady paused, reining her horses, when she saw Lotus Flower.

Diego looked with interest at the woman's sculpted hairdo, which resembled two round loaves, at the glittering robe of silver and blue and the priceless emerald earrings. Lotus Flower inclined her head gracefully. The courtesan nodded, her sharp eyes glancing quickly from the girl she had rescued to the foreigner who stood so protectively at Lotus Flower's side. With a moue of pleasure Hsu Lan drove on to her home in the suburbs. "Who was that woman?"

"That was Hsu Lan. She is the most expensive courtesan in the city, perhaps in all the world."

"You should not discuss such matters. It does not befit a lady."

Lotus Flower loved upsetting the Venetian's equilibrium. She prolonged her enjoyment of the situation by telling a lie. "I know Hsu Lan well. When I returned to Peking it was she who smuggled me past the guards at the gate."

Diego was uncertain whether Lotus Flower was teasing him.

The girl looked up at Diego and pointed to the Street of the Almond Blossom. "That is the street where my house is situated, sire."

"It is a beautiful street with wondrous fine blossoms."

Lotus Flower unlocked the gate and told Diego to enter. Then she left him, calling as she entered the house that she would return if he would wait for her by the fountain.

Diego looked over the house which was of stately proportions, with blue-tiled roof and a terrace of painted wood. The garden, though overgrown, was scented with the fragrance of lemon, lily and jacaranda. In the center of the clearing there was a fountain with water gushing from the mouth of a silver dolphin. And in the pool below the fountain Diego saw fish swimming around yellow water lilies. He thought how lazy and peaceful the scene was, how like Venice or any other civilized city of the world, until one went through the gate to the street beyond. There one found a city ruled by a despot where fear was the password and caution the wise man's constant companion.

Diego sat on the edge of the fountain, admiring the lines of the house, which was so different from the shacks he had seen around Chagan Nor. As he daydreamed, Li-Huei appeared and stood staring in amazement at the stranger. The old man's curiosity amused the Venetian, who calmly bade him good day.

"You are a foreigner, are you not, sire?" the gardener asked, with a modest bow of respect.

"I am Diego Mazzarini, Count of the Venetian Empire."

"I am Li-Huei, manservant and gardener to the lady Lotus Flower."

"I understand you have served the Sung family since your youth. I am happy to have this opportunity to meet you."

Li-Huei beamed a toothless smile, charmed by the manners of this visitor from another world. He showed Diego around the garden, pointing out the plants he was preparing, the weeds he was fighting and the walls he was mending with bricks made in the traditional Hang-t'u manner. The Venetian expressed interest and made suggestions. Some of them were new to Li-Huei and he was happy to acquire such clever ideas. They were pondering the problem of squirrels breeding in the trees when Hanan appeared and announced that her mistress was ready to receive the visitor.

Li-Huei bowed low as Diego departed. Then he hurried back to his shed, shaking a grizzled head, amazed to find that not all foreigners were oafs and lunatics. Count Mazzarini was obviously a gentleman and a brilliant conversationalist. Li-Huei wondered if his mistress was enamored of the Venetian, but such a thought seemed impossible and he chided himself for speculating like an old woman.

Hanan whispered her own greetings as she led Diego through the garden. "We are honored to receive you, noble

128

sire. The house still ails from neglect, but my lady wishes to offer you her hospitality. I shall go at once to prepare a room for you. Please join my lady in the green salon, sire. The one at your right."

Diego pushed a bamboo door aside and entered a room of faded elegance that had marvelous carved cedarwood panels on the walls and a floor of inlaid wood now damaged by flood water. Once it had been a beautiful home, full of beautiful objects. Diego was sad that it had so wantonly been allowed to deteriorate. Turning, he saw Lotus Flower sitting on a rose silk couch. She was dressed in a white satin robe painted with lilac flowers, at her throat a choker of emeralds to match her eyes. There were orchids in her hair, and she held a branch of lotus blossom, which she offered to Diego with a teasing smile. "This is for you, sire. I give it with the plea that you look after it well."

Diego looked down at the flower, then back to the enchanting creature on the couch. "Is this a symbol?"

"It is if you choose to make it so."

Diego sighed impatiently, longing to know the true feelings of the woman he adored. When he spoke, Lotus Flower listened intently. "In Cathay it is the people's habit to talk in riddles. In Venice when a man tells a woman he loves her she may make fun of him or she may slap his face for his audacity or she can tell him his feelings match her own."

"Then what must she do?"

"Then, if he asks her, she marries him. We call this asking for the hand in marriage a proposal."

Lotus Flower rang a bell, and Hanan appeared with tea, colored sugar sweetmeats and coconut cakes. Diego sat on a cushion, watching as the tea was prepared. He kept looking to Lotus Flower and marveling at the change in her appearance. Her cheeks were lightly powdered, her lips rouged, her body perfumed with the intoxicating scent of magnolia; only her hands betrayed the harsh years of exile. Diego longed to grasp them and kiss them, because they reminded him of their first meeting, by the wildfowl lake of Chagan Nor. He sipped the scented tea and asked Lotus Flower to tell him her plans.

"I intend to remain in Peking. I still have some of the gold you lent me," she said.

"And you have jewels which will keep you for the rest of your life. You are lucky they were not stolen when the house was confiscated." He looked at the necklace she wore.

"I shall never sell my mother's jewels."

Diego digested this statement, loving Lotus Flower the more for her sentimentality. He was surprised when his companion continued to explain her plans.

"At the summer's end you will return to Peking with the Khan's entourage. At that time I shall be happy to receive you so you may make me your proposal."

Diego's heart pounded with disbelief. Lotus Flower continued as if she had not noticed his astonishment.

"After we marry we can live in this house. You will go in search of the treasure you seek to renew your fortune, and I shall bear children to warm our old age."

"And what of Kublai Khan?"

"He will die of the gout or the dropsical swellings."

"And if he does not?"

"Then we shall flee to your city by the sea and I shall endeavor to become a Venetian lady."

"I have not said I wish to propose to you."

Lotus Flower spoke slowly and patiently as though to an idiot. "I did not slap your face when you told me you loved me and I did not make fun of you. I therefore imagined that you knew that I wished you to propose to me."

"Do you love me, Lotus Flower?"

She looked past Diego to the garden.

"I think of you when you are not here. I dream of you every night, and I should be in agony if your life came to an end, therefore I must love you."

"Do you want me as a woman wants a husband?"

"I do not know. I am a lady and I do not know about such things, and as a gentleman you should not ask me."

Diego was torn by sudden uncertainty. Was Lotus Flower still a child who dreamed of love without understanding its meaning? Did she need a husband as a society woman needs a parasol, one that is better and different from those which other women carry?

The Venetian shook his head wryly as Lotus Flower skipped gleefully toward him.

"I have something to show you, sire. It is a secret no one else knows."

She ran to her room, returning with the pebbles that had been buried in the garden. Diego smiled indulgently as Lotus Flower knelt at his feet, looking expectantly into his eyes. For a moment her feet became entangled in the hem of her robe and she blushed at her clumsiness. "I am not yet used to being the lady! Now, sire, can you tell me what these pebbles are?"

Diego looked at the stones curiously, rolling them back and forth in his hand and weighing them carefully.

"I have never seen anything like them. They are not natural pebbles. They have been made by a master craftsman, though for what purpose I cannot imagine."

Disappointed, Lotus Flower threw the pebbles to the ground. "I am sick of riddles!"

They looked in surprise as the pebbles cracked in two. Lotus Flower ran to the corner and retrieved the broken pieces, calling out excitedly as she found, freed from their cunning covering, six of the largest pearls she had ever seen.

Diego took them in his hand, his face flushed with pleasure. "These are pearls of the greatest value. Where did you find them?"

"They were buried in the garden. My father told me about them before he died."

"I have never seen pearls like this before. My dearest, your house is saved and your future forever assured. Even the Emperor has nothing of such worth."

"He has, but no one has ever seen the Khan's pearls. Some say he gets them out only on the night of the full moon when he has a blind musician serenade them."

"I'll wager they will not match these beauties."

"What shall I do with them, sire?"

"You must decide. It is not for me to tell you."

"Then I shall sell them and live in prosperity forever."

"I think not."

"What then?"

"If you have other jewels, sell those and use what you gain

131

to renovate the house and to buy food and the necessities of life. Keep the pearls safe, hide them away and never speak of them to anyone, for I promise you they could inspire men to murder. I wonder where your father bought them and how many others know of their existence."

Excited by the find, the lovers walked together in the garden, listening to the sound of crickets and inhaling the scented air. Diego told Lotus Flower about his brother and the rich noblewoman who kept giving Pierluigi rubies for his collection. He told of Pierluigi's desire to marry, and Lotus Flower laughed till her body shook with merriment.

"You will win the race to the marriage bed if he does not hurry and make up his mind."

"I can imagine my brother's astonishment when I tell him how you instructed me to make my proposal of marriage."

"I did not instruct you, sire!"

"You surely did, my lady."

In the cool of the evening they dined on roast peacock and quails' eggs dipped in gold dust. As the curfew tolled they toasted the future in tawny spiced wine. Then Lotus Flower played the mandolin and sang for her guest. And all the while Diego marveled at her beauty. He kept wishing that Lotus Flower would give him some sign that she knew how it felt for a woman to want a man. If only he could be sure that this was not the game of a girl thrust suddenly into the realities of the world and in need of diversion from the unpleasantness of the past.

That night Diego lay awake, listening to the howl of wolves prowling the edge of the city. Suddenly Lotus Flower appeared, walking barefoot in the moonlight, dressed only in a diaphanous robe. Not wishing to startle her, Diego breathed deeply as if he were asleep, his body tensing as she knelt at his side. First Lotus Flower kissed his hands, then his chest, then his throat and the curly gold beard. Then, hungrily, she sought his mouth, and Diego knew that it was not the kiss of a child but that of a woman impatient to be loved. Feeling the hardness of her nipples against his body, Diego grasped her and kissed her as he had always wanted to kiss her. Lotus Flower responded like a newly kindled flame and lay panting with longing on Diego's chest. Then she freed herself and slapped his face so hard the Venetian saw stars in the darkness. With a wicked chuckle she was gone, leaving her lover alone to rub his cheek and conclude that if he didn't see Lotus Flower again for twenty years he could identify her by the weight of her disapproving touch.

Despite the admonition, Diego was ecstatic. The woman he loved wanted and needed him. She had come to his room to steal a kiss and had returned his response with desire. A crescent moon looked down on the perfumed garden, lighting dew-touched lilac trees with silver. For a moment Diego enjoyed the magic scene. Then he fell asleep, wondering what the morning would bring.

Lotus Flower rose before dawn and walked alone in the garden, determined to calm herself before the Venetian appeared. For an hour she immersed herself with brush and scroll, writing a letter to her aunt in Hangchow, telling of her father's death and of her own return to Peking. The letter would be dispatched by horse messenger as soon as Li-Huei could deliver it to the post station.

Next she gathered lilies to put on the table where she and her guest would eat the morning meal. As she sniffed their heady perfume she thought of the night and the strange weakness of the body which her lover's kiss had provoked. Blushing with pleasure, Lotus Flower looked longingly toward the peach blossom near the wall. Soon the flowers would disappear, to be replaced by the budding fruits of summer. Lotus Flower longed as she had never longed before for the leaves to turn red and for the chrysanthemums to bloom, because when the year waned Diego would return to make his formal proposal. She would have a new dress made for the occasion, one that would take the Venetian's breath away. She would wear her mother's emeralds and be the queen such a nobleman deserved, untouched by any other. Lotus Flower hurried inside to see Hanan and to check that the table on the terrace was impeccably prepared.

For three days the couple enjoyed each other's company. They made few excursions from the house except in the pre-dawn darkness when they rode together to the south of Peking to shoot duck in the marshes. The rest of the time was spent making plans for the restoration of the house, enjoying games of chess, which Lotus Flower loved, and feasting in the moonlit silence disturbed only by the sound of crickets. It was not long before Hanan realized that her charge was deeply in love. She vowed to keep this secret until Li-Huei approached her in the dusk of the second evening and poured out his own fears.

"My lady loves the foreigner. Have you seen it, Hanan?"

"I have and I am glad she is happy."

"Will she leave us and return to his land?"

"I am sure she will remain here if she is able, but I do not know, because my lady has not yet confided in me."

"But what of the Khan?"

"Who can tell? We must be ready to protect my lady."

The two servants made plans for smuggling Lotus Flower away from the Emperor's soldiers if they came to arrest her. From that day on, Hanan's son slept in a newly constructed hut by the gate. At his side there was a brass bell for him to ring to signal danger. For her part, Hanan uncovered a cupboard underneath the kitchen floor, once used for storage, where she planned to hide her mistress if the necessity arose. As Diego's visit neared its end, Hanan was torn by regret. The Venetian was strong and in love with Lotus Flower. Instinct told her he would fight to the death for his loved one, and that eased the ache in her heart. But without Diego Mazzarini the house would be empty, the nights long and full of fear. Hanan looked in the mirror and frowned. At forty she was already old, and the tension of the past weeks had made her complexion turn gray. She went to the kitchen and prepared the last dinner before the Venetian's departure. She was thinking sadly that she wished she had the power to look into the future so she could save herself much apprehension.

In the morning, Lotus Flower prepared a bag of sweetmeats and another of wine and savories for Diego's journey. She readied them with her own hands so he would taste the love she bore him as he ate. Her tears fell on the roast fowl and the grapes as she wrapped them, and often she paused and looked into space. Lotus Flower was thinking of the day before when she and the Venetian had gone to a lake a morning's ride from Peking. There they had fished for trout, which she had cooked over the fire as she had first cooked for him at Chagan Nor. In the afternoon they had galloped home and arrived in Peking within minutes of the curfew. Then Diego had taken her in his arms and kissed her with an urgency so great she had felt his heart beating against her own. Lotus Flower remembered the longing Diego's touch had provoked, the excitement of being wanted, needed, loved. Her father had been right. Love was a blessing so precious it must be nurtured like a rare plant. Thinking herself wanton, Lotus Flower covered her face with her hands. Then she ran to the garden to give the food she had prepared to Diego.

As the sun rose in the heat of early summer, Diego rode away, back to the road that would take him to Chagan Nor. Lotus Flower retired to her room to cry, and Hanan visited an astrologer, who told her that she would soon be leaving her new home on an unwelcome journey. When Hanan asked how long it would be before she returned to Peking, the astrologer shook his head regretfully.

"You will stay forever in the swampy place of your exile."

"And what of my lady?"

"She will also go to the same place, which is a camp in a marshy area."

"And will she return?"

"I see armies led by two men who love my lady."

"*Two* men, but there is only one."

Hanan waved her face furiously with a paper fan. Looking closely at the astrologer's face, she wondered if his predictions were no longer as accurate as in former times.

The astrologer continued gravely, "There are two men who love your mistress and another who wishes to harm her. These men will fight for possession of the beautiful one."

Hanan paled visibly, her hands trembling like aspen leaves.

"How is his bearing, this enemy of my mistress? Tell me so I shall know him if I see him."

"He is not of this land and not of our faith. Indeed, he is a heathen and you will know him because his face is the face of evil which cannot be described. He wears a strange hat with fanlike pieces over the ears and rides a horse as if he knows not how."

Hanan hurried home and locked all the doors. Then, knowing that Lotus Flower was in her room crying, she went to the kitchen and confided what she had learned to her son. They discussed what could be done, and concluded that there was very little. The astrologer had been unable to say when the problem would be resolved. He had said only that it would come and that there would by many men involved, perhaps an army.

Hanan prepared food she knew she would not be able to eat with a tray for Lotus Flower. She knocked on the door of her mistress's room, begging the girl to nourish herself. Minutes later she returned to the kitchen and looked at the food so lovingly prepared which no one could eat.

That night the Sung house was silent. Li-Huei was asleep in the garden shed, Hanan's son in the lodge by the gate. Hanan herself had elected to lie on a quilt outside her mistress's room. There she tossed and turned, her ears constantly straining for the sound of alien approach. But nothing disturbed the peace of the house...yet.

The man who stood outside watching the courtyard of Lotus Flower's home was content. The foreigner had gone, leaving the girl and her nurse alone and unprotected. It was time to arrange what he had traveled so far to accomplish. He had enjoyed the thought of this mission ever since the dark night when he had first seen Lotus Flower leading her horse through the Suburb of the Prostitutes. Her beauty had added to his desire to take what must be taken with skill and daring. By dawn the man had completed his plan and was content that it was faultless. He rode away from Peking in search of his men, his face a grim mask of pleasure.

Lotus Flower rose and debated what to do with the day. In Chagan Nor there had been endless work to accomplish in order to stay alive. In Peking, now that she had sold some of her jewels, there was nothing to fill the hours. The gentle pursuits of former times bored her. Surely, she thought ruefully, she was no longer suited to the life of a lady. Impetuously, she put on her faded trousers and jacket, so that she could ride to a lake where she and Diego had fished. There she would play the boy until she felt recovered from the Venetian's departure. Mounting her horse, she galloped away from the city, unaware that she was being followed. As she rode, she sang a tune Diego had taught her in the Venetian dialect. Lotus Flower thought of her lover and was content. Life was good, and soon, if she kept busy, it would be time for his return. She rode swiftly on, her face radiating with the sweetness of love.

Chapter Eight:

Shang-tu

Diego rode past a field where men were digging black stone out of the ground. When he inquired what they were doing he was told that the stones were used to fuel fires in the courtyards of local communities. Intrigued by the discovery, Diego collected some of the stones to be used that night as he camped by the river. As he rode on, he wondered what had happened to the spies the Khan had sent to follow him. Had they been punished for their lack of concentration or had they lied about his activities, pretending that they had not lost him? Nearing the junction of the road to Shang-tu, Diego learned the answer to his question.

The spies had returned to the crossroads where travelers took one of two tracks to reach the summer palace of Shang-tu. For five days the two men had camped there waiting and praying for the Venetian to reappear. When they saw Diego approaching on the highway, they galloped to meet him, throwing themselves at his feet and kowtowing with their foreheads on the ground.

"Count Mazzarini, have mercy upon us," they wailed plaintively.

Surprised by this exhibition of humility, Diego told them to rise. "What ails you that you need my mercy?"

"We are soldiers of the Khan's army, sire, trained to spy for him."

"And you were sent to spy on me?"

"Yes, sire, but we lost you after the girl appeared, and we have remained here since that day, knowing that at this point of the road you must turn to take the only track to Shangtu."

"Why did you not tell the Emperor you had lost my trail?"

The two men looked at each other, then back to the Venetian. One of the spies explained that they had agreed to entrust Diego with their lives. "If the Khan knew that we lost you, he would have us executed as an example to the others in his employ."

Diego, who was shocked by the severity of the punishment, asked, "Why did the Khan wish to know my intentions?"

"He trusts no one, sire."

"He trusts my brother, Pierluigi, who goes on diplomatic missions representing the Emperor. He trusts young Marco Polo, who is the vainest fellow I have ever met. Why does he not trust me?"

The spies rode at Diego's side until he camped by the river. Then one of them took his bow and went into the woods to shoot birds for their supper. The other told Diego about the rumors he had heard in the royal palace.

"For over a year the Emperor has been besotted with a young girl he met near Chagan Nor. She is a peasant, I believe, who hunts and fishes like a lad. The Khan's passion for her has caused him to be much ridiculed. Last year, at the height of his passion, the Omnipotence sent soldiers to lie in wait and apprehend this girl, but they returned empty-handed, and as they were unpacking their saddlebags they found lotus flowers the minx had placed there. Obviously the girl had known she was being watched. The Khan was so angry many feared for their lives."

Diego laughed out loud at Lotus Flower's cheek. "Then what happened?"

"Throughout the winter the Khan remained in a foul humor. He would see only Jamui, his favorite wife, and the concubines became so frustrated through lack of use that they took to playing forbidden games. Then, sire, and this is but my own suspicion, the Khan met this girl again, last month, at the time of his journey to Shang-tu. Now he is mad in love with her. He cannot sleep and is often heard screaming at the astrologers because they have not told him what he wishes to know. Though he is old, the Khan has never loved before and the experience is destroying him. In my opinion, the girl is a sorceress, able to bind his mind so steadfastly to her image."

Diego concealed his amusement and asked again why the Emperor had sent spies to follow him.

"The Khan is afraid, sire. He has forbidden anyone in the court to ride in the vicinity of Chagan Nor in case they should meet the exquisite one and become besotted with her."

"But I asked leave to ride to Peking."

"Obviously the Emperor did not believe you, sire. I do not know why."

Darkness fell, and Diego piled some of the black stones on the campfire, praising their orange glow, to the amusement of his companions. As he ate, the Venetian explained that he had been to Peking to visit a lady and that he had stayed in her home, visiting and speaking with no one but her servants. Then Diego mentioned his brief glimpse of the courtesan Hsu Lan.

One of the soldiers laughed loudly. "In the last year Hsu Lan has ruined three of the Khan's administrators with her demands. I wish I were rich enough to enter her salon. I would surely tire her for a week."

The other soldier contributed what he knew of the temptress. "Hsu Lan is a woman of Suchow, not from Peking, and some say she will retire there shortly. There are also rumors that when she was young she had a child by a nobleman whose name she has never divulged. I know of this because

141

the rich man for whom my father works visited the courtesan, and he told his friends that her gaiety is blinding like the sun, but that in the night she sheds tears for her lost child. Truly, sire, the lady's smiles hide a thousand tears. I saw her only once, in the Street of the Singing Voices, and for a month I could not control my bodily urges. Women like Hsu Lan are prizes to be revered above gold. I dream of the day when I shall see her again, if only for a brief moment—even if she scowls at me."

In the morning the three men were wakened by the sound of voices speaking a language they could not understand.

Diego cautioned his companions to silence as they watched through the dense bushes bordering the river. On the road there were men dressed like brigands, with scarlet bands around their heads. They were armed with curved swords, and some had bows, nets and axes. Diego saw that the Khan's spies were troubled, but neither spoke until the strangers had disappeared down the road.

"Do you know who those men are?" Diego asked.

"They are Japanese warriors, sire, sent by the Khan's mortal enemy, the Shogun of Kyushu."

"The guide was talking of treasure to be retrieved and a life to be extinguished."

"They plan to kill the Omnipotence, sire. The Shogun of Kyusha has tried many times before."

Diego walked to his horse, pausing as he mounted to say, "We shall outride the Japanese if we hurry. Come quickly— we must warn the Khan that trouble approaches the palace of Shang-tu."

Three of the Khan's senior army officers, who had been summoned, arrived at the palace, riding on the backs of elephants, their heads shielded from the sun with golden umbrellas. Reaching the Emperor's presence, they bowed to the ground and presented their insignia. The Khan looked to the three generals, who arranged themselves on the silver chairs their rank permitted them to use in council.

"Who are the finest riders in the world?" the Khan demanded.

The spokesman of the three answered, "The Mongols, sire. Your Golden Horde has the finest riders ever known."

"And who are the best fighters?"

"The same, sire. The Mongols."

"And on the sea, am I also Master of the World?"

The general looked uneasily at his companions, aware that the Khan knew nothing of the sea and less about ships.

"You have not been much tried on the sea, sire."

"Who would dare try me?"

"The Japanese, sire," the general answered without hesitation. "They are masters of the sea because the islands where they live are surrounded by the waves."

At last the Khan revealed what Diego had told him. "I am informed that Junichiko Minamoto, the Shogun of Kyushu, has sent men to kill me. My spies also report that there are but few men, though I cannot believe this. The Shogun is not fool enough to send a dozen men to kill Kublai Khan who commands Tartars and Uighurs, men of the Naiman and Merkit, of Ongut and Onggirat, as well as those of China and Korea."

"Sometimes it is easier to remain undetected when there are but a few men, sire. The strategy is original."

"I dislike the Shogun's strategy." The Khan spoke angrily.

"Yes, my lord."

The Khan looked at his generals with narrowed eyes. "Prepare my horsemen at once."

"Where must we command them to ride, sire?"

"They must remain here in Shang-tu awaiting my orders."

"All of them, sire?"

"All of them. I am sick of the Shogun's taunting. I intend to have his head before the week is out."

When the generals had gone, the Khan invited Diego and members of the Venetian party to his private suite. There he presented his new ally with a casket of gold pieces. The casket was so heavy that four men were needed to carry it into the presence.

Diego bowed low, his face alight with pleasure at this unexpected bounty. "I am grateful for this token of your es-

143

teem, sire. I shall do my best to warrant your trust at all times."

"Thank you, Count Mazzarini. Now tell me of your visit to the city of Peking."

Servants brought ice from underground caverns to cool the drinks of those in the Emperor's presence. Nobles served tasty morsels of smoked deer and spiced fish sliced as thin as paper. Diego settled on a footstool at the Khan's feet and described what he had seen. Now and then the ruler nodded in agreement at the opinions passed, and when Diego described his admiration for the royal palace, the Khan roared enthusiastically.

"Soon, Count Mazzarini, you will see inside the inner walls of the imperial city. My palace in all its splendor will be your winter home."

The Khan was interrupted by the arrival of an imperial messenger. The man bowed low, and the Khan signaled for him to speak.

"Say what you have to say."

"I have a message for Count Mazzarini of Venice, sire."

Diego felt his pulse quickening. Only the members of Lotus Flower's ménage knew where he was. Lotus Flower would not send a message in so brazen a manner. So what was the meaning of this intrusion?

The messenger explained: "The message is from the servant Li-Huei, who is grievously ill from a sword wound. He begs to inform you that on the night after your departure from Peking a band of men appeared in the Street of the Almond Blossom. When they demanded entrance to the Sung house, Li-Huei refused to open the gate, so they climbed over the wall. Then, having wounded the gardener, they killed the son of the other servant, whose name is Hanan. That servant and her mistress have been abducted. The abductors left a message which says that the Shogun Junichiko Minamoto presents his compliments to the Emperor and requests the return of his pearls."

Stunned by the news, Diego was silent. The Khan too was silent, struggling to remember what it was he should know about the Street of the Almond Blossom. When Diego spoke, the Khan noted with approval that there was murder in his eyes.

"How long ago did you say that this happened?"

"On the night after your departure, sire."

"And when did Li-Huei send this message?"

"On the same night, sire, by imperial messengers riding in relays. The servant insisted that the Emperor be informed of this affront to a lady who is a friend of his guest."

"Who is this servant that he instructs my messengers so boldly?" The Khan leaned forward to inquire about Li-Huei.

"He thought you would be concerned, my lord. That is why he presumed to instruct the messengers."

"Why should I be concerned? Who is this woman?"

"She is the daughter of Wen-Fai of the House of Sung, sire. The girl has a true name which she does not use. Instead she calls herself Lotus Flower."

The Khan ordered everyone but Diego from the room. Then, without warning, he fell unconscious to the ground. The imperial physician appeared and administered salts. The Khan groaned, as though in pain, and Diego realized that despite his power and divine authority the ruler was old. When the Emperor was seated again on his throne, he looked in dull anger at the Venetian.

"It was to this girl's house that you went, was it not, Count Mazzarini?"

"It was, my lord. I met the lady Lotus Flower in Chagan Nor and was smitten by her beauty. But no sooner had I met her than she informed me that she was returning to Peking. Her father had died and she was left alone in the world."

"And so you encouraged her in her plan?"

"No, my lord. I forbade her to return to Peking, but she went of her own willfulness. It is no easy matter making my lady Lotus Flower obey."

The Khan moaned in dismay. "Oh, for the strength of the days of my youth."

Diego drew near, speaking softly so the servants could not hear. "I have enough strength for both, sire, and it is yours to command."

"You are my rival, Count Mazzarini. I tell you true, for

I intend to have this girl, who has haunted my dreams ever since the day I first looked into her eyes."

Diego remained calm in the face of the Khan's fury, and the ruler admired his courage. He listened as Diego spoke, sighing wearily at the truth of the statement.

"We shall have but a dead body to admire if we do not act at once, my lord."

The Khan nodded. "What say you, Count Mazzarini? Where shall we find these villains?'"

"When their mission is over they will wish to return to their islands. We must therefore put troops along the coast and others to hound them to the beaches."

The Khan thought of Lotus Flower, and his eyes filled with tears. "I shall do it at once. And now be gone or I shall forget that you are my friend."

Diego bowed and made his way to the door, where he paused and turned to face the Emperor.

"My lord, I am in love with the lady Lotus Flower. I shall not displease you by pressing my suit further at this time. But if she lives I shall beg you to allow *her* to choose her path in life. I would not wish an unwilling woman on myself or on the Ruler of Half the World."

The Khan watched as the Venetian withdrew. Despite his anger he was taken by Diego's diplomacy and the calm he had shown in the face of the imperial anger. He recalled Diego's ashen pallor at hearing the news of Lotus Flower's abduction and knew that his rival was deeply, irrevocably in love. For a moment the Khan closed his eyes, willing the pain to vanish from his chest. Then he called for messengers to ride night and day to give instructions to army commanders in every region of the Eastern Provinces.

Five hundred men rode as they had never ridden before, relieved by another five hundred waiting at staging posts all over the land. Each man rode sixteen miles, replaced by another with a fresh horse at the next staging post. In this way the Khan's orders were relayed like lightning throughout the kingdom. Within four days, 360,000 Mongols were ready to ride from Shang-tu. And along the coast, within the week, soldiers came from Manchuria and Korea, from Manzi and the borders of Chambo, half the Khan's entire manpower of three million. Then the Mongols formed a line along the beaches to prevent the invaders from escaping.

The Khan had not slept for days. He was gravely disturbed by the lack of news and by the thought of Diego's passion for Lotus Flower. He was about to march with his army to the coast when he was told that a Japanese envoy was approaching. The Khan received the man with due ceremony, noting the envoy's impeccable manners, which belied the bloodthirsty look in his eyes.

"Emperor of China, greetings from my master, the Shogun of Kyushu."

"My greetings to you. What news do you bring?"

"My master requests the return of his treasure in exchange for that which you desire."

"And what does he wish me to give him?"

"He demands the twelve pearls stolen many years ago from the Temple of Shiatsutu."

The Khan paused imperceptibly before replying. "I have but six pearls of sufficient splendor to warrant such a mission."

"This my master knows, sire."

"Does he expect me to give what I do not own?"

"My master wishes you to send men to make Li-Huei tell where his master hid the other six pearls. It was Wen-Fai, Prince of the House of Sung, who bought the superior pearls, sire. You received only what he refused."

The Khan strode away to consult with his advisers. Within minutes he returned to speak with the envoy.

"If the servant knew where the pearls were hidden, he would have told you to save his mistress's life."

The Japanese officer bowed assent.

"We must assume, therefore," the Khan continued, "that he does not know. I also do not know. What then can I do?"

"You must send an envoy to request his further orders, sire."

The Khan looked haughtily down at the envoy. "The Ruler of Half the World does not take orders!"

An experienced envoy was dispatched with the Shogun's representative to bargain for Lotus Flower's release.

For a week the Khan waited impatiently for the diplomat's
147

return. Then, one evening, the guards called that riders were approaching. The Khan hurried to the audience room prepared for a long, hard bargaining session. He was surprised when the soldiers appeared alone.

"Where is the negotiator?"

The captain of the guard came near and informed the Khan of the latest news. "The Shogun's envoy sent back the negotiator, sire."

"Where is he? Bring him to me at once!"

"The Shogun instructed his envoy to tell you that he was delivering food for your dinner, sire."

"But where is the negotiator?" The Khan roared impatiently at the delay.

"The Shogun roasted him alive, sire. That is the food of which the envoy spoke."

There was a hollow silence in the audience room at the insult to the Omnipotence. Many were remembering what had happened on a previous occasion when the Shogun had sent back envoys roasted to a turn and glazed to a sheen. Apples had been placed in their mouths and savory stuffing inserted to replace their innards, as if they were animals cooked by the Emperor's chefs. Before anyone could speak, the Khan swept from the room, ignoring his stunned subjects and the guards at the door. Once inside his private suite, the Khan sent for Badriak, the imperial horsemaster.

"Ride with men from my Special Squadron and bring back the Shogun's envoy," the Khan instructed Badriak.

"It is already done, my lord. When I saw the negotiator's body I knew you would wish to challenge the Shogun."

"Take the envoy to the torture chamber and hand him to the head inquisitor. I wish to know the location of the Shogun's camp. If the envoy dies before he speaks, the inquisitor too will die."

The Khan dismissed members of his entourage and sat alone in the marble hall. Visions of the girl from the wildfowl pool danced before his eyes, and he wondered despondently if Lotus Flower was still alive. Or would he be forced to witness the arrival of her body roasted over the heathen's fire? Hate filled the Emperor's heart, and he began to make

148

plans for an invasion of the Japanese Islands and tortures unmentionable with which to punish Junichiko Minamoto.

An hour passed, but there was still no news from the torture chamber. The Khan called for wine, and for Diego Mazzarini to share his vigil. No sooner had the Venetian arrived than the guard from the torture chamber was announced. The Khan bade him speak.

"The Shogun's envoy told what he knew, sire."

"Where is his master?"

"He claims he does not know, sire. The messenger was sent by Ariki, the Shogun's champion, who is on this mission with a party of soldiers trained to conduct warfare in alien lands. The men are hiding in the marshes of Yua."

"Give the inquisitor my compliments and a gift of silver."

"Yes, my lord."

"Does the envoy live?"

"No, my lord, he bled to death."

"You may leave the Imperial Presence."

The guard kowtowed and backed from the room, leaving the Khan looking questioningly at Diego.

"What say you, Count Mazzarini? I say we surround the marshes of Yua and force the Japanese to hand over their captive."

"They would cut Lotus Flower's throat before our eyes if they saw your force advancing."

"And I would cut their throats if they allowed themselves to be seen."

"Who will speak with the heathens, sire?"

"I, Kublai Khan, will speak."

"I beg leave to accompany you on your mission, my lord."

"I am pleased to permit it, Count Mazzarini."

The Khan left Shang-tu with a group of two hundred chosen men. The riders dismounted a mile before the marshes of Yua and made their way surreptitiously to the high ground around the hollow where Lotus Flower was imprisoned.

Diego and his brother, Pierluigi, accompanied the Mongol party, crawling on their bellies the last half mile until they were able to look down on the raiders hidden in the clearing.

Pierluigi strained his eyes to see what was happening.

"The light is already failing. I fear a storm is brewing, brother Diego."

"The Khan will advance with the royal bodyguard at any moment."

"He is too old to fight. What will he do if he is challenged? I have heard fearsome stories of Ariki's abilities."

"The Emperor will accept, and no one can advise him otherwise," Diego explained.

"They say the Emperor's heart is failing, worn out by the burden of his great weight."

"The Emperor will give his life if only he can retrieve Lotus Flower and prove that he remains the Omnipotent in his kingdom. The Shogun has made a fool of him more than once, that much is obvious."

Pierluigi looked closely at his brother and was overcome with pity for Diego. "And you? Will you also give your life? For it is unlikely we shall survive if we tread incautiously in that foul black mud."

"I do not wish to die when life is sweet and we are on our way to a new fortune. But I am in love with the lady Lotus Flower. If she dies I shall not want to live, because she is the sun, the moon, and everything I ever thought perfect."

Pierluigi put his arm around his brother's shoulder, saying, "I never thought to see you so stricken. I was sure you would forever enjoy your philandering."

Bugles sounded. The Emperor, who rode in a howdah atop a ceremonial elephant panoplied in cloth of gold, wore robes of yellow silk, and at his waist a sword studded with diamonds and topazes. He was surrounded by tame cheetahs, and behind him stood a hundred foot soldiers. The Emperor's face was unnaturally pale, but his voice echoed as he called his challenge to the enemy.

"I, Kublai Khan, Emperor of China, Lord of the Mongol Horde, Ruler of Half the World, am here to collect what is mine."

A man appeared out of the marsh, and Diego leaned forward, the better to see Ariki, the Shogun's champion swordsman. He recoiled in horror at the evil face of the Khan's adversary. The Shogun's champion was a giant; his body rippled with muscle under a brightly colored robe.

Observing that the Emperor remained on firm ground, not venturing his elephant on the marsh, Ariki called tauntingly, "I ask for my master's property if you can find it in your heart to part with it in return for the woman."

The Khan took out twelve pearls and showed them one by one to Ariki. The swordsman bowed and retreated into the marshy area. Minutes later he returned, dragging Lotus Flower behind him. "Is this your property, my lord?"

"That is my property."

The Khan gazed impassively down, showing nothing of his inner turmoil. Diego stared at the unconscious girl's face, which was white and blotchy with crying. His heart thundered as Ariki called again to the Emperor.

"My master replies that as you have been in possession of his property for many moons, he will retain the use of this concubine until the same time has passed. Then and only then will he return her, for she pleases him greatly. In the meantime, I am instructed to refuse your offer of the pearls until the time is right."

The Khan's voice trembled with emotion. "Where is your master? I will speak only with him."

Suddenly, out of the yellow mist of the marshes, the Shogun rode along the path toward his champion. He was as young as the Khan was old, as wild as the Khan was impassive, but his bearing was regal and the Emperor knew that at this moment the Shogun felt omnipotent.

A look of hatred lit the Shogun's face as he ordered his champion to lift Lotus Flower onto his horse. Then he called to the Khan in a harsh, staccato voice, "I am Junichiko Minamoto, Shogun of Kyushu. I expected you to offer me much land on which my people could settle, as well as the pearls I demand. I thought this woman was valuable to you, Emperor of China."

The Khan ordered his archers to make ready to fire. In reply the Shogun pointed to the hills beyond the marsh. Suddenly the air was full of the rattling of swords on shields, the hissing of whips and the thud of clubs as the Japanese force menaced the Mongols. The Emperor knew that it was no small party of raiders. It was an invasion of his territory by a hundred thousand Japanese. The Khan looked with contempt on the Shogun, frowning at the shapeless scarlet wrap, the conical hat and gaudy leggings.

"Think again, Shogun of Kyushu. This is *my* land and that is *my* woman."

"Too late, noble lord. I have already made her my own, and in time I hope to train her as you have trained your wild animals."

With that contemptuous statement, the Shogun turned to ride away with Lotus Flower. He was surprised to see a tall figure in leather armor standing on a hill before him. Reining his horse, the Shogun weighed the Venetian's expression and knew that his life was in danger. He made to gallop on.

Diego called to him, "I claim the right to fight on the Khan's behalf for the woman who is your prisoner."

An interpreter translated, and with a savage smile the Shogun urged his champion forward. Ariki drew his sword and ran menacingly toward the hill where Diego stood. The Venetian saw that the giant was half a body taller than all the other men in the plain. He recalled the Khan's envious comment that the Shogun's swordsman could cut any man in half with one sweep of his scimitar and his lament that no one had ever survived conflict with Ariki. The giant called for Diego to draw his sword. Instead, the Venetian drew his bow and shot the champion between the eyes with a silver-winged arrow. Ariki fell with a howl of pain, his body rolling down the hill into the marsh, where it sank slowly into the black mud.

The Shogun screamed with rage, and Pierluigi, darting out quickly from behind the bushes, pulled the half-conscious Lotus Flower from the Shogun's saddle. Within seconds the silence of the marsh became raucous with noise. The Khan called for his Mongols to pursue the Japanese. The Shogun galloped away, disappearing into the mist. And Diego, seeing his enemy escaping, threw up his arms and cried out in anguish.

At that moment there was a clap of thunder and a flash of lightning which illuminated the Shogun's hiding place. The Venetian galloped in pursuit, leaving the Khan staring in astonishment at his guest who could call on the elements to assist him. Another flash of lightning revealed a line of

Mongols advancing on the Japanese position. With the cunning for which he was renowned, the Khan had ordered his main force to lie back, hidden from view, until the signal to commence the charge. There were cries from the hill as the Mongols engaged. Then the thunderous roar of hooves as they forced the Japanese to retreat.

As the sun set and darkness came, the Emperor saw Diego riding toward him.

"Did the dog die?" he cried out hopefully.

Diego proffered a bloody souvenir of the encounter. "This is the right hand of your enemy, my lord. It is my sadness that he escaped into the darkness before I could bring you his head. It would have given me much pleasure to have taken it."

The Khan looked down on his trophy and smiled a cruel smile. Now he would show the Shogun of Kyushu how well he trained his animals. He ordered the hand to be shown to the cheetahs. Then, when they had taken the scent, he ordered them to pursue and kill. Soon twelve lithe bodies leaped unerringly through the marshy terrain and disappeared from view. The Khan lay back idly on the velvet cushions of his litter, looking at the sky and wondering superstitiously how the Venetian had called on the gods of lightning. Suddenly, he heard the demented screams of a man being torn apart. The Khan laughed and called for his lieutenant to go in search of the Shogun's body. Piece by piece it was brought to him, as one by one the cheetahs returned, their eyes flashing, their feline limbs twitching with excitement. The Khan belched loudly. Then he ordered the Shogun's hand to be wrapped in muslin and taken at once to the imperial embalmer for a cast to be made. Remembering the duties of battle, the Khan ordered his soldiers to annihilate the entire Japanese force.

Diego rode to where his brother was trying to revive Lotus Flower. He saw that no entreaty made the girl speak, no appeal touched the glazed expression in her eyes. Diego kissed her tenderly, lifted her on his horse and rode away with her on the stony path leading to Shang-tu.

Pierluigi tried in vain to comfort his brother. "My friend, the widow Li-Len, will care for my lady. She will understand what to say and what to do in these terrible circumstances. Do not cry, Diego. My lady needs our courage, not our tears."

Diego rode on without a word, tears streaming down his cheeks. The poet had, in love, become a soldier, and he did not like the feel of his new image. Once more Diego longed for the beauty of Venice, where culture went hand in hand with pleasure and the company of loyal friends. His heart hardened against the perils and intrigues of Cathay, against the Emperor whose presence bred hate and the Chinese who loathed their ruler despite his good works. Diego remembered his reason for coming to the East and knew he must play a double game for a few more months, until the Mazzarini fortune was sufficient to last for generations. Then, and then only, would he leave this alien land and return home to cherish Lotus Flower in the house by the sea. Diego held his love close, kissing her hair and whispering that he would always adore her. Lotus Flower did not hear. When Diego spoke, her eyes stared into space as though she were deaf to his promises and blind to the possibility of love.

The Khan's soldiers pursued the Shogun's army to the place where they had hidden their ships. Five thousand Japanese officers escaped before the Mongols arrived. The remaining ninety thousand were hacked to pieces. When the prisoners had been killed, the Khan dismissed his men. Then he stood on the shore, looking with distaste at the sea and cursing the one who had dared damage the woman he loved. Rain poured down as a storm raged, and the Khan called to the spirits of the air to crush the Shogun's ships. Then he rode back to Shang-tu with the imperial bodyguard.

As he rode, the Emperor thought of Diego Mazzarini, who had broken every rule of warrior's conduct by shooting the Shogun's champion with an arrow. The Khan's Mongol soul relished the memory of the champion's corpse sinking into the mud of the marsh. His pride was assuaged by the thought that he had the hand of his enemy and the twelve pearls with which he had tried to buy back his love. They were not the pearls the Shogun had demanded, but they were fine and valuable specimens. The Khan decided to have a gold cast made of the hand. It would be studded with rubies and displayed for all to see so none could deny his continuing Omnipotence. As a sign of his gratitude, he would bestow the twelve pearls on Pierluigi Mazzarini for his daring part in the rescue of the lady Lotus Flower. To Diego he would give a fortune in rubies and a casket of the finest diamonds ever brought to the kingdom of Cathay. Everything he would give but the woman he adored.

The Khan frowned apprehensively, recalling Diego's shout of anguish which had brought thunder and lightning from the sky. It was said that misfortune followed those struck by the white light of the storm. The Khan considered what he knew of the Venetian. Was Mazzarini a man or one of those with the power to call on spirits so powerful they could not be defied? By the time he reached Shang-tu the Emperor had decided it would be wise to bestow on Diego *everything* he desired.

Diego sat at Lotus Flower's bedside, trying to make her understand that she was safe. Lotus Flower lay staring at the gilded ceiling, her face an expressionless mask, and it seemed to the Venetian that she might never wake from her stupor. Unable to eat, Diego had begged the Khan's permission to forego the evening feast in order to remain at Lotus Flower's side. When it was dark the sick girl fell asleep. Hopeful that she might be hungry when she woke, Diego ordered food to be placed at the bedside. Then he prayed fervently for her recovery.

In the small hours of the morning the widow Li-Len appeared.

"Leave my lady with me, sire. She will need time to recover from her ordeal and will be reluctant to look on the man she loves until she is cleansed from the touch of the heathen who has defiled her," the widow explained.

"But how can she be cleansed?"

"It will be done, sire, I promise. Then my lady Lotus Flower will laugh and sing again, because she will be happy. Go now and sleep, for in truth you look like a phantom and will frighten the child if she should see you."

Diego returned to his suite and fell exhausted on the bed. Deeply distressed by the fact that he had killed and maimed so easily, Diego longed to visit the church near his home in

Venice to confess that he had become as great a barbarian as any in Cathay. Then, remembering the attitude of the champion and the murderous encouragement of the Shogun of Kyushu, Diego thought that if he were faced again with the same situation he would change nothing. For Lotus Flower he would upturn his life, his beliefs, his hope of salvation. Exhausted, he slept fully clothed until a servant came to bathe him.

Lotus Flower slept restlessly, watched over by the widow Li-Len. She was unaware that the widow had dropped on her lips a substance said to produce dreams which rid the troubled mind of its purgatory. Lotus Flower licked her lips and slept on, deaf to the sound of the nightingales. Soon she dreamed she was at home in the Street of the Almond Blossom. She imagined herself struggling to be free from a giant whose hands had touched her as no man had ever dared. She heard again his cruel laugh and cried out as she had cried out on that unforgettable night.

"Do not touch me. I beg you not to touch me."

Lotus Flower cried frantically as she relived Ariki's reply. "Have no fear, my lady. Virgins do not amuse me, though my master the Shogun will relish that which you guard."

Lotus Flower had been bound and gagged, then tied on a horse and taken to a marshy area miles from her home. She dreamed next of her first meeting with the Shogun, trembling violently as she felt his eyes appraising her body, his hands touching her breasts in full view of his mercenaries. The soldiers had laughed at her tears, and some had begged their leader to pass the girl on once he tired of her. When Hanan had protested, the Shogun had run her through with a sword. Lotus Flower howled in anguish when her nurse was killed. Then she fought as the Shogun carried her away to his tent on the hillside.

Imagining herself once again in the heathen's presence, Lotus Flower lay panting. In her dream she watched the Shogun disrobe and oil his body, which was strong, though his face was lined with the evil of his ways. She began to plead in her dream, as she had pleaded when the Shogun tore off her clothes. Then she fell silent, breathing hard and moaning as she relived what had followed.

First the Shogun had smoked a pipe of strange-smelling herbs. This he had thrust into her mouth so she was forced to draw on the contents, which made her dizzy. Lotus Flower felt herself become weak and incapable of resistance, watching helplessly as the ruffian parted her thighs and explored her inner folds. She cried in terror as she imagined the Shogun taunting her, screaming as he entered the place where no man had been. Lotus Flower remembered every thrust of the loathsome body and the quickening friction that had driven the Shogun wild. She rolled back and forth, her arms outstretched as she tried to push away the inevitable. Then, with one last scream of horror, she cowered on the bed, rolled in a tight ball and muttering that she wanted to die.

For two days the Shogun had used her until she believed the torture would never end. Then, tiring of her tears, he had promised her to his champion, Ariki. Lotus Flower sobbed as she remembered the swordfighter's boast: "Tonight you will lie with one whose manhood can split your precious body in two. You will enjoy me or I shall beat you until you can enjoy no other."

Lotus Flower woke from her dream at last, and looked around the room. Pink silk hangings painted with cherry blossoms were fluttering in the breeze of early morning. There were roses everywhere, on the bed, the stool and the window sill. Apricots, peaches and pomegranates had been placed in a bowl on the satin bed cover. And nearby a pretty woman sat sewing.

When Lotus Flower stirred, the widow rose and reassured her. "I am Li-Len, friend of my lord Pierluigi Mazzarini."

"Is the Venetian, Diego Mazzarini, here? Where am I?"

"You are in the palace of Shang-tu."

Lotus Flower burst into tears. "I want Count Mazzarini. I am afraid the Khan will force me to his pleasure."

"Count Mazzarini awaits you, have no fear. He and the Emperor rode with an army to rescue you from the evil one. Do you not remember, my lady?"

Lotus Flower turned away, remembering her shame.

"I have changed my mind. I cannot see Diego Mazzarini
157

and I can no longer hope to be his wife. Tell him what I have said in the kindest way, for to see him would break my heart."

"The Venetian will not accept your decision, my lady."

"I have been used by the Shogun Junichiko Minamoto. I am fit only for the Suburb of the Prostitutes."

Li-Len took a deep breath and told the lie she had been instructed to tell. "Count Mazzarini's brother told me that in his country men prefer women who have already been loved."

Lotus Flower's eyes widened in disbelief.

"It is true, child. I do not lie. Apparently it is so in other countries also. Only in China do we value so highly the barrier of innocence."

Lotus Flower looked uncertainly at her companion. Then she slid her hand over the satin cover and took Li-Len's hand in hers.

"I did not like love at all, and I fear I would not be a good wife. Can you teach me how to please? If you cannot I must not marry for I should be but a stone in the bed of my love."

"Your husband will teach you to please him as mine once taught me. And do not worry that you did not enjoy what happened. What you experienced was the lust of a heathen inflicted by force, not the love of a man who adores you. Only a fool enjoys humiliation."

"Still, I fear I shall fail Diego, and I am afraid. I cannot bear to think of sharing a man's bed. I am soiled and damaged forever."

"I will arrange for you to be tested to see if you are truly unsuited to passion."

Lotus Flower wiped her eyes, marveling at the older woman's wisdom. "How can I be tested?"

"I will send for one of the concubines from the imperial harem. Tatiana will know how to define your abilities, because it is she who tests the virgins who come to the harem each year from the province of Onggirat."

The concubine appeared with a picture book and a bowl of ripe yellow plums. As Lotus Flower ate she stared at the girl's orange hair and wide blue eyes. The concubine's musky perfume bemused her, and the painted fingernails and fabulous sapphires drew gasps of admiration. The concubine kissed Lotus Flower affectionately and consulted her book.

"I am Tatiana, one of the Emperor's favorite concubines. My lady Li-Len had asked me to visit you to test your talent for passion in the marital bed. With this book I can apply the same tests that I apply to the virgins from Onggirat and thus know if you are suitable for matrimony."

Lotus Flower did not answer. She was staring open-mouthed at the paintings in the book Tatiana held. The woman's list of requirements stated that points were to be awarded to each girl for the quality of her hair, the symmetry of her face, the smoothness of her eyebrows and each feature of her body. Further inspections were made to check the girl's breath and body odor. Those who failed this test were discarded and sent to the sewing rooms. Then one of the ladies of the court was made to sleep with the remaining applicants to make sure they did not snore. On this point Tatiana assured Lotus Flower that she had nothing to fear. The widow Li-Len had vouched that she did not snore. Then the book of pictures was displayed and its effects noted.

Tatiana explained that when an applicant's face became flushed and her breathing quickened she was marked as having a passionate nature. On examining the pictures in the book, Lotus Flower had flushed to the color of camellia flowers. Tatiana explained the significance of each of the delicate erotic drawings and made Lotus Flower repeat what she had learned.

Within two hours the Shogun's victim was reassured that she remained in every way the ideal wife. She could sing and sew. Her breath and body odors were sweet, her features perfect, her nature almost without flaw. Of her passion there was no doubt. Tatiana stayed for an hour to play chess with Lotus Flower.

"You are a princess, my lady Lotus Flower. No one can change what you are, not even the Shogun of Kyushu. I hope you will be very happy in your future life, and that fortune will always smile on you," Tatiana said.

"I am grateful to know that I am not permanently damaged by my experience. Thank you for all you have done for me."

The concubine went at once to inform Li-Len that she had been successful in convincing the innocent one of her continued perfection. Li-Len hurried back to her suite, carrying in her arms a basket given to her by Diego.

Handing the basket to Lotus Flower, she said, "My lord Diego Mazzarini instructed me to give you this basket of flowers. He said it would teach you another sound with which to summon him to your side. I did not understand this statement, my lady."

Lotus Flower, gazing at the rosebuds and moon daisies in the basket, was startled to see one of them move. Curious, she put her hand beneath the flowers and found a kitten with fur the color of cinnamon. Around the kitten's neck was a collar with a bell attached. With the gift there was a note brush-painted in Diego's inexpert hand: "This is a savage beast to guard you during my absence. If I hear him call in the night I shall rush at once to your side."

Lotus Flower laughed merrily as the kitten rolled around her bed. Then she read the note again and hid it under her pillow. *This is a savage beast to guard you during my absence.* She looked again at the kitten, which promptly fell asleep as she stroked its neck.

It was seven days before Li-Len allowed the impatient girl to receive visitors. First the Khan appeared with a gift of rare black pearls. Then some ladies of the court paid a call, their curious eyes taking in every line of Lotus Flower's face, every flicker in her fascinating green eyes. Li-Len dismissed the ladies, displeased that they were more curious about the Shogun of Kyushu than about the victim's health.

Impatiently Lotus Flower waited for Diego to appear, but he stayed away until nightfall. Just when her newfound confidence was turning to despair, she heard the squirrel chirrup she had made long ago to tell the Venetian of her presence. She answered in the same manner as Diego walked through the archway of her room. His arms were full of presents, his face eager with love. For a moment they stood at opposite ends of the room.

Then Diego spoke, surprising Lotus Flower with a crisp statement of fact. "I am here on important business."

Crestfallen, she walked toward him, her eyes disappointed to hear this sudden formality. "I had thought you would be anxious to see me, sire. I expected you this morning."

Diego concealed a smile. "When a gentleman of the Venetain Empire proposes, he does it formally and in the most eloquent manner. It takes him many hours to prepare his speech, so he is not free to visit until nightfall."

Lotus Flower threw herself in Diego's arms, and they kissed. "Tell me what I must do when you propose."

"You need only remember to say yes very loudly when I ask if you are willing to marry me. If I do not hear you say yes I may be tempted to leap out of this high window."

Tears of happiness fell down Lotus Flower's cheeks as Diego knelt before her.

"Lotus Flower, Princess of the House of Sung, I love you and wish you to be my wife. I am not the richest man in the world—indeed, I am working hard to make a new fortune—but I love you more than all the rubies in Cathay, more than all the clouds in the sky and more than my life. Will you marry me?"

"Yes! I shall be honored to be your wife."

Lotus Flower's voice echoed ecstatically in the night. Then she knelt at Diego's side, putting her hands together as if in prayer. "I am deeply proud that your love for me is so great you can accept me despite all that has happened. I adore you and will be devoted to you for as long as I live and even after when my soul flies to another's body. Then I pray I shall meet you again and be allowed to love you, for we two must never be parted."

Diego handed Lotus Flower the presents he had brought, a bale of silk for her wedding robes, a luster pot of scented lilies for her bedside, a book of poems illuminated by the Khan's calligrapher. Finally he handed her a box in which he had placed a wedding ring and the ring that would signify their agreement to marry.

Lotus Flower looked wonderingly at the band of gold etched with a design of swans and flowers. At its side she saw a creation of pearls, diamonds, rubies and rose quartz in the shape of a lotus flower. The excitement of the moment was too much, and suddenly she cried like a child.

Diego took her in his arms, reassuring her that he understood. Then he put the rose ring on her finger and took the other away to be used on the day of the marriage ceremony.

Lotus Flower looked in sudden puzzlement at her companion, and asked, "How did you persuade the Khan to give us permission to be married?"

"I waited until the night when a storm was brewing to ask the Emperor's permission."

"How did you know a storm was brewing?"

"I am a Venetian and trained to observe the weather."

"Did the Khan agree at once?"

Diego shook his head. "First he refused, saying he wanted you for his own."

"And how did you argue?"

"I swore I would never rest until you were happy. I told him I foresaw thunderstorms and pestilence in his land if you were forced yet again to do something against your will."

Lotus Flower began to laugh. "Then what did the Emperor say?"

"I did nothing more, because it was not necessary. As my voice rose, the greatest storm of the last hundred years broke, washing away the pleasure gardens of the palace and the bricks made by the builders for the new stables and the Bamboo Pavilion itself. The morning after this calamity, the Khan sent word that he gave his permission for us to marry."

Lotus Flower wiped tears of mirth from her eyes. "When will the ceremony take place?"

"It is to be in Peking when the leaves have fallen. The Emperor wishes to hold an elaborate ceremony in your honor, a ceremony befitting a princess of China."

"But I am no longer a princess."

"The Khan has restored your lands and all your possessions. At this moment men are working to restore your house in Peking. Li-Huei has agreed to oversee the work, while he recovers from his wound, and I have no doubt he will enjoy being the taskmaster."

Lotus Flower looked into Diego's eyes and said, "You are a worker of miracles, my love."

"And you, my lady, are my inspiration."

Until the end of the summer Lotus Flower remained in the palace of Shang-tu under the protection of the Emperor. Soon she began enjoying her peaceful life, and gradually she recovered from the horror of her ordeal. By the end of the summer the widow Li-Len was able to report that her charge no longer screamed in her sleep and that she was not so frequently given to bouts of weeping about the death of her nurse.

The Khan's spies also kept watch on the beautiful one, informing the Emperor of everything they heard. Often the Khan went to a secret chamber from which he could observe Lotus Flower playing in the garden with her kitten, and daily his desire grew until he could scarce control it. The Khan knew he must take care, not only for fear of the Venetian's magic, but because he could not bear to equate his own desire with the animal lust of the Shogun of Kyushu. Nothing, he swore, must ever be allowed to inflict suffering on the girl who had saved his life.

When the chrysanthemums bloomed, Diego returned to Changchow to collect his servant, Giorgio. Taking advantage of his rival's absence, the Khan began visiting Lotus Flower. They passed the time, playing games of double-six, jug, chess and checkers. Although the Khan was an expert at cheating he never won a game, because Lotus Flower was by far the most accomplished cheat he had ever met. Her audacity amused the Emperor, who was used to being allowed to win. And often his laughter could be heard all over the palace. Each night when he left Lotus Flower, the Khan lay in his suite plotting new ways to outwit the temptress. But none of his plans worked, and soon he owed her a fortune, which he paid in pearls and sapphires, much to Lotus Flower's delight.

As time passed the Khan thought of sending Diego on a diplomatic mission, the better to have time to persuade the bewitching one to love him. But fear and superstition haunted the imperial mind, and the Emperor decided he would be wise to bide his time, giving no sign of the fever that ruined his sleep. Once Lotus Flower was married, the Khan believed she would become addicted to the sweet sensations of love. Then, if her husband was absent for a long period of time, she would seek gratification from another man, as did most of the women of the court. The Khan planned to be that other man. He would have her yet, his nymph of the wildfowl pool.

163

He would draw her slender body onto his own like a glove on the hand and make her eyes shine like stars. Overwhelmed by his fantasies, the Khan called for opium pills and his concubines.

When the Emperor's birthday feast had passed, Lotus Flower packed her new clothes and the jewels given her by the Khan. She had hidden her winnings in a hollow ornament, chuckling that she had managed to elicit such a fortune from the Omnipotence. Lotus Flower was happy to be returning to Peking. Impatiently she ran to the window, where she could see the elephants and horses, the nobles and their families, the procession of bearers, sorcerers, wizards and servants preparing for the journey back to the capital. Then, taking one last look around the room where Diego had made his proposal, she followed the widow Li-Len to the carriage. As she passed the Venetian, Lotus Flower dropped a frond of scented blossom in his path. Then she walked to the head of the procession and stepped into a four-horse carriage studded with precious stones, where she waited for the conch-shell summons to depart.

First the Khan anointed the assembly with mare's milk. Then he assuaged the spirits of the air with more milk so his party would have safe passage, untouched by demons and calamities. He gave the signal for the conch shells to be sounded, and slowly the party moved away from the palace of Shang-tu. The Khan sat atop his elephant, enjoying the warmth of the sun, conscious that his love was traveling nearby and thankful that he had found her again. The Khan longed for Lotus Flower to be married so he could proceed with the next part of his plan. As he rode he began to speculate about the wedding feast. He would arrange a spectacle the likes of which had never been seen in Peking, a wedding that would never be forgotten or equaled. The Khan looked back, inclining his head as he caught Lotus Flower's eyes. Then he reached into a pillbox and fed himself more opium pills.

Lotus Flower held Li-Len's hand and chattered merrily all the way to the outskirts of Chagan Nor. At that place of many memories she fell strangely silent, thinking of the family who

164

had died there, of her first meeting with the Venetian near the wildfowl pool, and of the moment when she had known she loved him. That night as the Khan's party went to sleep under the stars, Lotus Flower dreamed of being married and loved above all women. In her dream, she thanked the spirits of the mysterious outer world for delivering her from poverty and loneliness to the adoration of Diego Mazzarini.

Chapter Nine:

Peking

Lotus Flower quivered with excitement as the maid dusted her face with rice powder and blushed her cheeks with pink balsam leaves crushed in alum. Looking intently at her reflection in a polished metal mirror, Lotus Flower saw the face of a stranger, no longer the childlike sprite of past times but a woman deeply in love. She hung perfumed sachets around her underrobe so the scent of magnolia would follow her everywhere. Then she put on slippers of gilded white leather. The bridal robe was red silk with voluminous sleeves and a train that flowed behind her like a stream. The sash was lotus pink, embroidered with doves of peace. On her head Lotus Flower pinned an oblong hat in a deeper shade of pink which had, suspended from its underside, three long flowery trailers that swung back and forth on either side of her face. Normally these streamers were made of fresh blossom, but

Lotus Flower's were a gift from the court jeweler and made of pearls, rubies and diamonds.

Lotus Flower's kitten yawned sleepily, unaware that this was a special day. Outside, in the Street of the Almond Blossom, the atmosphere was already festive. Colorful lanterns were hung from every window, ho-p'ans of joss paper burned outside the houses, and children paraded excitedly up and down calling greetings and banging gongs. Paper artists had cut images of Lotus Flower to be hung across the roadway from one balcony to another. Neighbors, who stood in groups waiting excitedly for the bride to appear, pointed to the thousand expertly cut "images" of Lotus Flower rustling in the crisp breeze of a sunny autumn day.

Lotus Flower wandered through the house she loved, marveling at the transformation that had taken place during her absence in Shang-tu. Rare aloe and sandalwood scented the atmosphere with the calming odor of wealth. The decayed floors had been replaced with mahogany boards inlaid with silver in the pattern of lotus flowers. In the bedroom Japanese pine and ivory provided coolness and a happy atmosphere, and in the once-overgrown garden bluebirds flew to rustic cotes by the fountain, which had been enlarged so it gushed over rocks to an ornamental pond. Lotus Flower longed fervently for the moment when she would share all this with Diego. Soon, she would return home with him, away from the clamor of the court and the endless gossip and intrigue of the nobles. Despite the Khan's kindness, she disliked life in the royal palace and had been relieved to learn that they had been given permission to live in the Sung house and not in one of the pavilions reserved for noblemen.

At midday the litter bearers arrived. Lotus Flower walked through the garden, bowing to Li-Huei, who presented her with a white rose.

"May the gods bless you with good fortune, my lady."

"My good fortune will always be shared with you, Li-Huei."

Lotus Flower stepped into the litter and was carried away. Diaphanous curtains billowed out in the breeze as she passed children playing with crickets, toy peddlers, sweetmeat vendors and legions of the curious. When she waved a regal greeting the onlookers bowed, and there was great rejoicing at Lotus Flower's return to favor. Soon the litter bearers were admitted to the core of the imperial city, and Lotus Flower felt her heart quickening with excitement. She looked out curiously as they passed guards stationed in the first circle of land between the outer walls and the nobles' homes. Ahead, within the inner wall, was the Khan's own palace of four hundred rooms. At the palace, Lotus Flower stepped down and walked up the marble steps to a room where the Khan's chamberlain greeted her.

"The Emperor has given permission for the ceremony to begin, my lady. He bids me accompany you to the hall."

"I thank you, sire."

Lotus Flower listened patiently as the chamberlain explained what was going to happen. "First there will be a short ceremony in your language. Then there will be a Catholic blessing, said by one of the Venetians in the tongue of Count Mazzarini. The tributes will be brought to you after the ceremony. And finally the Khan will present his own gifts, before the commencement of the feasting."

Lotus Flower nodded, wishing suddenly, inexplicably, that she were home again and that she could have married Diego in a simple ceremony. The bridal procession moved slowly, majestically down the center of the hall. As she entered, Lotus Flower saw that the nobles were all dressed in scarlet, cyclamen and peach. The women wore no jewels, by imperial decree, so they could not outshine the Emperor. Instead, each lady had flowers in her hair or pins of jade and ivory. The noblemen wore cloaks made of feathers, and these undulated in the breeze as the entrance door opened, making a moving spectacle of gaudy splendor. The ceiling was draped in scarlet silk, the floor strewn with red roses. Ahead, on either side of the Khan's gold throne, were two silver chairs. On one sat Diego Mazzarini, simply clad in white wool. Over his shoulders, Diego wore the silver cloak he had worn on the day of his first meeting with the Khan. In his hand he held the box containing the wedding ring.

Lotus Flower felt tears in her eyes as she admired the Venetian's aristocratic simplicity, comparing it with the barbaric appearance of the Khan's gold tunic and yellow cloak of a thousand diamonds.

The ceremony was short and simple. First the Khan's chamberlain spoke.

"By the power vested in me by my lord Kublai Khan, Emperor of China, Lord of the Mongol Horde, Ruler of Half the World, I proclaim that you are united."

Then the assembly heard the soft tones of the Venetian nobleman and priestly scholar, Arturo de Mirafiori.

"Do you, my lady Lotus Flower, Princess of the House of Sung, take this man as your spouse, to be yours forever until death do you part?"

"I do."

"Do you, Diego Giovanni Veneziano Mazzarini, take this woman as your spouse, to be yours forever until death do you part?"

"For always, I do."

Tears fell like dew down Lotus Flower's cheeks as Diego put the ring on her finger. Then, the important words were said: "By the grace of God and in the eyes of the Holy Catholic Church, I pronounce you man and wife."

Silver bells tinkled their acknowledgment of the union. And in the palace grounds a six-hundred-piece orchestra began the cymbal-crashing march of the tribute givers. Men and women of the city guilds formed lines with nobles, members of the Khan's army, Chinese inhabitants and merchants of the city, astrologers and soothsayers, all joined to deliver their gifts. It was a moment of respect and, for those of the Chinese community, pride.

Lotus Flower and her husband sat on the silver chairs, separated by the figure of the Omnipotence, as the tribute givers came forward to lay their gifts on the ground: a hundred skeins of silk from the Ogodai, scrolls of great antiquity from the noblemen, soap made from peas and scented herbs given by the soapmakers' guild, ornaments of bronze, jade and silver from the craftsmen, bales of silk from the ladies of the court, a musical casket full of seed pearls from the concubines, gold hair ornaments for Lotus Flower in the form of birds and phoenixes from the jewelers' guild, a girdle of leather with knife, purse, abacus, dagger and compartments for carrying gold for the bridegroom from the leather workers' guild.

The Emperor yawned and stole a glance at the flushed face of his beloved. That morning he had been obliged to take six opium pills to sooth his choler before the ceremony began, and they had made him sleepy. Diego too stole a glance at Lotus Flower, his heart thundering with passion because he thought her fragile perfection unique in this room of gaudily clad courtiers. Then he looked at the Khan and saw desire in the intent appraisal of the bride. Loath to consider the possibility of trouble on such a happy day, Diego told himself he must not be jealous. But trouble he knew could come, and disaster, too, if the capricious whim of the Omnipotence turned from favor to fury. Diego looked back to the proceedings in the hall, struggling to conceal his apprehension.

The gift bearers continued to come forward, each one dismissed by a regal nod from the Omnipotence. Soon the center of the hall was stacked high with valuables and the nobles were calling for the feasting to begin. The Khan silenced them with a wave of the hand. Then he ordered his own gifts to be brought. With a fanfare of trumpets two white horses were led forward followed by two white camels, each with magnificently bejeweled bridles. Then gold and silver plate, which had been transported to the palace on the backs of a thousand elephants, was stacked in a mound of splendor.

Unable to believe his eyes, Pierluigi whispered frantically to his brother, "The new Mazzarini fortune is made, brother Diego. I had better make haste back to Venice with these trinkets before the Khan changes his mind!"

Lotus Flower gasped as the Khan walked down the steps and with a sweep of the dazzling cloak presented his own final gift, the diamond of Jaipur, a stone as large as the palm of her hand which sparkled and shimmered in its magnificence. Lotus Flower bowed to the Emperor. Then, taking the stone from him, she kissed the hand that gave it with a caress like the touch of a butterfly wing.

The Khan smelled the delicate fragrance of Lotus Flower's skin and grew so mad with desire he turned his back and called for the feasting to begin. Bearers carried the wedding gifts away, to be locked in the cellars of the country property returned to Lotus Flower. The diamond was placed on a velvet cushion and carried behind her as she disappeared into the banqueting hall. When the couple had left, the Khan threw off his cloak and sat struggling to control his feelings. How tempting the girl was, how soft her body through the silk of the robe, how bright the sparkle in her eyes as she kissed the imperial hand. If a gift of diamonds made her so amenable, he would give her every diamond in the treasure house, but he must have her soon. The Khan closed his eyes in ecstasy at the thought of such perfection. Then he strolled to the banqueting hall, beaming with sudden good humor at the thought of the stir the feast would cause. He had excelled himself in the arrangements for the wedding, not in tribute to his rival's happiness but to show Lotus Flower what his wealth could provide. The Emperor took his place at a table above the members of the court and clapping his hands ordered the food to be served.

There were forty courses of fish, shrimp, pork, goose, duck, pigeon and peacock, twenty kinds of vegetables and nine varieties of rice. Then servants appeared with the dessert, pies, fruit and sweetmeats. Lichee, honey and ginger drinks were served to the ladies, rice wine and spiced mare's milk to the noblemen. The Khan drank koumiss, made from camel milk spiced with nutmeg and coriander. As he drank his lust increased, and he watched Lotus Flower with eyes full of longing. Soon, the Khan thought, she will be in her marriage bed, squealing with delight and giving enticing looks that would make the gods weak. The Khan drank to drown his sorrow and again to hide his feelings. He was uninterested in the entertainment that followed the meal and ordered the astrologers not to speak. The nobles were afraid. Surely, they said, something is seriously amiss with the Emperor.

It was dark by the time Diego led his bride from the banqueting hall. The courtiers bowed as the couple disappeared from view, led by the chamberlain to a carriage in which they would drive home to the Sung house. As the carriage passed through the deserted streets, Diego was silent, still bewildered by the magnificence of the feast and sumptuousness of the gifts. He had also seen envy in the Emperor's face, and knew that what Pierluigi had said was true. The Mazzarini fortune was made only if it could be delivered safely from Peking to Venice. And, most important of all, his love was secure only as long as the Khan controlled his desire to possess *everything* in the kingdom.

Then Diego thought of the simple ceremony he had planned, the calm of the countryside where he had hoped to become Lotus Flower's husband. He was startled when she spoke wistfully, with a trace of reproach.

"You and I should have married in secret, for we did not enjoy that lavish affair. I kept thinking of the lake to the south of the city where you kissed me when you first came to Peking. My heart longed to be alone with you, Diego, away from the Emperor's covetous glances and the envy of the noblewomen."

Diego took Lotus Flower in his arms and kissed her neck, her ears and the softness of her cheeks. "Shall we go now to the lake and marry again—just we two, in secret?"

"Now the curfew will prevent us passing the gate."

"The Khan gave me this tablet so we would avoid challenge."

When the couple arrived at the Sung house the servants were startled to see Lotus Flower rush to her room to change into the shabby jacket and shapeless trousers. None of the ritual procedures of the newly married had been carried out, none of the traditional offerings made, and yet the two seemed ecstatically happy. The new maid, Sanay, stared at her mistress as Lotus Flower wiped rice powder and rouge from her cheeks. Then, before the maid could protest, Lotus Flower ran outside to join Diego.

Within minutes the two lovers were clear of the city. As they rode through the bronze autumn landscape of Cathay, Lotus Flower sang a merry song. Diego, tucking the fur around her so she would not take a chill, thought how lovely she was, and he wondered suddenly if Lotus Flower would be overwhelmed by his passion. Would memories of the Shogun of Kyushu rise when the time came for love? Diego looked again at his wife's radiant face and was reassured that she was happy.

He whispered his adoration as she sat before him on the horse. "I feel free whenever I am out of Peking and a prisoner whenever I am in it. And I feel like a giant when I am with you and a dwarf when I am not. You are my life, Lotus Flower, never forget it and never be tempted to trifle with my love."

"Are you jealous, Diego?"

"As jealous as a thousand men. I have always despised others foolish enough to suffer from such pangs, and now I am one of them."

"I am glad. I should dislike a husband who did not care if his wife flirted with other men. I do not intend to flirt, but I shall enjoy knowing it would torture you if I did."

In the dawn light they sat together by the trout lake, grilling fresh-caught fish for breakfast. When they had eaten they caught more fish. Then they lay in the deserted stillness, enjoying the warmth of an Indian summer. Diego watched as Lotus Flower slipped off her cloak and spread it on the ground. He caught his breath as she lifted the jacket over her head and pulled down the trousers she pretended to loathe but which he knew she adored. Then, she was gone, skipping toward the reeds at the edge of the pool and plunging into the water to cool herself. Diego flung off his tunic and fur-lined jerkin, then his riding boots and sheepskin leggings.

Soon they were together, happy as children, calling and splashing and diving low in the water to kiss under the lily leaves. They were happy as they listened to the frogs croaking, the birds singing, happier than they had ever been in the gilded corridors of the Imperial Palace. As the sun rose the lovers lay together on the bank, hidden from view by rushes, grass and a hedge of honeysuckle. Diego touched the petal skin of his wife's thigh, kissing it gently, then passionately. He smoothed the droplets of water from Lotus Flower's breasts, excited when the nipples rose to a point under his fingers. From the look in her eyes he knew that she was ready for love, that the memory of her ordeal had faded into insignificance at that moment. Smothering her with kisses, Diego pulled her to him and they became one, two beings with a single thought, a forceful longing, a mutual need.

Lotus Flower had never dreamed that love would be so intoxicating. Any fears she had felt vanished when Diego entered her body and she was happy to surrender to the titillation of his touch. The culmination of love reminded her of spring buds bursting into bloom, and she cried out in ecstasy, clinging to Diego as though she could not bear to let him go. Then she smiled as he not not seen her smile before, the smile of a woman after love, replete and deeply content. Hands entwined, they repeated their vows to the sun and the birds and the lake. It was done. They had married again in their own fashion. Content, they dressed and walked together around the edge of the lake, looking shyly at each other and laughing at nothing at all.

On the way back to Peking, Diego told Lotus Flower his thoughts about the Emperor's failing health and his plan to send Pierluigi back to Venice with the newfound fortune. He explained his reasons for doing this, and Lotus Flower became suddenly serious.

"I have thought as much myself, Diego, for I know that the Khan's benevolence could end abruptly if we displease him. I am the one who will displease him, for I know the Emperor still desires me."

"I saw desire in his eyes during the wedding ceremony. I said nothing of it for fear of frightening you."

"What shall we do? We cannot hide forever from him."

"We shall leave Cathay as soon as possible. First I must make sure that my brother gets out of the country in safety. We Venetians prefer to travel by ship and not by land, so I shall hire a vessel and crew to take Pierluigi to Burma or to the coast of the great land beyond about which the Khan has spoken. From there he will sail to Venice."

"I shall be sad to leave my home, but it will upset me more to leave Li-Huei, whose family has served mine for many years. Who knows what vengeance the Khan will wreak on him if we disappear?"

"We shall not leave Li-Huei behind. We shall ask him and his family to accompany us."

That night the couple slept soundly. The hesitations of new love were over. Every moment was a moment to enjoy, every day a day to be spent in harmony, making secret plans. Lotus Flower had never been so happy, so secure in the knowledge that she was adored. When she woke in the night she sat up on one elbow, tracing a finger along Diego's face and whispering as he slept: "I love you, I love you, I love you...

why do you not wake and love me?" Diego turned to kiss her, and soon they were lost in passionate embrace.

As the autumn sun faded and the cold winds of winter came, Lotus Flower and her husband closed the doors of their home and ordered braziers to be lit around the terrace. Often Pierluigi visited them to tell of happenings in the Imperial Palace. And one day Giorgio returned from a long journey to Changchow full of exciting news.

"Guess what I have done, sir. I have been overwhelmed by a stroke of genius."

"Tell me of your brilliance, my good Giorgio."

"I have brought back the spy, Ho Shan."

When Diego looked askance at this statement, Giorgio made haste to explain, "Ho Shan no longer wishes to spy in the Khan's pay. Your influence upset his conscience, sir, and he has had as much appetite for the work as a hen for a cannon ball. So I proposed that he come here. He and I will lodge in the new quarters above the stable. I am teaching Ho Shan our language so I shall not lack for an entertaining companion."

"And what of Ho Shan?"

"He wants to return with us to Venice, sir. In the meantime, in order to help you, he will engage a ship for your brother, taking care not to arouse the suspicions of the men who spy for the Khan. Then he will spy on the Khan so we can know if the Mongol has any bad intentions toward us."

"The Emperor has been kind since my arrival in his land."

"Sir, do not deceive yourself, and forgive me for stating what many know. The Khan is kind because he desires my lady. If you will not share her with him he may decide to put you in the iron collar or to have a gold cast made of your manhood as he did of the Shogun's hand."

Diego paced the room, displeased by his servant's presumption. "The Khan will surely know of Ho Shan's arrival."

Giorgio beamed. "Of course he will know. Ho Shan has accepted a post as assistant in the workshop of the imperial calligrapher. The post will enable our friend to know everything that is happening in the court. On occasion he will tell tales on those who make plots against the Khan, thus earning the ruler's trust. To us he will tell tales about the Emperor so we shall be able to protect ourselves. We have thought of everything, Ho Shan and I. Have no fear, sir. It is our life's desire to keep you and my lady safe."

When Giorgio had gone, the Venetian thought over what he had been told. After a while he felt pleased by his servant's audacity. Ho Shan knew how to elicit information and perhaps could save their lives. Then Diego thought of the new servants in his own household and wondered if they were spies in the pay of the Emperor.

Sending for Li-Huei, he questioned the gardener. "The new servants, where did they come from?"

"The cook is my youngest sister, Fan-Tai. The houseboy is my grandson, Chang-Chi, and the woman who looks after my lady is my grandson's wife, Sanay. I have been very careful, sire. I trust none but those I love."

"You are a wise man, Li-Huei, and I hope to reward you well someday."

"When we go to Venice, sire, you will perhaps buy me a small house so my family cannot be turned out on the street like beggars."

Shocked by the casual revelation of his plans, Diego questioned the gardener. "What makes you think it is my intention to go to Venice?"

Li-Huei covered his mouth with his hand and chuckled. "I know because Sanay told me. She listens at doors, sire, a very bad habit to be sure, but she speaks of what she has heard only to me and my grandson. She was very excited to learn that she will be visiting your great city. When I told her that Venice was surrounded by water she went at once to her husband and asked him to teach her to be buoyant so she will not drown."

Diego sighed, wondering how a houseful of servants could be expected to keep such a secret.

Li-Huei reassured him. "Count Mazzarini, my family have many reasons to be afraid of the Omnipotence. My sister's previous master was a Chinese nobleman who volunteered to act as tutor to the children of members of the Emperor's court. One day he displeased the Khan by reciting the true history of our land. For this reason his tongue was cut out so he could never say such truths again. Before that the Khan

177

had showed kindness to this noble because he was willing to humble himself by teaching the Mongol children. Then, suddenly, the Khan's demeanor changed. It is often so, I am told. As he grows old he becomes capricious and more the Mongol."

"Do you know why we may have to leave Cathay?"

Li-Huei paused to think before replying, and Diego admired the old man's diplomacy. "My lips are sealed, sire."

"My lady's life could depend on your secrecy, Li-Huei. Tell that to your relatives in this house and see they mark it well."

The winter was long and icy, with fierce winds, snow and insidious yellow mists. The snow lasted from the shortest day of the year to the White Feast of the New Year, which was held about one month before the start of the hunting season. On the day of the White Feast, Diego and Lotus Flower were invited to the palace to dine with the Khan and his noblemen. As they dressed in ceremonial white, Lotus Flower asked what she should do if the Emperor tried to arrange a tryst with her.

"I am troubled, my love. I know the Emperor's patience will soon come to an end."

"I shall not leave you, have no fear."

"But what if he insists that you leave me, Diego?"

"I had not realized that you were troubled by thoughts of the Khan. In future, when you are afraid, you must confide in me."

Lotus Flower sat down, resting her head on Diego's shoulder and looking sadly into his face. "The winter is almost over. Soon the Khan will depart for the hunting grounds and you will have to go with him. If he should return during your absence I shall be alone and unprotected. For days I have been thinking of this, and my mind has found no solution to the problem."

"I shall not go hunting with the Khan."

"You may be ordered to go."

"I shall plead infirmity."

"He will not believe you."

Diego walked to the window and watched Li-Huei's grandson shoveling snow into a pile against the wall. The winter was almost over, and he was glad that it was. He turned to Lotus Flower and told her what he had just learned from Ho Shan.

"Before the end of the hunting season my brother will sail home with our fortune to Venice. It is all arranged, and the Khan has given his permission because Pierluigi agreed to take with him gifts for the Pope and the cardinals of the Roman Church."

"And will your brother return to Cathay?"

"Never! Once the Mazzarini fortune is back in Venice, Pierluigi intends to build himself a new house near my own. Then he will marry."

"And the widow Li-Len will cry that she sees him no more."

"The widow is already tired of my brother. She has set herself to win young Marco Polo and has already given him lavish gifts."

Lotus Flower enjoyed such scandalous talk.

"Diego, Marco loves only himself and the sound of his voice. They say that he pauses before every mirror in the palace, and you know there are many, so that he can look at himself and preen. In my opinion the widow Li-Len will long for him in vain. But tell me what you plan for *our* safety after the departure of your brother."

Diego whispered, unwilling to entrust this secret to the servants' ears. "In the spring, one month and a half from now, we shall go to Shang-tu with the Khan's party as we have been invited. When we have been there for some time we shall make an excuse to return to Peking. Then we shall flee in a ship which I will order to wait for us on the coast."

"And where shall we sail?"

"We shall go to Burma, then to the Malabar Coast, where we shall stay until we have recovered from the voyage. Then we shall either go overland to Tabriz and Acre or we shall sail to Venice, if I can find a ship."

"Then I shall see your house with the yellow blossom." Suddenly the smile vanished from Lotus Flower's face and she spoke dispiritedly. "But what of now?"

"I will protect you, Lotus Flower, have no fear."

Members of the imperial court were dressed in white. The ceremonial hall was draped in silk, the Khan's dais in dia-
179

mond-studded velvet. As Diego and his wife made their obeisance before him, the Emperor smiled regally, eyeing the object of his longing with affectionate curiosity. The girl's face was unchanged but for a sparkle in the eye which had not been there before. Nights of passion had made Lotus Flower more lovely, more tempting and less childlike in her ways. The Khan's eyes followed as Lotus Flower glided gracefully at her husband's side, and he knew that the moment was near when he would possess her. The plan was made and could not be faulted.

The Emperor was bored by the tributes that were carried to his feet, gifts of gold and silver, ivory, camels, elephants and spices from all the lands of the East. Only the traditional offering of white mares thrilled his heart, and the Khan strode to the window, calling for his nobles to admire some of the animals as they were led around the courtyard. Then he called for the feasting to begin, and servants appeared bearing steaming dishes for his approval.

Diego and his brother sat on either side of Lotus Flower as though conscious of the need to protect her. She ate sparingly, her body tense because she could feel the Khan's gaze constantly upon her. It brought back unpleasant memories of the Shogun, and her heart fluttered painfully. Then, as the astrologers appeared, the Khan forgot her, leaning forward to listen intently to the forecasts.

How solemnly he waits, Lotus Flower thought, as if to hear something of great import. I hope it is not of me that he waits to hear, for I shall *never* love him. She looked apprehensively as Tai Cheng took to the floor.

Suddenly there was a hushed reverential silence while the Chinese made his prediction. "I see for you, sire, the culmination of a wondrous longing. At the moment of your triumph, thunder will roar in your ears and you will feel as you have never felt before. It will be soon, sire, very soon, and it is that for which you have waited many weeks."

The Khan's face was wreathed in smiles and he flushed like a young boy at the moment of first love. The culmination of his longing could mean only one thing. The Khan ordered his treasurer to reward Tai Cheng with gold.

The old man looked perplexed to be so suddenly dismissed. "Does my lord not wish to ask of the journey to Shang-tu?"

The Khan waved him away with a kindly nod. "You may leave the Imperial Palace and take with you your reward."

The astrologer bowed obsequiously, his face impassive, his voice gently reassuring. "I am honored that my humble prediction pleases the Omnipotence."

The Khan called to Diego to join him in an antechamber. The Venetian waited warily for the ruler to speak, his mind mulling over Lotus Flower's fears that he was about to be sent away. Handmaidens poured wine for the two men, then disappeared with seductive sidelong glances at the Venetian.

The Khan began by asking about Pierluigi's journey. "Is your brother ready to depart?"

"He is, my lord. He waits only the warmer weather and less unruly seas."

The Khan grimaced, and Diego saw a shudder pass through his body. "I do not care for the sea. It moves when it is not bidden and cannot be forced to obey. It is impossible to predict and often injurious to the health."

Diego smiled assent as the Khan continued.

"When your brother is gone, I invite you to join me in the hunting grounds."

"I thank you, my lord, but my wife is afraid to be left alone in Peking. I feel obliged to remain here to quiet the fears that still haunt her."

The Khan looked with pleasure at his rival's uneasy face, delighted to see that the Venetian feared being ordered to accompany him to the hunting grounds.

"My lady need have no fear. I shall post guards in the Street of the Almond Blossom so she can never again be molested."

Diego swallowed hard, unable to say that what his wife feared most was the Emperor's own lust.

The Khan prepared to spring his trap. "Perhaps it is best that I do not insist that you accompany me to the hunting grounds, Count Mazzarini. You would be absent for at least one month, and Lotus Flower would be discomforted. Instead, I ask but one indulgence which would keep you absent for only two or three days from the capital. I shall be at the hunting grounds with my nobles and unable to entrust the task to another."

"I agree, of course, my lord."

The Khan rubbed his hands gleefully. "I have need to collect a secret message from one of my spies in a remote area ten hours' ride from Peking. On the appointed day you will collect this message for me, Count Mazzarini, with a parcel which will contain a gift from a foreign power. That is all."

Relieved that he need be absent only for two or three days, Diego readily agreed. He began to tell the Khan of his plans for the summer in Shang-tu, though he knew he was planning to be en route to the Malabar Coast by the middle of the summer. However, as he wished the ruler to think him safely and happily a prisoner in Cathay, he continued to list his intentions. The ruler laughed uproariously as Diego described Giorgio's seasickness and the wife his servant had left behind. The Khan's eyes sparkled as Diego described Arya, and he wondered whether to send soldiers to capture a few of the women of that village who were as big as men and twice as strong.

At last the Emperor returned with his guest to the banqueting chamber. For an hour there was a demonstration by the court illusionist which pleased the Khan.

Diego begged permission to withdraw, and within minutes he and Lotus Flower were on their way home. As soon as they were clear of the palace grounds she asked, "What did the Khan ask of you?"

"He wished me to go with him to the hunting grounds."

"I knew he would insist upon it."

"At first he did. Then something changed his mind and he said I should stay here with you. He asks only that I absent myself from Peking for two days to collect a message from a place ten hours' ride from the capital."

Lotus Flower was silent as she struggled to work out the meaning of the Khan's action, but soon she understood. The Khan had threatened to make her husband absent himself from the capital on a long hunting trip so that Diego would readily agree to absent himself for two days. Lotus Flower wondered what the ruler planned for her during that brief

182

unprotected period. Then she tossed her head in defiance. She had outwitted the Khan before and she would do so again. She would *not* live constantly in fear of the Omnipotence. She asked Diego calmly if Pierluigi would stay in the house during his absence.

"If he is still in Peking, my brother will be happy to watch over you."

"I should be happy in his protection."

The days grew humid as the hunting season drew near, and those who lived in the capital spread wicker mats over their windows in an effort to keep out the damp mist. Ceiling ventilators were operated feverishly by servants, and ladies fluttered paper fans to make air where there seemed to be none. The trees came suddenly into leaf, and there was blossom everywhere in the streets of Peking. Flies buzzed around the heads of those who ventured out, and fleas bred in the poorer areas, spread through the city via markets and busy teahouses. The newly arrived beauty of spring was marred by the reappearance of the yellow mist, which lasted many weeks, obscuring views and trying all but the hardiest souls.

It was on such a morning that Lotus Flower woke to find Diego beckoning her to come and say goodbye to his brother. She put on a wrap and went shyly to the courtyard.

"Next time we meet, my lord Pierluigi, you will think me a fine lady of Venice."

"I should know you were a princess no matter where we met, my lady."

"And now you are leaving us?"

"I must take the new Mazzarini fortune home."

"You are young to have such a heavy responsibility, sire."

Pierluigi picked a frond of winter jasmine and handed it to Lotus Flower. "I am young, but in the years since my departure from Venice I have aged considerably in wisdom."

"And you will marry when you return to Venice?"

"If the lady is not spoken for I shall propose at once, my lady."

"What is her name?"

"She is called Renata di Francesco, my lady, the youngest sister of my best friend, Edouardo. When I was seven years old I vowed to wed Renata, and in truth I think my judgment was better then than later."

When his brother had gone, Diego felt suddenly lonely. He kept thinking of the dangers of the journey and wondering if Pierluigi would see Venice again. That thought provoked Diego to wonder if *he* would ever see La Serenissima again, and his longing for the city increased until it felt like an ache in the heart. Determined not to upset his wife by his ill humor, Diego left the house and walked aimlessly around the city. Here and there he paused to purchase gifts for Lotus Flower. Soon four small boys loaded with merchandise were following the Venetian's every move, and still he continued to buy. When he returned home he found an imperial messenger waiting for him in the garden.

Diego put his seal on the letter and dismissed the messenger. Then he called for Sanay and asked her to take the gifts to her mistress. Breaking open the parcel, Diego found a coded letter and a bronze tablet to wear around his neck giving him the Khan's authority. The instructions stated that he must leave at first light the following morning to pick up the message on behalf of the Khan.

Diego went inside the house to greet his wife, smothering her with kisses as he explained that he would leave that night, the sooner to be at his destination, the sooner to return. Lotus Flower realized that the moment she had feared for so long was here. But she concealed her anxiety and returned Diego's kisses eagerly.

"I shall be impatient for your homecoming, my husband, and I pray you will never leave me again."

"I promise that I shall not."

Pleased by that, Lotus Flower made her own promise. "I promise never to be parted from you."

Before the curfew Diego rode away, and Lotus Flower went to her room, where she lay longing for the dawn. The night was cold, and when she rose at first light her face was pale with exhaustion. She chose her clothes carefully. Then she powdered her face and rouged her cheeks to hide the telltale signs of tension. After a hearty breakfast, she called her servants together to receive their instructions. There was much hilarity when Lotus Flower explained what she wanted, and Li-Huei's laughter could be heard from the other side of the wall.

Throughout the morning Lotus Flower waited on the terrace, seated at her easel. She was painting the purple orchids at the far end of the garden and the reflection of water on the old stone wall. As she painted her fears receded, and by the time the bell rang and a familiar voice demanded admittance Lotus Flower was quite calm. She had formed a plan. All that was needed was the nerve and skill to carry the plan to its conclusion.

The Khan strode into the courtyard and through the arch into the garden, pausing to look approvingly at the peaceful scene with its willow trees and rippling fountain. He was surprised by the calm demeanor of the girl he had desired for so long and puzzled at the pleasure in Lotus Flower's face as she ran forward to greet him.

"I am honored that you deign to come to my humble home. My servants also are honored, for they revere you."

The Khan wondered if Lotus Flower realized why he had come to visit her. Was it possible she did not know he intended to ravish her? He received the members of Lotus Flower's staff, each of whom kowtowed to him. Then Li-Huei presented the Emperor with the gift of a rare plant in a lacquer bowl. The Khan looked in wonder at the single delicate flower with its pointed, starlike petals and heady perfume. As he touched a petal, pleased by the velvety texture that reminded him of a woman's skin, the sharp point of one of the gray, powdery leaves stabbed his finger.

The Khan hurried to put the plant down and, roaring with annoyance, called for a kerchief with which to absorb the blood from his scratch.

The Khan looked warily at Lotus Flower's dancing smile. "The flower is dangerous. It should not be given as a gift to the unsuspecting."

"It is beautiful and rare, my lord. A flower fit for an Emperor."

"It cut my imperial finger!"

"Often that which is lovely is also perilous, my lord."

The Khan eyed his companion with increasing admiration. Was she warning him not to touch her? He burst into peals of laughter, shaking his head ruefully because he was delighted by her audacity.

"The Ruler of Half the World is not afraid of beauty and the perils therein."

"Of course not, my lord. And now to business."

The Khan looked at Lotus Flower's face with something approaching apprehension, his mind racing to grasp her meaning. Had there ever been such a mystifying demon?

Lotus Flower continued calmly to pour wine for the ruler and to hand him green lime-sugar cakes, which she knew he adored.

"You are here, sire, because you wish to possess me. You have sent my husband away in a most devious fashion so you can approach me when I am without his protection. This is true, is it not?"

The Khan nodded. Lotus Flower sipped her tea and continued. "As I am a princess and also a virtuous wife, I cannot give myself to you. And as you are the Emperor, a revered and cultivated scholar and Ruler of Half the World, you cannot stoop to taking me by force like the heathen Shogun of Kyushu."

Lotus Flower paused to see what effect her words were having, pleased to note that the Khan was at least made speechless by her logic. "Therefore we must find a solution, my lord."

The Khan put down his goblet and struggled to voice his feelings. "Have you found any way for us to be together?"

"I have, my lord."

"How can it be accomplished?"

"You must buy my services for one hour and I must agree to sell myself to you. Tomorrow at noon is the time I have arranged. My price is the six pearls of the Shogun of Kyushu."

The Khan leapt to his feet, outraged by her cheek, flattered by her assessment of him and provoked to desperation that this was the only way that he could possess the woman he craved without incurring the Venetian's wrath. For a moment he stood towering above Lotus Flower, who continued calmly to sip her tea.

"Your price is high, higher than reason and any woman's worth!"

186

"Quite so, my lord. But that is my price."

"I shall not pay it."

"Then there is no solution. May I offer you more wine, my lord?"

"Enough of this comedy. I shall return at noon tomorrow."

The Khan rushed out of the house and through the garden, ignoring Li-Huei, who bowed as he passed. Lotus Flower rang for the servants to remove the sweetmeats and cups. Then she gave her instructions for the following morning. Li-Huei, who was still laughing at his mistress's nerve in giving the Emperor such a harmful gift, was puzzled by her words.

"By noon you must all be far from this house. Before you leave, you must open the secret gate in the far wall and tie my white horse near it. Not the horse the Khan gave me but the one I brought from Chagan Nor."

"Yes, my lady. But will the barbarian return?"

"I do not know his intentions. I must therefore be prepared to elude him, and I cannot answer for the consequences of his wrath if you and your family are still here."

Left alone, Lotus Flower thought hard about her predicament. She had gambled everything on the fact that the Khan would be unwilling to hand over the pearls, which he valued above all the riches in his kingdom. The gamble had been lost. Now she would have to make a plan to extricate herself from the trap she was in. Lotus Flower's first thought was to run away. This she rejected, because she knew it would result not only in her own execution but in Diego's and that of every member of the household. Her second thought was to surrender to the Khan in the hope that a brief dominance would satisfy him. But she knew she could not do it. Many hours later Lotus Flower formed a plan by which the Khan would seem to have been allowed a certain license but which would fall short of the culmination of his longing. She wondered how to execute her plan, admitting that she did not have the knowledge to bring it to fruition.

As dusk came to the city streets, Lotus Flower made her decision. Donning a cloak and mask of carved ivory, she made her way to the Suburb of the Prostitutes. As she was carried to the courtesan's residence, Lotus Flower wondered what the next hour would bring. She told herself there was no other way, that she must do what had to be done in order to protect herself and her family. Hsu Lan had offered help if ever it was needed. Lotus Flower hurried to the door of the House of Violets, praying the courtesan would remember her. She was admitted at once to Hsu Lan's presence.

The courtesan watched as Lotus Flower took off her mask. Then she walked in stately appraisal of her unexpected visitor, noting Lotus Flower's trembling hands, the ashen pallor of her face and the rapid rise and fall of her chest. The innocent one was afraid!

Hsu Lan spoke gently. "There is nothing to fear, my lady. I am your friend and will not speak of your visit to my home."

"You offered help if ever I should need it."

"I am at your disposal, my lady. No doubt you need my assistance desperately or you would not have risked your reputation by coming here."

The two women talked for an hour in secrecy. Then Lotus Flower accepted fine wine and delicate food from the courtesan. She saw nothing strange about being at ease in Hsu Lan's presence; her only concern was that her arrival in the area had been detected. Hsu Lan took care to reassure her visitor.

"When you leave this house my bearers will take you in a covered chair to the city center. There you must engage a public bearer who will carry you to your home. No one will know you have been here. On that you have my word. You did well to consult me, for no one else would have kept your secret."

"Thank you, my lady. I am indeed grateful to you for your kindness and your honesty."

Lotus Flower looked at the courtesan with sudden interest. "May I know *why* you are my friend? I have not lived long enough to know much of the world, but I do know that ladies of your world and of mine rarely meet and can never be friends."

Hsu Lan hesitated. Then she faced her visitor with a dazzling smile. "I am an admirer of your courage, my lady. Courage in a woman is something to be helped at every opportunity."

Satisfied by the reply, Lotus Flower rose to take her leave.

"I do not know how I can ever repay what you have done for me, my lady Hsu Lan."

"It is my pleasure and my honor to help you."

That night Lotus Flower slept contentedly, dreaming of Diego standing outside his Venetian mansion overlooking the lagoon.

On the far side of the city Hsu Lan also lay dreaming, though she was wide awake. She was remembering the day she had handed her newborn babe to its father, her first and only true love, Wen-Fai, Prince of the House of Sung. Again, she heard his words. "This child will be called Mo-ch'ou, which means 'Do not grieve,' and that is what I counsel you. The daughter born to my wife died a few days ago. As my lady has been in a long, unnatural sleep she does not know the child is dead and will never be told what I have done. She will therefore love this little one as her own, and I will love her because Mo-ch'ou is the only one of my children born of true love."

The Prince of the House of Sung had never returned to see his young mistress in the suburbs of Peking. Then Hsu Lan heard from a mutual friend that Wen-Fai's heart had been weakened by a rare illness. From that moment he could only walk a few steps in his garden. For years she had hoped to receive news of her daughter, but none had arrived, and in time Hsu Lan had tried to forget the sadness that haunted her every waking hour.

Now, sixteen years later, the rejected mistress had become the omnipotent courtesan, but still the mother longed for the child she had never known. Still she yearned to tell the secret she had kept for so long, but this she knew she could not do for the agony it would bring to her daughter. Hsu Lan went over her conversation with Lotus Flower, admiring the girl's courage and treasuring the confidences they had shared. It took wit and an iron nerve to dare to try to evade the Omnipotent persistence. With a cunning smile Hsu Lan thought of the draught she had given Lotus Flower. Then she prayed that all would go well and that her daughter would be safe from further unwelcome attentions.

At noon the Khan strode into the garden of the Sung house. He looked around to see if any of the servants were about. No one was there, only a clumsy piebald cart horse munching grass near the gate. The Khan patted the horse as he passed by. Then he hurried up the steps into the house. The Emperor was in a state of considerable excitement, and beads of perspiration dripped constantly from his chin. Impatiently he wiped himself with a silk handkerchief, and wandered around the house, wondering if Lotus Flower had escaped. He was about to return to the palace to order the arrest of all members of the Mazzarini staff and family when Lotus Flower drew back the doors of the salon and invited him to enter.

"I have sent my servants away. I thought you would prefer to meet me in private."

The Khan stared at the supple body outlined through a transparent robe of orange gauze. He marveled at the scent of the tiger lilies in Lotus Flower's hair and wondered if there was ever such a temptress. The Khan sat on the gilded couch and accepted a goblet of amber wine, which Lotus Flower told him was a rare aphrodisiac. He drank quickly, urging her to refill his glass again and again. Then, when his thirst was sated, he looked expectantly at Lotus Flower, wondering when the proceedings for which he had waited so long were to begin.

Lotus Flower held out her hand. "Are the pearls hidden about your Imperial Personage so I must search for them?"

Smiling at her cheek, the Khan took three pearls from a chamois purse, and handed them to Lotus Flower.

She rolled the pearls around her hand, looking sharply, questioningly at the Khan. "There are but three pearls here."

"You will receive the others after we have been united."

"And not before?"

"Certainly not before."

Lotus Flower skipped from the room, returning with a jeweled tambourine and some strands of scented ribbon which she placed on the ground. To the Khan's delight she began to dance a bell dance, tossing her heels and inclining her head this way and that until the watcher was mad with longing.

Then, grasping the tambourine and the ribbons, Lotus Flower whirled around and around the Emperor's figure, brushing her thighs against his body. She trailed the scented ribbons over his face and clashed the tambourines, startling him, until he was provoked to reach out for her, roaring with desire. He tore pieces of the orange gauze from wherever he could reach. The elusive figure continued to revolve, and the Khan shouted for Lotus Flower to disrobe.

Lotus Flower kept looking at the Khan's face, searching for signs of sleepiness, but there were none. The plan had gone wrong. The sleeping draught was not working! For a moment she was filled with panic. Unnerved, she slipped as the Khan caught hold of her leg and tore the flowing trousers that covered her. Lotus Flower gasped as the Khan snatched off the veils she had wound around her body to conceal her breasts. She was conscious of sweat pouring from every pore; her mouth became dry and she began to tremble. Her condition excited the Khan all the more, because he took her trembling for passion, her cries of fear for cries of abandon. With one sweep of the hand the Emperor tore off the remaining gauze veil and feasted his eyes on her nakedness.

With an effort, Lotus Flower rose and backed away from the Khan, taking a wrap from the chair as she made her way to the door. The Khan called for her return at once.

She replied, "I can go no further without the remainder of my payment."

The Khan threw the three pearls into her hands. Then, with surprising agility, he rose and, towering above her, removed the wrap. "It is time, my lady Lotus Flower. I have waited too long to love you."

Lotus Flower was surprised the Khan's touch was gentle and his breath scented with jasmine oil. Momentarily dazed by the horror of her unexpected predicament, she darted away, pursued by the Emperor, who was roaring like a lion and hurling his outer robes onto the floor. They ran around the room. Then Lotus Flower made for the door, knowing that this was her last chance to reach the horse that could take her to safety.

Suddenly the Khan grasped a cabinet for support, his eyes staring wildly at the walls, which seemed to be revolving around him. Loud noises like thunder bellowed in his ears and pain burned his chest. As he fell to the ground the Khan remembered the prediction of the Chinese astrologer. In the moment of fulfillment he was feeling as he never had before, but *not* as he had hoped to feel in the sublime hour of fruition. The

Khan's eyelids fluttered and he gave a long, trembling cry and fell unconscious at Lotus Flower's feet.

For a moment, Lotus Flower stood frozen in fear. Then she looked closely at the Khan, certain he was dead. Trembling uncontrollably, she debated what would happen to her and to Diego if poison was suspected. Forcing herself to think calmly, Lotus Flower raised the Khan's body to a sitting position. She put her ear to his chest and sighed with relief when she heard the beating of his heart. Then she ran to her room and dressed, hiding the torn veils and destroying the garland of tiger lilies. Returning to the salon, she removed all evidence of the nature of the meeting, wrapping the Khan's outer robe around his body and holding salts under his nose.

Her mind raced wildly. Had Hsu Lan given her something other than a sleeping draught? Was this a slow-acting poison? Lotus Flower was unaware that the courtesan had given her a draught guaranteed to raise the pressure of the blood, causing the Emperor's collapse. When the Emperor did not recover, Lotus Flower ran to a neighbor's house, begging the son to bring the physician. Returning to the salon, she poured away the remainder of the wine and replaced it with fresh wine after she had washed the flagon meticulously.

By the time the physician appeared, Lotus Flower was sitting primly on the terrace under a pink-flowered white silk parasol. She bowed respectfully to the physician and led him to the Emperor.

"My lord Kublai Khan came to visit me and fell ill shortly after his arrival."

The Khan struggled to hear the voices that sounded so far away. When he opened his eyes he saw Lotus Flower dressed in sugar pink, a white flower in her hair, a parasol in her hand. He shook his head in disbelief. Was it possible he was suffering from delusions? Where were the orange veils he had torn from her body and the lilies wreathed around her head? The Khan groaned in confusion, and the physician ordered that he should not be moved until a draught of distilled foxglove had been administered. A boy was sent to the apothecary, and within minutes the Khan had taken the medicine. Then the physician called the imperial bearers, ordering them to take the Emperor back to his palace.

When the physician had gone, Lotus Flower looked at the Khan and curtsied primly. She handed him the pouch containing the six pearls. "You must not forget these, my lord."

The Khan looked questioningly into the temptress's eyes. "They are yours now, my lady."

"No, my lord, they are still yours. Perhaps someday if your heart grows stronger we shall renew our acquaintance."

As the Khan was being carried back to the palace on a gilded litter, he saw Diego returning home.

He pulled the curtains hastily around himself and leaned back on the cushions, gasping. Was he too old for passion, too old for what he dreamed of doing? Anger made him breathless and disappointment made tears come to his eyes. He decided to send for a famous physician who lived in Manchuria and who was said to know the secret of preserving a man's virility. With luck, if he obeyed all the physician's instructions, he would be well and fit for all he sought to accomplish. Heartened by this resolve, the Khan closed his eyes and tried not to think how his chest was hurting.

Diego arrived at the house to find Lotus Flower sitting on the terrace. He paused to admire the pink and white of the parasol, the shimmer of the satin robe and the pleasure in her eyes.

"I am happy to be home, my lady."

"I have missed you, sire. Life is dull when you are not here."

They walked arm in arm to the salon, where Lotus Flower regaled her husband with stories of the lonely hours spent without him. She mentioned that the Emperor had visited the house but said that he had been taken ill shortly after his arrival. Diego listened to the quaint singsong voice, his heart full of love. As the sun waned and the day drew to its close, he thought of the night when he would lie at Lotus Flower's side, intoxicated by her caresses and the sweet scent of her body.

Lotus Flower smiled happily. She had played a dangerous game and won. It was possible that the game was not over, but for the moment she was safe. Soon she would be in the Venetian's arms, and he had promised never to leave her again. It was enough. The sacrifices of the afternoon had been worth every moment of fear and apprehension.

At the Imperial Palace, doctors were puzzled by the Emperor's illness. Some thought he had been poisoned. Others were sure his heart was damaged. The Khan glowered at the physicians and sent them away, preferring to suffer his pain in solitude. It would take months for him to be well, on that all the advisers were agreed. The Khan was angry at his predicament. Soon his spies would report rumors of invasion, of civil disobedience and unrest. It was always so whenever he was indisposed.

As night fell, the Khan made a decision. He would send Diego and his wife away so he would not have to suffer the tempting proximity of the lady Lotus Flower. He would send the couple to Hangchow, where Diego could negotiate new trade treaties, and visit Yangchow, Ch'uanchou and other ports in the kingdom, inspecting the new ships being built for the Khan's navy. The Venetian would know how to advise the Khan about his navy, and the period apart from Lotus Flower would give him time to recuperate. Then, when spring came again to the capital, he would visit the Sung house and love the exquisite one as she had never been loved before. Resolved, the Khan ordered the Manchurian physician to be sent for with all speed. Then he slept, his chest a mass of pain, his dreams full of women with emerald eyes and devious ways.

Chapter Ten:

Hangchow

\

Hangchow, once the capital of China, was surrounded by water, with a river on one side, a lake on the other and the sea beyond. The streets were paved with stone kept scrupulously clean by the public authorities. The main squares housed thrice-weekly markets, and there were many bridges to provide passage over the interlacing canals. The canals were full of barges loaded with merchandise en route to Chamba, Malaya and India. Copper, silver, lead, tin and the renowned brocade of Hangchow were exported, rare woods, ivory, camphor, incense and cardamom brought in.

The people of Hangchow were cultured and friendly, and to the visitor there were marked contrasts at every turn with the Mongol capital, Peking. In Hangchow citizens hurrying to and from the public bathhouses took pride in their appearance. In Peking, lice-covered peasants rid themselves of their infestations by eating the insects that bit them. Hangchow's pleasure gardens were full of men and women enjoying the beauty of the lake, a meal on one of the pleasure craft or a tryst in a blossom-covered retreat. Peking's gardens were full of male courtesans, vice-ridden aristocrats and women of doubtful reputation. The pursuit of perfection was inherent in the heart of every resident of Hangchow. In Peking the Mongols admired only killing, drinking and horsemanship, and considered those who lived in the former capital foolishly cerebral, weak and given to decadent pursuit.

Diego liked Hangchow because it reminded him in many ways of Venice. Often he walked alone to watch the sunrise or to enjoy the freedom, the beauty and the gentleness of the city of artists and scholars. Whenever he remembered Peking, he thought of the barbaric splendor of the court and the stifling atmosphere that pervaded the very air of the capital. The Venetian and Lotus Flower enjoyed their lives in Hangchow, far from the watchful eye of the Khan. They were happy to stay in the city until the time came to leave China, though they had no idea if they would be allowed to follow their desire.

On one particular morning, Diego rose at dawn and made his way toward the shipyards. The inhabitants of Hangchow, who rose as early as four or five, were already hard at work. Monks walked the streets calling the weather: "the sky is clear, it will be a wondrous fine day." The aroma of breakfast delicacies sold by vendors along the Imperial Way filled the air and Diego sniffed the tempting smells of fried tripe, hot pancakes, steamed mutton and goose. He passed the vegetable market, already a hive of activity, and the crab market on the banks of the river, which bustled with servants, vendors and children watching the proceedings with eyes full of wonder.

Diego quickened his step. Today he would be told when the ship he had ordered for his escape would be ready. It was the eighth month of the year, a few days before the celebrations of the Khan's birthday far away in the palace of Shang-tu. After the feasting the Omnipotence would return to Peking, as was his custom, and Diego knew he would be called there to give an account of the progress on the vessels being built for the Khan's new navy. Diego had decided to leave China before he received the Khan's summons, because he knew there could be no useful purpose in returning to Peking. He was sure the Emperor's desire would in no way have diminished, and further contact with Lotus Flower could only breed danger. But what of the ship he had ordered? Summer in the province of Manzi had been unusually hot, with constant humidity. The weather conditions had slowed work on the ship, and only in the last seven days had the workmen returned to their duties. Each morning Diego went to see how the work was progressing, to encourage the owner of the yard and to reward particularly keen craftsmen. As he neared the yard Diego looked down, happy to see how close to completion the ship was.

The owner met Diego with a bow and a polite greeting. Then, looking cautiously from side to side, he begged the Venetian to take tea with him. Once inside the privacy of his office the shipbuilder closed the door and checked that no one was loitering below the window. Then he spoke to Diego in a grave voice.

"My lord, I must tell you that something strange has happened. I hope you will be able to throw light on the matter."

Diego saw that the owner's hands were trembling and that his face was unusually pale.

The shipbuilder continued apologetically, "This morning when I rose at the fourth bell, I noticed men walking around your ship, inspecting it and making diverse comments."

"Who were these men?"

"One was from Cathay. The others were Mongols, spies in the pay of the Khan, of that I have no doubt."

Diego's face betrayed nothing of the inner turmoil he felt. "Did you approach these men?"

"I did, sire, and they informed me that the Emperor had been told by his astrologers that his favorite woman would be spirited away from him by sea. So the Khan sent riders to inspect every boatyard in the city and to inquire the name of any man who has ordered a ship capable of riding the waves of the deep green ocean. He also wishes to know of anyone who has purchased such a vessel or who might have inquired about buying an existing vessel. Only five new ships

197

are being built at this moment, sire, yours and the others for the Khan. No one else has attempted to purchase a seagoing vessel, and so the Mongols requested your name and the particulars of your residence."

Diego sighed, despair filling his mind. The gamble he had taken was lost. Once the Khan knew *he* had ordered a seagoing vessel he would be arrested. Diego was relieved to hear the owner reassuring him.

"I told the Mongols that the man who ordered this vessel was a foreign merchant from Yunnan. I gave his address in Hangchow as the Street of the Jewelers' Guild. Then I sent one of my sons with a message to friends in that area. If the spies inquire for this merchant they will be told that he is away from the city, traveling around the province of Manzi."

The owner poured more tea for Diego and handed him an opium pill. "Do not worry, sire. In the province and especially here in the city of Hangchow we have little love for the Mongol. Indeed, some of us dream of rebellion, and I personally have longings to inflict the death of a thousand cuts on Kublai Khan. I have lied for you, thus placing myself at risk. Will you now enlighten me as to the reason for this inquiry? Why does the Khan seek you? Why does he wish to prevent your leaving his country, and who is this woman for whom he craves?"

Diego walked to the window and looked at the ship which would take him and his wife to freedom. Then he turned to the owner and confided his situation.

"The Emperor is besotted with my wife, my lady Lotus Flower. He desires her and is unwilling to consider the possibility of being denied. My wife is the daughter of Wen-Fai, Prince of the House of Sung. As a child she was forced into exile with her family, but before our marriage the Khan deigned to restore her title and all her lands. He has also been generous to me and to my family. Now I fear he grows impatient to love Lotus Flower, and no doubt he consults the astrologers frequently. For him, the future is interesting only if it hastens the fulfillment of his desire. That is our situation. That is why I ordered this ship from you. It is my intention to return in it to my homeland with my wife. If the ship is not ready I will be taken prisoner by the Khan and my wife will be at his pleasure."

The owner sighed at Diego's predicament. "The barbarian can no more alter his ways than a dog can change his bark, sire. You have done well to make plans for your escape, and I shall endeavor to assist you in every way. Today I will engage more workers and within fourteen days your ship will be ready for the ocean."

Diego bowed his acknowledgment of the builder's cooperation. "I shall owe you my life, sir, and that of my wife."

"I shall honor that which you entrust to me, Count."

Despite the shipbuilder's reassurance, Diego left the yard full of foreboding, his mind wrestling with the thought of what would happen if the Mongol spies questioned the workmen in the yard. What if a description of the "merchant" were given? Diego knew that their stay in Hangchow must end as quickly as possible, that at any moment he and Lotus Flower might have to escape to avoid arrest. He pondered how to tell his wife what had happened.

As he passed through the busy thoroughfare, Diego continued to wrestle with his problem, pausing outside a tea house to watch a group of wealthy merchants who were learning to play musical instruments. How peaceful the city seemed, despite the Mongol garrison at its gates, how far removed from the spy-ridden deviousness of the capital. Yet here too there were spies in the pay of the Khan, searching, inquiring, threatening his safety and that of Lotus Flower. At the corner of the street, Diego saw a young man in the leg stocks being pelted with eggs for throwing household refuse in the crystal-clear waters of the lake. For a moment he forgot his troubles and enjoyed watching the gleeful faces all around. In a tree-lined square, a traveling theater company was performing a comedy and loud hilarity greeted the actors' every move. Diego thought of the actors in the Venetian theaters and longed fervently for his home. As he skirted the lake he saw, in a shady courtyard, a courtesan walking in her garden, picking a peach and yawning languorously.

Diego sat on a bench and looked out on the shimmering water, working out plans for their escape and trying out ways to tell Lotus Flower what she must be told. Finally he decided to tell his wife the truth, as was his custom. There was nothing to be gained by trying to lessen the blow. Satisfied that he had made the best decision, Diego hurried on down the Street of the Green Ferns, surprised to find the gate of his house open and horses in the courtyard. Hurrying inside, he came face to face with Giorgio, who was followed closely by Ho Shan. Both men looked troubled. As the Venetian hurried inside the house Giorgio explained, "Ho Shan arrived in Hangchow at dawn, shortly after you left for the shipyard, sir. He has been riding like a Mongol and suffering on that accursed river for days."

Diego clasped the former spy to his chest. "I am happy to see you, Ho Shan."

"And I you, sire."

"Tell me what you know."

"In Peking the Emperor was told by one of his astrologers that his beloved was about to escape from the kingdom. For days he was demented, sire, and the astrologer fled to the hills for fear of losing his life. As you know, the Khan's love for my lady Lotus Flower is the subject of much gossip in the capital. I hope it will not enrage you if I presume to speak of such matters."

Diego bowed his assent.

"When he had considered the prediction, sire, the Khan sent men to Hangchow to find out who might abduct my lady. I persuaded the spies to let me join them on their journey, and here I am. When the Mongols arrived in the city they first visited the two shipyards. It did not take long to check the vessels being built, because in the eighth month there is little such activity."

Diego led Ho Shan to the salon where Lotus Flower was waiting. The spy continued his account.

"The ships being built here are for the Khan, except one which is for a foreign merchant. There are no others in Hangchow who could brave the oceans of the edge of the world."

"And what of the merchant?"

"The spies did not believe the shipbuilder's statement, sire. They intend to return to the yard when they have checked what he said. Then, if he lied, he will be arrested and tortured until he tells them who *really* ordered the other ship. I know from Giorgio that it is you, sire, and I beg you to tell me how I can help you."

Diego was silent. Then, seeing Ho Shan's distress, he revealed his plans. "I am indeed awaiting a ship which will take us all back to Venice. Its interior is not yet complete, so it is not yet ready for the far reaches of the ocean."

Ho Shan paced the room uneasily. "The Mongols intend to destroy your ship, sire. If they do not find the merchant about whom the builder spoke, they will damage the ship so no one can use it."

"I must go at once and warn the shipbuilder of the spies' intentions."

"You cannot go there, sire. The Khan's men are all around the yard."

"How can I tell him what he must know?"

"Leave it to me. I can go there without suspicion."

"I owe you a great deal, Ho Shan."

"You have given me back my self-respect, sire. The debt is long repaid."

"Eat with us before you leave, my good friend."

Shellfish cooked in rice wine, goose with apricots and fruit in peach liquor were served to the silent assembly.

Lotus Flower picked at her food, troubled by the news and preoccupied by the secret she had been keeping from her husband. She had been told that she was expecting a child, good news for one who longed to be a mother but unwelcome in the light of what had happened. Thoughts of a voyage to the other side of the world made Lotus Flower apprehensive, but the consequences of remaining in China were too terrible to consider. She ate what she could, holding herself erect and smiling graciously as Ho Shan struggled to make conversation.

Within the hour, Ho Shan was on his way to the boatyard, and Lotus Flower rested contentedly in Diego's arms. The sun shone brightly through the paper-thin blinds, lighting the room with flickering gold patterns.

Lotus Flower kissed Diego's cheek and snuggled against his chest. "Do you know how long our journey will take?"

"Many weeks, perhaps months. There is no way to tell what the sea will do."

"Shall we always be in sight of land?"

"For much of the way we shall, but not when we cross the uncharted ocean to the Malabar Coast."

"I would rather we were always in sight of land."

Diego smiled at her fears. Then, sensing that Lotus Flower was close to tears, he studied her face and said, "You were not afraid before when I spoke of the voyage."

"Then everything was different."

"How was it different?"

"*I* was different."

"How were you different?"

"I was alone. Now I have a companion who must travel with me on the perilous seas, and I fear we may never reach Venice."

Diego crushed Lotus Flower to his chest, as understanding filled him with love. The voyage would have to be postponed. Diego did his best to conceal his apprehension. Rising, he took a gift from the ebony cabinet, knelt at her side, and handed it to her.

"I bought this a few days ago, intending to give it to you to celebrate the anniversary of your birth," he explained.

"Are you not angry at my news?"

"I am without doubt the happiest man in the world."

Lotus Flower threw her arms around Diego's neck and hugged him. Then she unwrapped her gift, a gold chain on which diamonds shaped like stars glittered in profusion. Diego fastened the chain about her neck and lay cradling his wife in his arms, stroking her head.

"What are we to do about the Khan's spies?" Lotus Flower asked anxiously.

"We shall change our plan and leave in the springtime of next year. In the meantime we must outwit those who seek to harm us. On Ho Shan's return I will ask him to ride with a message for the Omnipotence."

"What will the message say?"

"You will write it at my dictation, my lady."

Lotus Flower laughed with delight, leaping up and hurrying to bring her brush and pot of ink wash. Diego spoke solemnly as his wife painted the strokes, pausing now and then to smile at his cunning.

My lord Kublai Khan, Emperor of China, Ruler of Half the World. I am writing to tell you my glad tidings so you will be the first to know my news. I am with child and will be delivered by the time the hunting season comes, in the days of the almond blossom. The physician has forbidden me to travel, so I shall be unable to return home for the New Year Feasting. I beg you to make offerings on my behalf. Please also send me a message to reassure my fears, caused by the news that you believe I am about to be abducted. I appeal for your protection, noble lord, and put my trust in your Omnipotence. In obeisance and trembling, your subject Lotus Flower, Princess of the House of Sung, Contessa Mazzarini.

A flower decorated the scroll, a seal closed it.

Then, as Lotus Flower looked questioningly at Diego, he explained, "If the Khan thinks you cannot travel he will be reassured, and as you have begged his protection, he will surely give it."

"But he will send soldiers to guard me, and I will never be able to escape."

"He may send soldiers. He will certainly inform the garrison of Mongols in Hangchow that you are a special person of privilege who must be looked after like a queen."

Lotus Flower waited expectantly, but Diego remained silent. Then, seeing her impatience, he explained the significance of his strategy. "If the Khan's men are guarding you, he will be satisfied that little harm can come to you and will settle for waiting for you to return to Peking."

"But how can we escape from the Khan's kingdom if we are watched at every hour of the day by a thousand eyes?"

"We shall not attempt to escape. We shall remain here in Hangchow until the start of the hunting season, enjoying a quiet life and awaiting the birth of our child."

"Then what?"

Diego led Lotus Flower to the garden, and together they

sat on a marble seat, watching butterflies flutter about the maple leaves.

"When we tell the guards of our intention to return to Peking they will accompany us, traveling a short distance ahead as is their custom. We shall follow with the servants and sail up the Yangtze River."

"*Across* the Yangtze River?"

"Across the river leads to Yangchow, Sulsien and eventually to Peking. We shall sail *up*river to the sea."

Understanding made Lotus Flower gaze at Diego with eyes full of admiration. "Is it really possible to escape so easily, my love? Will the Khan's soldiers not follow us?"

"The Mongols are the greatest horsemen in the world, but we Venetians are the greatest seamen. We shall escape, believe me. The ship will be ready-provisioned, and we shall take on water at Zaiton. I have thought of everything. Then we shall sail in peace through the dark-green seas."

"What shall we see on our voyage?"

"We shall see the Southern Provinces of China, then the wilds of Chamba and the island of Sumatra, where birds can be taught to speak like men. We shall cross a mighty ocean and come, with God's help, to the Malabar Coast, where we shall rest awhile before continuing our journey."

Lotus Flower kissed Diego's hands and looked dreamily into his eyes. "If I could command the days to pass quickly I should do so, but I fear they will pass like a snail along a wall."

"We have many things to do before our departure. I think I can promise that you will not notice the time dragging."

When Ho Shan arrived with Giorgio at the shipyard, the Khan's spies looked with interest at their comrade's swarthy companion. They drew near and began to question Ho Shan about the identity of the stranger. As arranged, Giorgio walked away from the group on the pretense of examining the ships. When he was far enough away from the spies the owner drew near to speak with him and Giorgio was able to hand him a note written by Ho Shan. Then he sauntered back to the group, bowing and nodding affably to the puzzled Mongols.

Having perused the contents of the note, the shipbuilder

gave instructions to his foreman and his brothers, who were in the wharfside office. Then he disappeared with a crew of seamen he had just engaged. Distracted by Giorgio's presence, the Mongols did not notice the shipbuilder's departure.

Ho Shan explained to Diego's servant what he had told the Mongol spies. "They think you are the merchant's servant, and I have offered to question you."

Giorgio nodded and sat eagerly on the ground. The spies grouped around him as Ho Shan began the "interrogation." Not understanding a word of the Chinese language, Giorgio answered in his own tongue, and the Mongols, not understanding a word of the Venetian dialect, turned helplessly to Ho Shan for a translation. Ho Shan looked resolutely at his Venetian friend and then back to the group.

"This servant says his master has gone on a mission to Foochow. And this fellow was left behind to tell the shipbuilders he no longer wants the vessel they have begun to build."

The spies discussed this puzzling piece of information, arguing among themselves about what should be done. Finally, their leader decided that he and a chosen lieutenant should leave at once to report to the Emperor in Peking. The other spies would be left to keep watch on the shipyard and to wait for the return of the foreign merchant. Ho Shan bowed gravely and wished them safe journey. Then he dismissed Giorgio, urging him to return to the Mazzarini home as soon as possible. Once Giorgio had departed, Ho Shan walked around the boatyard, pausing here and there as though to examine something of importance. He made a pretense of scrutinizing some scrolls in the boatbuilder's office, and for a while the spies watched him closely. Then they grew bored and adjourned to a nearby tavern. When Ho Shan was sure they were paying him no further heed he hurried back to Diego's house.

Diego was pleased with the news. Ho Shan, who agreed readily to deliver Lotus Flower's letter to the Emperor, was invited to spend the evening. As they were dining, a message was delivered from the shipbuilder. Ho Shan read it to Diego.

My lord Count Mazzarini. My humble thanks for the warning which you sent me. I am leaving the city at once with my family. We shall sail in your ship up the coast to the yard of my brother in Changchow, where work on its interior will be completed. When it is safe for me to return to Hangchow, I trust I shall receive some sign from you. In the meantime, I am your ally and, I beg to hope, your most respectful friend, Chen-Yu.

Giorgio chortled joyfully at the thought of the Mongols returning from the tavern and finding the vessel vanished, the shipbuilder gone and the yard they had been ordered to watch deserted. The three men talked until the middle of the night, forming plans and exchanging information about the Emperor's activities. Then Diego retired, leaving Ho Shan and Giorgio to sleep in the servants' quarters.

The following day, Ho Shan began the journey back to Peking. He was content that he had been able to do the Venetian a favor and hopeful that it would not be the last.

At the beginning of the twelfth month of the year an imperial messenger arrived in Hangchow with a casket containing one of the famous pearls as a gift for Lotus Flower. The messenger also delivered a scroll written by the imperial calligrapher: "To Count Mazzarini and his lady, the Princess Lotus Flower. The Emperor Kublai Khan, Lord of the Mongol Horde, Ruler of Half the World, sends this gift in friendship and to express his Omnipotent pleasure at the news you have sent him."

When Diego questioned the messenger about the Khan's health he was surprised by the man's reply.

"The Khan seems suddenly young again, my lord. Some say it is due to the influence of a physician brought from Manchuria. After the Emperor's last illness some feared for his life, but now he is reborn."

"What manner of man is this physician?"

"He is a tyrant, sire, who gives orders to the Khan as no other would dare. I swear you would not believe your eyes if you were to witness the indignities the Emperor suffers in recovering his well-being."

"What regime has the physician set?"

"He forbids certain foods, sire, even koumiss, which the Khan drank at every hour of the day before this physician appeared. He forces the Khan to exercise as if he were a young lad and to ride three hours each evening as well. They say it is to make his heart strong, and surely the plan is working."

Lotus Flower listened uneasily. If the Khan was reborn and as fit as a lad she would do well to stay away from him. She begged leave to retire and withdrew from the room.

Innocent of her concern, the messenger continued, "As you know, sire, the Khan had ceased to use the concubines for fear of damaging himself. Now he tires them all so they cannot stay awake, and the hundred virgins newly arrived as well. He is indeed miraculously changed, sire. I wish I knew the physician's secret so I could train myself in a similar fashion when I am old."

Lotus Flower crept to her bedroom, her eyes wide with alarm. The Khan's body was renewed! Memories of the past flickered through her mind, troubling her. Then she looked at herself in the polished shell mirror, noting her thickening waist. She patted her body, happy that the child for which she longed had saved her from being forced to return to Peking. When the cherry blossom bloomed and birds sang their spring song, she would give birth to their baby. Then she and her loved ones would escape to a land far away, a land no Mongol would ever see. As she daydreamed about Venice, Lotus Flower took out the miniature she had found long ago on the cave floor. She touched the portrait of Diego's mother with her finger and looked again at the painting of the Mazzarini palazzo. Her heart pounded with excitement as she thought of entering the house for the first time. She wondered wistfully if she might appear strange in the eyes of the Venetian's servants as they would seem strange to her. She debated whether she would adopt Venetian dress, but rejected the idea because she knew her husband loved her as she was.

When she had robed herself for the night, Lotus Flower walked to the window to look out on the moonlit garden. She was startled to see a shadowy figure dodging behind a tree. Looking more closely, she saw the silhouette of a man and knew that someone was watching the house from within its walls. Terrified, she ran back to the salon and told Diego what she had seen.

"There is a man in the garden, my lord. I saw only his shadow, but I know he is there. Who can he be? I fear he is a heathen come to abduct me!"

Diego ran from the house to the garden. Lotus Flower returned to her room, where she paced back and forth in fear and turmoil. First she hid the pearl given her by the Khan in a bowl of white jade roses. Then she knelt and prayed at the shrine near her bed. A sudden draft made her turn, and as she did she saw a man standing by the window. She recognized him as a Mongol from the Khan's imperial guard.

Backing away from the intruder, she made an effort to speak in a firm voice. "You have no right to be here. You must leave at once or it will be to your peril."

The Mongol advanced and, grasping Lotus Flower by the hair, whispered menacingly, "Give me the pearl the Khan sent you or I shall call men to kill your husband."

Struggling to free herself from his grasp, Lotus Flower tried to discover if the man was alone, or working with others who could kill her husband. The intruder's hands tightened around her neck, and Lotus Flower screamed a warning to Diego. Then she fell unconscious to the ground.

Diego drew his sword and ran into the house. He saw that the thief was holding a net in one hand, a ball of spiked iron on a chain in the other. As the Mongol swung the weight, Diego lunged forward, dodging death by inches. Overturning furniture, he pursued the thief. The two men battled furiously, and the sound of crashing steel woke the servants, who came running to see what could be done.

Soon, blood was pouring from Diego's shoulder and from the Mongol's side. Still they stalked each other, hate making them fearless as they tried desperately to kill. The imperial messenger stood watching helplessly on the terrace. Then, as the Mongol turned his back on the garden, the messenger took a chance and crashed a bronze urn on the intruder's skull, felling him with one blow.

Wiping the blood from his face, Diego ran to Lotus Flower's side. His face paled as she moaned and clenched her fists in agony. Returning to the terrace, Diego called for Li-Huei to go at once for the physician. When he had instructed the messenger to tie the intruder's hands and feet, Diego returned to his wife's side and lifted her gently onto the couch. Then he waited silently for the physician to arrive.

Through the long night vigil, Diego remained alone in his room, finding strength in prayer. As he waited, he remembered all the happy times he and Lotus Flower had spent together and vowed there would be many more if only she would live. The physician came often to report what was happening, reassuring the Venetian that he was making every effort to save Lotus Flower's life.

"The child is lost, my lord, and there will be no more. But my lady fights like a tiger for her life, and, with the indulgence of the gods, I believe I can save her."

Dawn came, lighting the sky with yellow. Diego knelt again to pray, his face looking up at the heavens, as if to question God himself about the unfairness of what had happened. In the distance, the city came to life with a faint hum of human activity, and outside the wall monks called the weather. The physician appeared at last, and Diego sighed in relief that he was smiling.

"My lady is saved, sire. She wishes to see you at once. I beg you say nothing of what I have told you, for she is severely disquieted by her loss."

"I thank you with all my heart for what you have done, doctor."

"I shall return later, Count Mazzarini."

Lotus Flower opened her eyes and saw Diego kneeling at her side, holding out a bunch of butterfly orchids. She took the flowers and sniffed them, struggling to find words to comfort her husband.

"I am feeling well, Diego, and soon I shall be as strong as ever I was. The physician promised it."

"Of course you will. You are young, and the young mend easily."

"And I shall have more children for you someday."

"Of course you will, my dearest."

Suddenly Lotus Flower's eyes filled with tears and she sobbed with pent-up grief. "I shall never have another child.
209

I heard the physician talking to his nurse. He thought I was asleep, but I heard everything he said. I am destroyed, my lord, I fear I shall never smile again."

Diego gathered her into his arms, holding her so tightly she gasped, and told her, "You are the one I love, you are the one I cannot be without. If we are not to be blessed with children, so be it. We must accept the will of God with good grace. For my part, I care only that you are by my side."

"I love you, and I shall never stop loving you."

"Try to sleep now, dearest. I shall stay at your side until the physician returns."

Lotus Flower closed her eyes and fell instantly asleep. The Venetian watched her, noting the flush in her cheeks and the uneven rise and fall of her chest. As he guarded his wife, Diego thought of the plans they had made for the future, the hopes they had had for their child. But, he thought defiantly, all that mattered was for Lotus Flower to recover her health. If he could not provide an heir for the Mazzarini title his brother would surely do so. As Diego thought of the baby that had been lost, he wiped tears from his eyes. Then he bent over the bed and kissed Lotus Flower's burning forehead. Bathing her face with rose water, he whispered endearments though she could not hear them, because he could not resist telling her how much he adored her.

When the physician returned, Diego joined the imperial messenger for lunch. The two men barely spoke at first, so drained were they by the events of the previous night. When the meal was over, Diego dictated a message to be given to the Emperor:

My Lord Kublai Khan, Emperor of China, Ruler of Half the World: It is with a heavy heart that I inform you of the illness of my wife, the lady Lotus Flower. She thanks you for the generosity which prompted you to send her one of the pearls taken from the Temple of Shiatsutu. Sadly, the gift brought with it a villain who sought to steal the gem. The thief now lies in your imperial prison in Hangchow. As a result of his attack, my lady has lost the child we hoped to present to you on our return to Peking.

210

My Lord, you alone will understand my feelings. I trust that you will be able to ascertain the origin of this villainy and that you will send no further valuables to provoke damage on my lady's person. I remain, your obedient servant, Diego Mazzarini, Count of the Venetian Empire.

Within a month, Lotus Flower was able to rise from her bed. There was snow on the ground, so she could not sit in the garden. Instead Diego ordered Li-Huei to plant a miniature garden of jasmine and evergreens in the inner courtyard of the house. There, warmed by braziers and covered with quilts, Lotus Flower recovered from the loss of her child.

Often she and Diego talked of their first meeting in the wilds of Chagan Nor, and their laughter could be heard all over the house as Lotus Flower described the Khan's awe on first seeing the Venetian. As she grew stronger, Diego took to walking with his wife in the garden. There he pointed out the icy splendors of winter, the frozen fountain glittering in the sun, the trees heavy with snow, the hungry birds fluttering along the pathway. As they walked, Diego talked of the imminent journey, thrilling Lotus Flower, who was as impatient as ever to leave China. Sometimes, to restrain her desire to leave at once, Diego would discuss her favorite subject, the house by the sea in Venice.

"Tell me more of the house where we shall live."

"I have told everything I know of my home and still you ask for more."

"Tell it all again, for I love to hear it."

"Will you never tire of my tales?"

"I shall want them until the day I see Venice for myself. As I listen to you I imagine I am already there. I am *so* impatient for the journey to commence. In the last few days I have thought of nothing else."

The winter was cold and traffic to and from Hangchow had almost ceased. It was rumored that the River Yangtze had frozen, and merchants grumbled that food supplies would soon be frozen too. It was therefore a shock to Diego one bright chilly day to hear that a visitor was demanding admittance to the house.

Lotus Flower covered her body with another quilt, and puzzled by the insistent clanging of the bell, asked, "Who can it be? We have invited no one. And why does he ring the bell in such an unmannerly fashion?"

"No doubt we shall soon know the name of this vulgar fellow."

At that moment the Khan strode into the room. Diego bowed low. Lotus Flower's cheeks flushed with shock. And the Khan, looking down on her, observed the signs in her face that still hinted of her recent brush with death. His heart contracted with pity, and he knew then that he loved Lotus Flower more than anything in the world and that he always would.

Courageously, Lotus Flower struggled to welcome the Omnipotence in a suitable fashion. "My lord, forgive my appearance. I am not yet strong enough to emerge from my winter wrappings, but I bid you welcome to our home."

Diego placed a couch at the Khan's disposal. "I am deeply honored to see you, my lord."

"You look tired, Count Mazzarini. Obviously the foul air of Hangchow does not suit you."

Diego thought of the humid air of Peking but did not argue with the Emperor's statement.

"And you, my lord, seem ten years younger than when we last had the honor of meeting you."

The Khan beamed at the compliment.

"I am rejuvenated by a new physician who comes from Manchuria. He is a cruel fellow, unused to the kindness of my cultivated ways. Indeed, when first he treated me I thought to have his head for the pains he gave me with his regimes. But now I see his is truly the way to well-being, and I have rewarded him with a fine estate."

Lotus Flower smothered a laugh at the Khan's rouged cheeks. Was it possible the Emperor was as young inside as his outer appearance suggested? Or was the transformation due to the use of paint and powder by an expert cosmetician?

The Khan looked meaningfully at Lotus Flower and said, "I shall be relieved when you are home again in Peking, my lady. The province of Manzi is a lawless place which even I cannot control. In the last year four of the six attempts on my life were made by natives of Hangchow. I have debated whether to raze the city to the ground and annihilate the inhabitants, but I fear such an action would only bring more trouble."

Diego inquired about the Mongol thief who had caused such sadness in his home.

The Khan dismissed the question with a flicker of the eyelids and a wave of the bejeweled hand. "He is dead, of course, as are his conspiring friends, three officers of my imperial guard. Their heads now blacken on the spikes outside the city wall as a lesson to anyone foolish enough to consider such audacity. I fear it took them long to die. My sleep was disturbed for nights because of their ignominious wailing. Sometimes I ask myself why I must suffer so, but such is the price of greatness which cannot be avoided."

Servants appeared with scented water, and the Khan washed his hands. Lotus Flower ordered sugar cakes, preserved fruit and candied rose petals, which she knew the Omnipotence loved. And all the while the Khan gazed in admiration at her beauty. Then Lotus Flower inquired the reason for the Khan's visit, and the Emperor rose and postured before her, his scarlet cloak billowing out as he made dramatic gestures.

"I came in answer to your request for protection, my lady. My conscience troubled me that I had failed you and that as a result of my failure you have suffered a grievous loss. Suddenly, I knew what I must do."

"To have traveled so far in these harsh days of winter was more than kind, my lord. I am touched by your concern."

The Khan bowed, his face glowing with pleasure. Then he turned to Diego. "And you, Count Mazzarini, will you now be able to show me the ships of my new navy? How goes the work?"

"Slowly, sire, but I shall be honored to show what progress has been made. Two of the ships are complete and the others almost so."

A sudden premonition made Lotus Flower speak. "How long will you stay in Hangchow, my lord?"

The Khan looked at her keenly, grinning as he revealed the true reason for his arrival. "I shall stay until you and
213

Count Mazzarini are ready to travel. It is my intention to bring you *personally* back to Peking with an escort of the imperial bodyguard."

Lotus Flower was stunned to silence, so Diego spoke up to distract the Khan's attention. "My lady will not be able to travel for at least a month, sire."

"Then I shall wait, and willingly. You see, Count Mazzarini, I fear some ill might befall you and your wife on the journey back to Peking. One of my astrologers, curse his abject soul, informed me that my lady Lotus Flower would be taken away from my kingdom by sea. I cannot think who would wish to abduct her, but it would be easiest done while she is returning to Peking, because you must cross the river which leads to the ocean. That is why I came with my force to protect her. I could remain no longer in the capital, for my unease and distress at the prophecy have made me suffer much unwelcome torment. The nights are long and I believe the physician's work will be undone, as I cannot sleep."

"You are most kind in your concern, my lord."

Diego turned away so the Khan could not see the alarm in his eyes.

The Khan spoke with exaggerated concern. "You are my friend, Count, and Kublai Khan loves his friends above all things."

For a moment the two men looked challengingly at each other, then the Khan turned to Lotus Flower, who was struggling to collect her thoughts. Servants entered the room at that moment and served food and wine.

Lotus Flower handed a goblet to the Khan and asked him, "Did you travel with many men, my lord?"

"I brought a hundred thousand of the finest. Enough to see us all safely back in Peking." The Khan roared with laughter at the memory of his soldiers' reaction to the news that they would be leaving Peking. "How they grumbled at leaving the capital. I fear my Mongols are growing soft. They live too much in the city and not enough on the plains. I am hoping that this expedition will harden their bodies."

Diego sighed, wondering if there was any hope left of escaping the Khan's clutches. They would have to leave Hangchow before the time came for the Khan to accompany them back to Peking. In the capital every wall had ears, every window eyes, and the actions of foreigners were reported directly to the Emperor. Once in Peking it would be impossible to escape.

Diego looked at his wife and saw that she was wiping tears from her cheeks. Relieved that the Khan had not noticed her condition, Diego asked for news of the court and was delighted to learn that his brother had sent a letter from Persia. The Khan handed the letter to Diego with an unctuous smile.

"Your brother has arrived in Persia. By now he will be safely home in Venice. The lieutenants appointed by me gave him safe passage through the lands which I govern, and your brother thought to send this note via one of the riders. It has taken many moons to get here but was delivered by one of the tribute collectors. Your brother is a fine man, a true and noble personage I am proud to call a friend."

Diego read the letter, his thoughts wandering to the house by the sea.

My dearest brother, I do not know if you will ever receive this note but I will give it to one of the Emperor's tribute collectors to deliver into your hand. The journey has mercifully been uneventful. I am safe and will start tomorrow on the final stage of the passage. You will enjoy the Malabar Coast. Indeed, I was sorely tempted to remain there, but I was conscious of my obligations. Give my respects to my lady Lotus Flower and my grateful thanks to the Khan for making the journey through these harsh lands so peaceful. Without his influence I should surely have perished. I am, as always, your loving brother, Pierluigi Mazzarini.

Diego understood the letter's implication. Hidden in its guileless words was a warning that without the Khan's blessing the journey would be harrowing.

As Diego mulled over the contents of his brother's note, the Khan talked with Lotus Flower. "Your home in Peking is in good order, my lady. I took the liberty of ordering my craftsmen to inspect it thoroughly before I left the capital."

"You are most kind, my lord."

215

"And I have built a magnificent pavilion for you and your husband within the wall of the imperial city."

Lotus Flower looked at her hands, uncertain how to react to that unwelcome news. The Khan continued to describe the pavilion, as though unaware of the lady's sidelong glances at her husband.

"It is built of the finest stone and lined with your favorite sandalwood. There are lotus flowers in the garden and rare shrubs that attract butterflies to their branches in profusion. These shrubs have been trained to cover the walls of the pavilion, and I have no doubt you will find the place enchanting."

"When shall I dwell in this pavilion, my lord?"

The Khan looked warily toward Diego.

"If Count Mazzarini should leave Peking on a mission he will wish you to come to the palace so you can be under my imperial protection. Also, when you and your husband attend one of my feasts you will be able to retire to your own pavilion by the lake, far away from the foolish gossip of the nobles. It is an enchanted place, my lady. I cannot wait to show it to you."

The Khan thought of all the times during the past few months that he had gone to the lovenest to sit alone dreaming of Lotus Flower.

"It was a fine idea, my lord. I thank you for your kindness and consideration," she said, trying to smile.

The Khan rose and made his way to the door.

"I thank you both for your hospitality. I have elected to stay in the palace that once belonged to the chamberlain of this city. I shall return tomorrow with the gifts I brought for you from Peking, and before the moon is new I shall expect you to come to dine with me."

"We shall be most honored, my lord."

Lotus Flower looked toward Diego, wondering how he managed to remain so calm. Diego accompanied the Emperor to the gate, bowing low as the Khan rode away followed by his soldiers, his horsemen and a legion of retainers. The memory of the ruler's lascivious glances at Lotus Flower made Diego fume with anger, and for a moment he considered challenging the Khan to a duel. Then he realized that this was foolish pride. Lotus Flower was his wife of her own free will. But what did free will matter in a land ruled by a man whom none could deny?

Violent feelings swirled around in the Venetian's mind, and he decided he had to visit the boatbuilder to make the final arrangements for the journey. When he saw Lotus Flower's distress, Diego's anger melted, and he knew he must do only what was best for her.

Lotus Flower put her hand on her husband's shoulder and lay with her eyes closed, whispering questions for which Diego had no answer. "What shall we do, my lord?"

"I need time to reconsider my plans."

"I will *not* go back to Peking. I would rather die than occupy the pavilion that presumptuous fiend has built for me. It is obvious he intends to send you away. Then he will persist in trying to make love to me."

"I shall not leave you, my lady."

"If you refuse to obey the Khan he will imprison you. I fear you and I are no match for the Omnipotence."

Lotus Flower sighed at the thought of the Khan's continuing lust. Diego walked to the cabinet where he kept his maps and charts of the sea.

"I am sorry you should think me no match for the barbarian."

"Can we not sail away now, this day, without telling anyone but our servants?"

"You are still not strong, and the weather at this time of the year is unpredictable."

"I would rather die with you on the ocean than in that man's arms! Do not be angry with me, my love, for what I say. The Khan has five million men spread over half the world, he has spies and experts who foretell the future with accuracy. How can we outwit him? It seems always as if he knows what we are doing before we do it. That is why he has come to Hangchow."

"You outwitted the Khan when he pursued you near the wildfowl lake. Are you less able now to think of such strategy?"

Lotus Flower smiled at the memory of the Khan's displeasure. "Since my illness I have felt tired. Once I am completely well I hope to be able to think of schemes and plans as devious as the Khan's."

"In the meantime I shall spend the evening considering our problem. Tomorrow, I promise I will tell you how we can escape the kingdom."

"Do not let the Khan take me back to Peking."

"I promised many months ago that we should never again be parted, and I intend to keep my word."

That night, as Diego sat considering his dilemma, Giorgio came to talk with him.

"My lord, Ho Shan is here. He arrived with the Khan's party."

"Why did he not come to greet me?"

"He is ill with a fearful pain in the gut. When he reached the house he was so unwell I gave him a draught of opium and he retired at once to his bed."

"What news did he bring, my good Giorgio?"

"Bad news, my lord."

Diego looked at his servant, noting the white hairs fast replacing the black and the troubled look that clouded Giorgio's face.

"Tell me what you know, Giorgio."

"We must leave Hangchow at once, sir. The Khan knows where the shipbuilder is hiding, the one who is constructing your ship. I do not know how he discovered his hiding place but apparently it is so. Ho Shan has sent a trusted friend to warn the builder. He has also presumed to instruct Chen-Yu to provision the ship and to engage a crew for our escape. It is Ho Shan's opinion that the Khan suspects it is *you* who will take my lady Lotus Flower away from him. That is why he has journeyed this great distance in such unspeakable conditions."

"The Khan called me his friend when he visited this house."

"You have what he most desires, sir, so you are his enemy and not his friend. Of course, it is possible that Ho Shan is mistaken. But it is strange that he should bring with him one hundred thousand Mongols to accompany a woman and one man back to Peking."

For a moment Diego was silent. Then he turned to Giorgio and asked resignedly, "What has Ho Shan arranged?"

"Your ship will lie anchored in the inlet which you know. The shipbuilder says he has already arranged the place with you."

"He has indeed. But how shall we travel there if we are forever observed?"

"Ho Shan will remain behind and supply information to the Khan's spies that will send him in the wrong direction."

"The Khan would subject our friend to the death of a thousand cuts for his perfidy. No, my good Giorgio, we shall not leave Ho Shan behind. Indeed, if the Khan suspects me he will also suspect Ho Shan and believe nothing he says."

Giorgio shrugged his shoulders disconsolately, and the two men sat in silence drinking spiced wine and trying to work out how best to save themselves. Then Diego had an idea that he considered to be so subtle and ingenious it could have come from the Khan himself. He explained it to Giorgio, who slapped his thigh and roared with laughter.

"Damn, sir, you are becoming as roundabout as a Mongol!"

"The Khan will believe what he is told, will he not?"

"He will. Shall I wake Ho Shan and tell him what you propose?"

"No, let him sleep. He will need all his strength before we are back in Venice. And now deliver this note to the lady I mentioned. See that you do not loiter in her court or I promise that you will lose all desire to leave Hangchow."

"I shall never lose my desire to leave China, my lord, for I am fearfully homesick for Venice."

"And what of Arya?"

"My wife will accompany me there, of course."

"And if she will not?"

"I shall carry her there by force."

Recalling Arya's girth, Diego burst into peals of laughter, and Giorgio was cheered to see him so relieved of his despondency. After another goblet of wine, the servant left the house.

As he walked down the dark city street, Giorgio was pleased to see that he was being followed by two of the Khan's spies.

The courtesan Hsu Lan had recently retired from business in Peking to live in an opulent mansion in Hangchow. Thrilled by the prospect of enjoying her days in newfound leisure, she nevertheless allowed two lovers to visit her perfumed court. Each man paid a fortune annually for the privilege of being known as one of her chosen companions. Gossip still surrounded the courtesan, but her vast fortune and influence in the highest offices in the land placed her in a different sphere from any other woman in her profession. As she no longer accepted clients, Hsu Lan was displeased to hear that she had an unknown caller. At first she ordered Giorgio to be sent away, but when he insisted on delivering his message into her own hands, she observed him through a peephole. Recognizing him as Diego Mazzarini's servant, Hsu Lan ordered him to be admitted.

Giorgio stared at the floor of the drawing room, which was covered in gold brocade. Then his attention wandered to the walls hung with priceless tapestries. He was coughing nervously as Hsu Lan walked regally down the steps toward him. The courtesan's piercing eyes and silvered lids mesmerized the servant, and when she asked his business Giorgio could find no voice with which to reply. He continued to stare in amazement at the scarlet lips and long pointed nails, starting nervously when Hsu Lan rapped on the table with her ivory fan.

"Come, sire, you did not visit me to gape like a yokel! Give me the message you carry."

Giorgio handed over the scroll. Hsu Lan read it quickly, her face hardening as she understood its meaning. With a look of cold disdain, she threw the scroll on the fire and for a moment stood watching as it burned. Then she turned to Giorgio and nodded curtly.

"Tell Count Mazzarini he may visit me in the morning. And now goodnight to you, sire."

With an autocratic nod the woman swept past Giorgio, disappearing in a wave of intoxicating fragrance. Giorgio looked again around the room, shaking his head in wonderment at the satin couches, the tinkling fountains and the musicians playing in trancelike serenity. What a place it was, like no other he had ever seen. And what a woman, magnificent and beautiful and terrifying.

Giorgio hurried back to the Mazzarini house to report what had happened. "The spies followed me, sir, just as you said they would. Your plan is going to work, of that you can be sure."

"I am glad, my good Giorgio. And how did you find my lady Hsu Lan?"

Giorgio stared at the brazier in the corner of the room, blinking perplexedly at the memory. "Like hot coal, sir, able to burn the very innards from any man. She seemed angry at the contents of your note and I feared for myself."

"Why should she have been angry?"

"I do not know, sir, but she was. She threw the note on the fire and stamped her foot hard as she watched it burn."

The next morning Diego rode to the house of the courtesan Hsu Lan. Behind him, Giorgio rode as escort, carrying a chest of gold plate. When he had carried the chest into the house, Giorgio withdrew, chuckling at the faces of the spies across the street. Soon, he thought, they will tell their tales to the Omnipotence, whose choler will surprise them. Giorgio hurried home to tell his mistress that the Khan's spies were behaving just as they anticipated.

Hsu Lan's servants took Diego's cloak and his surcoat and bade him enter the drawing room. The Venetian strode confidently to meet the woman about whom he had heard so much. He saw an impressive figure above average height, dressed in cloth of gold. Her dark hair sparkled with emeralds, her fingers with exotic pearls. Diego bowed, looking uneasily to the corner of the room, where a musician was playing, then back to the woman, who smiled and held out her hand.

"I have heard so much of your journey to China, Count Mazzarini."

"And I have heard so much of you, my lady."

"And now at last we meet."

"It is an honor to be welcomed to your house."

Hsu Lan wondered why the Venetian kept looking so apprehensively at the musician. "Shall I dismiss my servant, sire?"

"If it pleases you, my lady."

Hsu Lan clapped her hands and the musician withdrew. Diego walked to the door to make sure that none of the servants was listening, then to the window to be sure he was not overheard.

Hsu Lan smiled mockingly, taking in the luxurious silk velvet of her visitor's tunic, the rubies on his fingers and the taut expression on his face. "You take much care not to be discovered, Count Mazzarini. Are you always so cautious?"

"What I have to say is in the greatest confidence, my lady."

"That is what all my visitors say."

Diego looked down on the courtesan with an expression of barely concealed annoyance. When he spoke his tone startled Hsu Lan, and she looked more closely at her visitor.

"I am Diego Mazzarini, Count of the Venetian Empire, and I am not in any way like the others who visit you."

Hsu Lan looked into the defiant blue eyes and wondered what Diego wanted of her.

Suddenly softening in his attitude toward her, the Venetian sat on a footstool at Hsu Lan's feet. "My wife is Lotus Flower, Princess of the House of Sung."

Hsu Lan nodded, and Diego wondered why she was so tense. He continued, "My wife told me that you helped her enter Peking after the hour of the curfew. Is that true, my lady?"

"That is true, sire."

"Why did you help her?"

"I saw her wandering alone with a white horse in a forbidden quarter of the city. Obviously she was very young and very lost."

"I feel sure you had more reason than that for your action. I have been in China for many months and I have learned the ways of your country. A woman of your world would *never* presume to speak with a lady of Lotus Flower's importance."

"She was dressed like a lad. How was I to know she was a princess?"

"I'll wager you had more reason than you say for your action, my lady."

"Perhaps I did, perhaps not."

"Could you tell me your true reason?"

Displeased by the inquisition, Hsu Lan poured herself more wine. "You have come here at great expense, Count Mazzarini, because you wish to love me. Surely you do not intend to waste time discussing my attitudes and feelings for your wife, my lady Lotus Flower."

Diego's reply shocked the courtesan.

"I have no intention of touching you, my lady. I love my wife and would love no other. My reason for coming here is to establish a pattern of daily action for the benefit of the Emperor's spies, who persist in following me. I intend to stay in your house until midday. Then I shall return home. Furthermore, with your permission, I shall return twice each week on the same days and at the same hour."

"Why are the Khan's spies following you?"

"The Khan does not trust me, my lady. He has come from Peking to accompany me and Lotus Flower back to the capital for our safety. At least that is what he told me."

"And for that he needs one hundred thousand Mongols?"

"That is what the Khan said."

Hsu Lan rose agitatedly and poured more wine into Diego's goblet. "Why do you wish the Khan to think you are my lover?"

"I cannot tell you why, my lady. This much I will tell: If I can visit you as I have said for the next month I shall succeed in my aim, which is to establish in the minds of the Khan's spies, and thus in his mind too, the fact that I come to you on the same days of each week and that I am devoted to you. Then one day when they expect me to be here in your home I may take the opportunity to be far away from this city."

"It is your intention to escape the kingdom, Count Mazzarini?"

"I intend to risk my life to ensure the safety of my lady Lotus Flower, who is coveted by the Emperor above all else."

Hsu Lan covered her face with her fan to conceal the conflicting emotions she was feeling. As she sat silently at Diego's side she kept trying to think of a way to make him trust her.

"I was interested in the welfare of the lady Lotus Flower because I admire her beauty and her courage."

223

"How did you come to admire my wife? I'll wager you had never seen her before that night."

"I cannot say...I..."

Diego saw a tremor in the pale hands and a tear in the courtesan's eyes. Suddenly he had a moment of intuition that shocked him so harshly he could say nothing at all. For a while he was silent, considering the possibility of his thoughts more thoroughly.

Finally, Diego rose and looking down on Hsu Lan asked gently, persuasively, "My lady, anything you deign to tell me will be *our* secret, will it not? I swear, on all that is precious to me, that I will never tell another. Now, may I ask you a question which may grievously offend you?"

Hsu Lan sighed. "You may ask, sire."

"There are rumors in Peking that you had a daughter in the days of your youth, when first you came to live in the city. Is it true?"

"It is, sire."

"Is my lady Lotus Flower your daughter?"

Hsu Lan looked up at the tall, dignified young man before her and knew that this was the moment for sharing a confidence. Her daughter was in danger and this man sought help in saving her.

"She is my daughter, sire," Hsu Lan said in a whisper, "and I would kill anyone who told her of her origin. Wen-Fai, Lotus Flower's father, was my lover, the only man I have ever truly loved and the first who touched my body. When the child born to his wife died, Wen-Fai took my daughter and raised her in his own home.

"He loved Lotus Flower more than all his other children, and though I rarely saw her again, so did I. I had long wished to see my daughter when I met her that night as she was leading her horse through the Suburb of the Prostitutes. I recognized my child only because I had seen Lotus Flower with her father on the day before they were sent into exile. When I saw her there, dressed like a beggar, my heart leaped and before I knew it I had spoken to her."

Understanding filled Diego's heart, and he poured out his troubles to the courtesan. "I thank you for your confidence. Be sure I shall never speak of what you have said. Now, if

I may, I would like to tell you my plan of escape. If you can make corrections to it, please do so, because we need every help in our effort to evade the Khan's displeasure."

For hours Diego and Hsu Lan talked about his strategy, about the Khan's desire for Lotus Flower, about Lotus Flower's illness and her future in Venice, the city by the sea. The courtesan's eyes moistened as she heard of her daughter's distress at the loss of her child. Then she grew happy again when Diego told her about life in Venice, of the mansion where Lotus Flower would live, the servants she would have, the luxury that would always be hers.

Romance had entered Hsu Lan's life only once, bringing with it sadness and shame. She was determined that her daughter's life should be idyllic and that nothing would prevent her from living in complete security. Hsu Lan made suggestions, amending Diego's plan. Diego accepted the suggestions eagerly, praising the courtesan for her inventiveness and laughing with her at the riddle the Khan might never solve.

When it was time for the Venetian to leave, Hsu Lan accompanied him to the gate, and as he mounted his horse she whispered, "My humble thanks for all you have confided, sire. This is the first I have learned about my daughter's life, and I shall cherish what you have told me for the rest of my life. Know that I will do *anything* I can to help you in your endeavors."

"I thank you, my lady."

"We are playing a dangerous game, Count Mazzarini, for the Khan has power like no other on the face of the earth. Nevertheless, I am hopeful we shall succeed."

Hsu Lan curtsied as Diego rode away. Across the paved road the Khan's spies were grumbling at the hours they had waited for the Venetian to emerge. As Hsu Lan disappeared into her home the spies hurried to the Khan's palace to report what they had seen to the Omnipotence.

Chapter Eleven:

Hangchow

The Khan rose early and dressed with particular care. He had been in Hangchow for almost a month and was making the final preparations for his journey back to Peking. Below, in the courtyard of the palace, Mongol horsemen were exercising their horses. The Khan looked fondly down on the animals and their riders. Then he returned to his chamber and read once more the report of his spies on the activities of Diego Mazzarini. The Khan flushed with indignation on behalf of Lotus Flower. For the past month the Venetian had been visiting the courtesan Hsu Lan, sometimes remaining all day in her presence, sometimes only a few hours. These visits were regular, and it was obvious that the Venetian was the courtesan's lover.

The Khan sat on a gilded couch, wondering how the Venetian could stoop to desert his beautiful bride for the favors of the greatest scheming harlot in all of China. With a shudder, the Khan remembered the day when he had ordered Hsu Lan to report to the Imperial Palace to bestow her favors on his Omnipotence. She had demanded gifts and made so many conditions that he had been foul-tempered by the time of her arrival and unable to enjoy her. Each time the Khan remembered Hsu Lan's hard eyes and the sinuousness of her body he wanted to know more of her. But each time he recalled her rapaciousness he postponed the pleasure.

To choose passion with such a monster instead of the caresses of the lady Lotus Flower seemed the act of a madman. Roaring for the astrologer, the imperial barber and zither players to calm his disposition, the Khan strode to the withdrawing chamber.

When an astrologer appeared, the Khan ordered him to tell what he saw for the immediate future. The astrologer immediately annoyed the Omnipotence by saying what could not be done.

"It is not possible to know *when,* my lord, only *what* is going to pass."

"Then say what you can say and do not inflame my imperial temper."

"There is going to be a curious happening, my lord, a gathering or feast or performance of play-acting. You will watch this with much pleasure."

"Where will it take place?"

"Here, my lord. I see a street hung with lanterns, and a woman with green eyes."

The Khan smiled and rewarded the astrologer. "What more do you see of my Imperial Personage at this feast?"

"I see nothing more of the feast, sire, but I see a voyage on water for you, my lord."

Alarmed, the Khan roared at the astrologer, "I do not place my Imperial Personage upon the sea. You are undoubtedly seeing through clouds."

"No, my lord. You are on the sea and it is written that you will be many days there and in a great tempest."

The Khan cursed the astrologer vehemently. "I do *not* go on the sea. I am Kublai Khan, Lord of the Mongol Horde, the finest horseman the world has ever known and the greatest general. I am *not* given to voyaging on waters which are good only for fishes and Japanese."

"Yes, my lord."

"You were mistaken, were you not?"

"I was, my lord."

"Tremblingly, obey me!"

"Yes, my lord."

The astrologer withdrew, trembling as ordered. The Khan closed his eyes and listened to the sound of the zithers gently playing, while the barber trimmed his beard. Then the Emperor went to the courtyard and rode his horse back and forth for an hour, as ordered by the physician. When he made his way back to his suite, one of the spies was waiting with the latest report on Diego Mazzarini's activities.

The spy's face was jubilant. "My lord, I have news. Tomorrow the Venetian is to throw a celebration for my lady Hsu Lan."

"I cannot believe his effrontery!"

"Tonight also there are to be festivities because it is Hsu Lan's birthday."

"Ha! That is why she is so ill-natured. I cannot abide women born in the third month of the year."

"Tonight, Count Mazzarini has been invited to attend the celebrations, and tomorrow he will give his own tribute. Truly, sire, he is besotted with the courtesan. There are rumors he has spent his fortune on her."

"Have you arranged a place from which I may witness these celebrations?"

"Better still, my lord. My lady has invited you to honor her house at the feast this evening."

The Khan's eyes glittered with satisfaction at the thought of the chagrin Diego Mazzarini would feel at being discovered in his infidelity. The Khan told the spy to signify his acceptance of the invitation. Then he hurried away to prepare for the feast. First he called the imperial jeweler to arrange a suitable gift for Hsu Lan. After that was arranged, the Khan took his annual bath in cinnamon-scented water, immersing himself for a few seconds before calling for protective oils to keep him from the cold.

For the first time in months the sun shone, and by late afternoon it was apparent that spring was on its way.

The Khan dressed in a robe of jade-green velvet lined with sable, a surcoat above it; a lynx-fur cloak completed the ensemble. It would not do for him to shiver in the chill air of evening, as the festivities reached their height, and it would be galling to be surpassed in splendor by the Venetian. The Khan admired himself in a mirror of polished shell. Then he placed a square cap on his head and strode regally from the palace.

The imperial procession was greeted by an astonishing sight as it neared Hsu Lan's home. Thousands of scarlet lanterns fluttered in the breeze on either side of the road. Children rang silver bells as the Emperor approached, calling greetings and falling in obeisance as he passed by. Delighted by this surprising welcome, the ruler threw silver pieces to the crowd, bowing regally and beaming with pleasure. As he entered the courtesan's estate, trumpeters sounded a fanfare and Hsu Lan swept down the marble steps toward him. The courtesan was dressed in black with a necklace of rubies and a cloak made from the feathers of five thousand peacocks. Impressed by her style, the Khan acknowledged Hsu Lan's greeting and handed her his gift, a pair of ruby earrings. The courtesan's eyes glittered with pleasure at the splendid tribute, and she took the Khan's arm and led him to a terrace overlooking the ornamental lake.

The sun was low in the sky, and its orange light made the costumes of those in the procession about to pay homage glow as though engulfed in flame. At a signal from Hsu Lan, an orchestra began a martial march. The music with its banging drums and clanging cymbals delighted the Khan. The courtesan noted with satisfaction that the spies were standing at the edge of the clearing, watching the arrival of Diego Mazzarini.

The Khan also noticed Diego's arrival and called loudly for everyone to hear, "Ah, my dear Count Mazzarini. Come join me as I review this fine procession. I had not expected to find such a devoted husband as you at such a gathering."

Giorgio led his master's horses and covered carriage away through the gate, passing children with windbells and bamboo pipes. This first section of the procession marched to the steps below where the Emperor was sitting and laid flowers at his feet. Looking down, the Khan saw that the flowers spelled out a loyal message. Touched, he rose and bowed his approval, nodding graciously as the children cheered him. The children were followed by members of Hsu Lan's household, first the men in charge of furnishings and scrolls, then those in charge of liquors and teas, banquets and feasts. The tribute givers were followed by chefs and women of the household, responsible for buying incense and perfumes, for cleaning and playing the zither. To the rear of this group, the Khan saw chess experts, craftsmen, experts in calligraphy and tellers of amusing riddles employed from time to time by Hsu Lan.

Astonished by this revelation of his hostess's wealth, the Khan exclaimed, "Surely you keep a larger household than I!"

"It is my pleasure to give employment to as many of my fellow countrymen as possible, sire."

The Khan viewed his companion with new respect, thinking that she was certainly a most astonishing creature.

Soon, another procession appeared, commanding the Emperor's attention. In this group young women bizarrely masked in silver were costumed as animals. Some pawed their ears like cats. Some crawled like caterpillars. One had the ambling gait of a donkey and another slid sinuously on her stomach like a snake. These enticing creatures excited the Khan as they pranced and trotted and crept and clawed their way past his dais. Hsu Lan observed the Emperor's face with satisfaction, and her attention wandered to the edge of the clearing, where she was pleased to note the spies engrossed in the proceedings.

Next a fire eater performed, his arms shimmering with oil, a satin cloak lined with stars calling attention to the rippling muscles on his body. The audience watched intently as the fire eater swallowed flames from torches at the edge of the clearing. Then, to everyone's amazement, he spat the flames out, igniting a thorn bush which burned fiercely.

The Khan leaped up and called to the performer, "I command you to do that again."

"I shall obey, sire."

Every eye was fixed on the fire eater as he walked solemnly to the edge of the clearing and swallowed the flames from three more burning brands. Then, with a flourish, he ran to the lake in the center of the garden and spat with such vigor the water itself was briefly ignited. Shouting his approval, the Khan threw a purse of silver to the man, who bowed and left the arena.

Still amazed by what he had seen, the Emperor turned to Diego, who was watching the performance with an unusually solemn face. "What ails you, my friend? You look fearsomely out of countenance. Has my company disrupted you?"

"Indeed not, sir. I am honored to be in your Imperial Presence."

"Have no fear, Count, I shall not inform my lady Lotus Flower of your duplicity."

Diego bowed his gratitude, and the Khan smothered the urge to laugh out loud at his rival's unease. The procession continued with the appearance of a troupe of dervishes. They were followed by a puppeteer whose lascivious dolls provoked the assembly to bouts of irreverent laughter. Then a conjurer, reputed to be the finest in the land, provided one of the high spots of the evening when he drew from the Khan's robe a white dove, from his ear a silver ball and from his sleeve a wriggling green snake. The final act of the entertainment was a dancer whose abandoned performance made the Khan tense with lust. The dancer threw herself at the Emperor's feet, urging him to feel the skin of her thighs and the firmness of her breasts. A reward of gold greeted the end of the girl's performance.

Leaning toward Hsu Lan, the Khan issued his instructions. "I will see that beauteous creature on my return to the palace."

"Of course, my lord. It is already arranged."

As the procession ended the orchestra began to play and some of the masked dancers reappeared to divert the audience. Servants had placed sheep, goat, kid and roe deer on spits over the fire, and the air was heavy with the smell of sizzling meats. The Khan watched the proceedings with satisfaction, pleased to have been invited. He was still pondering the welcome he had received in this normally hostile city, unaware that every invited person had been paid by Hsu Lan and given instructions to cheer the Khan every time he glanced in their direction.

To further divert the crowd until the food was ready, a pickpocket appeared to exhibit his expertise, removing valuables from the guests' sleeves, jewelry from the ladies' hands and an earring from the courtesan Hsu Lan. The Khan applauded loudly, laughing joyously at the surprised expression on his hostess's face. When he had rewarded the pickpocket, the Khan was charmed to be given back his own gold chains, his hat and the belt from his velvet pelisse.

That night two hundred guests ate dinner with the royal visitor. Then, as darkness came and the air grew cold, Hsu Lan signaled to her servants. Retainers appeared with torches which they put to an invisible circle painted around the perimeter of the clearing where the celebration was taking place. Suddenly the circle burst into flames, and instead of feeling the chill everyone declared that it was as warm as a summer's day. Flames rose like an orange sparkling curtain around the assembly, and there were cheers of approval from the guests.

The Khan rose and said, "I toast your wit and ingenuity, my lady Hsu Lan."

The courtesan acknowledged the tribute with one of her own. "My lord, your presence here has honored my humble dwelling. I venture to hope it will not be the last time you will visit me."

The Khan stole a sidelong glance at the courtesan, wondering if at last Hsu Lan was willing to submit to him without endless bargaining. Then he remembered the cavorting and contorting of the exotic dancer who had excited him earlier in the evening and decided to postpone approaching the courtesan.

As the flames died down, the guests began to take their leave, dispersing quietly until only Diego, the Khan and his spies remained. The ruler looked quizzically at Diego. "You will be late home, Count Mazzarini."

"Since her illness my wife sleeps soundly, sire. She will

233

not wake until the morning, and by then I shall be at her side."

With a bow, the Khan bade Hsu Lan goodnight. When he reached his carriage he found inside the dancer who had impressed him. Calling excitedly for his driver to hurry, the Emperor returned at full speed to the palace.

The spies watched as Diego kissed Hsu Lan's cheek and led her to the door of the house. As they passed inside the courtesan exclaimed in a voice loud with excitement, "I am delighted to have you as my guest, sire. It will be exciting to watch the sun rise in your presence."

The spies yawned wearily, resigned to yet another endless vigil. Across the street from the courtesan's house they huddled in a doorway, shivering in the bitter chill. Before long an old woman appeared and offered them some homemade spirit. The two men gulped the burning liquid and felt warmer. They thanked the old crone, who bowed politely and went on her way. Within minutes the spies were asleep and snoring loudly. The old woman returned and removed the jug of liquor. Then, singing raucously, she returned to her dockside shanty, a silver piece in her pocket from Hsu Lan.

The Khan rose at dawn, having made an important decision. If the Venetian could not respect his wife he did not deserve to have her as his own. He ordered the captain of the guard to be ready to return to Peking within the hour. The weather was warm, buoying his spirits further, because spring had come without warning, as often it did in the province of Manzi. For breakfast the Emperor enjoyed pigeon, quail and rice, accompanied by his favorite hot sauces. When he had finished the savory dishes he ate some raisins soaked in rice spirits and figs fermented in peach-blossom wine. Then he called for servants to bring his new clothes, the ones made by the imperial needlewomen. The Khan put over his robe a sleeveless surcoat of velvet lined with the skins of baby foxes. Finally, he sprayed amber perfume into his mouth and ordered his horse to be saddled. When he was ready to depart, the Khan encountered one of the spies who had come to make his report.

"My lord, Count Mazzarini has spent the night with my lady Hsu Lan and is still in her house."

The Khan dismissed the spy, fuming his annoyance to the chamberlain. "The scoundrel. He cares nothing for his wife's tender feelings. I shall have his head for this affront to my lady Lotus Flower."

The Emperor descended to the courtyard and rode away with an escort of a hundred men. At Lotus Flower's home, a Mongol guard clanged the bell loudly with ever increasing impatience. When no one answered the summons, the Khan himself rang, roaring to be admitted.

"Open the gate at once. I, Kublai Khan, Emperor of China, demand to be admitted."

But no one answered the imperial summons, no voice spoke in reply to his call. At first the Khan was puzzled. Then panic filled his heart and he wondered if the Venetian had harmed the lady he had once loved. The Khan gave orders for the gates to be broken down. Soldiers hurried forward with axes and hammers, and soon the Emperor was able to ride into the courtyard. There he looked helplessly around at the emptiness. Birds were twittering in the cherry trees. A solitary cat sat taking the sun on the terrace, and everywhere there was silence. The Khan ordered his men to search the house, and as they fanned out he walked in the garden, examining rows of newly planted seeds. In Li-Huei's shed, the Khan found a chart which showed, by signs and symbols, the date of the planting of each variety. The Khan noted with increasing concern that the last had been planted only two days previously. Shaking his head in confusion, he tried to work out how everyone had vanished without his having been informed. Was it possible the spies had not seen the servants leaving? How could that be when the Mazzarini residence had been under surveillance for months by his most experienced men?

Minutes later one of the soldiers ran to inform the Khan that the house was empty. The Emperor gave orders that his soldiers surround the outer wall of the property. Then he wandered alone through the rooms where Lotus Flower, until recently, had lived. In her bedroom he found a twig of faded jasmine fallen from a vase by her couch and a stick of incense in the shrine where she had prayed. He took the flower and sniffed it longingly. Then he strode out of the house and rode with a dozen men to the home of the courtesan, Hsu Lan.

The Khan was admitted to the lady's presence at once. He found Hsu Lan taking a lesson in playing the reed pipes. The courtesan looked up in surprise as the Khan entered.

"My lord, I am honored that you return so quickly to visit me."

"Can you tell me where Diego Mazzarini has gone?"

"My friend left here one hour ago."

"Did he say where he was going?"

"Yes, my lord, he did."

"Tell me at once so I can avoid a calamity."

"Count Mazzarini said he was going to join his friends at the shipyard. I believe he is planning to return to his own country after the feast he has prepared in my honor later this day."

The Khan groaned. He had been told nothing of the Venetian's plans to return to his own country. His spies had said only that Mazzarini's servants lived quietly with the family, talking of returning to Peking and the home they adored. They had also said that the Venetian's outings were limited to visiting the courtesan Hsu Lan. The Khan swallowed hard, vowing to have the head of every spy in the kingdom if they had given him the wrong information. He rose abruptly and bowed to Hsu Lan with something akin to affection.

"You have been most helpful, my lady. I shall reward you well."

"It is my pleasure to be of service to you, sire."

The Khan returned to the palace to assemble his men. Soon the courtyard was full of Mongol warriors impatient for action. The Khan spoke in a voice ringing with emotion.

"The Venetian, Diego Mazzarini, must be found. My spies tell me he has gone to a shipyard. I demand news of him within the hour. Go now and find him for me."

When his men had gone, the Khan sat alone in his suite, cursing Diego's duplicity and bemoaning his own love for Lotus Flower. He thought bitterly of the gold and jewels with which he had rewarded Mazzarini and of the fortune Pierluigi had taken with him when he sailed home to Venice. The Mazzarinis had grown rich from his bounty, and all he had

236

expected in return was the body of the lady Lotus Flower. The Khan thought of the woman for whom he craved and was sick with apprehension that he might never see her again.

The time passed slowly until the Khan heard the welcome sound of riders approaching. He ran to the parapet to watch his men ride in. Their faces told him what he wanted to know and he flung on a cloak and went down to meet them.

"What have you to tell me of the Venetian?"

"He has escaped, my lord."

The Khan hesitated, unable to believe his ears. The soldiers were touched to see the ruler's face turn pale in anguish. When he was able to speak, the Emperor asked, "Where has the Venetian gone?"

The Mongol commander stepped forward. "The Venetian set sail with others in a ship he has secretly built."

The Khan cried out in anger. His distracted gaze made his officers wonder if he would recover from this latest affront to his pride. For some time the Khan stood as though turned to stone. Then he made an effort to rally himself, looking up at his commander and questioning him again. "Which shipyard did the Venetian sail from?"

"From the one your spies reported on many months ago, sire."

"And the owner of the yard?"

"He also has vanished, sire."

"How do you know all this?"

"We met an old woman who lives at the wharfside. It was she who said she had seen the Venetian sailing from the yard."

"Did she say when he sailed?"

"She could not remember, my lord. The woman is old and her sight is not the best. She knew only that many men had sailed in the Venetian's ship."

The Khan looked at the sky, then back to his Mongol horsemen. The Venetian had outwitted him by using the sea as an ally. The Khan had had men watching the shipyard, the Venetian, the courtesan, and *still* he had failed to know what was happening. The Khan assumed correctly that the ship had been moved in the dead of night and incorrectly that

237

it had sailed on the first tide, confounding all surveillance. Bitter fury rose in the Emperor's throat, and he trembled with the ferocity of his rage. Then, suddenly, he knew what he must do, and he gave orders for one of the new warships to be provisioned and crewed by Chinese mariners who were familiar with the waters of the dark-green sea.

Boldly the Khan called to his commander, "We shall pursue the Venetian to the very last."

Aghast at this suggestion, the Mongol replied, "On the sea, sire?"

"Do you think I will permit myself to be outwitted by Diego Mazzarini?"

"No, my lord, of course not. I never thought anything of the kind."

"Or that I cannot rule the waves as I have ruled the land?"

"Of course you can, sire."

"Take men and hasten to make my ship ready, for we leave at sunset. Use your own men to help those who provision the ship, and choose a hundred of the finest to sail with me."

The Khan returned to Hsu Lan's home, his head aching, his heart thundering with anger. The courtesan welcomed him reassuringly and provided tasty food and drink, which was served by beautiful young girls. The Khan forgot his troubles for a moment and enjoyed the ambiance of the lady's home.

When they were alone, he explained what had happened. "You will have no festivity this day, my lady. The Venetian has vanished, and none can find him."

Hsu Lan answered with a sigh, "I received this from Count Mazzarini shortly after you left. A child was paid to bring it to me."

The Khan read a scroll in Diego's hand:

My lady, forgive this unreasonably sudden departure but circumstances force me to change my plans. I am commencing my journey back to Venice and will be obliged to forgo the pleasure of your company at the festivity. Instead, I send you a gift with my grateful thanks for your affection and for all the hours we have spent together. Think of me on the high seas and pray

for my safe arrival in Venice. Diego Mazzarini, Count
of the Venetian Empire.

The Khan spat contemptuously into an urn, closing his
eyes and trying to remember the lessons taught him by the
new physician. He had been warned to control his emotions
and to keep a tight rein on his temper. He had obeyed all the
physician's demands in order to become well enough to enjoy
Lotus Flower's favor. Now, without her, he felt suddenly very
old and tired. Nothing mattered any more except seeing her
again. The Emperor looked wearily at Hsu Lan and saw that
she was watching him closely.

"What will you do, sire?"

"I intend to pursue the Venetian on the ocean."

"How can you pursue him? Have you a ship here in
Hangchow?"

"I have already given orders for a ship to be provisioned.
We sail on the evening tide."

"I wish you safe journey, sire. I shall pray for you."

"I trust I shall survive the sea and have the pleasure of
your company on my return, my lady."

The evening was cold with a stiff breeze that tossed the
waves into eddies of pounding white foam. The Khan stood
beside his horse at the quayside, looking in dismay at the
rocking gangplank. For a moment his resolve wavered. Then
with a defiant cry he walked on board and was welcomed by
the Chinese captain of the vessel. The Khan accepted a flagon
of wine and some pomegranates and explained to the captain
that he was pursuing a Venetian across the ocean and that
his investigations had led him to believe that his enemy had
sailed only a few hours before him. The captain bowed politely
and departed for the bridge, as his ship sailed slowly out of
harbor. Below, in his cabin, the Khan moaned loudly because
his innards were already pitching and tossing.

Throughout the night two doctors attended the ruler, to
the amusement of the Chinese crew. Ten servants were kept
busy running back and forth to the galley demanding wine,
cold compresses, buckets and sedatives to dull the agonies
provoked by the storm. The Khan thought of the astrologer's

prophecy that he would be at sea for many days and chastised himself for not having believed it. But how many days was "many"? Two, three, four or more? The Khan called on the spirits of the sea to save him from the rigors of his ordeal.

Three days later the Khan was forced to accept that there was no sign of the Venetian's ship. He ordered his warship to put into port for supplies. As the Khan sat on deck thinking of how he had suffered for his love of Lotus Flower, his Mongol commander hurried to his side and kowtowed.

"The harbormaster gave me this to give to you, sire. He was given it by the brother of the treacherous shipbuilder from Hangchow."

The Khan tore open the silk-wrapped folder and saw inside a portrait of Lotus Flower drawn on vellum. A note in her hand said only:

I leave you this, my lord, so you will have a souvenir of our friendship. That which is yours awaits you in the palace of Hangchow. Lotus Flower, Princess of the House of Sung, Contessa Mazzarini.

Suddenly the Khan felt as he had felt when he played games of chance with Lotus Flower. He did not like the feeling now, though it had amused him before. He stroked the portrait of his love and whispered to the face that looked so enigmatically into his own, "Have you tricked me into pursuing you on the sea when you are not on the sea at all? Wicked one, have you manipulated me like a cricket on a string?"

The Khan could not help admiring the lady. He, who prided himself on being the most devious mortal on earth, was lost, confused, rushing here and there in pursuit of the invisible.

One week later the Khan arrived back in Hangchow and made his way to the palace. The chamberlain presented him with an ivory box that had been delivered the morning after his departure by ship.

The Khan hurried to his private suite and opened the box. He found inside the pearl he had given Lotus Flower and a poem he recognized as one of his favorite ones about lost love:

*The fragrance has not disappeared...but she does not return
...and I keep loving her while the leaves fall....The palaces
of China had never seen such beauty, dressed in her veils,
frailer than a swallow.*

The Khan buried his head in his hands and wept.

In early evening a young boy was ushered into the Emperor's presence. The Khan looked down at the child, then at the captain of the guard.

"Why have you brought this child to me?" he asked.

The captain of the guard nudged the boy. "Tell the Omnipotence what you saw."

"I saw a lady with green eyes riding a white horse on the bridge that leads to the wild desert."

The Khan handed the boy a jade tablet.

"Show this to my horsemaster and he will let you ride one of my imperial horses."

Alone again, the Khan pondered the child's statement. The only woman to ride a white horse in his kingdom was Lotus Flower. Chinese girls were not permitted to run, let alone ride horses, for fear of jeopardizing their virginity. The Khan tried desperately to think like Lotus Flower and at last he made his decision. Calling the commander of the guard, he gave orders which involved the dispatch of a hundred imperial messengers. When the Japanese Shogun had sought to escape his kingdom, Diego Mazzarini had given the Khan good advice, and the ruler had covered the beaches with soldiers blocking his enemy's retreat. Now the Khan decided to use the same strategy against the Venetian and his party. This time he would spread men through Chamba, Burma and the mountains leading to the uncharted territory. There would be no escape from the Mongol Omnipotence.

Within a week a million of the Khan's men were on their way south and southwest. As they rode they combed the countryside for news of strangers seeking safe passage to the coast. The Khan rode at battle speed ahead of another army of 500,000 through Shuhsien to Paoki and Changtu to Yaan. As he rode his spirits rose, because in the saddle he knew he was invincible. It was his chance to show the Venetian the daring and skill that had made him Ruler of Half the World. There would no hiding place, no cave or castle, village or forest that would not be combed, searched and revisited in the imperial hunt. If Diego Mazzarini was on the earth he would be found.

Soon the Khan's southern borders were sealed by lines of soldiers stretching as far as the eye could see. He surveyed his legions and knew that no one could hope to pass without being apprehended and none could challenge this dazzling display of power.

In the dawn of a new day the Khan walked alone on the mountainside and cried into the breeze: "You seek to escape me, Venetian. You trick me into believing that you are on the sea when you ride on the land. Now match yourself against my Mongol army and know who is Omnipotent Master of the Earth!"

Chapter Twelve:
The Yangtze River

For weeks Diego and Lotus Flower had been traveling on the Yangtze River. Until they had reached Wuhan, on the inland sea, they had traveled in their own new ship. Then, from Wuhan, the shipbuilder and his family had returned east to the ocean in Diego's ship, leaving the Venetian's party to continue west on the narrower stretches of the river in a dhow, rented with its crew after lively negotiations. It was Diego's plan for the shipbuilder, his family and a crew of expert mariners to travel down the coast of China to Malacca, then to the island of Ceylon and on to the Malabar Coast of India, where they would wait for his arrival. If the ship was boarded by the Khan's spies Diego and Lotus Flower would not be aboard. When Diego's party reached that coast they would join the ship and sail to Hormuz on the Persian Gulf. Then they would travel overland to Acre before embarking on a trader for the Venetian lagoon. Everything had been planned in fine detail. Now all that was needed was the luck to carry the plan to fruition.

Diego lay in the dhow, thinking of the night Lotus Flower had escaped Hangchow by hiding on the floor of his carriage as he made his way to the courtesan's house for the birthday feast. Dressed as one of the masked dancers pretending to be animals, Lotus Flower had pranced past the Khan and his spies to the far reaches of Hsu Lan's grounds, where a horse was waiting to take her with Giorgio and Ho Shan to the river. Diego had joined them in the early hours of the morning, having ridden like a Mongol from Hsu Lan's home. The gardener, Li-Huei, and his family had left Hangchow three days previously in a farm cart and were waiting to be picked up at a bend in the river.

Holding Lotus Flower in his arms now, Diego told her he adored her and that she was without doubt the cleverest woman in the world. Occasionally he looked through the canvas flap to make sure no one was following the dhow, but the landscape was peaceful and soon Diego began to hope that their escape had been successful.

The Chinese crew respected the Mazzarini party and treated them with deference and kindness. At each village men from the dhow inquired of local people the latest gossip and reported what they had heard to the Venetian, because they knew he feared pursuit by the Mongol Khan. As the dhow with its billowing scarlet sail passed on toward the arid lands empty of inhabitants, the crew began to feel less nervous. Hatred of the Khan had made them accept the Venetian's offer to take him and his wife downriver. But fear of the Emperor's cruelty and his limitless power had also kept them constantly afraid for their lives.

Part of the journey had been on stretches of the river as wide as any sea, crowded with sampans, junks and barges. Any of these boats could have carried a spy, and the captain of the dhow had suffered endless worry. Now a new danger faced the party. The landscape at this ever-narrowing part of the river was deserted, and the captain knew that the scarlet sails stood out against the colorless background like a tiger lily in a bed of weeds. Blue mountains rose like walls of a citadel all around the narrow channel. The villages were small and far apart, the inhabitants intensely curious about strangers. To safeguard the fugitives, the captain suggested that Diego and his group conceal themselves each time the dhow put in for supplies so the locals could not mention their presence if questioned.

"The Khan has spies everywhere, Count. It will be best if you remain hidden."

"We shall do as you ask, Captain."

"Next we shall come to a village close to the border. There, if anywhere, we shall encounter danger. My crew is well armed but no match for a Mongol patrol."

The Venetian had secured some rough plans of the area drawn by one of the Khan's generals. From these he was able to ascertain that a mountain range divided the far reaches of the Khan's land from the coast. Diego knew his plan involved the members of his party in some risk, but he could find no other solution to reaching the sea and the distant Malabar Coast. He had decided that they would leave the comparative safety of the river only at the end of the waterway. From there they would travel to the mountains into the uncharted land. Diego often sat trying to work out the problems he would encounter on the overland section of the journey. The only thing he could not overcome was his fear that the mountain border would be guarded with a Mongol legion. If they were confronted by a patrol of the Khan's soldiers it would be over for them all.

Each day the scenery grew wilder, the waters more boisterous. With the advent of spring, the mountain snows had melted, swelling every river in the area. The air was fresh and free from flies, and soon Diego saw that Lotus Flower's health was visibly improved. Ho Shan was feeling better, too. His pains had vanished on leaving Hangchow, and Diego wondered if the former spy was being poisoned by the Khan's officers. The party continued peacefully along the river until one morning when Diego heard the crew shouting excitedly above him on the deck. He rose only to be cautioned by Lotus Flower, who was gazing in awe at the distant plain.

"Look, Diego. The Khan has brought his Mongol Horde to guard the borders."

Diego saw, to his horror, that the valley was full of heavily armed soldiers. The Khan rode at the head of this mighty force, and, as Diego watched, he saw that the mountainside was also infested with Mongols, its wooded slopes gleaming silver, gold and brown as the sun touched the swords and shields of men hidden in the trees.

"Sire, there must be a million Mongols on the plain and in the mountains. What shall we do?" the captain asked.

"Tell Giorgio to collect the members of my party and put them below, out of sight of the men in the hills. Tell your crew to behave as they always behave at this hour of the day, for if they should arouse the Khan's suspicions with their feverish chatter we shall all lose our heads."

"Yes, my lord."

"And Captain, when we sail through the narrow pass that lies ahead, there will be Mongols on either side of us. Some will be close enough to touch. Tell your men to kowtow to the Khan."

The captain listened to Diego's instructions, smiling as he understood the Venetian's intentions. He hurried away, and soon Diego and Lotus Flower heard the usual sounds of morning, the cook clanging his brass bell, the oarsmen singing, the captain calling instructions, the lookout shouting his observations. Diego pulled down the canvas flap to conceal himself and his wife from the Mongols camped at the narrowest part of the river. Then he drew his sword, and continued to watch the scene through a hole in the side of the canvas. As they passed the line of Mongols that spread along the valley as far as he could see, Diego told Lotus Flower what was happening.

"We are almost abreast of the Khan at this moment. If you were to raise your voice he would hear you."

Though she was trembling with tension, Lotus Flower could not resist a smile at the situation in which they found themselves. The Khan was clever. He had discovered that they were not on the ocean and was riding to block the borders of the southwestern territories. How he must have ridden! Lotus Flower marveled at the thought of such determination and superhuman endurance. Then she asked herself if the Khan would think to search the boats sailing on the Yangtze

River. Would a Mongol, whose heart so loved the earth, be able to think like a Venetian, whose soul adored the water? Lotus Flower prayed that they would pass the soldiers without being challenged, that the plan Diego had worked out in the winter nights could outwit the Ruler of Half the World.

At the narrowest point of the channel, where the rocks jutted far out into the water, a Mongol captain was frying fish over the campfire. He was joined by some of his colleagues, who waited impatiently for the first meal of the day. On the river a dhow drifted by, its crew running back and forth, busily accomplishing the tasks of morning. The Mongols ignored the dhow. Then, suddenly, they were startled to see the approach of the Emperor.

The Khan dismounted and stood for a moment looking approvingly up at the mountains whose slopes were full of his soldiers. Then he looked down at the water and at the dhow, which was drawing level with the spot where he stood. While admiring the color of the sails and the swell made by the wind in the rustling scarlet silk, he was gratified to see the crew kowtowing to him and surprised by this unsolicited mark of respect in so hostile an area. The Khan inclined his head graciously, smiling as the vessel slipped slowly by and on toward the mountains of the uncharted land. Then, smelling the fish cooking, he felt hungry. He thought how good it was to be in the open air, to be with his men, living the life of a Tartar warrior. The Khan sat apart from the soldiers, eating and calling questions to the men as they waited for their food. Above the Emperor's head birds sang a song of springtime, which cheered him and made him happy, so he did not notice the scarlet-sailed dhow vanishing into the sunlight.

For three days and three nights, Diego, Giorgio and Ho Shan kept watch for Mongol patrols. They saw nothing, and soon the captain informed them that he was sure they were no longer in the Khan's lands.

That night Diego stood on deck, looking out into the moonlit stillness as he questioned the captain. "Have you ever been in this area before?"

"Only once when my brother sailed to the end of the waterway."

"What did you find there?"

"We saw mountains, sire, high mountains full of game and wild animals. You are lucky to have come at this time of year, for it is beautiful on the slopes during the summer. In the cold months men's bodies freeze like ice in a matter of moments and the passes are so deep with snow none can travel to the lands beyond."

"Who rules those lands?"

"I do not know, sire. The Khan believes that all the South is his and indeed half the world too, but I think it is not so. Those who live in this area do not heed the Mongol. They do not even consider themselves part of our country and are forever rebelling. I think the Khan is prone to believing only what he wishes to believe and not what is really true."

Amused by the captain's insight into the Khan's character, Diego continued to question him.

"How long will it take us to cross the mountains?"

"I met a traveler once, sire, who came from the country on the other side of that range. He told me that he traveled twelve days through the mountains and that the greatest danger to his person came from the wild animals he encountered there. He traveled at this time of year and was loud in his praise of the beauty of that area."

"I am impatient to put those mountains behind me. I shall not feel safe until I am far from the Khan's lands."

"You will be leaving this vessel in three or four days, for we shall come to the end of the river. Then you and your friends will be able to make your way in peace to the uncharted land."

The Khan paced the campsite near his imperial tent. For days he had waited, but still there was no news of the Venetian. His soldiers were growing restive and he had lost confidence in the belief that the Mazzarini party would try to escape by land. Again and again the Khan went over the facts. Somehow, Diego Mazzarini had spirited his wife and servants away from the house in Hangchow, contriving to make it seem that he traveled on the sea. But when the Khan had followed them he had found no trace of the party. Therefore they must have traveled by land and would be heading for the border. Had he judged the Venetian's intentions wrongly? Had Mazzarini ridden northwest and taken his party through the desert? Had he considered taking the beautiful one through such impossible country? The Khan remembered his astonishment when told of Diego's association with Hsu Lan. If the Venetian was besotted with the harlot, why was he risking his life by escaping from the kingdom with his wife? Such behavior was not reasonable or logical to the Khan's mind, and its inconsistency troubled him.

"Send the imperial messengers to ride in relays to Hangchow. There they must order the commander of the garrison to arrest the courtesan Hsu Lan."

"Yes, my lord. And when they have taken her, what must be done?"

"She must be questioned about the escape of Diego Mazzarini."

"Will torturers be required, my lord?"

"I think it likely. I care not how the information is extracted. When you have discovered everything she has to tell of her complicity in this matter, have riders return at once to report to me. They must ride at battle speed night and day, mark you. My life may depend on what is told by that wicked creature."

"I will use the express relay, sire, and obey your orders with the greatest urgency."

That night the Khan could not sleep. For hours he went over and over the conundrum of Diego's escape. Gradually, grudging admiration stole into the ruler's mind and he could not help respecting the man who had learned so quickly to think with the deviousness of a Mongol.

As dawn came over the mountains, the Khan walked to the perimeter of his camp, still trying to find answers to the questions in his mind. He sat disconsolately on the grass, resigning himself to the fact that nothing was certain except that the Mazzarini party had left Hangchow. The Khan returned to his tent and called for the old Chinese astrologer.

When Tai Cheng was summoned to appear before the Khan, his face betrayed none of the inner turmoil he was feeling. He had already looked into the stars and had known

249

for days that Diego Mazzarini was destined to journey both by ship and by land.

Tai Cheng thought of the home he would never see again, of his daughter who had cried when he was taken away by a Mongol captain. Soon he would die surrounded by the barbarians who had conquered his beloved China. And all this because of the Khan's obsession with the lady Lotus Flower, who loved her husband as a woman should. Tai Cheng thought of the Venetian, who adored his wife so fervently he was risking his life and hers rather than remain under the influence of the Khan.

The old man rose and went to the Emperor's tent, bowing low and commencing his prediction. "I have seen something of Count Mazzarini's journey, sire."

"Tell me what you know."

"I see the Venetian in a ship on the sea, sire."

The Khan leaped up, his eyes gleaming with rage. "So! He has tricked me twice into following him in the wrong direction. What duplicity after all the kindness I have shown him! Where is he going? Can you see anything of the lands to which he sails?"

"I see first a port busy with the ships of many nations. There are rocks leading from the harbor to the sea, which is dark-green and fathomless in its depths."

Knowing this to be Zaiton, on the eastern coast of China, the Khan moaned in frustration that he had relinquished his pursuit on the sea.

"Continue. Pay no heed to my suffering."

The astrologer concealed a smile, delighted to have been able to inflict hurt on the man who had destroyed so many of the inhabitants of China. The old man took a breath and continued, "Next I see the ship continuing to an island in the midst of the sea. There... there..."

The Khan urged Tai Cheng to make haste and say what was on his mind. The astrologer hesitated, as he always did when about to give bad news. Fear gripped the Khan's heart and he roared for the prediction to be made.

Tai Cheng's voice grew faint as he proceeded: "On this island, the natives will damage the Venetian's ship so it cannot return to the ocean. Then they will kill Count Mazzarini and all his party. I see blood running on the decks of the ship and staining the sea red. None will survive, my lord, and rightly so, for such is the fate of *all* who disobey your Omnipotent will."

The Khan felt as if he had been struck by a sword through the heart. For a moment he stared into space. Then, Tai Cheng was shocked to see the imperial frame racked by sobs. He retreated hastily, unnoticed by the Emperor.

In his tent, the astrologer thought of the metamorphosis that had taken place before his eyes. Within seconds the Emperor's shoulders had sagged, his face had paled, and he had grown old, irrevocably old, so that all the paint in Cathay could not remedy the dejection of his pallor.

Tai Cheng felt few pangs of conscience at the lies he had told. He thought of Lotus Flower, who had once consulted him about her love of the Venetian. As he remembered her bright face and the generosity she had shown him, Tai Cheng knew he had done the right thing. The astrologer closed his eyes wearily. The excitement and tension of the past weeks had drained him of what little strength remained. Now he had done all he could for the Mazzarinis it was time to pray for the gods to receive his soul. Outside the tent, Mongol soldiers were eating their midday meal. Tai Cheng listened to their raucous voices, and grew happy as the sounds began to fade into oblivion.

Hours later, when the Khan's servant came to call the astrologer again, he found Tai Cheng dead on the couch, a smile of contentment on his wizened face.

The following day the Khan gave orders for his Mongol soldiers to return to their territories. Many noted the Emperor's ghastly complexion and the look of anguish in his eyes, but none dared inquire what had caused the sudden change in the imperial disposition.

At great speed the Emperor's party made its way back to Hangchow, through Tali and Toloman, from Luchow to Chunking, camping at night by the river and riding by day with the relentlessness for which they were famous. At Chunking they met the imperial messengers returning from Hangchow with news of the courtesan. The Khan ordered his

251

soldiers to make camp. Then he asked that the messengers inform him of the result of their inquiry.

The leader spoke in a hushed voice. "The courtesan Hsu Lan, about whom you asked, my lord Emperor, could not be found. She was not at her estate in Hangchow nor in her home town of Suchow, where she has a retreat. Express riders went to Peking to ascertain if the lady had returned to the capital, but she had not."

"I left spies to watch the courtesan. What do they report?"

"On the night after your departure with the army, the lady Hsu Lan invited your spies into her house. They have not been seen since, sire."

"Have you no other information for me?"

"None, sire. Only that Hsu Lan has taken with her all the gold, the jewels and valuables for which she is famous. Nothing but furniture and some worthless objects remained in the house."

"And what of her servants?"

"They are all gone, my lord. The lady would surely have needed a ship to move such an assembly, and that she did not have."

The Khan nodded regally in dismissal of the messenger. Then he retired to ponder what he had been told. Suddenly he knew he was growing old. To have been outwitted was bad enough, but to have been twice outwitted and this time by the most expensive courtesan in China was almost too much for him to bear. Or had it all been part of a plan masterminded by Lotus Flower? The Khan believed that it had. Yet again he longed for her, remembering their first meeting by the wildfowl pool. He thought of Tai Cheng's prediction and cried in anguish throughout the night for his loved one.

By morning the Khan had decided to erect a palace in Lotus Flower's memory, placing it near the lake of Chagan Nor. Each year, on the anniversary of their first meeting, he would go and stay alone in its marble halls to commune with the spirit of the departed one.

As the Khan came near to Hangchow, he was met by Badriak, the imperial horsemaster. Badriak's face was ashen pale, and the Khan knew that he was profoundly disturbed. He took the horsemaster into his tent and having made sure that they could not be overheard asked his friend to reveal the source of his distraction.

Badriak knelt before the Emperor. "I do not know how to break this news to you, sire."

"We have been friends for so many years. There is nothing you cannot say."

"One of your new warships has been stolen, sire."

"Is that what troubles you?"

"It is, my lord."

"What care I for warships? I shall build ten more and ten times ten if it pleases me!"

Badriak explained what was on his mind.

"There is evidence pointing to the fact that the ship was stolen by those in the pay of the courtesan Hsu Lan. The woman has used the ship to escape and to travel far in pursuit of the Venetian party. One of the dockers who assisted when the ship embarked on its journey swore that he heard the courtesan say she was heading for the Malabar Coast of India."

The Khan cried out, his face purple with fury. Then suddenly he fell at Badriak's feet, and the horsemaster was obliged to call the imperial physician.

Throughout the night Badriak sat at the Khan's side, urging him to recover his will to live, his desire for revenge and his determination to pursue. The Khan said nothing, so great was his anger, so enormous his shock at this latest affront to his imperial dignity. When he was well enough to speak he would comment only: "Say nothing of this, Badriak, for if it should ever be known I shall pay with my life." Badriak assured the Emperor that he would never speak of what had happened.

Slowly, the Emperor made his way back to Peking. He was not seen for weeks as he recuperated in the imperial suite, pampered and fussed over by Jamui. Despite all that had happened, the Khan still spent his nights thinking of Lotus Flower, admiring her more every day, for he was sure she had devised the wicked plan that had fooled him. There would never again be such a woman in the kingdom. And he would never again know the feeling of love. Secretly, sadly, the Khan continued to dream of lost love.

* * *

While the Emperor of China grieved for Lotus Flower, Diego and his party passed through the mountains that divided Mongol territory from the uncharted areas. They had no guide and no accurate map of the mountains. Diego led his party with a light heart and a cautious eye, ever wary of Mongol patrols, ever watchful for the lions, bears and lynxes which had made the nights at the beginning of the journey perilous.

Soon the pathways were no longer bordered by precipitous drops but linked by gorges lined with juniper trees. Lotus Flower was happy to be with her husband in the clean air of freedom. Already the past was fading in her mind, and she looked forward with joy to arriving in Venice. Ho Shan made notes on everything he saw, entertaining Giorgio each night over the campfire with observations of life in the area. When the other members of the party were sound asleep, Giorgio dreamed of his wife, Arya, who would be waiting for him somewhere in the mountains beyond the clouds. Giorgio had no idea how he would return to the village where he had married, but he awaited his reunion with Arya with all the eagerness of a young boy.

At one of the villages en route to the valley, the Venetian party were given a resounding welcome. Young girls sprang from mud huts and fathers brought their daughters and pressed them on the men of the party. Gradually, Diego came to understand that in this village the most desirable women were the ones who had been with the most men. Tokens adorned the unmarried girls' necks, and some had twenty or more, each signifying that she had given herself to a different man. The girls were proud of the fact that their beauty had inspired such admiration. Virgins were regarded with horror and considered unlucky enough to be displeasing to the gods.

In early evening Giorgio and Ho Shan disappeared with some of the most persistent dusky ladies of the village. Diego retired with Lotus Flower, who was delighted to learn that there were indeed places in the world where a maiden's virtue had no value.

For three days the party remained in the village, eating and drinking and being entertained by musicians and the relentlessly sensuous women. Then, at Diego's insistence, they moved on and began the descent into the undulating plain below. Soon they were in a beautiful valley where orchards of peach, plum and orange scented the air with heady perfume. The fields were bordered by pomegranate trees and walnut bushes, the hillsides golden with broom. To the exhausted travelers this fertile place seemed like paradise.

Lotus Flower watched as women with muslin turbans walked along a track followed by their children. The women wore long coats, belted at the waist, the men were barefoot, the children's hair decorated with silver rings. In the doorway of a mud hut at the approach to the village, a young lady stroked a snakeskin fiddle with a yak-hair bow. As the party walked by, they were offered tea from copper kettles and paste made from barley flour and yak butter.

Only Ho Shan could make himself understood in this area, and he reported what he had ascertained. "These people are Tibetans, sire. Their ruler has diplomatic links with the Khan, who conquered this land some time ago. But the ruler cares nothing for the Mongol Khan. We are safe here, and if you will tell this man where you want to go he will provide us with a guide."

"Have you asked where we are and what lies below if we continue this descent?"

"We have traveled along the Yangtze River and on one of its tributaries, sire. If we go directly south we shall reach a country ruled by the Khan where the natives report everything to the Omnipotence. In the other direction, beyond the mountains to our rear, is the Kush, and toward the sun is the sea and an enchanted place where flowers bloom in profusion. I think it is best that we ask to have the guide take us there."

"And then how shall we reach Thana, where we must embark on my ship?"

"Thana is south of the enchanted place, sire. To get there we must travel through a burning plain to get to the Malabar Coast. But that journey will be nothing to the one we have just accomplished."

Diego looked thoughtfully around the village. It would not please Lotus Flower to stay long in such a place, and it was wise to put the greatest possible distance between his party and the lands governed by the Khan. Diego agreed with Ho Shan's decision and instructed him to speak at once with the village elder about a guide.

The journey continued at a leisurely pace in ever-increasing heat. Often Diego ordered a halt so they could refresh themselves in mountain pools surrounded by rocks velvety with moss. The nights were loud with the sound of bullfrogs and merry with the glimmer of fireflies. The dawn hours were noisy with the sound of birdsong and the high-pitched shouts of natives working in the fields. Lotus Flower had never been so happy. Only once did the fears of the past intrude on the contentment of the present, when they saw a line of Mongol riders hastening above them on the high ground.

Ho Shan reassured his companions, "They are tribute collectors riding back to Peking with the valuables they have taken. Have no fear; they ride toward the sun so their eyes are blind to our presence."

The party continued through fields of feathery grass glistening gold in the sunlight. Often they paused at wayside shrines to pay tribute to the gods of those who guided them, and always they were greeted with friendly curiosity by those they met. The hills were blue with larkspur and scented with lilies. Sheep and musk deer approached to view the strangers, their tameness surprising Diego. With each new day the scenery became more beautiful until Giorgio exclaimed what they had all been thinking.

"Surely, sir, I think I am in paradise!"

Diego covered his eyes and looked ahead through the oscillating heat of midday to the sepia plain.

"Once we are beyond that high pass we shall be able to breath easily, my good Giorgio. I believe we are the luckiest beings in the world to have escaped so easily from the Omnipotence."

Part Three:

India

Day after day spring's glory vies with the glorious sun.
Sloping roads to the hill city smell of flowering
    almond.
How long before the heart's threads, all cares gone,
Float free for a hundred feet with the gossamer?

—Li Shang-Yin (812–858)

Chapter Thirteen:

The Tree House

Lotus Flower was sitting on the terrace of the tree house painting a blue peacock strutting below on the beach. It was midsummer, and though the heat was like a burning furnace all around her she looked relaxed and happy. When they had first arrived in India, Lotus Flower had felt isolated and afraid that the Khan's army would come riding across the flatlands that stretched as far as the eye could see. But since Diego had moved his party south to the Malabar Coast she had been at peace. With feverish excitement she had watched the house taking shape as palm, bamboo and aloe woods were cut into the form of a machan, or platform, built into the widespread branches of a dragon tree. The Venetian had designed this strange dwelling to please his wife and had personally supervised its construction.

Under the shelter of an overhanging roof of palm fronds,

Lotus Flower looked down on a beach of pale-gold sand and sea that was green as an emerald under the sun. Twenty miles south, Diego's ship was waiting to deliver the party to Hormuz. But Lotus Flower felt the need for rest, because the journey from China had exhausted her more than she cared to admit. So Diego had ordered the house built, and Lotus Flower was happy to remain in its shelter until Giorgio returned from his journey north to collect Arya.

Diego arrived home as the sun was setting and the tree house was bathed in a glow of red light. Below, on the sand, Lotus Flower walked among the peacocks and parrots which followed her everywhere. She was looking intently out to sea as though trying to diminish the distance between her temporary home and the Venetian lagoon. This she did each evening, like a ritual, and Diego loved her for it. He hurried to her side, and together they walked in the cool of evening to a rocky point some distance from the house.

"What do you think of as you gaze out to sea?" Diego asked.

"I think of Venice and wonder when I shall see it."

"Giorgio will be back within the month."

"How can you be sure of that?"

"It is time he returned, and I know he will not linger in the mountains for fear of meeting a Mongol patrol."

"I am curious to see his wife."

"I can promise you will never have seen a woman like Arya."

"Shall we go fishing again tomorrow?"

"If the sun is not too hot for you."

"I saw the catch some of the fishermen brought for Fan-Tai to cook. The fish were scarlet and black and silver. Some had claws and bulging eyes, others had swordlike spines along their backs. I never tire of their variety and their strange beauty."

"You see beauty in everything, my love."

"Shall we go in the canoe tomorrow or shall we ride to the lagoon?"

"The lagoon is lovely at this time of year, and there will be cover for us under the tree ferns when the sun becomes too taxing."

They ate lampuka fish cooked on skewers, lamb roasted

with mint, rice and flat loaves of bread. A local boy acted as Lotus Flower's page, hurrying to her side with the choicest morsels and choosing fruit for her desert with meticulous care. Grapes, figs, cherries, musk melons and apricots were served in a bowl scooped from the trunk of a coconut tree. When the meal was over, Diego led his wife to the terrace of the house, and together they looked out at the green, phosphorescent sea. Diego held Lotus Flower close to his heart as they listened to the night calls of this alien land. Below, local fishermen were lashing logs together in the form of a rough raft. As they pushed the raft out to sea, the men called a greeting to the couple and sang a song purported to attract the most powerful creatures of the deep.

That night, as she lay half asleep, Lotus Flower heard a snake slithering along the roof fronds. She spoke apprehensively, and Diego knew she was afraid.

"That snake reminds me of the Khan, sire."

"Do you think often of the past?"

"Sometimes I think of my home in Peking. Sometimes I think of the Emperor and fear his power. But often I forget the past because there is so much to look forward to in the future."

"The worst of our journey is over. Soon we shall sail in triumph to Venice, and I promise you will love my city."

"Tell me again about the house by the sea?"

Diego told the story he had told so many times.

"In the house by the sea there are many people who will love you. The garden is full of flowers and trees, and there is a gazebo where you can sit and watch the gondolas on the lagoon. Your bed will be carved from chestnut wood in the Chinese style, and from your window you will see the islands and smell the lemon blossom."

Lotus Flower's eyes closed, and she fell asleep on her husband's shoulder. The Venetian kissed her and held her tightly as if to keep her safe from any dangers lurking in the night. For some reason Diego was unable to sleep, and for hours he thought over the events of the past six years. By the time he returned home to Venice he would be thirty, a man who had traveled to the far corners of the world, who had seen what others had not seen and accomplished what few dreamed of achieving. He had suffered in the desert and risked his life in perilous mountain passes. He had been given a new fortune by the Khan of the Mongol Horde and had succeeded in seeing his wealth safely out of the kingdom. And, most important of all, he had found love and contentment with Lotus Flower and had been able to escape with her from China despite insurmountable odds. Diego looked toward the horizon, where the sun was rising like a ball of fire over the water. Though he had said nothing to his wife, he was impatient to leave the Malabar Coast and to set sail for Venice. Often he scanned the path that led north from the village, longing for Giorgio's return.

The lagoon where Lotus Flower liked to fish was surrounded by coconut palms. A band of green water led from the secret place to the rice paddies farther south. Violet bougainvillea bloomed in profusion, and insects with gleaming silver bodies darted on the water. As they approached the lagoon, Lotus Flower saw a brilliant yellow shikara. The boat was canopied against the heat of the sun, and she recognized it as one of the craft used by rich rulers in the Northern Provinces.

"Where did this charming boat come from?"

"I put it there for you. I thought it more suited to your beauty than a fisherman's canoe."

"It is lovely. But where did you find it?"

"One of the traders sold it to me."

Delighted by the surprise, Lotus Flower ran aboard the craft and soon was lying on velvet cushions under the awning.

"I am so comfortable I fear I shall not find the energy to fish."

"I will fish for both of us."

"You spoil me as if I were a child."

"You are everything to me, my love."

Lotus Flower lay back looking at the exotic vegetation of the area, at scarlet orchids and yellow cockatoos, at hibiscus blooms and white-faced monkeys leaping between the branches. A kingfisher flew toward her, perching on the rail of the boat and inclining its head in puzzlement as Lotus Flower mimicked its call.

Diego caught a fish with a rainbow-striped body. As his wife watched, he held it up for her to admire. Within two hours he had a dozen silvery bodies strung on a line. Then, putting his fishing rod aside, Diego lay at his wife's side and kissed her cheeks, puzzling at the faraway expression in her eyes.

"If I ask what you are thinking, will you tell me you think of Venice?"

"I am not thinking of Venice."

"Then you are thinking of the home you left behind in Peking?"

"I am thinking I am hungry and that I am feeling much stronger than when I first arrived on the Malabar Coast."

Diego rummaged in a basket and brought out wild duck, bread and wine with a pot of fresh apricots swimming in syrup.

"Fan-Tai said you would soon be hungry, so she made food for us. Eat your fill, my love. We shall stay here until dusk, because I do not wish to ride back in the heat of midday."

Diego pulled down the blinds on either side of the boat, enclosing them in a sunlit cell. He untied the robe Lotus Flower was wearing and traced a finger over her body, enjoying the shudder of anticipation and the eagerness in her eyes. As they made love, the boat rocked gently on the water, and they forgot everything but the sensuous warmth of their surroundings.

It was dusk when Diego tied the boat to the stump of a tree by the side of the lagoon. Bats wheeled overhead in the scented evening air, and the surrounding land was alive with the shriek of nightjars and the croaking of treefrogs. Diego walked back through the undergrowth to where he had left the horses. The animals were gone. Surprised, he searched until it was dark, but the horses had vanished without trace. He returned to his wife, and Lotus Flower knew that he was angry.

"Someone has stolen the horses!"

"But the natives live by fishing or by growing rice. What use would they have for horses?"

"Then how have they escaped? They were secure and had water within easy reach."

"I do not know. But now we must walk back to the house."

"It is dark and we have no lantern."

"We shall see by the light of the moon."

Diego hesitated. He had not brought his sword and was loath to pass through the strip of woodland without the means of protecting his wife. On the other hand, if they stayed the night on the boat, they had no food, no water, no wine and no means of making fire. In the morning when they were parched with thirst they would face the long walk back in the heat of the sun. Diego made his decision, and returning to the boat took the string of fishes and the few remaining drops of wine.

"We shall return to the beach together. But first you must drink what remains of the wine."

"You drink first."

"I am used to thirst, you are not. Drink, Lotus Flower."

Diego led his wife through the woodland bordering the lagoon. Within minutes they were on the rough stone ground of a small farm. Diego helped Lotus Flower as she stumbled, admiring her for not complaining though she was wearing the lightest shoes. He was angry that the perfection of the day had been marred by the disappearance of the horses. When they had been walking for an hour, the couple heard the pounding of waves on the shore. Smiling, they hugged each other and ran toward the ghostly line of surf breaking on the sand. Then, sure that Lotus Flower was exhausted, Diego picked her up and carried her the rest of the way to the tree house.

"We are lucky to return home unscathed by the dangers of the night."

"I love you, Diego, and I love adventuring with you. Life has been exciting since we have been together. I even like the bad moments, for they make the good ones seem sweeter. When I am old I shall talk of these days, but I do not know if I shall believe that they really happened."

When they reached the house, Diego saw that Li-Huei had placed lanterns on the sand to light the way. He put Lotus Flower down, brushing a fly from her neck as it clung tenaciously to the skin. Then he saw that his own hands were covered with the same flies, and, dislodging them impatiently, he helped his wife into the house.

Li-Huei was waiting to speak with his master when Diego descended to the beach. "Sire, I waited up for you because we knew you would be troubled by the disappearance of the horses. Something must have frightened them, a tiger perhaps, for they broke their fastenings and returned home without you. They are now tethered and calm again."

"We walked home, and I am relieved we saw no tigers, for I left my sword behind."

"I have asked Fan-Tai to prepare food for you, sire. Also I wish to inform you that some fiendish flies have appeared this day, the likes of which I have not seen before. They are black and they cling to the skin like limpets, drawing blood. I have placed gauze over my lady's bed so she will not be devoured, and tomorrow I will ask the natives what manner of flies these are and what we must do to be rid of them."

"My thanks to you, Li-Huei."

"I will retire now, sire, though I doubt I shall sleep for the excitement of the day. Truly I had begun to wonder if you and my lady would ever return to us."

The next morning a party of traders arrived from the north. Lotus Flower purchased brocade and perfume, rare spices and gold amulets studded with turquoise. The traders sat on the beach looking out to sea as their animals rested, and Lotus Flower enjoyed trying to communicate with them. She was assisted by her page, a native boy whose quick ear had picked up enough of her language to enable him to translate.

As the men spoke, the boy turned to Lotus Flower. "These men have traveled far, my lady, through the plateau at the center of the country. They speak of seeing Mongols. Do you think Count Mazzarini's servant will be safe? Shall I inquire where they saw the Mongols?"

Lotus Flower turned to Diego, who considered the traders' swarthy faces. Diego spoke cautiously.

"It is best to ask nothing. Wherever they go these men will pass on news to any who might ask. We would do well to say as little of ourselves as possible."

For three hours, until the sun began to sink in the sky,

the traders remained on the sand, cooking fish bought from local men and drinking their fill of coconut milk and rice spirit. To Diego's relief, they took their leave in the friendliest fashion, tying their merchandise on the backs of the camels and elephants that had accompanied them. Then they formed a picturesque silhouette against the red evening sky and the caravan moved on. Diego watched their departure thoughtfully. The traders had said they were traveling east to the far coast of India and then to land bordering the Khan's territories. The journey would take months, and Diego worried because he knew the traders would gossip of a Chinese princess they had met on the Malabar Coast and her husband, a man with golden hair who lived in a strange house of driftwood, waiting for the day when he would sail home to his land beyond the horizon.

Diego looked again to the north, shielding his eyes from the sun, willing Giorgio to return. But there was no sign of his servant, and he wondered if Giorgio had come to harm. Giorgio had insisted on traveling with only one guide, two beaters and Ho Shan, who was eager to see as much of the country as possible. Giorgio had reckoned on riding like a Mongol, pausing only to rest the animals. So why had he not returned? Diego knew that his party would not be secure until they reached Venice. He thought wistfully of his brother, smiling as he envisaged the moment of arrival in the Venetian lagoon under a sail of scarlet and gold. It would be good to see Pierluigi again, to have news of Venice and to meet all his friends.

In the early dawn hours Diego woke with a start, shocked to hear screaming below on the beach. He leaped up and ran outside, calling to Li-Huei's grandson, who was on the sand, looking in horror out to sea.

"What is wrong?"

Chang-Chi pointed out to sea, and following his gaze Diego saw a ship anchored in the bay. His heart missed a beat as he realized that the vessel was one of the Khan's warships. Angrily Diego turned to Li-Huei. "Tell your grandson and his wife to control their feelings. I will not give the Khan the satisfaction of knowing his arrival has destroyed us."

Li-Huei nodded and spoke sharply to the sobbing couple

on the beach. Then he watched as Diego hurried back to the tree house to tell Lotus Flower what had happened. The sun came over the horizon, lighting the beach with a bright-yellow light, and looking up, the Venetian saw his wife on the terrace, staring in apprehension at the ship in the bay.

When Lotus Flower spoke her voice trembled with anger. "That devil will follow us to the end of the earth. But how has he found us when we are half the world away?"

"I do not know. I only know he is here, and as I see men lowering a boat I must dress and prepare to receive the Khan."

Lotus Flower followed Diego inside and stood looking despairingly out to sea. "He will make us return with him to Cathay."

"I shall refuse."

"Then he will take us prisoner."

"We shall leave tonight and ride over the mountains."

"Will this *never* end? Will the Khan follow us even to Venice?"

"Do not despair, my love. Tell me you are still the vixen who made fun of the Emperor when he tried to enslave you. Tell me you will never give in to his demands."

"I shall ride at your side until we are far away from the Khan. And I shall happily die at your side if we cannot escape him."

A startled cry came to Diego's ears, and looking out, he saw Li-Huei waving from the water's edge.

"Count Mazzarini, come quickly! Sire, my lady, come at once! The gods be praised, we are delivered."

Diego and Lotus Flower ran from the house to the beach, where they stood looking out to sea. Suddenly they smiled with relief, because in a boat being rowed toward the shore was the courtesan Hsu Lan. The lady carried a parasol of imperial yellow, and they saw that her face was flushed with pleasure.

The sailors jumped out and dragged the boat onto the sand. Then they lifted Hsu Lan out and deposited her by the Venetian's side. The courtesan looked at Diego and then to Lotus Flower, who was crying with joy at this reprieve from further flight. Hsu Lan bowed graciously, and as she explained herself Lotus Flower's tears turned to laughter.

"My lord Count Mazzarini, my lady Lotus Flower, I am *so* happy to be reunited with you. You cannot imagine what adventures I have had. Your plan worked as well as you expected. The Khan rushed to his warship and pursued your party down the coast of China. Then, when he realized he had been tricked, he returned to Hangchow just as we expected. Within a few days he had decided to ride for the border with a million of his Mongol Horde summoned from every corner of the land. I was so relieved at his departure that I threw a celebration for all my friends in Hangchow."

"But why did you leave Hangchow, my lady?"

Hsu Lan looked appealingly into Diego's eyes.

"My lord, fate dealt me a shocking blow. Just when I imagined that life had settled into its peaceful routine, I was visited by an imperial inquisitor accompanied by two of the Khan's men. These surly fellows informed me that the Khan suspected me of assisting you and my lady in your escape."

Lotus Flower's eyes widened at the thought of the inquisitor, and she spoke in a breathless voice, "What did you do, my lady Hsu Lan?"

"With the aid of my friends I managed to incarcerate these men in the cellar of my home. Then *I* questioned *them*. It became obvious that my days in Hangchow were over. I would no longer be able to live there and indeed would no longer be safe anywhere in the Khan's kingdom."

Diego held his wife close as they led Hsu Lan into the tree house.

Hsu Lan continued her story. "I knew I must make haste to escape, so I mobilized my servants and every friend I had in Hangchow. First we arranged for the Khan's warship to be stolen. Then I engaged an expert Chinese crew, who loaded the ship with my valuables, my servants and some people wishing to escape the kingdom. We sailed at full speed down the coast in the direction you had mentioned. We have had many adventures, sire, and I can tell you that I have not enjoyed most of them. But the day I sailed into the harbor of Cochin and was told that your ship was lying farther north on that same coast was, without doubt, the happiest day of my life. Now here I am. I beg your forgiveness for terrifying the servants. No doubt they thought the Emperor had arrived to persecute them."

Diego poured wine and admitted wryly, "That is what we all thought, my lady."

"May I ask if you and your wife would like to visit my ship? I would be honored to entertain you."

Diego called for more wine, amused to hear Lotus Flower questioning the courtesan about her future plans.

"May I ask what you are going to do now, my lady Hsu Lan?"

"I intend, with your permission, to sail with you to Venice."

Lotus Flower covered her face with a fan to conceal the confusion she was feeling.

Hsu Lan explained her intentions more fully. "My past is such that I must now leave it behind, and I pray that you and Count Mazzarini will help me in my resolve. It is my intention to sail in the warship at the same time as you sail in your ship to Hormuz, then to travel overland with you to Acre. I shall arrive in your company in Venice, and from that moment will behave as a lady would behave. I shall invent a new past for myself so as not to shame you, because I wish to have the pleasure of your friendship in the noble city of Venice. Will it be possible? Can a woman like me be accepted in society, or must I forever remain an outcast?"

Lotus Flower answered at once. "It is possible, is it not, my lord? We must help you as you have helped us. If you had not been willing to risk your life we would still be in China and I would be in the Khan's harem. We owe you everything, my lady Hsu Lan, and we shall fulfill our obligations with pleasure and humility."

As he ate, Diego thought of the irony of the situation. Hsu Lan needed a new identity, a respectable name and reason for being with Lotus Flower which could not be questioned. The obvious one was the truth, but he had sworn never to tell his wife that the courtesan's interest in her was maternal.

Diego thought aloud, hoping Lotus Flower would agree with his reasoning. "We shall arrive in Venice with Chinese servants and I with a Chinese wife who would normally be accompanied by her mother and members of her family. As my lady's parents are dead it would be advantageous for her to appear to have someone of her own kin. If you agree, my lady Hsu Lan, I think it would be wise to pretend that you are my wife's aunt."

Hsu Lan blushed, suddenly fearful that her daughter would reject any suggestion that associated them. She was surprised when Lotus Flower agreed readily and made her own suggestion.

"How clever you are. My lady Hsu Lan can be my aunt. We shall say that as my family are all dead my one remaining relative accompanied me to Venice. As I am a princess, the custom would be for me to travel with many of my family, so I am sure everyone will believe what we say."

Hsu Lan closed her eyes, willing herself not to cry tears of joy. She had journeyed through heat and storm to be near the daughter she loved. Now she would live out her days close to Lotus Flower, able to advise and guide her through the problems of settling in an alien land. When Hsu Lan opened her eyes she saw Lotus Flower watching her with a knowing affectionate gaze. For a moment the courtesan was afraid the Venetian had told his wife her secret, and she looked toward him suspiciously. But Diego was unaware of her tension.

Relaxing, Hsu Lan spoke further of her plans. "My friends from Hangchow disembarked on the far coast of India, where they intend to make a new life for themselves. My personal staff remain with me, and the crew are loyal. It is my intention to sell the warship on reaching Hormuz. Then I will release the money in equal divisions to the crew so they can make their own way in life. Having finished my business with the crew, I shall accompany you to Venice with my jewels and my finest belongings. Those who work for me know what I intend to do and they have given me every encouragement. We shall have our stories well rehearsed, Count Mazzarini. You need have no fear that we shall falter when we arrive in your city."

During the next few days, Diego and Lotus Flower visited the ship in the bay for dinner, or Hsu Lan was rowed to the shore by her sailors. The summer was drawing to a close, and often Diego looked at the sky with a worried expression, aware that the season of rains was approaching.

Seeing her husband's unease, Lotus Flower tried hard to comfort Diego. "Do not worry. I am sure Giorgio is safe and that he will soon be home."

"Come and sit down and tell me what my lady Hsu Lan has told you of her journey."

"When she talks of the journey I laugh so much my sides ache."

Diego drew Lotus Flower to him and stroked her hair as she described Hsu Lan's adventures. "Do you know how my lady stole the Khan's warship?"

"I cannot imagine how much money Hsu Lan had to pay to bribe the guards to release it," Diego admitted.

"She paid nothing at all. She sent one of her friends with an imperial seal and a scroll bearing the imperial cipher. The guards at the shipyard believed the message, and Hsu Lan's crewmen were able to provision the vessel and sail it out of harbor."

"Where did she obtain the seal and the cipher?"

"The seal was stolen from one of the Khan's messengers. Hsu Lan herself obtained the cipher when she visited the palace to ask news of the Emperor. She has an admirable ability to remain calm in the most unnerving circumstances. Also she knows how to steal the robe off a man's back without his realizing the loss. My lady said she was taught this trick by the finest thief in Cathay. She also stole the Khan's imperial umbrella—the yellow one with silver decorations. She told me she had always wanted an imperial umbrella so she took it at the same time as the cipher."

Diego was distracted only momentarily by Hsu Lan's adventures, for he was still worried about Giorgio's safety and impatient to be home in Venice. As he lay next to her he traced a finger over Lotus Flower's cheeks and whispered his plans into her ear.

"When our good Giorgio returns we shall sail away to La Serenissima. How I am looking forward to showing you my home and all the places I have described to you. I love you, my darling. Without you even Venice would be hell."

Chapter Fourteen:

Giorgio

As Giorgio drew near the village where he had met his wife he was puzzled by the deathly silence of the forest. No birds sang in the early-morning light, no animals fled as he approached. Giorgio stood for a moment weighing the hollow stillness. Then the guide turned anxiously to him and voiced his thoughts.

"Something is wrong, sire."

"How can you tell?"

"There is no noise in the forest."

"That I know, but why is there no noise?"

"I do not know, sire."

"Perhaps there has been an eruption in the mountains."

Giorgio rode resolutely on, followed by Ho Shan and the guide. As they passed the place where he had been attacked by the tiger, Giorgio shuddered, and Ho Shan comforted him.

"I perceive that you are upset, friend Giorgio. Do not worry. If there has been a disturbance of the earth we shall follow those who have moved from the village. If not we shall ascertain what has happened."

"You are a good friend, Ho Shan. I feel myself lucky that you are with me."

As they rode into the village, Giorgio examined the houses that circled the clearing and the river where local men used to fish. He thought of Arya and how she had immersed him to save him from the Mongols. Everything was as it had been except that the village was empty, devastatingly, eerily empty of life. Loath to shout out or to make his presence felt in case there were Mongols nearby, Giorgio walked back and forth, searching, examining, puzzling this unexpected sight. In what had been Arya's hut he found cooking pots, a child's rattle, a pile of cotton wrappings and a bowl containing the remains of some cooked rice. In the other huts there were simple possessions and decayed food but no evidence of recent occupation. Giorgio went to the center of the clearing and examined the fire pit, which was as dry as sand. Nothing had burned there for days. He was about to order his men to make camp for the night when he heard something rustling in the branches above his head. Looking up, Giorgio saw a small boy peering down at him from the safety of a banyan tree.

"Come down here at once!" he called to the boy.

The child stared impassively at the intruder. Then, taking his bow and arrow, he shot at Giorgio, missing his head by inches. Roaring with annoyance, Giorgio ordered the boy to be brought to him, and watched with increasing anger as the bearers struggled to bring the boy down. He was startled to see the little boy fighting so fiercely and snatching back the bow when it was taken from him. Finally, the two stood facing each other, and Giorgio saw contempt in the child's eyes as he motioned for the native guide to question the boy.

"Ask this horrible child where the people from the village have gone."

The guide squatted at the boy's side and spoke in a sing-song voice. Giorgio edged closer, trying to catch the expression in the child's face, but he saw only defiance.

"What does he say?"

"He says that his mother was taken away with the other women of the village by a party of soldiers."

"When did this happen?"

"He does not know, sire, but such a small boy could not live long in the forest."

Giorgio looked at the child's thin arms and the stomach distended with hunger. Then, disdaining to question the boy further, he ordered the fire to be lit. Soon wild ducks were cooking in the embers and yams, rice and eels stewing in a pot. Giorgio stirred the food, watching as the boy edged closer, his eyes wild with hunger. Pity filled the servant's heart and he took a leaf and put some of the food on it. This he handed to the boy. Returning to the fire, Giorgio turned the meat, picking off crisp pieces of meat and licking his lips with relish at the subtle taste.

As darkness fell, the boy crept nearer to Giorgio until he was sitting directly behind him. Each time the servant turned, the child ran away and hid in the bushes. But once Giorgio's attention returned to the food, the boy crept back and sat so close to him he could feel bony feet pressing against his back. Giorgio smiled indulgently, remembering his own childhood and his shyness when young. He had hidden under tables or behind his father's back in order to avoid friends who visited the house. Then he turned so swiftly the child could not escape. Grasping the boy's shoulders, Giorgio peered into the dark, sad eyes. The child began to cry, terrified that the stranger was going to harm him. Giorgio called to the guide, who came running to his side.

"Ask this child what his mother is called."

The guide addressed the boy. And as Giorgio waited with bated breath, the child replied, "Arya."

Giorgio stared in disbelief at the boy, at the guide and then back to the child. Sensing that something was wrong, Ho Shan hurried over to see what had happened. When Giorgio explained his suspicions, Ho Shan asked the guide to question the child again.

"Ask the boy to tell you his favorite story—the one his mother told him each night before he slept."

For a long time the boy sat very still, and Giorgio imagined he was remembering the happier days with his mother. Finally, haltingly, the child told his favorite story.

"My mother told me of a warrior with golden hair who rode over the mountains at the roof of the world and went in search of treasure. He was accompanied by another warrior, my father, who was tall and handsome and braver than the lion. Someday I shall see those warriors again, and each morning I climb the highest tree to watch for their return."

Tears streamed down Giorgio's face as he handed the child more food. "Ask the boy again where the villagers have gone. Tell him we are friends and that we shall take him to meet the warrior with golden hair."

The guide spoke swiftly, but the child shrugged.

"He does not know, sire. He was asleep in a hammock hung in one of the trees. When the soldiers rode into the village, his mother told him to stay where he was. Then she and the other women were taken by the soldiers. Some of the men escaped into the jungle, the others were enslaved. The boy has been living on the food from his mother's house. Now there is no more food, only the remains of some rice."

That night Giorgio and Ho Shan discussed the events of the day. Aware of his companion's deep depression, Ho Shan reassured Giorgio. "The boy is your son, my good friend. He will therefore come to love you as a son."

"He expects a warrior, not an aging servant!"

"He will love you all the same. Count Mazzarini will know how to find a way to make the child see you as his mother said."

Giorgio paced the clearing, unable to bear the thoughts racing through his mind. "We must return with all speed to the coast, Ho Shan. If the soldiers the boy saw were Mongols, they cannot be far away. Let us pray they were not riding south."

"Will you bring the boy back with you to Venice?"

"I cannot even speak to him!"

"I will teach him your language. He is not stupid, he will learn."

Giorgio looked at the small figure lying by the side of the fire. Then he shrugged. "We cannot leave him here, so we will return with him to Count Mazzarini's camp."

"Are you not pleased with your son, my good friend?"

"All my life I have longed for a son. All my life I have dreamed of teaching my son the things I was never taught and of guiding his youth and enjoying his childish ways. But now I have a son who speaks the language of a foreign land, whose mother has told him I am a warrior and who will soon see me for the servant I am. He will be disappointed in me to his dying day, and I am too old to learn to please him. That is why I am distressed, Ho Shan."

"You are but six and forty, and you *are* a wondrous adventurer. You have been where few have been and can tell tales like no other. The privations of the journey have tired you, my good friend. Once you return to Venice you will be reborn and your son will respect you for what you are."

The next morning Giorgio rode away with his party, pausing only once in the nearby settlement to inquire what had happened to the people of Arya's village. The elder confirmed that the women had been abducted by Mongol soldiers and that the men had been enslaved. Giorgio asked in which direction the Mongols had been traveling, and was relieved when the elder pointed to the east.

Giorgio rode on at the head of his small group, thinking of Arya and trying to accept that he would never see her again. For years he had dreamed of their reunion. Now that moment would never come. Instead he had a son with whom he could not converse, a boy who fired arrows at him and who refused to come near except to sit behind him like a shadow. Giorgio sighed, looking out of the corner of his eye at the boy, who was sitting in front of Ho Shan on a Mongol horse. The child returned his gaze, looking away as though distressed or disappointed by something Giorgio could not understand.

Later in the day the party stopped for food by the side of a lake. Giorgio fished for trout, returning to the camp with a string of silver bodies. As he unhooked the fish he felt his son watching him, but he made no attempt to communicate. Again the lad crept to where Giorgio was sitting and crouched behind him, snatching bits of fish when they were offered and eating hungrily. When the time came to ride on, Giorgio found the boy on his horse.

"Did you put the lad on my horse?" Giorgio asked Ho Shan.

"I did not. He chose to ride with you, and I did not attempt to change his mind, for he is as stubborn as his father."

Giorgio rode on, his mind full of contradictions. He knew he should love his son, but he barely knew him. And yet he was proud of the way the boy had fought on seeing strangers in his village. He was a brave boy, of that there was no doubt, a young warrior of the finest order. Giorgio held the boy a little closer, touched when the boy's hands rested on his on the reins.

As night fell, they saw ahead the light of a campfire. Giorgio debated whether to ride on in the hope of hospitality, but the possibility that the fire belonged to a Mongol patrol chilled him and he ordered his men to halt. Alone, Giorgio crept forward until he was within earshot of the group. He eyed their swarthy faces and the curved scimitars at their belts, shuddering when he recognized the men as pirates from the Malabar Coast. Giorgio retreated hastily almost tripping over his son, who had crept behind him. Without a word he lifted the boy on his shoulder and hurried back to the waiting group.

Ho Shan ran forward to meet Giorgio. "Are they Mongols?"

"They are the pirates of the Malabar Coast. I have heard stories of such people and do not wish to dally with them. We must make a detour and ride swiftly to put distance between us."

All night they rode until they came to a pink shell beach. In the light of dawn Giorgio lit a fire. He was tired and hungry, but first he prepared food for the members of his group. Then when they had all eaten, he rolled out a padded blanket and fell instantly asleep. The boy crept to his side, entwining his legs around Giorgio's to make sure he could not be left behind.

Ho Shan watched the pair, smiling with amusement at his friend's predicament. Giorgio was going to have to learn to live with a child as stubborn as himself. Ho Shan thought of Giorgio's depression and decided to write down everything he knew of the Venetians so he could read the stories to the child and make him understand that his father *was* a warrior, just as he had been told. While the others slept, Ho Shan walked along the beach, shielding his eyes from the sun. He was barely fifty paces from the camp when he saw a cloud of dust in the distance and a glint of silver that made his heart leap with fear.

Hurrying back, he woke Giorgio and told what he had seen. "I have observed a cloud of dust which comes from many riders. And I saw shimmering silver, perhaps from the shields of soldiers. I do not know if they are Mongols, but we must avoid an encounter when we are so near to our destination."

Giorgio eyed a native canoe on the shoreline, wondering to whom it belonged. Then he looked at the horses, aware that they were tired and past their best. Tethering them where the boat had been, he urged Ho Shan, the guide and the bearers into the water. For a moment Giorgio forgot his son. Then he noticed the boy hiding behind a tree, his body shaking with apprehension at the thought of being immersed in the ocean. Giorgio threw back his head and laughed, delighted to have been blessed with a son so like himself. He lifted the boy on his shoulder and waded out to the waiting craft, forgetting his own loathing of water in his anxiety not to upset the child.

Giorgio saw that the tide was in his favor, running south down the coast in the direction of the Mazzarini camp. He took one of the oars and handed the other to the guide. Within minutes they were skimming swiftly through the sea.

"What shall we call the boy?" Ho Shan asked.

"God knows!"

Giorgio looked at the boy's pale face, conscious that he was uneasy on the water. As he talked with Ho Shan, the child came and sat behind him, snuggling against his back.

Giorgio stroked his son's head, and Ho Shan said enviously, "He is your shadow, my good friend. He ignores the rest of us and feels safe only with you. What wondrous instincts children have for their own preservation."

"I shall call the boy Lucca after his grandfather and Giorgio after me and Pescari, which is our family name."

"That is a fine name," Ho Shan agreed.

By nightfall they were within sight of the Mazzarini camp. Giorgio looked apprehensively at the Mongol designs on the prow of Hsu Lan's ship, his heart thundering as he debated if the Khan had followed them half across the world. Then he saw the courtesan walking on deck with Lotus Flower. Giorgio grinned as Hsu Lan's voice echoed across the water.

"Welcome back, my good man. We have been waiting impatiently for your return. Count Mazzarini is in the beach house plotting our route for the last part of the journey."

"I am happy to be safely back, ma'am. My greetings to you, my lady Lotus Flower."

Later, over the campfire, Giorgio told of his adventures. There was a hushed silence as he explained that his wife had been abducted by Mongols and thrilled exclamations when Lucca was presented.

"And your son, Giorgio—will he learn the Venetian language?" Lotus Flower asked.

"Already Ho Shan is teaching him, my lady."

"Why do you not teach him?"

"I am a servant, not a scholar, my lady."

"But you taught Ho Shan all he knows!"

Giorgio explained how Arya had made the boy believe his father was a warrior. His voice became mournful as he described his predicament. "I am depressed that Lucca will be disappointed to learn I am only a servant."

Seeing Giorgio's chagrin, Hsu Lan spoke sharply. "If you tell Lucca you are a warrior he will believe you, because you are his father. If you make apologies for yourself he will think you a fool, and he will be right. Look how peacefully the child sleeps. He is happy here and safe too. We shall embark on our voyage soon, and when Lucca realizes the extent of your journey he will know that his mother spoke the truth and that you *are* a great warrior."

The following morning Giorgio walked with Diego on the beach. They were discussing their departure when they saw Lucca watching from the steps of the tree house. The child was staring as though dumbfounded, and Giorgio called to the guide to ask the boy what was troubling him.

The native returned, grinning broadly. "Small one says he has now seen the warrior with golden hair about whom his mother spoke and also the man who rides with that warrior—the man who is as brave as a lion."

Giorgio blushed and walked away from his master. The guide called after him.

"Small one has only just realized you are his father, and he wonders how to beg your forgiveness for trying to shoot you when you came from the roof of the world to rescue him in his distress."

Giorgio nodded curtly. Then, seeing the boy's anxious glances, he smiled reassuringly and walked toward the small figure standing uncertainly by the tree house. At first Giorgio walked slowly. Then, as his son ran to meet him, Giorgio rushed over the sand and grasped the boy, whirling him around ecstatically. As Lotus Flower stepped out on the terrace she heard the child cry the only word in the Venetian language he had been taught.

"Papa! Papa! Papa!"

For the rest of the day Giorgio walked up and down the beach as if he had seen a vision. His son considered him a warrior. Overwhelmed, Giorgio could not bear to let the boy out of his sight. He kept imagining Lucca growing up in the Mazzarini household, and hoped that Diego would arrange for the boy to be educated so he could rise from being a servant to being the owner of a business on the quayside of Venice. Giorgio had never been ambitious, but now he longed for Lucca to prosper. Throughout the afternoon he sat looking out to sea, dazed by the joys of fatherhood. Diego had promised him a bounty from the new Mazzarini fortune as a reward for his support on the journey to Cathay. For the first time in his life Giorgio appreciated the importance of financial stability.

In the late afternoon a strange sound came to the ears of those on the beach. Puzzled by the high-pitched whining noise, Li-Huei and his grandson stepped out of their makeshift kitchen onto the sand. Hsu Lan was being rowed to the shore when she too heard the sound. She looked around, saw nothing, but, fearful of a tidal wave, ordered her sailors to make haste to the beach. Lotus Flower was stroking the head of her pet peacock and marveling at the color of its body. The peacocks of China were dark green, but those on the Malabar Coast were as blue as the depths of the sea. Lotus Flower looked up when she heard the mysterious sound.

281

She called to Diego, who was inside the tree house writing his journal. "I think a swarm of bees is approaching."

Diego stepped outside and walked to the edge of the water, tilting his head and scanning the horizon for some clue to the ugly sound. Within minutes he saw what looked like a round black cloud approaching over the sea.

Narrowing his eyes to see better, Diego called in horror to Lotus Flower, "Run inside the house and cover yourself with the netting. The noise is coming from a swarm of flies."

Lotus Flower and Diego ran toward the tree house.

Hsu Lan stepped onto the beach and, seeing Diego's anxiety, called to him, "What ails you, sire?"

Diego pointed to the approaching swarm, and Hsu Lan saw as they drew nearer that they were black-winged and shiny-bodied. She hastened after Diego, calling to the rest of the party, "Cover yourselves! Those dangerous flies are swarming, and they will reach the beach shortly."

Lotus Flower hurried to the tree house and paused to recover her breath. Then she ran inside to look for the net she covered herself with each night. As the droning became louder, Diego adjusted the net so it covered every inch of their bodies. Then, suddenly, the air was full of the black-winged creatures. Lotus Flower clung to her husband, praying the torment would soon be over. She closed her eyes, listening to the sound of her husband's voice as he reassured her.

"Do not cry, my love. This will soon be over. Giorgio is back and we are all ready to leave the Malabar Coast."

Soon Diego was able to announce, "The flies have tired of their game and are flying away to plague another part of the coast."

Gingerly they emerged from the netting and looked questioningly at each other. Diego's face was pale with apprehension, and Lotus Flower kissed him to soothe his anxiety.

"Do not worry. I am well—they have not touched me," she said. But as she held out her arms for Diego's inspection, Lotus Flower saw small puncture marks at the wrist and elbow. She dropped to her knees and looked helplessly at the netting.

"There must be a hole in the gauze. The mice are forever eating our belongings."

"The bite of the flies is not always fatal, have no fear."

Lotus Flower fell silent, and Diego knew she was afraid for her life. Diego comforted her as well as he was able. Then he explained what had happened to Hsu Lan. The courtesan's face was a mask of calm, and the Venetian could not help but admire her courage. While Diego checked that the rest of the party were well, Hsu Lan entered the tree house and spoke to her daughter.

"Count Mazzarini told me you have been bitten by those accursed flies. Do not worry, my lady. I am sure that you will not be harmed."

"I intend to ignore what has happened."

Hsu Lan saw tears in Lotus Flower's eyes and knew that her words were untrue. Determined to take the girl's mind off what had happened, she made a suggestion. "Tonight is our last night in this country. Shall we arrange a celebration to welcome Giorgio's son?"

"I would like that, and I am sure Lucca will enjoy being feted."

Lotus Flower followed Hsu Lan to the beach, where they discussed the requirements of the evening with the cook, Fan-Tai. A houseboy was sent to bring musicians from the nearby village and women to paint screens with rice paste in the traditional designs of the area. Hsu Lan took charge, keeping Lotus Flower so busy she had no time to think of the ominous happenings of the day. Hsu Lan described the menu for Lotus Flower's approval, and called orders to Diego's staff as if she had known them for years.

"We shall eat that fine turtle your maid upturned on the beach and drink a sherbet to make us all merry. Li-Huei, kindly make sure there are plenty of yams to please your master. Chang-Chi, make a fire for roasting the turtle." To another boy, she called, "Row to my ship and bring the musicians back. They are growing lazy from having nothing to do, my lady, but we shall keep them busy this evening."

The night sky was violet-tinged, the air scented with clove. Torches lit the clearing and a fire dominated the feasting area. Local people, fishermen and members of the Mazzarini party joined hands and sang songs of their homeland. Lotus Flower watched happily, forgetting her fears as she listened to the lapping of the waves and the rise and fall of the chorus of voices. Diego observed his wife closely, his face full of love, his hand stealing to hers as the moon slipped behind a cloud. They ate hungrily from turtle meat, gulls' eggs, parrotfish and rice from the area farther south. The feast was proclaimed a success, and Li-Huei's family were congratulated on the quality of the food.

After the meal, native drums beat out a rousing rhythm and women of the village sang a chant which was greeted with enthusiastic applause. Hsu Lan's musicians played the flute and the three-stringed guitar, their impassive faces contrasting oddly with the volatile faces of the fishermen.

Lotus Flower watched Lucca, warmed by his childish delight in the proceedings and by the fact that his hand was entwined tightly with his father's. Finally a group of young children sang a lullaby, their high-pitched voices piping the age-old melody. Lotus Flower yawned and, turning to Diego, begged leave to retire.

"I have so enjoyed the feast. I shall remember it always and treasure it close to my heart."

"I will accompany you, my lady."

Inside the tree house, Diego sat stroking Lotus Flower's face.

"How do you feel, my love?"

"I am tired."

"We must rise at first light."

"Sanay packed all my belongings yesterday, and I put away my jewels before retiring. They are in the velvet casket you gave me and the key is around my neck."

"Why are you telling me this?"

"Since the flies marked me I am afraid. If I should die, I want you to take my jewels back with you to Venice so at least some part of me will see your city."

"Do not speak so foolishly."

"Hold me close, Diego. I want to feel the beating of your heart."

The sky lightened to rose as the sun came over the horizon. Diego dozed for an hour. When he woke he was still holding Lotus Flower close to his chest. Impatient to start the journey, Diego placed her carefully on the quilt so as not to wake her. Then he dressed, looking out to where Giorgio was getting his son ready to leave. Chang-Chi stood lighting the fire, and Li-Huei finished buying fish for breakfast from the fishermen.

Turning to wake his wife, Diego saw that she was lying very still, her eyes open, her mouth struggling to form words he could barely decipher.

"Are you ill, my love?"

"I am tired unto death."

Diego gathered Lotus Flower into his arms, shocked to find her body burning feverishly.

She whispered desperately, "Remember always that I love you and that it is my belief that we shall not long be separated."

"I will send men to bring water from the spring of Ratnagiri. It will make you well as it made you well before."

"It is too late, my love. I feel my body growing weak."

"Do not give in, Lotus Flower."

"I am not Lotus Flower. I am Mo-ch'ou, which means 'Do not grieve, and that is what I say to you.... Now tell me about your house by the sea...."

Before Diego could speak, Lotus Flower sighed and was still. Unable to believe that she was dead, the Venetian clutched her to his chest, urgently trying to say all that was in his heart. "You are my life, do not leave me! My plans for the future are for *us,* my hopes and ambitions revolve around you! Without you there will be no sunlight, only days of darkness and despair.... Lotus Flower! Lotus Flower! *Why* have you gone away?"

Li-Huei was standing on the beach watching the tree house as Diego walked dazedly down the steps. When he saw the Venetian's stricken face the old man knew what had happened. It had been written in the stars that Lotus Flower would not reach Venice. Now he must forget his own anguish and comfort the Venetian. The old man hurried across the sand to where Diego was standing looking out at the horizon.

"It is time for us to leave, sire."

"My lady Lotus Flower is dead. I cannot leave her alone in this accursed land."

"But my lady's soul has already flown like a white dove into the soul of another, born this fourth day of the eighth

285

month of the year, sire. Only my lady's remains lie in the tree house."

"She always said that she would return to me someday."

"My lady was determined to see the house by the sea, sire. Who knows, perhaps she will in time find her way there."

"Send your grandson to tell my lady Hsu Lan what has happened and ask Giorgio to come to me."

"At once, sire."

Giorgio left his son with Ho Shan and hurried to the beach. When he saw his master's face he fell on his knees.

"My lord, I beg you not to let this calamity ruin you. You are young and there are many lives yet for you to lead, many seas to cross and many who will love you. I know no one can ever replace my lady in your heart, but in time someone may try."

"I have been thinking of your future, my good Giorgio."

"My future is with you, sir."

"When you return to Venice you will have enough money to set yourself up in business. You must buy a house by the Rialto and use the lower floor for business and those above for living quarters."

Stunned by the mechanical tone of his master's voice, Giorgio was silent.

"Your son will be given a fine education, and with luck he will be able to enlarge any business you start. Who knows, my good Giorgio, you may end by being richer than all the Mazzarinis."

"Sir, I am grateful for your consideration, but at this time you need me near you. I have been with you for many years and intend to stay with you. There will be much to do on our return to Venice, and..."

"Someday I may return to Venice, but not yet."

Aware that this was no time for argument, Giorgio concentrated on the needs of the present.

"My lord, may I speak of what must be done? I think it best that you go to the ship."

"First I must return to the tree house. My lady charged me to return to Venice with her jewels, and I shall, but I do not know when I can leave her. You had better go with your son and the rest of the party."

"We shall *all* leave the coast today, sir. I will not leave you here pining for the past."

"I will not leave Lotus Flower."

"Sir, my lady's body must be burned, as is the custom of her land."

"I will not allow it."

As Diego's voice rose in anger, Giorgio realized that grief had taken away his reason. He looked sadly at the Venetian and said calmly, "I will bring my lady's jewels, sir."

"No! I must go. The key is around her neck."

"Stay here, sir. After all these years you know that you can trust me to have respect for my lady."

As Giorgio climbed the steps to the tree house, he saw vultures grouping on the branches of the surrounding palms. He collected Lotus Flower's jewel case and the key from around her neck, looking down on the pale face so peaceful in death. Giorgio thought how all his master's love had been lavished on this exotic lady from Cathay, all the Mazzarini hopes and plans for the future based on the Count's desire to make his wife proud. The servant shook his head wearily. Where would it end? What chance was there of keeping his master sane? Giorgio walked from the house, pausing to inform Ho Shan what had happened and giving instructions for a funeral pyre to be made of the tree house. Then he saw Hsu Lan approaching the beach in her boat.

Hurrying back to Diego's side, Giorgio offered the jewels and the key. "Here you are, sir, as you instructed."

"My lady Hsu Lan is bringing her boat to collect the members of our party. I order that you accompany her and leave at once."

"And you, sir?"

"I cannot leave here. I must stay with my lady Lotus Flower."

"My lady is dead, sir."

"For me she will always be alive."

"I beg you, lead us home to Venice."

"You can lead our friends, my good Giorgio. There is no longer any need for me."

Giorgio put down the jewel case and the key and looked

287

sadly at Diego. "You know, sir, that I have always respected you and that I have obeyed you without question."

"Indeed you have and I am deeply grateful."

"Then you will forgive me if I tell you that I cannot obey this order you have given me."

"It is my life, and I can do with it as I wish."

Giorgio closed his eyes, said a prayer, and aimed a resounding punch at his master's chin. The Venetian fell without a cry. Giorgio felt tears falling down his cheeks as he looked down on the unconscious form of the man he had served for so long. Hsu Lan's angry voice broke into his thoughts.

"Do you brawl on such an occasion?"

"Count Mazzarini refuses to sail with us, my lady. He has set his mind on remaining here to die with his wife."

Hsu Lan spoke with sudden compassion. "You are a fine man, Giorgio. Do what must be done here. Then bring everyone to my ship in the longboat. My men will carry Count Mazzarini back to the ship, and I shall accompany them. Have no fear that he will escape. I have prepared his suite and will guard the key on my own person."

"Thank you, my lady."

Giorgio stood alone on the beach as the tree house burned. Long-forgotten prayers came to his mind, and he whispered them softly, reverently, his mind wandering back to visions of Lotus Flower riding like the wind on the plains south of Peking. Would Diego Mazzarini ever find her like again? Giorgio shook his head sadly. When only the blackened shell of the tree house remained, Giorgio walked to the canoe and rowed himself out to the ship in the bay. As he rowed he looked sadly to the receding shoreline, which was shrouded in mist. The sun shone on the gold of a distant temple, and the land seemed dreamlike and ethereal. Suddenly, the past was like an illusion, a dream or nightmare soon forgotten. Giorgio turned resolutely and rowed toward the warship.

On the deck Hsu Lan stood waiting to welcome the last member of the Mazzarini party. She was dressed in deep mourning and still pale with shock. As Giorgio stepped on board, she said, "I have ordered my captain to sail at once."

"How is Count Mazzarini, my lady?"

"He is distracted. He refuses food and wine and has twice tried to break down the door. I shall be relieved to be away from here."

Below, in his suite, Diego stood looking in horror at the tree house, its blackened remains stark against a storm pink sky. His eyes filled with tears, and he sat on the narrow bed and gave way to grief. It had all been for nothing. The Mazzarini fortune had been saved and he could return with honor to a secure future in Venice. But the luck that had accompanied him for so long had vanished, taking with it the most important person in his life.

Diego recalled his first meeting with Lotus Flower and the chirruping noises she had made, like a lively cricket. He remembered her in all her splendor, a true princess of China, on the day of their wedding. Finally Diego thought of his wife in the yellow boat on the fishing lagoon, threading her hair with orchids and eating hungrily like a young boy instead of the elegant lady he adored. How long would it take for grief to subside? Would it last forever, leaving him old before his time? Diego could think of nothing but the moment of death, the brief shudder when life had passed away. Sadly he admitted that he wanted to think of nothing but Lotus Flower, remember in detail every word she had ever said to him, every joke she had played, every kiss she had planted on his cheek. As the ship sailed on, Diego continued to muse in lonely melancholy.

Members of the party kept inquiring about Diego, who would see no one but Hsu Lan. Some of the crew whispered that the Venetian was deranged. Others believed he was willing himself to die. Rumors were rife that Diego screamed in his sleep and that he had nightmares about swarms of flies from which he could not escape.

Giorgio racked his brain for a solution to the Venetian's sadness, but there was none. The transfer from one ship to another was made without incident. Diego greeted his own crew. Then he disappeared below deck, unable to bear company, unwilling to think of anything but the loss of his wife. The green coast of India gave way to the sandy deserts of Baluchistan. Still Diego remained aloof, barely eating and showing no interest in his surroundings. Giorgio looked despondently out to sea, fearful that the Mazzarini luck was lost and that his master, who had shown such wondrous courage during the previous six years, had allowed his will to vanish with it. Sadly, Giorgio asked himself what the future held for him and his son and for the man he had always revered.

Part Four:

The Homecoming

Keep away from sharp swords, •
Don't go near a lovely woman.
A sharp sword too close will wound your
*   hand,*
Woman's beauty too close will wound your life.

Meng-Chiao (751–814)

Chapter Fifteen:
The Homecoming

Pierluigi sat reading in the garden of his home when he heard a cacophony of sound below on the lagoon. Excited fishermen, crews of anchored merchantmen and crews of gondolieri were sounding bells and horns and waving flags of greeting to the crew of a ship sailing into port. Pierluigi saw that the ship's sails were black and that the sailors were lined in salute at the rails. A woman stood at the prow, looking up eagerly at the city. Pierluigi's heart missed a beat when he finally saw Diego outlined against the blue of the Venetian sky.

Calling to his servants, Pierluigi ran to the quayside and stood waiting impatiently for the ship to dock. Crowds surrounded the harbor's edge to witness the arrival of the ship, and there were rumors that another famous adventurer was returning to La Serenissima.

Once the ship docked, Pierluigi rushed aboard and flung himself on his brother's shoulder.

"My dear Diego, welcome home. Why did you not send a message with one of the captains? I am delighted to see you, but I had no idea you were on your way back."

Pierluigi broke off in midsentence, the smile vanishing from his face as he saw the change in his brother's appearance. The blond hair was speckled with silver, the face and body gaunt.

"Is something wrong, brother Diego?"

When Diego spoke his voice trembled with emotion. "My lady Lotus Flower died of a fever while we were on the Malabar Coast."

"And you, Diego, have you also been ill?"

"Only with grief. But today I am pleased to see you and to be home again in Venice. If you knew how many times I have dreamed of this moment..."

Pierluigi put his arms around his brother and led him to the prow of the ship, pointing up toward the hill. "That is my new home. I built it on my return from the East."

"Did you marry Renata?"

"I did, and we are happy. Renata has already given me twin sons, one of whom is named after you, and we hope we shall have another within the year."

"I am glad the Mazzarini title is not lost."

Pierluigi saw Hsu Lan approaching and was shocked by his brother's introduction.

"Pierluigi, this is my lady Hsu Lan, the mother of my late wife. My lady has left behind her life and home in Peking and intends to settle in Venice. Without her help, my lady Lotus Flower and I should certainly have been executed by the Khan. She, too, was forced to leave her home in Hangchow. We shall do her the honor of welcoming her as a close friend of our family."

"Indeed we shall, Diego. And now, where is our faithful Giorgio?"

Diego's face clouded for a moment. Then he called to his servant.

"It is because of Giorgio that you see me here today. He insisted that I leave India instead of staying behind with

Lotus Flower. My jaw ached for a month from his persuasion! At first I refused to speak with him, but now I am pleased to report that we are as good friends as ever."

Giorgio stepped forward and presented his son to Pierluigi. "This is Lucca Giorgio Pescari."

Pierluigi hugged the child to his chest and received in return a halting greeting in the Venetian dialect. Then he turned to his brother.

"And now Diego, come home with me so I can show you a real Mazzarini welcome."

Pierluigi led the way, followed by sailors and porters and the rest of the Mazzarini party. Diego looked up at the city, thankful to see Venice little changed. Despite his sadness, he smiled as he sniffed the air of his homeland, knowing that here, if anywhere, he would regain the will to live.

In a square near Pierluigi's house, men were practicing on the public archery targets, just as they had been on the day of Diego's departure. He touched the stone wall, reassured by its coolness. There was a tang of salt in the air and a subtle smell of lemon blossom. Diego savored the pleasure of being back in Venice, and as he made his way to Pierluigi's house he remembered all the times he had dwelled with longing on the sights, scents and vistas of La Serenissima in the spring.

As they entered Pierluigi's house, Diego saw a woman dressed in green waiting by the stairs. He recognized her as Renata, his brother's wife, and greeted her warmly, pleased by the welcome he received.

"Welcome home, Diego. My husband has been so impatient for your return, I vow he will exhaust you with all he wishes to discuss. May I first introduce you to my sons?"

"I shall be honored, my lady."

"Then I shall show you the new garden and the rooms we have prepared for your return."

While Pierluigi was entertaining the members of his party, Diego walked up the hill to his own home. For a moment he paused outside the gates, looking down at the iron key that had meant so much to him during his travels. Then he put the key in the lock and pushed the gate open. The mimosa was in blossom, throwing powdery yellow dust on the pathways. A kitten looked down at him from the wall, and everywhere there were irises fragrantly blooming in the sunlight of a spring morning. Despite all he had suffered, Diego's heart leaped with joy as he hurried inside the house. First he walked around the rooms on the ground floor. Then, almost reluctantly, he climbed the stairs to his bedroom and opened the window, remembering what he had told Lotus Flower of the house by the sea.... "From your window you will see the lagoon and smell the lemon blossom...." It was all unchanged, only Lotus Flower was not here to enjoy it. Diego sat on the bed, his sadness briefly diminished by the delight of being home again. How healing it was to the mind, how soothing to the senses. Diego put his feet up on the bed and closed his eyes. Within minutes he was asleep.

Diego woke to the sound of a gondolier singing. He leaped up and ran to the window. Then, realizing that someone had undressed him, he rang the bell. Duccio appeared, his face still swollen from the tears he had shed the previous evening at his master's return.

"My dear sir, God be praised that you are home."

"It is good to see you again, Duccio."

"Was your journey successful, sir?"

"It was, Duccio. The fortune is replenished. We shall never again lack for gold."

"Sir Pierluigi came to look for you last evening, and found you sleeping on top of the bed. He told me of your tragedy, and I beg leave to express my sympathy."

"I thank you, Duccio. Now, tell me, is your daughter well?"

"Maria-Innocenta married a sailor and lives on the island of Burano, in a yellow house on the quayside of which she is inordinately proud."

"I kept my promise and brought her a songbird and also some silk for dresses."

"On her behalf I thank you, sir. Now, my lord, what of the future?"

Diego put on a wrap and walked to the window, lingering yet again to watch the busy scene below. The water was noisy with activity, full of traders en route to the market, fishermen returning with their catch, gondolas transporting officials and travelers staring at the sights.

Diego turned to the old man. "I fear I shall spend the next few weeks staring out of this window. You ask of the future, Duccio. First I will have breakfast. Then I shall collect my lady Hsu Lan, the mother of my late wife, who will stay in this house until she finds a property to buy."

"My lady is already here, sir. She has lodged her servants in the far wing and has ordered me to serve her breakfast with yours. Your servants from the house in Peking have also been accommodated. One of them, the old man whose name is Li-Huei, is still laughing about his bed. I understand the people of his race sleep on quilts. Here the old man has a large bed, and last night I was unable to sleep for the noise he made leaping up and down upon it. I could have sworn he was but fifteen years old."

"I will dress and go down at once so I can eat with my lady Hsu Lan."

"Giorgio and his son also returned home last night, sir."

"I wish to see Giorgio at noon. Please ask him to visit me at that hour."

"Yes, my lord."

"And, Duccio, I am delighted by the way you have cared for this house during my absence, and I thank you."

"I hope to serve you for the rest of my life, sir, and to have the good fortune to help you to a happier frame of mind."

The cries of Venice warmed Diego's heart as he dressed, and he kept returning to the window to look at the busy scene below. There was much to be done before he could retire and be at peace with his thoughts. There were important matters to be settled for Giorgio and for Hsu Lan. There were reports to be written for the Doge, who had charged him, before his departure, to make a full account of his adventures for the grand council. Conscious of all he had to do, Diego descended the staircase.

In the dining hall he found Hsu Lan, who greeted him with a compliment. "Count Mazzarini, you did not tell me that your home was a palace. I am enchanted by what I see, and by your servants, who have been most kind."

"Welcome to Venice, my lady Hsu Lan. I hope this will be a happy city for you and the start of a new life full of contentment."

"I shall do all in my power to help you during the coming months, sire. You have suffered the loss of your wife and I have lost a daughter I traveled across the world to know. We must keep busy so we do not dwell too much on our sadness. And eventually I hope you will be right and that we shall *both* achieve happiness and contentment."

In the coming weeks, Diego and Hsu Lan searched for a home she could buy. At last they found something that pleased her, a small but elegant mansion of thirty rooms near the Palazzo Ducale. Hsu Lan was content to own a home so near the Mazzarinis and enchanted by her view of the lagoon. She threw herself energetically into furnishing her new home and was soon renowned in the area for her good taste, her insistence on quality and the stern way she dealt with traders who tried to take advantage of her limited knowledge of their language. It was not long before Hsu Lan remedied her ignorance of the Venetian tongue and it became known that she could not be tricked, except by fools who did not care for the safety of their skins. Venetian nobles clamored to be introduced to the newcomer, but Hsu Lan continued to wear deep mourning, refusing all invitations and visiting only Diego and his brother. The gossiping wives of Venice accepted Hsu Lan without question as a lady of the finest breeding. The former courtesan was well pleased. She had kept her promise and respected the Mazzarini name.

Next Diego purchased a house for Giorgio on the canalside near the Ponte di Rialto. There, where the air was scented with herbs and the pungent odors of the food stalls, Giorgio settled down. The house was a short walk from Diego's home, and Giorgio was happy to have Li-Huei and his family as neighbors. For the Chinese servants who had been so loyal, Diego purchased the house adjacent to Giorgio's, giving them sufficient money to commence in business. He arranged for Lucca to receive an education and gave Giorgio an annuity for life and a lump sum to ensure his independence. Predictably, Giorgio proposed a union with the Chinese, and the group went into partnership with a glassblower. Craftsmen at their workshop and furnace on the island of Burano were kept busy with orders for the designs drawn by the two Chinese women, based on objects from their homeland. These were exotic in Venetian eyes and instantly desirable. Giorgio left technical matters to the glassblower and artistic design to the Chinese. He assumed the role of salesman, visiting traders, wealthy customers and artistic guilds interested in promoting the unusual new products.

Each week Giorgio returned to discuss the progress of his business with Diego. Determined to rouse the Venetian from his grief, Giorgio explained what was happening in the city, how his son's lessons were progressing and what the latest gossip was. He was conscious that Diego barely listened but refused obstinately to allow his master to become a recluse. Someday, somehow, Giorgio felt sure he would find a way to tempt Diego's interest and perhaps his participation. Each night Giorgio prayed that his visits to the Mazzarini home would meet with a little success.

A blazing-hot summer was followed by a winter when snow fell on the islands of the Venetian lagoon. Diego withdrew into his home and locked the shutters. When he went out it was only to visit his brother or Hsu Lan. He shunned friends of past times and refused to attend public functions. Sometimes, Diego wondered if he was being ungrateful for the good fortune that had accompanied him on his travels. But deep in his heart the Venetian wanted only to be alone, to relive the perfection of his years with Lotus Flower. When match-makers tried to introduce him to eligible young ladies, Diego was unfailingly polite, but he met none of them and was adamant in his unwillingness to socialize. Gradually it became known that Count Mazzarini was living in seclusion, and soon many had forgotten him.

On sunny days, Diego walked alone in the garden, planning a terrace here, a shrub there, a fountain to be placed to cool the air. For hours each day the lonely man worked on his journal, finally bringing to a close the story of the momentous journey he had shared with his servant. Once, Diego took a small boat and sailed for months among the islands of the Venetian lagoon. Then he returned home to spend his days planning a future alone with his memories.

Time passed; Giorgio prospered, and Pierluigi had more children. Hsu Lan began to grow old, and one of the richest men in Venice fell madly in love with her. Her salon became famous, her acid comments and ready wit admired by the Venetians who frequented her home. When the Duke of Mantegna proposed to her, Hsu Lan accepted his offer of marriage. Society matrons felt that the Duke, who was known for his willfulness, had at last met his match. Only Diego Mazzarini remained suspended in time, a man unwilling to leave the past behind for the future.

Chapter Sixteen:

Fifteen Years Later

For the first time in many years, Diego agreed to attend a social function—the wedding of his nephew and namesake. Diego had just returned from a journey through Italy and was tanned and fit, though his hair had turned silver and his clothes were years out of date. Studying his reflection in the mirror, he frowned at the cut of his clothes. They were fine garments, ordered on his return from the East. He turned back and forth, amused to recall how in times past he had ordered new clothes as often as he could afford them. Now, when he had all the money he needed, he never thought of summoning the tailor.

Diego made his way to his brother's house to encourage the nervous bridegroom. As he walked he remembered the day of his own marriage and the exotic and astonishing gifts that had been piled to the ceiling in the Khan's palace in Peking. Sometimes, in the quiet of his home and the security of Venice, Diego found it hard to believe that he had ever lived through so many adventures. Time had softened and dimmed his memories so they appeared like mirages of the mind; only his recollections of Lotus Flower were clear, and even they were fading into the misty wasteland of memory.

At Pierluigi's house, he watched his nephew fussing over his appearance. Turning to his brother, Diego said wistfully, "All this concern with dressing reminds me of the Khan on the day of my own wedding."

Diego's nephew asked in a surprised voice, "I did not know you had ever been married, Uncle."

"I was married once, long ago."

"In Cathay?"

"In the court of Kublai Khan."

"That is what Antonella thought."

Puzzled, Diego questioned his nephew. "Who is Antonella? And what does she know of my life?"

"She says she knows everything about our family, but I do not believe her. She is the nosiest girl in Venice and renowned for her unconventional statements."

"How old is this monster?"

"She is sixteen, and I am glad I am not marrying *her!*"

Diego and his brother went downstairs and drank a glass of wine together.

Pierluigi explained about the family of Antonella di Volpe. "You will meet Antonio di Volpe at the wedding. He is a fine man and one of my best friends. I would warn you, however, that he will come with his three daughters, one of whom is young Antonella."

Amused by his brother's tone, Diego asked, "Must I be warned about these women?"

"They are lovely girls, but not like the women we are used to. Their mother died at Antonella's birth, and they have been brought up by their father and an aunt from Verona. They came to live in Venice only a few years ago—perhaps that is why they seem strange in our eyes. Until they came here they lived in the countryside outside Verona, and they prefer it to La Serenissima, as they will not hesitate to tell you."

"Why do they stay if they do not like our city?"

"They are good girls who love their father. Antonio di Volpe lives in Venice because it is a center of commerce and he has many ships."

"I shall avoid them. Indeed, I plan to withdraw soon after the ceremony."

"I wonder if you will, brother Diego."

The church was lit with a thousand candles. Stone madonnas looked down on altars covered with flowers in side chapels and the walls gleamed in the flickering amber light. Rose petals had been scattered on the ground, and at the center altar, on a cloth of the finest *punto in aria* lace, emerald-studded vases held orchids that scented the air with the exotic perfume of the East. The bride had a calm, sweet face and a slim, childlike figure. Diego recalled that his nephew disliked women with too much spirit. Glancing again at the bride, Diego knew that his namesake would have no such difficulty with the girl he had chosen.

A choir of young boys sang, and the incense of mass made the air thick with the scent of reverence. Diego sighed as the couple were pronounced man and wife, his mind drifting back to the moment when he had put the ring on Lotus Flower's finger and promised to love her until death and after. Diego decided to return briefly to Pierluigi's home to share the celebratory meal. When he had eaten he would congratulate the couple. Then he would return to the house by the sea. Already Diego was longing for the peace and solitude of his own home. Again he felt ill at ease in company.

As Diego left the church, he collided with a young girl dressed in violet silk. He apologized. The girl smiled, her green eyes sparkling with humor at his unease. Diego looked closely at her, remembering Lotus Flower's green eyes, and felt he was once again looking into the eyes of his loved one. The girl turned and walked from the church. Diego followed.

In the sunlight of an April day, Diego stood at his brother's side, his heart still pounding with shock at the strange feeling of recognition he had experienced. The girl's perfume had reminded him of flowers in the exotic gardens of Peking. Her manner and movements had stunned him because they were so like Lotus Flower's.

"I am surprised my lady Antonella did not berate you loudly for your clumsiness. I am told she has a fiendish temper, though I have been lucky enough never to have seen it," Pierluigi teased Diego.

"Was that the girl who knew I had once been married?"

"It was. She is lovely, is she not?"

"I barely noticed her."

"Then you are blind as well as stubborn."

As Diego hurried into the grounds of his brother's house, he was startled to see a score of white doves flying past his face to the roof. In Cathay that would have been seen as a sign that something unexpected was about to happen. Diego watched thoughtfully as the doves settled on the roof and preened their feathers.

Inside the house, the wedding guests were seated around a banqueting table, gossiping loudly, eating riotously and proposing numerous toasts. Pierluigi explained to his brother who everyone was, conscious that Diego barely knew a soul in the city where once he had known almost everyone.

"At the end of the table is Renata's father, and next to him her aunt, then Antonio di Volpe and his eldest daughter, Cosima, then the Contessa Favorini and her son Alessandro and..."

Suddenly Pierluigi realized that his brother was not listening. Following Diego's gaze, he looked across the table to where Antonella di Volpe sat with her sister Mariana. The girl was staring fixedly at Diego as though mesmerized by his gaze.

Pierluigi whispered to his brother, "Those are the other two daughters of the Volpe family. Cosima, who is sitting next to her father, is a fine musician. Mariana thinks only of marrying and returning to Verona. Antonella is a dreamer and a romantic who has a too vivid imagination."

Diego looked at the pale skin and heavy red-gold hair. The girl's mouth curved sensuously, making her appear more mature than her years. The looseness of her dress and the

304

severity of her coiffure were tantalizing, revealing nothing of the woman beneath.

Diego turned to his brother and apologized for not answering. "Forgive me, Pierluigi. I have lived alone for so long I have forgotten how to behave in civilized society."

"You are interested in the girl?"

"Only to know how she knew I had been married."

"Her father has twenty ships trading with the merchants of Constantinople and Izmir. It is possible Antonella has heard sailors talking about you. She is a romantic child and curious about everything, so they say. At this moment, brother Diego, it seems that she is interested in *you*."

Diego made an effort to converse normally with his brother, telling himself firmly that there was no reason to be interested in such a young and spoiled girl. There was nothing to be gained by involving himself with a woman when he could never forget Lotus Flower or replace her in his heart. Diego gave himself a dozen reasons for not looking again at the beautiful, watchful girl. But his eyes returned to dwell on Antonella di Volpe, and soon he was longing to be home, far away from the breathlessness which took him every time their eyes met. Diego barely touched his food, though he drank more than was his habit. Then, as the guests made their way from the dining hall to the salon, he said goodbye to his brother.

"I shall go and offer my congratulations to your son and to his wife. Then I will return home," Diego said.

"Come and eat with us on Sunday, Diego."

"I will come at noon."

"We shall look forward to your company."

Leaving the house, Diego found his way barred by Antonella di Volpe. The girl smiled playfully and curtsied as he looked down on her.

"Why are you leaving so hastily, Count Mazzarini? They are going to have an entertainment which promises to be amusing. Why not stay and enjoy it?"

"I am not accustomed to appearing in public, and the noise tires me."

"You speak as if you were old, but you are not."

"To a child all men above twenty are old, my lady."

305

"I am sixteen and not a child!"

"And I am forty-six and too old to argue with you."

Antonella picked a camellia and looked hard at Diego. "May I ask you a question, sir?"

"You may, my lady. I understand that you are much given to asking questions."

"I would like to ask why you have locked yourself away in that beautiful house for so many years."

"You seem to know a great deal about me."

"I know everything."

"Your chaperon will be worrying where you are."

"I do not have a chaperon. My sister Mariana accompanies me when I go to the opera or to the cathedral."

"May I pass, my lady? I wish to return home."

"Of course, sir. I would not detain you with my chatter, though I have long dreamed of meeting you. My only reason for being so forward was..."

Diego walked to the gate. Then, conscious that he had been rude, he turned and found the girl still watching him. Something in the sadness of her expression caught his heart, and he spoke more gently. "May I ask *why* you are so interested in me and how you have amassed such knowledge of my life?"

For a moment Diego thought she was going to tell her secret. Then, Antonella's face changed from appeal to anger.

"No, Count Mazzarini, you may not. If I tell you, you will think me as great an idiot as my father did when I confided in *him*. And now, good day to you, sir."

With a rustle of silk, the girl hurried back to the house, leaving Diego to his thoughts. He walked home, relieved to reach the garden where he was able to lock out the world. For an hour Diego wandered among the new shrubs that had been planted, enjoying the tinkling sound of the fountain. Then he stood looking out from the parapet overlooking the busy lagoon. Below, a gilded gondola passed by. In the craft the Venetian saw Antonio di Volpe and his three daughters. Diego stood quite still, uncertain whether he had been seen. But as the gondolier turned the boat into a waterway off the lagoon, Diego was surprised to see Antonella salute him with a stem of lilac, which she threw on the water so it landed by the wall below his house. Diego hurried inside, thoroughly disconcerted by the girl's forwardness and by the pounding of his heart.

The week passed quickly, and soon it was time for Diego to visit his brother's house. He dressed quickly, then stood peering out of the window at a foggy day full of the sound of ships' horns hooting. Before the clock struck midday, Diego arrived at Pierluigi's and was welcomed by Renata. He followed her through the hall to the salon, where he was met by Pierluigi, whose face was full of excitement.

Renata whispered to Diego, "Your brother has a surprise for you which has excited *him* beyond measure."

"I hope it is a pleasant surprise."

"I am sure you will find it so."

Diego saw that his brother had lit braziers to warm the vast room on this sunless morning. Then he noticed Antonio di Volpe sitting on the far side of the room, examining some charts of the Malabar Coast.

"I hope you will not mind, Diego—I invited my good friend Antonio di Volpe, who is knowledgeable about trade with the East and who has interesting news to tell us," Pierluigi explained.

Di Volpe rose and greeted Diego. "I am honored to meet you, sir. I have been telling your brother that my agents in Constantinople have encountered the Polo family, on their return from Cathay. I understand they are bragging that they alone have been to that country and that they alone know the route through the roof of the world. It will come as something of a shock to them when they find that you have told many here of that route and that in the Doge's Palace there is a set of maps that you drew showing the way to the East."

"Bragging was always young Marco's finest talent, so your news does not surprise me."

"I hope you will contradict the Polos, Count Mazzarini."

"Indeed I need not do so. I have passed the copy of my journal kept during the journey and my sojourn in Cathay to the grand council and it has been accepted."

"My daughter tells me your house is very beautiful."

307

"Your daughter seems to know more about me than I know myself, sir."

Di Volpe sighed, and Diego was curious as to the reason for his weariness.

"Count, may I ask you a great favor?" di Volpe said.

"Indeed you may, sir."

"Will you speak with my daughter Antonella for a moment? She has something to tell you, and when she has told it I would be obliged if you would correct her, for her utterances have caused much trouble in our house for many years. I do not know what to do with my daughter, for she talks as if she knows things she has not the means to ascertain. Will you put her to the test, Count?"

Puzzled, Diego waited while di Volpe went to bring his daughter. The girl blushed prettily on entering the room, her eyes downcast, her hands trembling with anticipation.

Di Volpe spoke sternly to his daughter. "Now at last I have an opportunity to end this game which it has been your whim to play all these years. Tell Count Mazzarini what you told me. Come, child, this is no time to be bashful."

Antonella sat on a stool, her beautiful hair falling over a dress of pink and white. At first she looked appealingly toward Diego. Then her eyes settled on a bowl of lemons, and she looked fixedly at it as though determined to concentrate. When she spoke, Diego admired the softness of her voice and the pleasing way she explained herself.

"When I was small I had dreams of a house built of stone and set in the middle of the sea. The house had a lemon tree in the garden, a fountain and a gazebo. I knew the place well, including the interior rooms, and I used to call it 'my home.' At first Papa was amused by my dream, but when I continued to talk of the house he became angry and told me never to speak of it again. When I arrived in Venice I was eleven years old, and one day I saw 'my home' and wished strongly to enter it. I told Papa what had happened and he learned that this house of my dreams belonged to you, Count Mazzarini."

Diego stared at the girl, half angry and suspecting a trick, half uncertain as to the meaning of her strange story.

"When you returned to Venice this last time, I thought I

should be allowed to see inside your house. Papa has refused my request many times because he is tired of this dream. I too am tired of it, because sometimes I can think of nothing else but that house by the sea. If I describe one of the rooms to you, will you tell me if my dream is only a childish invention or if the description is correct? If I am wrong I must try to forget my dream and to concentrate on recovering from this malady."

"Very well, my lady. Describe your own bedroom in my house."

Antonella's face softened, and she looked happy. Diego was shocked when she spoke.

"My bedroom has a lemon tree outside the window. The bed is carved of chestnut wood in a strange style I have not seen before. There are silk . . ."

Diego rose and paced the room. "Enough! The description is correct."

Antonella burst into tears. Surprised, Diego turned to her. "Why are you crying?"

"Now I shall be considered mad and sent to live with the nuns."

"I think not, my lady."

Diego was astonished by Antonella's fury as she turned on him.

"I am *sick* of dreaming of you and your house, Count Mazzarini. For years pictures have haunted my mind, and now you ridicule me. You are an enfeebled recluse who knows nothing of a woman's feelings and who cares even less. I despise you. I despise you and wish I had never met you."

With that, Antonella raised her hand and slapped Diego so hard on the cheek the sound echoed in the silent room. Then, weeping bitterly, she ran from the room. Diego stood quite still, his mind racing, his heart pounding, every muscle in his body tense with anticipation.

Antonio di Volpe appealed to Pierluigi for help. "How can I apologize? How can I redress such an insult?"

The two men turned toward Diego, surprised to see his face radiant with pleasure. He was remembering the night when he had first stayed in Lotus Flower's home in Peking, when she had stolen into his room in the middle of the
309

night to kiss him and then had slapped his face so hard he had seen stars for a few confusing moments. Antonella di Volpe had deep-emerald eyes like the eyes of Lotus Flower. She had a temper too and an ability to stun with a blow from her tiny white hand. Diego held his breath and thanked the mysterious gods of the East for sending his love back to him.

Pierluigi spoke with a lightness he did not feel. "Forgive the child, Diego. She is growing up and has fallen in love with you, I think."

"She is forgiven, of course."

Diego made for the door. Amazed by his behavior, Pierluigi tried to stop him. "Where are you going?"

"I am off to visit my tailor."

"Diego! What ails you? This is the Sabbath and none of the tailors will be working. In any case, you have not visited your tailor in fifteen years and he has been dead for ten of them."

"I have decided to order new clothes."

Diego turned to Antonio di Volpe and shook his hand. "My compliments to you, sir, on your lovely daughter. With your permission I would like to arrange a party in my lady Antonella's honor."

Stunned by Diego's change of humor, di Volpe did not reply. But once Diego left, di Volpe turned to Pierluigi and asked, "Is your brother always so sudden in his decisions?"

"Diego has been like a man half alive since the death of his wife, my lady Lotus Flower. Now it seems he is resurrected, and your daughter is surely the reason for the miracle. My good friend, I think I should warn you that Diego is in love with Antonella."

"God be praised. I have been sure for years that no sensible man would suffer her."

"She is beautiful. How could you underestimate her?"

"Antonella *is* beautiful, and clever too. She can be as quiet as a mouse when she chooses. But often she sits for hours looking at that accursed house by the water and trying to see the Count as he walks in the garden. Of late I have thought of locking her in her room for fear she would escape and pester him to death."

310

"Be happy, Antonio. The years of my brother's anguish are over. He has found what he seeks, and I think your daughter also has found what she has longed for without knowing the reason."

Chapter Seventeen:

Venice

Antonella walked slowly through the gates of the Palazzo Mazzarini. First she admired the doves in the cote by the lemon tree. Then she passed to the wall and looked out on the lagoon.

"How beautiful it all is, and just as I saw it in my dream! I am *so* happy that you decided to indulge me, Count Mazzarini, and I thank you from the bottom of my heart."

"I thank you for coming here, my lady."

Diego looked into the dark-green eyes and then at the pearls around Antonella's throat. How lovely she was. How perfect and unspoiled. His heart raced with excitement as he showed her the inside of his home. First they walked together through the downstairs rooms. Then the rooms on the first floor of the house. Finally Diego unlocked a room that he had shown no one before, a room on which men had worked in secret to a design he had specially prepared.

Diego stood aside, motioning for Antonella to pass. "I shall be interested to have your opinion on this room, my lady."

A glow of delight touched the creamy skin, and Diego saw joy in the wide green eyes. Antonella whirled happily around and around, taking in the carved chestnut-wood bed, the wall hangings of painted silk and the altar built into the wall. Then she hurried to the dressing table and stroked the jewel box of faded velvet.

"This is my room, Count. At least it is the room of my dreams, which I believed to be mine. This is the room I have longed to see for so many years."

"This *is* your room, my lady."

Antonella was suddenly serious. "Now I am here I shall not want to leave."

"You do not have to leave, my lady."

"Do not make light of me, sir."

Diego sighed, conscious that he must not frighten the girl with a too sudden revelation of his intentions. It was apparent that in some way the mind of Antonella di Volpe had been influenced by the spirit of Lotus Flower, who had died on the day of Antonella's birth. Diego led the girl downstairs toward the salon, where Renata and Pierluigi were waiting with Antonella's father. As they neared the room, Diego saw that his companion was wiping tears from her eyes.

"Why are you crying?"

"I do not know. Perhaps it is that I have waited so long for this moment. Now my heart feels as if it could burst."

"And what now, my lady?"

"Now I shall enjoy your hospitality, Count. Then I will return home and try to forget all I have seen, because it is obvious I have suffered a trick of the mind."

"I love your tricks of the mind."

"Do you like me?"

"I do, my lady. I like you and I love you."

Antonella looked up into the Venetian's face, and Diego forgot the past and the sadness that had haunted him for so long and drew her to his side. Their lips met, their eyes closed, and for a brief moment they breathed as one.

314

Diego led Antonella to the salon, whispering as they reached the door, "Is your father in a good humor this evening?"

"He is, sir."

"And you, do you feel strong enough to endure a shock?"

"My heart is pounding and I feel a little faint. But I shall look forward to being astonished by you, sir."

Pierluigi was surprised and impressed by the grand meal and the elegance of its service. Choice wine accompanied a banquet of venison, ptarmigan and suckling pig. Flowers had been made to form a bower on the terrace, and the servants were dressed in silk for the momentous occasion. Pierluigi was amazed by his brother's appetite and by the look on Antonella's face. At the end of the meal, as the servants poured fruit liqueurs for the guests, Diego proposed a toast.

"To the future happiness of my lady Antonella, whose beauty has made me conscious of the years I have wasted on my sadness," Diego said.

Di Volpe drank to his daughter, touched to see tears streaming down her cheeks. Then, at Diego's request, they adjourned to the study. When the two men rejoined the party, Diego was conscious that Antonella was watching him closely. As her father fell into conversation with Pierluigi, she came to Diego's side.

"My lord, I beg you to tell me what is happening," she asked.

"I am planning to ask you to marry me, my lady."

Antonella smiled a secret smile, and Diego caught her hand.

"Why do you smile so strangely?"

"I am happy that *all* my dream has come true."

"Will you accept me when I ask? I have wasted too many years to spend months persuading you to do something you do not wish."

"I shall accept you at once."

"Do you love me?"

"With all my heart. But do you love me? Or am I only a reminder of the lady from Cathay?"

Touched by her insight, Diego replied, "You are not at all like my lady Lotus Flower. Your background, nature and

315

mode of living are quite different. Only in your curiosity about this house do you remind me of her."

"I am glad you want me for myself, for I cannot change."

"I do not wish you to change at all."

In the weeks that followed, plans were made for the wedding ceremony. The di Volpe family had insisted on a lavish spectacle, though Diego would have preferred the quiet of a private ceremony. He recalled that once before he had acquiesced to an epic day of feasting and celebration. He had done so again because to refuse would be to disappoint the father of his bride.

Two days before the wedding, Antonella arrived at Diego's house. She was trembling from head to toe with excitement, and he was concerned that she was ill.

"What ails you, my lady?" Diego asked.

"I am nervous, sir. It has taken much scheming for me to accomplish what I have arranged for this day."

"What have you been scheming?"

"Trust me, please, and accompany me to the home of a friend."

Diego walked at Antonella's side to the home of Hsu Lan. "I did not know that you knew my lady Hsu Lan."

"My lady Hsu Lan, the Contessa di Mantegna, is one of my father's best friends. He plays chess with her and her husband and loses a fortune every week."

"You know that she is the mother of my late wife?"

"I know it, and to be truthful, of late I often feel she is a mother to me, because when I need wise counsel I go to her. I cannot ask my sisters for advice, and I do not have a mother. I cannot ask Papa either, because he worries so much about what others will think. That is why I go to the Contessa."

Diego greeted Hsu Lan, who led the couple to her garden. Turning to Antonella, she whispered, "I have done everything you asked, my dear. No one will disturb you, and the Monsignore is waiting in the gazebo."

With that, Hsu Lan disappeared, leaving the couple to admire the scene before them. The sun was shining through a lattice of moon daisies woven into a frame and placed as a canopy over a carpet of yellow roses. Doves perched on the hedge, watching expectantly.

Antonella turned to Diego and took his hand. "Diego, I am not happy with the idea of a wedding before many hundreds of guests and in full view of their curiosity. I have always dreamed of being married in a bower of blossom, alone with the man I love. I hope you will forgive this deception, but I have asked a priest here today to marry us. In two days we shall satisfy the wishes of my father by being married in the cathedral."

Diego kissed her, delight mixing with wonder that her longings were so like his own. "I am enchanted by your cleverness, Antonella, and by this beautiful place you have arranged."

"The Contessa helped me with everything."

"She is indeed the very finest friend."

Songbirds twittered in the branches and the faint echo of a gondolier's song came across the water as the priest intoned the words of the wedding ceremony. When the couple were man and wife, the priest withdrew to the house, where Hsu Lan and her husband were waiting to entertain him.

Diego and his bride stood hand in hand under the canopy of flowers. They kissed and held each other close, laughing at the thundering beat of their hearts.

Antonella spoke. "It was a wedding to cherish forever. I love you, Diego, indeed I love you so much I swear I could sing like a bird."

Diego was content. He was home in Venice and with his love. What more could any man ask?